ISAAC ASIMOV PRESENTS THE BEST HORROR AND SUPERNATURAL OF THE 19TH CENTURY

Also edited by Isaac Asimov,
Charles G. Waugh,
and Martin H. Greenberg

Isaac Asimov Presents the Best Fantasy of the 19th Century
Isaac Asimov Presents the Best Science Fiction of the 19th Century
The Science Fiction Solar System
The Thirteen Crimes of Science Fiction
TV: 2000

ISAAC ASIMOV

PRESENTS THE BEST HORROR AND SUPERNATURAL OF THE 19TH CENTURY

*Edited by Isaac Asimov,
Charles G. Waugh,
and Martin H. Greenberg*

BEAUFORT BOOKS, INC.
New York / Toronto

808.83
Isa

*No character in this book is intended to
represent any actual person; all the incidents
of the stories are entirely fictional in nature.*

*Library of Congress Cataloging in Publication Data
Main entry under title:*

*Isaac Asimov presents the best horror and
supernatural of the 19th century.*

*Sequel to: Isaac Asimov presents the
best science fiction of the 19th century.*
1. Horror tales   2. Fiction—19th century.
I. Asimov, Isaac, 1920–
II. Waugh, Charles G.   III. Greenberg, Martin Harry.
PN6120.95.H72718 1983   808.83'872   82-20794
ISBN 0-8253-0128-9

*Published in the United States by Beaufort Books, Inc., New York.
Published simultaneously in Canada by General Publishing Co. Limited
Designer: Ellen LoGiudice*

Printed in the U.S.A.   First Edition
10 9 8 7 6 5 4 3 2 1

CONTENTS

Introduction:
THE LURE OF HORROR

Isaac Asimov

In 1974, a book of mine was published which was a detailed annotation of John Milton's great epic, *Paradise Lost*.

In preparing it, I noted what seemed to me to be an interesting thing, something that was not emphasized in the commentaries I had seen.

Here were bands of angels in countless hordes, all living in unimaginable bliss in the company of a perfect and all-beneficent God, and yet one-third of them rebelled and fought desperately against the remainder. The rebels were defeated, of course (of course!) and were hurled into the unimaginable tortures of Hell, and yet not one of them (not one!) rebelled against Satan for having led them into this ultimate catastrophe. Not one expressed remorse or contrition. Not one suggested trying to truckle to God and seek pardon.

Why is that?

It is no use to fall back upon "sin" and say that sin had seized control of the fallen angels. Sin is just a one-syllable word that describes the situation. *Why* did sin seize control? How could it find entry under conditions of absolute perfection?

Nor is it enough to say that that was just Milton's idea. The epic poem could scarcely have been so universally praised if intelligent readers did not find something deep and satisfying in Milton's anaylsis of the situation.

So I looked, and here is what I found. In Book II of *Paradise Lost* the fallen angels gather in council to decide what must be done to retrieve the situation. Satan throws the floor open to discussion and several of the leading rebels state their disparate views, after which Satan comes to a rational decision, taking on the burden of its implementation himself. In

7

Book III, there is a council in heaven—but only God speaks, and the role of the angels consists of the equivalent of an endlessly repeated "Yes, Lord."

Again, after the council in hell is completed, the rebel angels proceed to amuse themselves as they can within the confines of hell. Some engaged in war games, some engaged in athletics, some in music, some in art, some in philosophy, some in exploration of their new domain. In short, they behaved as though they were rational beings. In heaven, the unfallen angels did not seem to have any role but to sing the praises of God and to follow his orders.

I could not help but think that an existence so limited as that described in Milton's heaven, however much it was *called* bliss, would produce that serious mental disorder called "boredom." Surely, given enough time, the pains of boredom, of dissatisfaction with an absolutely dull and eventless life, would gather in intensity to the point where any being with a rational mind would see it as worse than any conceivable risk that accompanied the attempt to end it.

So Satan and his angels rebelled, and when they found that, as a result, they ended in Hell, they were dreadfully distressed, but not one of them felt like returning to Heaven. After all, there was self-rule in Milton's Hell, and as Satan said, in the single best-known line of the epic: "Better to reign in Hell, than serve in Heav'n."

In short, then, one of the things that *Paradise Lost* explains, in very satisfying manner, is the lure of "horror" upon all of us. That this lure is very real is beyond doubt.

Consider the tale of adventure and daring deeds. That is a genre undoubtedly as old as *Homo sapiens*. Around Stone Age campfires, men surely told tales of danger and heroism that the listeners found not only entertaining but filled with social meaning. The heroes of the stories, whether those stories were exaggerated truth or outright fiction, were role-models to emulate, so that it made men more daring in hunt and more enduring in adversity. Such things therefore contributed to the advance of the tribe and of humanity in general.

Yet there is no question but that in these tales, those elements which encourage fear and dread, are more strongly emphasized than would seem necessary, and that, indeed, the popularity of such stories is increased in proportion to the efficacy with which such fear and dread is introduced.

The oldest surviving and the most continuously popular adventure story in the Western tradition is Homer's *Odyssey*. Does anyone doubt that the most popular portion of the epic are Books 8 to 12, Odysseus' tale of his wanderings through the terror-lands of the (then-unknown) western Mediterranean? (Indeed, I suspect that some who know only what they have heard of the *Odyssey* imagine that that represents the whole of the tale.) And, of Odysseus' tale, surely the most popular item is also the most terrifying, his encounter with the one-eyed cannibalistic giant, Polyphemus.

The tendency has continued through all the 28 centuries or so since the *Odyssey* was composed. We find ourselves fascinated with stories that inspire suspense, that induce in us increasing uneasiness. We read, without danger of satiation, adventure stories, mystery stories, gothics, and, always popular, those tales which distil out of all this just those elements which most efficiently arouse fear and dread. These are the so-called "horror stories" which confront us with the nearly unendurable.

Why should we read these when none of us wants to be thrown into real-life situations involving fear and dread. We don't want to face wild beasts, or spend a night alone in a haunted house, or have to run from a homicidal maniac. Of course, we don't want to. But a life filled with peace and quiet becomes dreadful and would drive us to these things if we did not find some way of exorcising boredom (as the rebellious angels could not).

We read about events which take place in the never-never land of fiction and for a while we are absorbed in them and feel the emotions they give rise to. We experience them vicariously without *really* being in danger and can then return to our peace and quiet with the risk of having to "break out" allayed.

This need to escape from the disagreeableness of the potentially unbearable quiet life would, in fact, seem to be deeply ingrained in human nature. Where is the child that does not love a ghost story? Where is the popular children's folktale that does not involve witches and spectacular dangers of all kinds? It may induce nightmares and persistent fear, but even that seems to be preferable to a life of utter peace. Children seem to agree with the rebellious angels; all of us do, in fact.

The modern horror story begins with *The Castle of Otranto* by Horace Walpole, published in 1764. The scene is an unlikely medieval castle with an impossible architecture that leaves room for interminable secret passages, and a plot that includes ghosts and supernatural influences of all kinds.

Many followed Walpole's lead, and the genre reached its peak in the 19th Century with Edgar Allan Poe, his predecessors and his many imitators. In this book, we present a collection from the 19th Century peak of the horror stories. Some, such as Poe's *The Tell-Tale Heart* have never lost their popularity, or their efficacy. Most, however, are not familiar, for fashions in horror have changed (as all fashions do).

Might we say that change has come because we no longer need ghosts and the supernatural in the 20th Century where the horrors of war and the chances of universal destruction are so much nearer than they ever were in preceding centuries?

Indeed? Surely, the unknown still terrifies. With advances in technology, we call upon vision to make real what, earlier, only imagination could embody. The 20th Century horror movies, such as *The Exorcist* and *Poltergeist* are a new version of the 19th Century horror tale, and the lure remains.

Return with us, then, to the horror of yesteryear.

Washington Irving (1783–1859)

Born in New York City, Washington Irving was a magnetic charmer whose good looks and diplomatic nature helped insure many of his successes throughout life. He received little formal schooling because of a sickly nature, but read widely in his father's library before turning to law.

Sketches he had submitted to his brother's newspaper, *The Morning Chronicle*, became his first book, *The Letters of Jonathan Oldstyle, Gent.* (1802–1903). His next book, Knickerbocker's *A History of New York* (1809), was a major success. The work which brought him fame and wealth, *The Sketch Book of Geoffrey Crayon* (1819–1920), was ironically undertaken out of necessity when the failure of his brothers' importing firm left him stranded in England.

Six years later, just as his money started running low again, he received an offer to travel to Spain to translate some papers about Christopher Columbus. During this stay he produced four books, including *The Legend of the Alhambra* (1832). In 1832 he returned to America, where he was to live for most of the rest of his life.

Because of "Rip Van Winkle" and "The Legend of Sleepy Hollow," Irving is often thought of as an American regional writer of charming prose and picturesque characters. However, the majority of his stories were set in Europe, and several of his American stories were based on German legends. Furthermore, he was capable of writing chilling horror stories, such as the "The Young Robber" or, our selection for this volume "The Adventure of the German Student."

THE ADVENTURE OF
THE GERMAN STUDENT

*O*n *a stormy night, in the tempestuous times of the French revolu*-tion, a young German was returning to his lodgings, at a late hour, across the old part of Paris. The lightning gleamed, and the loud claps of thunder rattled through the lofty narrow streets—but I should first tell you something about this young German.

Gottfried Wolfgang was a young man of good family. He had studied for some time at Göttingen, but being of a visionary and enthusiastic character, he had wandered into those wild and speculative doctrines which have so often bewildered German students. His secluded life, his intense application, and the singular nature of his studies, had an effect on both mind and body. His health was impaired; his imagination diseased. He had been indulging in fanciful speculations on spiritual essences, until, like Swedenborg, he had an ideal world of his own around him. He took up a notion, I do not know from what cause, that there was an evil influence hanging over him; an evil genius or spirit seeking to ensnare him and ensure his perdition. Such an idea working on his melancholy temperament, produced the most gloomy effects. He became haggard and desponding. His friends discovered the mental malady preying upon him, and determined that the best cure was a change of scene; he was sent, therefore, to finish his studies amidst the splendors and gayeties of Paris.

Wolfgang arrived at Paris at the breaking out of the revolution. The popular delirium at first caught his enthusiastic mind, and he was captivated by the political and philosophical theories of the day: but the scenes of blood which followed shocked his sensitive nature, disgusted him with society and the world, and made him more than ever a recluse.

13

He shut himself up in a solitary apartment in the *Pays Latin*, the quarter of students. There, in a gloomy street not far from the monastic walls of the Sorbonne, he pursued his favorite speculations. Sometimes he spent hours together in the great libraries of Paris, those catacombs of departed authors, rummaging among their hordes of dusty and obsolete works in quest of food for his unhealthy appetite. He was, in a manner, a literary ghoul, feeding in the charnel house of decayed literature.

Wolfgang, though solitary and recluse, was of an ardent termperament, but for a time it operated merely upon his imagination. He was too shy and ignorant of the world to make any advances to the fair, but he was a passionate admirer of female beauty, and in his lonely chamber would often lose himself in reveries on forms and faces which he had seen, and his fancy would deck out images of loveliness far surpassing the reality.

While his mind was in this excited and sublimated state, a dream produced an extraordinary effect upon him. It was of a female face of transcendent beauty. So strong was the impression made, that he dreamt of it again and again. It haunted his thoughts by day, his slumbers by night; in fine, he became passionately enamored of this shadow of a dream. This lasted so long that it became one of those fixed ideas which haunt the minds of melancholy men, and are at times mistaken for madness.

Such was Gottfried Wolfgang, and such his situation at the time I mentioned. He was returning home late one stormy night, through some of the old and gloomy streets of the *Marais*, the ancient part of Paris. The loud claps of thunder rattled among the high houses of the narrow streets. He came to the Place de Grève, the square where public executions are performed. The lightning quivered about the pinnacles of the ancient Hôtel de Ville, and shed flickering gleams over the open space in front. As Wolfgang was crossing the square, he shrank back with horror at finding himself close by the guillotine. It was the height of the reign of terror, when this dreadful instrument of death stood ever ready, and its scaffold was continually running with the blood of the virtuous and the brave. It had that very day been actively employed in the work of carnage, and there it stood in grim array, amidst a silent and sleeping city, waiting for fresh victims.

Wolfgang's heart sickened within him, and he was turning shuddering from the horrible engine, when he beheld a shadowy form, cowering as it were at the foot of the steps which led up to the scaffold. A succession of vivid flashes of lightning revealed it more distinctly. It was a female figure, dressed in black. She was seated on one of the lower steps of the scaffold, leaning forward, her face hid in her lap; and her long disheveled tresses hanging to the ground, streaming with the rain which fell in torrents. Wolfgang paused. There was something awful in this solitary monument of woe. The female had the appearance of being above the common order. He knew the times to be full of vicissitude, and that many a fair head, which had once been pillowed on down, now wandered houseless. Perhaps this was some poor mourner whom the dreadful axe had rendered desolate, and who sat here heartbroken on the strand of existence, from which all that was dear to her had been launched into eternity.

He approached, and addressed her in the accents of sympathy. She raised her head and gazed wildly at him. What was his astonishment at beholding, by the bright glare of the lightning, the very face which had haunted him in his dreams. It was pale and disconsolate, but ravishingly beautiful.

Trembling with violent and conflicting emotions, Wolfgang again accosted her. He spoke something of her being exposed at such an hour of the night, and to the fury of such a storm, and offered to conduct her to her friends. She pointed to the guillotine with a gesture of dreadful signification.

"I have no friend on earth!" said she.

"But you have a home," said Wolfgang.

"Yes—in the grave!"

The heart of the student melted at the words.

"If a stranger dare make an offer," said he, "without danger of being misunderstood, I would offer my humble dwelling as a shelter; myself as a devoted friend. I am friendless myself in Paris, and a stranger in the land; but if my life could be of service, it is at your disposal, and should be sacrificed before harm or indignity should come to you."

There was an honest earnestness in the young man's manner that had its effect. His foreign accent, too, was in his favor; it showed him not to be a hackneyed inhabitant of Paris. Indeed, there is an eloquence in true enthusiasm that is not to be doubted. The homeless stranger confided herself implicitly to the protection of the student.

He supported her faltering steps across the Pont Neuf, and by the

place where the statue of Henry the Fourth had been overthrown by the
populace. The storm had abated, and the thunder rumbled at a distance.
All Paris was quiet, that great volcano of human passion slumbered for a
while, to gather fresh strength for the next day's eruption. The student
conducted his charge through the ancient streets of the *Pays Latin*, and
by the dusky walls of the Sorbonne, to the great dingy hotel which he
inhabited. The old portress who admitted them stared with surprise at the
unusual sight of the melancholy Wolfgang with a female companion.

On entering his apartment, the student, for the first time, blushed at
the scantiness and indifference of his dwelling. He had but one chamber—an old-fashioned saloon—heavily carved, and fantastically furnished with the remains of former magnificence, for it was one of those
hotels in the quarter of the Luxembourg palace, which had once belonged to nobility. It was lumbered with books and papers, and all the
usual apparatus of a student, and his bed stood in a recess at one end.

When lights were brought, and Wolfgang had a better opportunity
of contemplating the stranger, he was more than ever intoxicated by her
beauty. Her face was pale, but of a dazzling fairness, set off by a
profusion of raven hair that hung clustering about it. Her eyes were large
and brilliant, with a singular expression approaching almost to wildness.
As far as her black dress permitted her shape to be seen, it was of perfect
symmetry. Her whole appearance was highly striking, though she was
dressed in the simplest style. The only thing approaching to an ornament
which she wore, was a broad black band round her neck, clasped by
diamonds.

The perplexity now commenced with the student how to dispose of
the helpless being thus thrown upon his protection. He thought of
abandoning his chamber to her, and seeking shelter for himself elsewhere. Still he was so fascinated by her charms, there seemed to be such
a spell upon his thoughts and senses, that he could not tear himself from
her presence. Her manner, too, was singular and unaccountable. She
spoke no more of the guillotine. Her grief had abated. The attentions of
the student had first won her confidence, and then, apparently, her heart.
She was evidently an enthusiast like himself, and enthusiasts soon
understand each other.

In the infatuation of the moment, Wolfgang avowed his passion for
her. He told her the story of his mysterious dream, and how she had
possessed his heart before he had even seen her. She was strangely

affected by his recital, and acknowledged to have felt an impulse toward him equally unaccountable. It was the time for wild theory and wild actions. Old prejudices and superstitions were done away; everything was under the sway of the "Goddess of Reason." Among other rubbish of the old times, the forms and ceremonies of marriage began to be considered superfluous bonds for honorable minds. Social compacts were the vogue. Wolfgang was too much of a theorist not to be tainted by the liberal doctrines of the day.

"Why should we separate?" said he; "our hearts are united; in the eye of reason and honor we are as one. What need is there of sordid forms to bind high souls together?"

The stranger listened with emotion; she had evidently received illumination at the same school.

"You have no home or family," continued he, "let me be everything to you, or rather let us be everything to one another. If form is necessary, form shall be observed—there is my hand. I pledge myself to you forever."

"Forever?" said the stranger, solemnly.

"Forever!" repeated Wolfgang.

The stranger clasped the hand extended to her: "Then I am yours," murmured she, and sank upon his bosom.

The next morning the student left his bride sleeping, and sallied forth at an early hour to seek more spacious apartments suitable to the change in his situation. When he returned, he found the stranger lying with her head hanging over the bed, and one arm thrown over it. He spoke to her, but received no reply. He advanced to awaken her from her uneasy posture. On taking her hand, it was cold—there was no pulsation—her face was pallid and ghastly. In a word, she was a corpse.

Horrified and frantic, he alarmed the house. A sense of confusion ensued. The police was summoned. As the officer of police entered the room, he started back on beholding the corpse.

"Great Heaven!" cried he, "how did this woman come here?"

"Do you know anything about her?" said Wolfgang eagerly.

"Do I?" exclaimed the officer: "she was guillotined yesterday."

He stepped forward; undid the black collar round the neck of the corpse, and the head rolled on the floor!

The student burst into a frenzy. "The fiend! the fiend has gained possession of me!" shrieked he; "I am lost forever."

They tried to soothe him, but in vain. He was possessed with the frightful belief that an evil spirit had reanimated the dead body to ensnare him. He went distracted, and died in a madhouse.

Here the old gentleman with the haunted head finished his narrative.

"And is this really a fact?" said the inquisitive gentleman.

"A fact not to be doubted," replied the other. "I had it from the best authority. The student told it me himself. I saw him in a madhouse in Paris."

Honoré de Balzac (1799–1850)

Considered to be one of the world's greatest writers, Honoré de Balzac helped develop the novel as a vehicle for serious social commentary. Born in Tours, France, he had an unhappy childhood. His illegitimate half-brother Henri was his mother's favorite. Still, she may have encouraged Balzac's life-long interest in supernatural phenomena and the occult because of her fascination with Swedenborg.

At his father's insistence, he studied law, then worked in a barrister's and solicitor's office. After receiving his license, he abandoned his career to become a writer.

A disasterous attempt at publishing and seven years of failure were to occur before he produced *Le Dernier Chouan* (1829), his first important novel. Then in 1834, Balzac conceived of *The Human Comedy*, on which he labored for the rest of his life. It was a grandiose attempt to organize all his works into a unified and interlocking view of French society from the Revolution to his day.

Wild and irresponsible financial ventures forced him to write quickly (he completed nearly one hundred novels), but his backgrounds were detailed, and he had a good ear for dialogue, and, at his best, his prose was rich and dynamic.

The "Philosophic Studies" section of his plan contains several supernatural pieces such as *The Magic Skin* (1831), *The Search for the Absolute* (1834), *Melmoth Reconciled* (1835). amd "Christ in Flanders." His horror stories include "Elixir of Life," "La Grande Bretêche," "The Revolt of a Sheep," and our selection of a man who preferred death to life, "El Verdugo."

EL VERDUGO

To Martinez de la Rosa

*M*idnight had just sounded from the belfry tower of the little town of Menda. A young French officer, leaning over the parapet of the long terrace at the further end of the castle gardens, seemed to be unusually absorbed in deep thought for one who led the reckless life of a soldier; but it must be admitted that never was the hour, the scene, and the night more favorable to meditation.

The blue dome of the cloudless sky of Spain was overhead; he was looking out over the coy windings of a lovely valley lit by the uncertain starlight and the soft radiance of the moon. The officer, leaning against an orange tree in blossom, could also see, a hundred feet below him, the town of Menda, which seemed to nestle for shelter from the north wind at the foot of the crags on which the castle itself was built. He turned his head and caught sight of the sea; the moonlit waves made a broad frame of silver for the landscape.

There were lights in the castle windows. The mirth and movement of a ball, the sounds of the violins, the laughter of the officers and their partners in the dance was borne toward him, and blended with the far-off murmur of the waves. The cool night had a certain bracing effect upon his frame, wearied as he had been by the heat of the day. He seemed to bathe in the air, made fragrant by the strong, sweet scent of flowers and of aromatic trees in the gardens.

The castle of Menda belonged to a Spanish grandee, who was living in it at that time with his family. All through the evening the oldest daughter of the house had watched the officer with such a wistful interest that the Spanish lady's compassionate eyes might well have set the young Frenchman dreaming. Clara was beautiful; and although she had three brothers and a sister, the broad lands of the Marqués de Légañès appeared to be sufficient warrant for Victor Marchand's belief that the young lady would have a splendid dowry. But how could he dare to imagine that the most fanatical believer in blue blood in all Spain would give his daughter to the son of a grocer in Paris? Moreover, the French were hated. It was because the marquis had been suspected of an attempt to raise the country in favor of Ferdinand VII that General G———, who governed the province, had stationed Victor Marchand's battalion in the little town of Menda to overawe the neighboring districts which received the Marqués de Légañès' word as law. A recent despatch from Marshal Ney had given ground for fear that the English might ere long effect a landing on the coast, and had indicated the marquis as being in correspondence with the cabinet in London.

In spite, therefore, of the welcome with which the Spaniards had received Victor Marchand and his soldiers, that officer was always on his guard. As he went toward the terrace, where he had just surveyed the town and the districts confided to his charge, he had been asking himself what construction he ought to put upon the friendliness which the marquis had invariably shown him, and how to reconcile the apparent tranquillity of the country with his general's uneasiness. But a moment later these thoughts were driven from his mind by the instinct of caution and very legitimate curiosity. It had just struck him that there was a very fair number of lights in the town below. Although it was the Feast of Saint James, he himself had issued orders that very morning that all lights must be put out in the town at the hour prescribed by military regulations. The castle alone had been excepted in this order. Plainly here and there he saw the gleam of bayonets, where his own men were at their accustomed posts; but in the town there was a solemn silence, and not a sign that the Spaniards had given themselves up to the intoxication of a festival. He tried vainly for a while to explain this breach of the regulations on the part of the inhabitants; the mystery seemed but so much the more obscure because he had left instructions with some of his officers to do police duty that night, and make the rounds of the town.

With the impetuosity of youth, he was about to spring through a gap in the wall preparatory to a rapid scramble down the rocks, thinking to reach a small guardhouse at the nearest entrance into the town more quickly than by the beaten track, when a faint sound stopped him. He fancied that he could hear the light footstep of a woman along the graveled garden walk. He turned his head and saw no one; for one moment his eyes were dazzled by the wonderful brightness of the sea, the next he saw a sight so ominous that he stood stock-still with amazement, thinking that his senses must be deceiving him. The white moonbeams lighted the horizon, so that he could distinguish the sails of ships still a considerable distance out at sea. A shudder ran through him; he tried to persuade himself that this was some optical delusion brought about by chance effects of moonlight on the waves; and even as he made the attempt, a hoarse voice called to him by name. The officer glanced at the gap in the wall; saw a soldier's head slowly emerge from it, and knew the grenadier whom he had ordered to accompany him to the castle.

"Is that you, Commandant?"

"Yes. What is it?" returned the young officer in a low voice. A kind of presentiment warned him to act cautiously.

"Those beggars down there are creeping about like worms; and, by your leave, I came as quickly as I could to report my little reconnoitering expedition."

"Go on," answered Victor Marchand.

"I have just been following a man from the castle who came round this way with a lantern in his hand. A lantern is a suspicious matter with a vengeance! I don't imagine that there was any need for that good Christian to be lighting tapers at this time of night. Says I to myself, 'They mean to gobble us up!' and I set myself to dogging his heels; and that is how I found out that there is a pile of faggots, sir, two or three steps away from here."

Suddenly a dreadful shriek rang through the town below, and cut the man short. A light flashed in the commandant's face, and the poor grenadier dropped down with a bullet through his head. Ten paces away a bonfire flared up like a conflagration. The sounds of music and laughter ceased all at once in the ballroom; the silence of death, broken only by groans, succeeded to the rhythmical murmur of the festival. Then the roar of cannon sounded from across the white plain of the sea.

A cold sweat broke out on the young officer's forehead. He had left his sword behind. He knew that his men had been murdered, and that the English were about to land. He knew that if he lived he would be dishonored; he saw himself summoned before a court-martial. For a moment his eyes measured the depth of the valley; the next, just as he was about to spring down, Clara's hand caught his.

"Fly!" she cried. "My brothers are coming after me to kill you. Down yonder at the foot of the cliff you will find Juanito's Andalusian. Go!"

She thrust him away. The young man gazed at her in dull bewilderment; but obeying the instinct of self-preservation, which never deserts even the bravest, he rushed across the park in the direction pointed out to him, springing from rock to rock in places unknown to any save the goats. He heard Clara calling to her brothers to pursue him; he heard the footsteps of the murderers; again and again he heard their balls whistling about his ears; but he reached the foot of the cliff, found the horse, mounted, and fled with lightning speed.

A few hours later the young officer reached General G——'s quarters, and found him at dinner with the staff.

"I put my life in your hands!" cried the haggard and exhaused Commandant of Menda.

He sank into a seat, and told his horrible story. It was received with an appalling silence.

"It seems to me that you are more to be pitied than to blame," the terrible general said at last. "You are not answerable for the Spaniard's crimes, and unless the marshall decides otherwise, I acquit you."

These words brought but cold comfort to the unfortunate officer.

"When the emperor comes to hear about it!" he cried.

"Oh, he will be for having you shot," said the general, "but we shall see. Now we will say no more about this," he added severely, "except to plan a revenge that shall strike a salutary terror into this country, where they carry on war like savages."

An hour later a whole regiment, a detachment of cavalry, and a convoy of artillery were upon the road. The general and Victor marched at the head of the column. The soldiers had been told of the fate of their comrades, and their rage knew no bounds. The distance between headquarters and the town of Menda was crossed at a well-nigh miraculous speed. Whole villages by the way were found to be under arms; every one of the wretched hamlets was surrounded, and their inhabitants decimated.

It so chanced that the English vessels still lay out at sea, and were no nearer the shore, a fact inexplicable until it was known afterwards that they were artillery transports which had outsailed the rest of the fleet. So the townsmen of Menda, left without the assistance on which they had reckoned when the sails of the English appeared, were surrounded by French troops almost before they had time to strike a blow. This struck such terror into them that they offered to surrender at discretion. An impulse of devotion, no isolated instance in the history of the Peninsula, led the actual slayers of the French to offer to give themselves up; seeking in this way to save the town, for from the general's reputation for cruelty it was feared that he would give Menda over to the flames, and put the whole population to the sword. General G——— took their offer, stipulating that every soul in the castle from the lowest servant to the marquis should likewise be given up to him. These terms being accepted, the general promised to spare the lives of the rest of the townsmen, and to prohibit his soldiers from pillaging or setting fire to the town. A heavy contribution was levied, and the wealthiest inhabitants were taken as hostages to guarantee payment within twenty-four hours.

The general took every necessary precaution for the safety of his troops, provided for the defense of the place, and refused to billet his men in the houses of the town. After they had bivouacked, he went up to the castle and entered it as a conqueror. The whole family of Léganès and their household were gagged, shut up in the great ballroom, and closely watched. From the windows it was easy to see the whole length of the terrace above the town.

The staff was established in an adjoining gallery, where the general forthwith held a council as to the best means of preventing the landing of the English. An aide-de-camp was despatched to Marshall Ney, orders were issued to plant batteries along the coast, and then the general and his staff turned their attention to their prisoners. The two hundred Spaniards given up by the townsfolk were shot down then and there upon the terrace. And after this military execution, the general gave orders to erect gibbets to the number of the prisoners in the ballroom in the same place, and to send for the hangman out of the town. Victor took advantage of the interval before dinner to pay a visit to the prisoners. He soon came back to the general.

"I am come in haste," he faltered out, "to ask a favor."

"*You!*" exclaimed the general, with bitter irony in his tones.

"Alas!" answered Victor, "it is a sorry favor. The marquis has seen them erecting the gallows, and hopes that you will commute the punishment for his family; he entreats you to have the nobles beheaded."

"Granted," said the general.

"He further asks that they may be allowed the consolations of religion, and that they may be unbound; they give you their word that they will not attempt to escape."

"That I permit," said the general, "but you are answerable for them."

"The old noble offers you all that he has if you will pardon his youngest son."

"Really!" cried the commander. "His property is forfeit already to King Joseph." He paused; a contemptuous thought set wrinkles in his forehead, as he added, "I will do better than they ask. I understand what he means by that last request of his. Very good. Let him hand down his name to posterity; but whenever it is mentioned, all Spain shall remember his reason and its punishment! I will give the fortune of his life to any one of the sons who will do the executioner's office. . . . There, don't talk any more about them to me."

Dinner was ready. The officers sat down to satisfy an appetite whetted by hunger. Only one among them was absent from the table—that one was Victor Marchand. After long hesitation, he went to the ballroom, and heard the last sighs of the proud house of Légañés. He looked sadly at the scene before him. Only last night, in this very room, he had seen their faces whirled past him in the waltz, and he shuddered to think that those girlish heads with those of the three young brothers must fall in a brief space by the executioner's sword. There sat the father and mother, their three sons and two daughters, perfectly motionless, bound to their gilded chairs. Eight serving men stood with their hands tied behind them. These fifteen prisoners, under sentence of death, exchanged grave glances; it was difficult to read the thoughts that filled them from their eyes, but profound resignation and regret that their enterprise should have failed so completely was written on more than one brow.

The impassive soldiers who guarded them respected the grief of their bitter enemies. A gleam of curiosity lighted up all faces when Victor came in. He gave orders that the condemned prisoners should be unbound, and himself unfastened the cords that held Clara a prisoner. She smiled mournfully at him. The officer could not refrain from lightly touching the young girl's arm; he could not help admiring her dark hair, her slender waist. She was a true daughter of Spain, with a Spanish complexion, a Spaniard's eyes, blacker than the raven's wing beneath their long curving lashes.

"Did you succeed?" she asked, with a mournful smile, in which a certain girlish charm still lingered.

Victor could not repress a groan. He looked from the faces of the three brothers to Clara, and again at the three young Spaniards. The first, the oldest of the family, was a man of thirty. He was short, and somewhat ill-made; he looked haughty and proud, but a certain distinction was not lacking in his bearing, and he was apparently no stranger to the delicacy of feeling for which in olden times the chivalry of Spain was famous. His name was Juanito. The second son, Felipe, was about twenty years of age; he was like his sister Clara; and the youngest was a child of eight. In the features of the little Manuel a painter would have discerned something of that Roman steadfastness which David has given to the children's faces in his Republican *genre* pictures. The old marquis, with his white hair, might have come down from some canvas of Murillo's. Victor threw back his head in despair after this survey; how should one of these accept the general's offer! nevertheless he ventured to intrust it to Clara. A shudder ran through the Spanish girl, but she recovered herself almost instantly, and knelt before her father.

"Father," she said, "bid Juanito swear to obey the commands that you shall give him, and we shall be content."

The marquesa trembled with hope, but as she leant toward her husband and learned Clara's hideous secret, the mother fainted away. Juanito understood it all, and leapt up like a caged lion. Victor took it upon himself to dismiss the soldiers, after receiving an assurance of entire submission from the marquis. The servants were led away and given over to the hangman and their fate. When only Victor remained on guard in the room, the old Marqués de Légañés rose to his feet.

"Juanito," he said. For an answer Juanito bowed his head in a way that meant refusal; he sank down into his chair, and fixed tearless eyes upon his father and mother in an intolerable gaze. Clara went over to him and sat on his knee; she put her arms about him, and pressed kisses on his eyelids, saying gaily—

"Dear Juanito, if you but knew how sweet death at your hands will be to me! I shall not be compelled to submit to the hateful touch of the hangman's fingers. You will snatch me away from the evils to come and.... Dear, kind Juanito, you could not bear the thought of my belonging to any one—well, then?''

The velvet eyes gave Victor a burning glance; she seemed to try to awaken in Juanito's heart his hatred for the French.

''Take courage,'' said his brother Felipe, ''or our well nigh royal line will be extinct.''

Suddenly Clara sprang to her feet. The group round Juanito fell back, and the son who had rebelled with such good reason was confronted with his aged father.

''Juanito, I command you!'' said the marquis solemnly.

The young count gave no sign, and his father fell on his knees; Clara, Manuel, and Felipe unconsciously followed his example, stretching out suppliant hands to him who must save their family from oblivion, and seeming to echo their father's words.

''Can it be that you lack the fortitude of a Spaniard and true sensibility, my son? Do you mean to keep me on my knees? What right have you to think of your own life and of your own sufferings?—Is this my son, madam?'' the old Marquis added, turning to his wife.

''He will consent to it,'' cried the mother in agony of soul. She had seen a slight contraction of Juanito's brows which she, his mother, alone understood.

Mariquita, the second daughter, knelt, with her slender clinging arms about her mother; the hot tears fell from her eyes, and her little brother Manuel upbraided her for weeping. Just at that moment the castle chaplain came in; the whole family surrounded him and led him up to Juanito. Victor felt that he could endure the sight no longer, and with a sign to Clara he hurried from the room to make one last effort for them. He found the general in boisterous spirits; the officers were still sitting over their dinner and drinking together; the wine had loosened their tongues.

An hour later, a hundred of the principal citizens of Menda were summoned to the terrace by the general's orders to witness the execution of the family of Légañés. A detachment had been told off to keep order among the Spanish townsfolk, who were marshalled beneath the gallows whereon the marquis's servants hung; the feet of those martyrs of their cause all but touched the citizens' heads. Thirty paces away stood the block; the blade of a scimitar glittered upon it, and the executioner stood by in case Juanito should refuse at the last.

The deepest silence prevailed, but before long it was broken by the sound of many footsteps, the measured tramp of a picket of soldiers, and the jingling of their weapons. Mingled with these came other noises— loud talk and laughter from the dinner-table where the officers were sitting; just as the music and the sound of the dancers' feet had drowned the preparations for last night's treacherous butchery.

All eyes turned to the castle, and beheld the family of nobles coming forth with incredible composure to their death. Every brow was serene and calm. One alone among them, haggard and overcome, leant on the arm of the priest, who poured forth all the consolations of religion for the one man who was condemned to live. Then the executioner, like the spectators, knew that Juanito had consented to perform his office for a day. The old marquis and his wife, Clara and Mariquita, and their two brothers knelt a few paces from the fatal spot. Juanito reached it, guided by the priest. As he stood at the block the executioner plucked him by the sleeve, and took him aside, probably to give him certain instructions. The confessor so placed the victims that they could not witness the executions, but one and all stood upright and fearless, like Spaniards, as they were.

Clara sprang to her brother's side before the others.

"Juanito," she said to him, "be merciful to my lack of courage. Take me first!"

As she spoke, the footsteps of a man running at full speed echoed from the walls, and Victor appeared upon the scene. Clara was kneeling before the block; her white neck seemed to appeal to the blade to fall. The officer turned faint, but he found strength to rush to her side.

"The general grants you your life if you will consent to marry me," he murmured.

The Spanish girl gave the officer a glance full of proud disdain.

"Now, Juanito!" she said in her deep-toned voice. Her head fell at Victor's feet. A shudder ran through the Marquesa de Légañés, a convulsive tremor that she could not control, but she gave no other sign of her anguish.

"Is this where I ought to be, dear Juanito? Is it all right?" little Manuel asked his brother.

"Oh, Mariquita, you are weeping!" Juanito said when his sister came.

"Yes," said the girl; "I am thinking of you, poor Juanito; how unhappy you will be when we are gone."

Then the marquis's tall figure approached. He looked at the block

where his children's blood had been shed, turned to the mute and
motionless crowd, and said in a loud voice as he stretched out his hands
to Juanito—

"Spaniards! I give my son a father's blessing—Now, *Marquis*,
strike 'without fear'; thou art 'without reproach.' "

But when his mother came near, leaning on the confessor's arm—
"She fed me from her breast!" Juanito cried, in tones that drew a cry of
horror from the crowd. The uproarious mirth of the officers over their
wine died away before that terrible cry. The Marquesa knew that Juanito's courage was exhausted; at one bound she sprang to the balustrade,
leapt forth, and was dashed to pieces on the rocks below. A cry of
admiration broke from the spectators. Juanito swooned.

"General," said an officer, half-drunk by this time, "Marchand
has just been telling me something about this execution; I will wager that
it was not by your orders—"

"Are you forgetting, gentlemen, that in a month's time five hundred families in France will be mourning, and that we are still in Spain?"
cried General G———. "Do you want us to leave our bones here?"

But not a man at the table, not even a subaltern, dared to empty his
glass after that speech.

In spite of the respect in which all men hold the Marqués de
Léganès, in spite of the title of *El Verdugo* (the executioner) conferred
upon him as a patent of nobility by the King of Spain, the great noble is
consumed by a gnawing grief. He lives a retired life, and seldom appears
in public. The burden of his heroic crime weighs heavily upon him, and
he seems to wait impatiently till the birth of a second son shall release
him, and he may go to join the Shades that never cease to haunt him.

Captain Marryat (1792–1848)

The son of a West India Merchant M.P., Frederick Marryat was born at Westminster, England, Unhappy at home, he repeatedly attempted running away to sea, finally becoming a midshipman in 1806. He rose through the ranks rapidly. In 1820-1821 he commanded a sloop guarding Napoleon's imprisonment on St. Helena. In 1828 he became a captain.

In 1830 he resigned suddenly. The peacetime naval routine may have bored him, and his first novel, *Frank Mildmay* (1829), had been successful.

In 1832 he assumed the editorship of *Metropolitan Magazine* and began filling its pages with his works. Juvenile sea stories such as *Peter Simple* (1834) and *Mr. Midshipman Easy* (1836) proved very popular. He became one of the most highly paid authors of his time, but his penchant for good living and bad speculations forced him to emphasize quantity, often at the expense of quality.

In the fantasy and horror field, he is primarily remembered for "The White Wolf of the Hartz Mountains." It is a tale of lycanthropy, an independent section of *The Phantom Ship* (1839), and just one of the many digressions sprinkled throughout his works. The novel itself is an interesting retelling of the Flying Dutchman legend.

Widely neglected is *The Pacha of Many Tales* (1835), a series of fascinating imitations of the *Arabian Nights*.[1] From this collection comes "The Story of the Greek Slave," an unforgettable tale featuring both Marryat's broad humor and his taste for the grotesque.

---

[1]These stories were serialized in *Metropolitan Magazine* from June 1831 to May 1835 (our selection was Chapter II). The first British edition appeared in 1835, but the National Union Catalog lists an American edition in 1834.

THE STORY OF THE GREEK SLAVE

The pacha called for coffee, and in a few minutes, accompanied, as before, by Mustapha and the armed slaves, was prowling through the city in search of a storyteller. He was again fortunate, as after a walk of half an hour, he overheard two men loudly disputing at the door of a small wineshop, frequented by the Greeks and Franks living in the city, and into which many a slave might be observed to glide, returning with a full pitcher for the evening's amusement of his Turkish master, who, as well as his betters, clandestinely violated the precepts of the Koran.

As usual he stopped to listen, when one of the disputants exclaimed: "I tell thee, Anselmo, it is the vilest composition that was ever drunk: and I think I ought to know, after having distilled the essence of an Ethiopian, a Jew, and a Turk."

"I care nothing for your distillations, Charis," replied the other, "I consider that I am a better judge than you: I was not a monk of the Dominican order for fifteen years, without having ascertained the merit of every description of wine."

"I should like to know what that fellow means by *distilling people*," observed the pacha, "and also why a Dominican monk should know wine better than others. Mustapha, I must see those two men."

The next morning the men were in attendance, and introduced; when the pacha requested an explanation from the first who had spoken. The man threw himself down before the pacha, with his head on the floor of the divan, and said: "First promise me, your highness, by the sword of the Prophet, that no harm shall result to me from complying with your request; and then I shall obey you with pleasure."

"Mashallah! what is the Kafir afraid of? What crimes hath he committed, that he would have his pardon granted before he tells his story?'' said the pacha to Mustapha.

"No crime toward your state, your sublime highness; but when in another country, I was unfortunate,'' continued the man. "I cannot tell my story, unless your highness will condescend to give your promise.''

"May it please your highness,'' observed Mustapha, "he asserts his crime to have been committed in another state. It may be heavy, and I suspect 'tis murder; but although we watch the flowers which ornament our gardens, and would punish those who cull them, yet we care not who intrudes and robs our neighbor—and thus, it appears to me, your highness, that it is with states, and sufficient for the ruler of each to watch over the lives of his own subjects.''

"Very true, Mustapha,'' rejoined the pacha; "besides, we might lose the story. Kafir, you have our promise, and may proceed.''

The Greek slave (for such he was) then rose up, and narrated his story in the following words.

I am a Greek by birth; my parents were poor people residing at Smyrna. I was an only son, and brought up to my father's profession, that of a cooper. When I was twenty years old, I had buried both my parents, and was left to shift for myself. I had been for some time in the employ of a Jewish wine merchant, and I continued there for three years after my father's death, when a circumstance occurred which led to my subsequent prosperity and present degradation.

At the time that I am speaking of, I had, by strict diligence and sobriety, so pleased my employer, that I had risen to be his foreman; and although I still superintended and occasionally worked at the cooperage, I was entrusted with the drawing off and fining of the wines, to prepare them for market. There was an Ethiopian slave, who worked under my orders, a powerful, broad-shouldered, and most malignant wretch, whom my master found it almost impossible to manage; the bastinado, or any other punishment, he derided, and after the application only became more sullen and discontented than before. The fire that flashed from his eyes, upon any fault being found by me on account of his negligence, was so threatening, that I every day expected I should be murdered. I repeatedly requested my master to part with him; but the Ethiopian being a very powerful man, and able, when he chose, to move a pipe of wine without assistance, the avarice of the Jew would not permit him to accede to my repeated solicitations.

One morning I entered the cooperage, and found the Ethiopian fast asleep by the side of a cask which I had been wanting for some time, and expected to have found ready. Afraid to punish him myself, I brought my master to witness his conduct. The Jew, enraged at his idleness, struck him on the head with one of the staves. The Ethiopian sprung up in a rage, but on seeing his master with the stave in his hand, contented himself with muttering, "That he would not remain to be beaten in that manner," and reapplied himself to his labor. As soon as my master had left the cooperage, the Ethiopian vented his anger upon me for having informed against him, and seizing the stave, flew at me with the intention of beating out my brains. I stepped behind the cask; he followed me, and just as I had seized an adze to defend myself, he fell over the stool which lay in his way; he was springing up to renew the attack, when I struck him a blow with the adze which entered his skull and laid him dead at my feet.

I was very much alarmed at what had occurred; for although I felt justified in self-defense, I was aware that my master would be very much annoyed at the loss of the slave, and as there were no witnesses, it would go hard with me when brought before the cadi. After some reflection I determined, as the slave had said, "he would not remain to be beaten," that I would leave my master to suppose he had run away, and in the meantime conceal the body. But to effect this was difficult, as I could not take it out of the cooperage without being perceived. After some cogitation, I decided upon putting it into the cask, and heading it up. It required all my strength to lift the body in, but at last I succeeded. Having put in the head of the pipe, I hammered down the hoops and rolled it into the store, where I had been waiting to fill it with wine for the next year's demand. As soon as it was in its place, I pumped off the wine from the vat, and having filled up the cask and put in the bung, I felt as if a heavy load had been removed from my mind, as there was no chance of immediate discovery.

I had but just completed my task, and was sitting down on one of the settles, when my master came in, and inquired for the slave. I replied that he had left the cooperage, swearing that he would work no more. Afraid of losing him, the Jew hastened to give notice to the authorities that he might be apprehended; but after some time, as nothing could be heard of the supposed runaway, it was imagined that he had drowned himself in a fit of sullenness, and no more was thought about him. In the meantime I continued to work there as before, and as I had the charge of everything I had no doubt that, some day or another, I should find means of quietly disposing of my incumbrance.

The next spring, I was busy pumping off from one cask into the other, according to our custom, when the aga of the janissaries came in. He was a great wine bibber, and one of our best customers. As his dependents were all well known, it was not his custom to send them for wine, but to come himself to the store and select a pipe. This was carried away in a litter by eight strong slaves, with the curtains drawn close, as if it had been a new purchase which he had added to his harem. My master showed him the pipes of wine prepared for that year's market, which were arranged in two rows; and I hardly need observe that the one containing the Ethiopian was not in the foremost. After tasting one or two which did not seem to please him, the aga observed, "Friend Issachar, thy tribe will always put off the worst goods first, if possible. Now I have an idea that there is better wine in the second tier, than in the one thou hast recommended. Let thy Greek put a spile into that cask," continued he, pointing to the very one in which I had headed up the black slave. As I made sure that as soon as he had tasted the contents he would spit them out, I did not hesitate to bore the cask and draw off the wine, which I handed to him. He tasted it and held it to the light—tasted it again and smacked his lips—then turning to my master, exclaimed, "Thou dog of a Jew!—wouldst thou have palmed off upon me vile trash, when thou hadst in thy possession wine which might be sipped with the Houris in Paradise?"

The Jew appealed to me if the pipes of wine were not all of the same quality; and I confirmed his assertion.

"Taste it then," replied the aga, "and then taste the first which you recommended to me."

My master did so, and was evidently astonished. "It certainly has more body," replied he; "yet how that can be, I know not. Taste it, Charis." I held the glass to my lips, but nothing could induce me to taste the contents. I contented myself with agreeing with my master (as I conscientiously could), "that it certainly had more *body* in it than the rest."

The aga was so pleased with the wine, that he tasted two or three more pipes of the back tier, hoping to find others of the same quality, probably intending to have laid in a large stock; but finding no other of the same flavor, he ordered his slaves to roll the one containing the body of the slave into the litter, and carry it to his own house.

"Stop a moment, thou lying Kafir!" said the pacha, "dost thou really mean to say that the wine was better than the rest?"

"Why should I tell a lie to your sublime highness? Am not I a worm that you may crush? As I informed you, I did not taste it, your highness; but after the aga had departed, my master expressed his surprise at the excellence of the wine, which he affirmed to be superior to anything that he had ever tasted—and his sorrow that the aga had taken away the cask, which prevented him from ascertaining the cause. But one day I was narrating the circumstance to a Frank in his country, who expressed no surprise at the wine being improved. He had been a wine merchant in England, and he informed me that it was the custom there to throw large pieces of raw beef into the wine to feed it; and that some particular wines were very much improved thereby."

"Allah Kebur! God is great!" cried the pacha. "Then it must be so—I have heard that the English are very fond of beef. Now go on with thy story."

Your highness cannot imagine the alarm which I felt when the cask was taken away by the aga's slaves. I gave myself up for a lost man, and resolved upon immediate flight from Smyrna. I calculated the time that it would take for the aga to drink the wine, and made my arrangements accordingly. I told my master that it was my intention to leave him, as I had an offer to go into business with a relation at Zante. My master, who could not well do without me, entreated me to stay; but I was positive. He then offered me a share of the business if I would remain, but I was not to be persuaded. Every rap at the door, I thought that the aga and his janissaries were coming for me; and I hastened my departure, which was fixed for the following day—when in the evening my master came into the store with a paper in his hand.

"Charis," said he, "perhaps you have supposed that I only offered to make you a partner in my business to induce you to remain, and then to deceive you. To prove the contrary, here is a deed drawn up by which you are a partner, and entitled to one-third of the future profits. Look at it, you will find that it has been executed in due form before the cadi."

He had put the paper into my hand, and I was about to return it with a refusal, when a loud knocking at the door startled us both. It was a party of janissaries dispatched by the aga, to bring us to him immediately. I knew well enough what it must be about, and I cursed my folly in having delayed so long; but the fact was, the wine proved so agreeable to the aga's palate that he had drunk it much faster than usual; besides which, the body of the slave took up at least a third of the cask, and diminished the contents in the same proportion. There was no appeal, and no escape. My master, who was ignorant of the cause, did not seem at all alarmed, but willingly accompanied the soldiers. I, on the contrary, was nearly dead from fear.

When we arrived, the aga burst out in the most violent exclamations against my master. "Thou rascal of a Jew!" said he, "dost thou think that thou art to impose upon a true believer, and sell him a pipe of wine which is not more than two-thirds full—filling it up with trash of some sort or another. Tell me what it is that is so heavy in the cask now that it is empty?"

The Jew protested his ignorance, and appealed to me: I, of course, pretended the same. "Well, then," replied the aga, "we will soon see. Let thy Greek send for his tools, and the cask shall be opened in our presence; then perhaps thou wilt recognize thine own knavery."

Two of the janissaries were dispatched for the tools, and when they arrived I was directed to take the head out of the cask. I now considered my death as certain—nothing buoyed me up but my observing that the resentment of the aga was levelled more against my master than against me; but still I thought that, when the cask was opened, the recognition of the black slave must immediately take place, and the evidence of my master would fix the murder upon me.

It was with a trembling hand that I obeyed the orders of the aga—the head of the pipe was taken out, and, to the horror of all present, the body was exposed; but instead of being black, it had turned *white*, from the time it had been immersed. I rallied a little at this circumstance, as, so far, suspicion would be removed.

"Holy Abraham!" exclaimed my master, "what is that which I see!—A dead body, so help me God!—but I know nothing about it—do you, Charis?" I vowed that I did not, and called the Patriarch to witness the truth of my assertion. But while we were thus exclaiming, the aga's eyes were fixed upon my master with an indignant and deadly stare which spoke volumes; while the remainder of the people who were present, although they said nothing, seemed as if they were ready to tear him to pieces.

"Cursed unbeliever!" at last uttered the Turk, "is it thus that thou preparest the wine for the disciples of the Prophet?"

"Holy father Abraham!—I know no more than you do, aga, how that body came there; but I will change the cask with pleasure, and will send you another."

"Be it so," replied the aga; "my slave shall fetch it now." He gave directions accordingly, and the litter soon reappeared with another pipe of wine.

"It will be a heavy loss to a poor Jew—one pipe of good wine," observed my master, as it was rolled out of the litter; and he took up his hat with the intention to depart.

"Stay," cried the aga, "I do not mean to rob you of your wine."

"Oh, then, you will pay me for it?" replied my master; "aga, you are a considerate man."

"Thou shalt see," retorted the aga, who gave directions to his slaves to draw off the wine in vessels. As soon as the pipe was empty, he desired me to take the head out; and when I had obeyed him, he ordered his janissaries to put my master in. In a minute he was gagged and bound, and tossed into the pipe; and I was directed to put in the head as before. I was very unwilling to comply; for I had no reason to complain of my master, and knew that he was punished for the fault of which I had been guilty. But it was a case of life or death—and the days of self-devotion have long passed away in our country. Besides which, I had the deed in my pocket by which I was a partner in the business, and my master had no heirs—so that I stood a chance to come into the whole of his property. Moreover—

"Never mind your reasons," observed the pacha, "you headed him up in the cask—go on."

"I did so, your highness; but although I dared not disobey, I assure you that it was with a sorrowful heart—the more so, as I did not know the fate which might be reserved for myself."

As soon as the head was in, and the hoops driven on, the aga desired his slaves to fill the cask up again with the wine; and thus did my poor master perish.

"Put in the bung, Greek," said the aga, in a stern voice.

I did so, and stood trembling before him.

"Well! what knowest thou of this transaction."

I thought, as the aga had taken away the life of my master, that it would not hurt him if I took away a little from his character. I answered that I really knew nothing, but that, the other day, a black slave had disappeared in a very suspicious manner—that my master made very little inquiry after him—and I now strongly suspected that he must have suffered the same fate. I added, that my master had expressed himself very sorry that his highness had taken away the pipe of wine, as he would have reserved it.

"Cursed Jew!" replied the aga; "I don't doubt but he has murdered a dozen in the same manner."

"I am afraid so, sir," replied I, "and suspect that I was to have been his next victim; for when I talked of going away, he persuaded me to stay, and gave me this paper, by which I was to become his partner with one-third of the profits. I presume that I should not have enjoyed them long."

"Well, Greek," observed the aga, "this is fortunate for you; as, upon certain conditions, you may enter upon the whole property. One is, that you keep this pipe of wine with the rascally Jew in it, that I may have the pleasure occasionally to look at my revenge. You will also keep the pipe with the other body in it, that it may keep my anger alive. The last is, that you will supply me with what wine I may require, of the best quality, without making any charge. Do you consent to these terms, or am I to consider you as a party to this infamous transaction?"

I hardly need observe that the terms were gladly accepted. Your highness must be aware that nobody thinks much about a Jew. When I was questioned as to his disappearance, I shrugged up my shoulders and told the inquirers, confidentially, that the aga of the janissaries had put him *in prison*, and that I was carrying on the business until his release.

In compliance with the wishes of the aga, the two casks containing the Jew and the Ethiopian slave were placed together on settles higher than the rest, in the center of the store. He would come in the evening, and rail at the cask containing my late master for hours at a time; during which he drank so much wine, that it was a very common circumstance for him to remain in the house until the next morning.

You must not suppose, your highness, that I neglected to avail myself (unknown to the aga) of the peculiar properties of the wine which those casks contained. I had them spiled underneath, and, constantly running off the wine from them, filled them up afresh. In a short time there was not a gallon in my possession which had not a *dash* in it of either the Ethiopian or the Jew; and my wine was so improved, that it had a most rapid sale, and I became rich.

All went on prosperously for three years; when the aga, who during that time had been my constant guest, and at least three times a week had been intoxicated in my house, was ordered with his troops to join the Sultan's army. By keeping company with him, I had insensibly imbibed a taste for wine, although I never had been inebriated. The day that his troops marched, he stopped at my door, and dismounting from his Arabian, came in to take a farewell glass, desiring his men to go on, and that he would ride after them. One glass brought on another, and the time flew rapidly away. The evening closed in, and the aga was, as usual, in a state of intoxication; he insisted upon going down to the store, to rail once more at the cask containing the body of the Jew. We had long been on the most friendly terms, and having this night drunk more than my usual, I was incautious enough to say: "Prithee, aga, do not abuse my poor master any more, for he has been the making of my fortune. I will tell you a secret now that you are going away—there is not a drop of wine in my store that has not been flavored either by him, or by the slave in the other cask. That is the reason why it is so much better than other people's."

"How!" exclaimed the aga, who was now almost incapable of speech. "Very well, rascal Greek! die you shall like your master. Holy Prophet! what a state for a Mussulman to go to Paradise in—impregnated with the essence of a cursed Jew!—Wretch! you shall die—you shall die."

He made a grasp at me, and missing his foot, fell on the ground in such a state of drunkenness as not to be able to get up again. I knew that when he became sober, he would not forget what had taken place, and that I should be sacrificed to his vengeance. The fear of death, and the wine which I had drunk, decided me how to act. I dragged him into an empty pipe, put the head in, hooped it up, and rolling it into the tier, filled it with wine.

Thus did I revenge my poor master, and relieved myself from any further molestation on the part of the aga.

''What!'' cried the pacha, in a rage, ''you drowned a true believer —an aga of janissaries! Thou dog of a Kafir—thou son of Shitan—and dare avow it! Call in the executioner.''

''Mercy! your sublime highness, mercy!'' cried the Greek. ''Have I not your promise by the sword of the Prophet? Besides, he was no true believer, or he would not have disobeyed the law. A good Mussulman will never touch a drop of wine.''

''I promised to forgive, and did forgive, the murder of the black slave; but an aga of janissaries!—Is not that quite another thing?'' appealed the pacha to Mustapha.

''Your highness is just in your indignation—the Kafir deserves to be impaled. Yet there are two considerations which your slave ventures to submit to your sublime wisdom. The first is, that your highness gave an unconditional promise, and swore by the sword of the Prophet.''

''Staffir Allah! what care I for that! Had I sworn to be a true believer, it were something.''

''The other is, that the slave has not yet finished his story, which appears to be interesting.''

''Wallah! that is true. Let him finish his story.''

But the Greek slave remained with his face on the ground; and it was not until a renewal of the promise, sworn upon the holy standard made out of the nether garments of the Prophet, by the pacha, who had recovered his temper, and was anxious for the conclusion of the story, that he could be induced to proceed, which he did as follows:

As soon as I had bunged up the cask, I went down to the yard where the aga had left his horse, and having severely wounded the poor beast with his sword, I let it loose, that it might gallop home. The noise of the horse's hoofs in the middle of the night aroused his family, and when they discovered that it was wounded and without its rider, they imagined that the aga had been attacked and murdered by the banditti when he had followed his troops. They sent to me, to ask at what time he had left my house; I replied, an hour after dark—that he was very much intoxicated at the time—and had left his sabre, which I returned. They had no suspicions of the real facts, and it was believed that he had perished on the road.

I was now rid of my dangerous acquaintance, and although he certainly had drunk a great quantity of my wine, yet I recovered the value of it with interest, from the flavor which I obtained from his body, and which I imparted to the rest of my stock. I raised him up alongside of the two other casks; and my trade was more profitable and my wines in greater repute than ever.

But one day the cadi, who had heard my wine extolled, came privately to my house; I bowed to the ground at the honor conferred, for I had long wished to have him as a customer. I drew some of my best. "This, honorable sir," said I, presenting the glass, "is what I call my aga wine: the late aga was so fond of it, he used to order a whole cask at once to his house, and had it taken there in a litter."

"A good plan," replied the cadi, "much better than sending a slave with a pitcher, which gives occasion for remarks: I will do the same; but, first, let me taste all you have."

He tasted several casks, but none pleased him so much as the first which I had recommended. At last he cast his eyes upon the three casks raised above the others.

"And what are those?" inquired he.

"Empty casks, sir," replied I; but he had his stick in his hand, and he struck one.

"Greek, thou tellest me these casks are empty, but they do not sound so; I suspect that thou hast better wine than I have tasted: draw me off from these immediately."

I was obliged to comply—he tasted them—vowed that the wine was exquisite, and that he would purchase the whole. I stated to him that the wine in those casks was used for flavoring the rest; and that the price was enormous, hoping that he would not pay it. He inquired how much—I asked him four times the price of the other wines.

"Agreed," said the cadi; "it is dear—but one cannot have good wine without paying for it: it is a bargain."

I was very much alarmed, and stated that I could not part with those casks, as I should not be able to carry on my business with reputation, if I lost the means of flavoring my wines, but all in vain; he said that I had asked a price and he had agreed to give it. Ordering his slaves to bring a litter, he would not leave the store until the whole of the casks were carried away, and thus did I lose my Ethiopian, my Jew and my aga.

As I knew that the secret would soon be discovered, the very next day I prepared for my departure. I received my money from the cadi, to whom I stated my intention to leave, as he had obliged me to sell him those wines, and I had no longer hopes of carrying on my business with success. I again begged him to allow me to have them back, offering him three pipes of wine as a present if he would consent, but it was of no use. I chartered a vessel, which I loaded with the rest of my stock; and, taking all my money with me, made sail for Corfu, before any discovery had taken place. But we encountered a heavy gale of wind, which, after a fortnight (during which we attempted in vain to make head against it), forced us back to Smyrna. When the weather moderated, I directed the captain to take the vessel into the outer roadstead that I might sail as soon as possible. We had not dropped anchor again more than five minutes when I perceived a boat pulling off from the shore in which was the cadi and the officers of justice.

Convinced that I was discovered, I was at a loss how to proceed, when the idea occurred to me that I might conceal my own body in a cask, as I had before so well concealed those of others.

I called the captain down into the cabin, and telling him that I had reason to suspect that the cadi would take my life, offered him a large part of the cargo if he would assist me.

The captain who, unfortunately for me, was a Greek, consented. We went down into the hold, started the wine out of one of the pipes, and having taken out the head, I crawled in, and was hooped up.

The cadi came on board immediately afterwards and inquired for me. The captain stated that I had fallen overboard in the gale, and that he had in consequence returned, the vessel not being consigned to any house in Corfu.

"Has then the accursed villain escaped my vengeance!" exclaimed the cadi; "the murderer that fines his wines with the bodies of his fellow creatures: but you may deceive me, Greek, we will examine the vessel."

The officers who accompanied the cadi proceeded carefully to search every part of the ship. Not being able to discover me, the Greek captain was believed; and, after a thousand imprecations upon my soul, the cadi and his people departed.

I now breathed more freely, notwithstanding I was nearly intoxicated with the lees of the wine which impregnated the wood of the cask, and I was anxious to be set at liberty; but the treacherous captain had no such intention, and never came near me. At night he cut his cable and made sail, and I overheard a conversation between two of the men, which made known to me his intentions: these were to throw me overboard on his passage, and take possession of my property. I cried out to them from the bung-hole: I screamed for mercy, but in vain. One of them answered, that, as I had murdered others, and put them into casks, I should now be treated in the same manner.

I could not but mentally acknowledge the justice of my punishment, and resigned myself to my fate; all that I wished was to be thrown over at once and released from my misery. The momentary anticipation of death appeared to be so much worse than the reality. But it was ordered otherwise: a gale of wind blew up with such force, that the captain and crew had enough to do to look after the vessel, and either I was forgotten or my doom was postponed until a more seasonable opportunity.

On the third day I heard the sailors observe that, with such a wretch as I was remaining on board, the vessel must inevitably be lost. The hatches were then opened: I was hoisted up and cast into the raging sea. The bunk of the cask was out, but by stuffing my handkerchief in when the hole was under water, I prevented the cask from filling; and when it was uppermost, I removed it for a moment to obtain fresh air. I was dreadfully bruised by the constant rolling, in a heavy sea, and completely worn out with fatigue and pain; I had made up my mind to let the water in and be rid of my life, when I was tossed over and over with such dreadful rapidity as prevented my taking the precaution of keeping out the water. After three successive rolls of the same kind, I found that the cask, which had been in the surf, had struck on the beach. In a moment after, I heard voices, and people came up to the cask and rolled me along. I would not speak, lest they should be frightened, and allow me to remain on the beach, where I might again be tossed about by the waves; but as soon as they stopped, I called in a faint voice from the bung-hole, begging them for mercy's sake to let me out.

At first they appeared alarmed; but, on my repeating my request, and stating that I was the owner of the ship which was off the land, and the captain and crew had mutinied and tossed me overboard, they brought some tools and set me at liberty.

The first sight that met my eyes after I was released was my vessel lying a wreck, each wave that hurled her further on the beach breaking her more and more to pieces. She was already divided amidships, and the white foaming surf was covered with pipes of wine, which, as fast as they were cast on shore, were rolled up by the same people who had released me. I was so worn out, that I fainted where I lay. When I came to, I found myself in a cave upon a bundle of capotes, and perceived a party of forty or fifty men, who were sitting by a large fire, and emptying with great rapidity one of my pipes of wine.

As soon as they observed that I was coming to my senses, they poured some wine down my throat, which restored me. I was then desired by one of them, who seemed to be the chief, to approach.

"The men who have been saved from the wreck," said he, "have told me strange stories of your enormous crimes—now, sit down, and tell me the truth—if I believe you, you shall have justice—I am cadi here—if you wish to know where you are, it is upon the island of Ischia—if you wish to know in what company, it is in the society of those who by illiberal people are called pirates: now tell the truth."

I thought that with pirates my story would be received better than with other people, and I therefore narrated my history to them, in the same words that I now have to your highness. When I had finished, the captain of the gang observed:

"Well, then, as you acknowledge to have killed a slave, to have assisted at the death of a Jew, and to have drowned an aga, you certainly deserve death; but, on consideration of the excellence of the wine, and the secret which you have imparted to us, I shall commute your sentence. As for the captain and the remainder of the crew, they have been guilty of treachery and piracy on the high seas—a most heinous offense, which deserves instant death: but, as it is by their means that we have been put in possession of the wine, I shall be lenient. I therefore sentence you all to hard labor for life. You shall be sold as slaves in Cairo, and we will pocket the money and drink your wine."

The pirates loudly applauded the justice of a decision by which they benefited, and all appeal on our parts was useless. When the weather became more settled, we were put on board one of their small xebeques, and on our arrival at this port were exposed for sale and purchased.

Such, pacha, is the history which induced me to make use of the expression which you wished to be explained; and I hope you will allow that I have been more unfortunate than guilty, as on every occasion in which I took away the life of another, I had only to choose between that and my own.

"Well, it is rather a curious story," observed the pacha, "but still, if it were not for my promise, I certainly would have your head off for drowning the aga—I consider it excessively impertinent in an unbelieving Greek to suppose that his life is of the same value as that of an aga of janissaries, and follower of the Prophet; but, however, my promise was given, and you may depart.''

"The wisdom of your highness is brighter than the stars of the heaven,'' observed Mustapha. "Shall the slave be honored with your bounty?''

"Mashallah! Bounty! I've given him his life, and, as he considers it of more value than an aga's, I think 'tis a very handsome present. Drown an aga, indeed!'' continued the pacha, rising. "But it certainly was a very curious story. Let it be written down, Mustapha. We'll hear the other man to-morrow.''

William Mudford (1782–1848)

Author and journalist William Mudford was born in London. At the age of eighteen he became assistant secretary to the Duke of Kent, resigning two years later to pursue a literary career. A conservative (or Whig) he served first as Parliamentary reporter for the *Morning Chronicle*, and then as assistant editor and editor for the *Courier*. When the *Courier* owners changed policy, Mudford withdrew rather than support their switch.

By now he had translated several works and written eight books including novels, essays, criticism, and history. But speculative losses and a growing family forced him to seek editorial positions once again.

First he served as editor and then owner of the *Kentish Observer* in Canterbury. In 1841 he assumed the editorship of *John Bull* in London, a post which he retained until his death.

During many of these years *Blackwood's Magazine*, a Scottish publication, was extremely popular and influential. Mudford was a prolific contributor, sometimes placing a story, a review, and a political paper all within the same issue.

Perhaps to protect his editorial positions, he published much of his work either under a pseudonym or anonymously. That includes both novels and *Blackwood* pieces such as *The Life and Adventures of Paul Plaintive, Esq, an Author* (1811), *Stephen Dugard* (1840), political articles by the "Silent Member," and, our selection for this volume, "The Iron Shroud," a story about a collapsing prison.

THE IRON SHROUD

*T*he castle of the Prince of Tolfi was built on the summit of the towering and precipitous rock of Scylle, and commanded a magnificent view of Sicily in all its grandeur. Here during the wars of the Middle Ages, when the fertile plains of Italy were devastated by hostile factions, those prisoners were confined for whose ransom a costly price was demanded. Here, too, in a dungeon, excavated deep in the solid rock, the miserable victim was immured, whom revenge pursued—the dark, fierce, and unpitying revenge of an Italian heart.

Vivenzio—the noble and the generous, the fearless in battle, and the pride of Naples in her sunny hours of peace—the young, the brave, the proud Vivenzio fell beneath this subtle and remorseless spirit. He was the prisoner of Tolfi, and he languished in that rock-encircled dungeon, which stood alone, and whose portals never opened twice upon a living captive.

It had the semblance of a vast cage, for the roof and floor and sides were of iron, solidly wrought and spaciously constructed. High above there ran a range of seven grated windows, guarded with massive oars of the same metal, which admitted light and air. Save these, and the tall folding doors beneath them, which occupied the center, no chink, or chasm, or projection broke the smooth black surface of the walls. An iron bedstead, littered with straw, stood in one corner; and beside it a vessel with water and a coarse dish filled with coarser food.

Even the intrepid soul of Vivenzio shrank with dismay as he entered this abode, and heard the ponderous doors triple-locked by the silent ruffians who conducted him to it. Their silence seemed prophetic of his fate, of the living grave that had been prepared for him. His menaces and his entreaties, his indignant appeals for justice, and his impatient questioning of their intentions, were alike in vain. They listened, but spoke not. Fit ministers of a crime that should have no tongue!

How dismal was the sound of their retiring steps! And, as their faint echoes died along the winding passages, a fearful presage grew within him, that never more the face, or voice, or tread of man would greet his senses. He had seen human beings for the last time! And he had looked his last upon the bright sky, and upon the smiling earth, and upon a beautiful world he loved, and whose minion he had been! Here he was to end his life—a life he had just begun to revel in. And by what means? By secret poison? or by murderous assault? No—for then it had been needless to bring him thither. Famine perhaps—a thousand deaths in one! It was terrible to think of it—but it was yet more terrible to picture long, long years of captivity in a solitude so appalling, a loneliness so dreary, that thought, for want of fellowship, would lose itself in madness or stagnate into idiocy.

He could not hope to escape, unless he had the power, with his bare hands, of rending asunder the solid iron walls of his prison. He could not hope for liberty from the relenting mercies of his enemy. His instant death under any form of refined cruelty, was not the object of Tolfi, for he might have inflicted it, and he had not. It was too evident, therefore, he was reserved for some premeditated scheme of subtle vengeance; and what vengeance could transcend in fiendish malice either the slow death of famine or the still slower one of solitary incarceration till the last lingering spark of life expired, or till reason fled, and nothing should remain to perish but the brute functions of the body?

It was evening when Vivenzio entered his dungeon, and the approaching shades of night wrapped it in total darkness, as he paced up and down, revolving in his mind these horrible forebodings. No tolling bell from the castle or from any neighboring church or convent struck upon his ear to tell how the hours passed. Frequently he would stop and listen for some sound that might betoken the vicinity of man; but the solitude of the desert, the silence of the tomb are not so still and deep as the oppressive desolation by which he was encompassed. His heart sank within him, and he threw himself dejectedly upon his couch of straw. Here sleep gradually obliterated the consciousness of misery, and bland dreams wafted his delighted spirit to scenes which were once glowing realities for him, in whose ravishing illusions he soon lost the remembrance that he was Tolfi's prisoner.

When he awoke it was daylight; but how long he had slept he knew not. It might be early morning or it might be sultry noon, for he could measure time by no other note of its progress than light and darkness. He had been so happy in his sleep, amid friends who loved him, and the sweeter endearments of those who loved him as friends could not, that in the first moments of waking his startled mind seemed to admit the knowledge of his situation, as if it had burst upon it for the first time, fresh in all its appalling horrors. He gazed around with an air of doubt and amazement, and took up a handful of the straw upon which he lay, as though he would ask himself what it meant. But memory, too faithful to her office, soon unveiled the melancholy past, while reason, shuddering at the task, flashed before his eyes the tremendous future. The contrast overpowered him. He remained for some time lamenting, like a truth, the bright visions that had vanished; and recoiling from the present, which clung to him as a poisoned garment.

When he grew more calm, he surveyed his gloomy dungeon. Alas! the stronger light of day only served to confirm what the gloomy indistinctness of the preceding evening had partially disclosed, the utter impossibility of escape. As, however, his eyes wandered round and round, and from place to place, he noticed two circumstances which excited his surprise and curiosity. The one, he thought, might be fancy; but the other was positive. His pitcher of water and the dish which contained his food had been removed from his side while he slept, and now stood near the door.

Were he even inclined to doubt this, by supposing he had mistaken the spot where he saw them overnight, he could not, for the pitcher now in his dungeon was neither of the same form or color as the other, while the food was changed for some other of better quality. He had been visited therefore during the night. But how had the person obtained entrance? Could he have slept so soundly that the unlocking and opening of those ponderous portals were effected without waking him? He would have said this was not possible, but that in doing so he must admit a greater difficulty, an entrance by other means, of which he was convinced there existed none. It was not intended, then, that he should be left to perish from hunger. But the secret and mysterious mode of supplying him with food seemed to indicate he was to have no opportunity of communicating with a human being.

The other circumstance which had attracted his notice was the disappearance, as he believed, of one of the seven grated windows that ran along the top of his prison. He felt confident that he had observed and counted them; for he was rather surprised at their number, and there was something peculiar in their form, as well as in the manner of their arrangement, at unequal distances. It was so much easier, however, to suppose he was mistaken, than that a portion of the solid iron which formed the walls could have escaped from its position, that he soon dismissed the thought from his mind.

Vivenzio partook of the food that was before him without apprehension. It might be poisoned; but if it were, he knew he could not escape death should such be the design of Tolfi; and the quickest death would be the speediest release.

The day passed wearily and gloomily, though not without a faint hope that by keeping watch at night he might observe when the person came again to bring him food, which he supposed he would do in the same way as before. The mere thought of being approached by a living creature, and the opportunity it might present of learning the doom prepared, or preparing, for him, imparted some comfort. Besides, if he came alone, might he not in a furious onset overpower him? Or he might be accessible to pity, or the influence of such munificent rewards as he could bestow, if once more at liberty and master of himself. Say he were armed. The worst that could befall, if nor bribe, nor prayers, nor force prevailed, was a desired blow which, though dealt in a damned cause, might work a desired end. There was no chance so desparate, but it looked lovely in Vivenzio's eyes compared with the idea of being totally abandoned.

The night came, and Vivenzio watched. Morning came, and Vivenzio was confounded! He must have slumbered without knowing it. Sleep must have stolen over him when exhausted by fatigue, and in that interval of feverish repose he had been baffled; for there stood his replenished pitcher of water, and there his day's meal!

Nor was this all. Casting his looks toward the windows of his dungeon, he counted but *five*! Here was no deception; and he was now convinced there had been none the day before. But what did all this portend? Into what strange and mysterious den had he been cast? He gazed till his eyes ached; he could discover nothing to explain the mystery. That it was so, he knew. Why it was so, he racked his imagination in vain to conjecture. He examined the doors. A single circumstance convinced him they had not been opened.

A wisp of straw which he had carelessly thrown against them the preceding day, as he paced to and fro, remained where he had cast it, though it must have been displaced by the slightest motion of either of the doors. This was evidence that could not be disputed; and it followed there must be some secret machinery in the walls by which a person could enter. He inspected them closely. They appeared to him one solid and compact mass of iron; or joined, if joined they were, with such nice art that no mark of division was perceptible. Again and again he surveyed them—and the floor—and the roof—and that range of visionary windows, as he was now almost tempted to consider them: he could discover nothing, absolutely nothing, to relieve his doubts or satisfy his curiosity. Sometimes he fancied that altogether the dungeon had a more contracted appearance—that it looked smaller; but this he ascribed to fancy, and the impression naturally produced upon his mind by the undeniable disappearance of two of the windows.

With intense anxiety, Vivenzio looked forward to the return of night; and as it approached he resolved that no treacherous sleep should again betray him. Instead of seeking his bed of straw, he continued to walk up and down his dungeon till daylight, straining his eyes in every direction through the darkness to watch for any appearances that might explain these mysteries. While thus engaged, and as nearly as he could judge (by the time that afterwards elapsed before the morning came in) about two o'clock, there was a slight tremulous motion of the floor.

He stooped. The motion lasted nearly a minute; but it was so extremely gentle that he almost doubted whether it was real or only imaginary.

He listened. Not a sound could be heard. Presently, however, he felt a rush of cold air blow upon him; and dashing toward the quarter whence it seemed to proceed, he stumbled over something which he judged to be the water ewer. The rush of cold air was no longer perceptible; and as Vivenzio stretched out his hands he found himself close to the walls. He remained motionless for a considerable time, but nothing occurred during the remainder of the night to excite his attention, though he continued to watch with unabated vigilance.

The first approaches of the morning were visible through the grated windows, breaking, with faint divisions of light, the darkness that still pervaded every other part, long before Vivenzio was enabled to distinguish any object in his dungeon. Instinctively and fearfuly he turned his eyes, hot and inflamed with watching, toward them.

There were *four*! He could see only four; but it might be that some intervening object prevented the fifth from becoming perceptible; and he waited impatiently to ascertain if it were so. As the light strengthened, however, and penetrated every corner of the cell, other objects of amazement struck his sight. On the ground lay the broken fragments of the pitcher he had used the day before, and at a small distance from them, nearer to the wall, stood the one he had noticed the first night. It was filled with water, and beside it was his food.

He was now certain that by some mechanical contrivance an opening was obtained through the iron wall, and that through this opening the current of air had found entrance. But how noiseless! For had a feather almost waved at the time, he must have heard it. Again he examined that part of the wall; but both to sight and touch it appeared one even and uniform surface, while to repeated and violent blows there was no reverberating sound indicative of hollowness.

This perplexing mystery had for a time withdrawn his thoughts from the windows; but now, directing his eyes again toward them, he saw that the fifth had disappeared in the same manner as the preceding two, without the least distinguishable alteration of external appearances. The remaining four looked as the seven had originally looked; that is, occupying at irregular distances the top of the wall on that side of the dungeon. The tall folding door, too, still seemed to stand beneath, in the center of these four, as it had at first stood in the center of the seven. But he could no longer doubt what on the preceding day he fancied might be the effect of visual deception.

The dungeon was smaller. The roof had lowered, and the opposite ends had contracted the intermediate distance by a space equal, he thought, to that over which the three windows had extended. He was bewildered in vain imaginings to account for these things. Some frightful purpose—some devilish torture of mind or body—some unheard-of-device for producing exquisite misery, lurked, he was sure, in what had taken place.

Oppressed with this belief, and distracted more by the dreadful uncertainty of whatever fate impended, than he could be dismayed, he thought, by the knowledge of the worst, he sat ruminating, hour after hour yielding his fears in succession to every haggard fancy. At last a horrible suspicion flashed suddenly across his mind and he started up with a frantic air.

"Yes!" he exclaimed, looking wildly round his dungeon, and

shuddering as he spoke—"Yes! it must be so! I see it!—I feel the maddening truth like scorching flames upon my brain! Eternal God!—support me! It must be so! Yes, yes, that is to be my fate! Yon roof will descend!—these walls will hem me round—and slowly, slowly, crush me in their iron arms! Lord God! look down upon me, and in mercy strike me with instant death! Oh, fiend—oh, devil—is this your revenge?"

He dashed himself upon the ground in agony; tears burst from him, and the sweat stood in large drops upon his face; he sobbed aloud; he tore his hair; he rolled about like one suffering intolerable anguish of body, and would have bitten the iron floor beneath him; he breathed fearful curses upon Tolfi, and the next moment passionate prayers to heaven for immediate death. Then the violence of his grief became exhausted, and he lay still, weeping as a child would weep.

The twilight of departing day shed its gloom around him ere he arose from that posture of utter and hopeless sorrow. He had taken no food. Not one drop of water had cooled the fever of his parched lips. Sleep had not visited his eyes for six-and-thirty hours. He was faint with hunger, weary with watching and with the excess of his emotions. He tasted of his food; he drank with avidity of the water; and reeling like a drunken man to his straw, cast himself upon it to brood again over the appalling image that had fastened itself upon his almost frenzied thoughts.

He slept. But his slumbers were not tranquil. He resisted, as long as he could, their approach; and when, at last, enfeebled nature yielded to their influence, he found no oblivion from his cares. Terrible dreams haunted him—ghastly visions harrowed up his imagination—he shouted and screamed, as if he already felt the dungeon's ponderous roof descending on him—he breathed hard and thick, as though writhing between its iron walls. Then would he spring up—stare wildly about him—stretch forth his hands to be sure he yet had space enough to live—and, muttering some incoherent words, sink down again, to pass through the same fierce vicissitudes of delirious sleep.

The morning of the fourth day dawned upon Vivenzio. But it was high noon before his mind shook off its stupor, or he awoke to a full consciousness of his situation. And what a fixed energy of despair sat upon his pale features, as he cast his eyes upwards, and gazed upon the three windows that now alone remained! The three!—there were no more!—and they seemed to number his own allotted days. Slowly and calmly he next surveyed the top and sides, and comprehended all the meaning of the diminished height of the former, as well as of the gradual approximation of the latter.

The contracted dimensions of his mysterious prison were now too gross and palpable to be the juggle of his heated imagination. Still lost in wonder at the means, Vivenzio could put no cheat upon his reason as to the end. By what horrible ingenuity it was contrived that walls, and roof, and windows, should thus silently and imperceptibly, without noise, and without motion almost, fold, as it were, within each other, he knew not. He only knew they did so; and he vainly strove to persuade himself it was the intention of the contriver to rack the miserable wretch who might be immured there with anticipation, merely, of a fate from which in the very crisis of his agony he was to be reprieved.

Gladly would he have clung even to this possibility if his heart would have let him; but he felt a dreadful assurance of its fallacy. And what matchless inhumanity it was to doom the sufferer to such lingering torments—to lead him day by day to so appalling a death, unsupported by the consolations of religion, unvisited by any human being, abandoned to himself, deserted of all, and denied even the sad privilege of knowing that his cruel destiny would awaken pity! Alone he was to perish! Alone he was to wait a slow coming torture, whose most exquisite pangs would be inflicted by that very solitude and that tardy coming!

"It is not death I fear," he exclaimed, "but the death I must prepare for! Methinks, too, I could meet even that—all horrible and revolting as it is—if it might overtake me now. But where shall I find fortitude to tarry till it come! How can I outlive the three long days and nights I have to live? There is no power within me to bid the hideous spectre hence— none to make it familiar to my thoughts, or myself patient to its errand. My thoughts, rather, will flee upon me! That so, in death's likeness, I might embrace death itself, and drink no more of the cup that is presented to me than my fainting spirit has already tasted!"

In the midst of these lamentations Vivenzio noticed that his accustomed meal, with the pitcher of water, had been conveyed, as before, into his dungeon. But this circumstance no longer excited his surprise. His mind was overwhelmed with others of a far greater magnitude. It suggested, however, a feeble hope of deliverance; and there is not hope so feeble as not to yield some support to a heart bending under despair.

He resolved to watch during the ensuing night for the signs he had before observed; and, should he again feel the gentle, tremulous motion of the floor or the current of air, to seize that moment for giving audible expression to his misery. Some person must be near him and within reach of his voice at the instant when his food was supplied; some one, perhaps, susceptible of pity. Or if not, to be told even that his apprehensions were just, and that his fate was to be what he foreboded, would be preferable to a suspense which hung upon the possibility of his worst fears being visionary.

The night came; and as the hour approached when Vivenzio imagined he might expect the signs, he stood fixed and silent as a statue. He feared to breathe, almost, lest he might lose any sound which would warn him of their coming. While thus listening, with every faculty of mind and body strained to an agony of attention, it occurred to him he should be more sensible of the motion, probably, if he stretched himself along the iron floor.

He according laid himself softly down, and had not been long in that position when—yes—he was certain of it—the floor moved under him! He sprang up, and in a voice suffocated nearly with emotion, called aloud. He paused—the motion ceased—he felt no stream of air—all was hushed—no voice answered to his—he burst into tears; and as he sank to the ground, in renewed anguish, exclaimed: 'O, my God! You alone have power to save me now, or strengthen me for the trial you permit.'

Another morning dawned upon the wretched captive, and the fatal index of his doom met his eyes. Two windows!—and *two* days—and all would be over! Fresh food—fresh water! The mysterious visit had been paid, though he had implored it in vain. But how awfully was his prayer answered in what he now saw! The roof of the dungeon was within a foot of his head. The two ends were so near, that in six paces he trod the space between them. Vivenzio shuddered as he gazed, and as his steps traversed the narrowed area.

But his feelings no longer vented themselves in frantic wailings. With folded arms, and clenched teeth, with eyes that were bloodshot from much watching, and fixed with a vacant glare upon the ground, with a hard quick breathing, and a hurried walk, he strode backwards and forwards in silent musing for several hours. What mind shall conceive, what tongue utter, or what pen describe the dark and terrible character of his thoughts! Like the fate that moulded them, they had no similitude in the wide range of this world's agony for man. Suddenly he stopped, and his eyes were riveted upon that part of the wall which was over his bed of straw. Words are inscribed here! A human language, traced by a human hand! He rushed toward them; but his blood froze as he read:

'I, Ludovica Sforza, tempted by the gold of the Prince of Tolfi, spent three years in contriving and executing this accursed triumph of my art. When it was completed, the perfidious Tolfi, more devil than man, who conducted me hither one morning, to be witness, as he said, of its perfection, doomed *me* to be the first victim of my own pernicious skill; lest, as he declared, I should divulge the secret, or repeat the effort of my ingenuity. May God pardon him, as I hope he will me, that ministered to his unhallowed purpose! Miserable wretch, whoe'er thou art, that readest these lines, fall on thy knees, and invoke as I have done, His sustaining mercy who alone can nerve thee to meet the vengeance of Tolfi, armed with his tremendous engine, which in a few hours must crush *you*, as it will the needy wretch who made it.'

A deep groan burst from Vivenzio. He stood like one transfixed, with dilated eyes, expanded nostrils, and quivering lips, gazing at this fatal inscription. It was as if a voice from the sepulchre had sounded in his ears, 'Prepare!'

Hope forsook him. There was his sentence, recorded in those dismal words. The future stood unveiled before him, ghastly and appalling. His brain already feels the descending horror—his bones seem to crack and crumble in the mighty grasp of the iron walls! Unknowing what it is he does, he fumbles in his garment for some weapon of self-destruction. He clenches his throat in his convulsive gripe, as though he would strangle himself at once. He stares upon the walls, and his warring spirit demands, ''Will they not anticipate their office if I dash my head against them?''

An hysterical laugh chokes him as he exclaims, ''Why should I? He was but a man who died first in their fierce embrace; and I should be less than man not to do as much!''

The evening sun was descending, and Vivenzio beheld its golden beams streaming through one of the windows. What a thrill of joy shot through his soul at the sight! It was a precious link that united him, for the moment, with the world beyond. There was ecstasy in the thought. As he gazed, long and earnestly, it seemed as if the windows had lowered sufficiently for him to reach them.

With one bound he was beneath them—with one wild spring he clung to the bars. Whether it was so contrived, purposely to madden with delight the wretch who looked, he knew not; but, at the extremity of a long vista, cut through the solid rocks, the ocean, the sky, the setting sun, olive groves, shady walks, and, in the farthest distance, delicious glimpses of magnificent Sicily, burst upon his sight. How exquisite was the cool breeze as it swept across his cheek, loaded with fragrance! He inhaled it as though it were the breath of continued life. And there was a freshness in the landscape, and in the rippling of the calm green sea, that fell upon his withering heart like dew upon the parched earth.

How he gazed, and panted, and still clung to his hold! Sometimes hanging by one hand, sometimes by the other, and then grasping the bars with both, as loath to quit the smiling paradise outstretched before him; till exhausted, and his hands swollen and benumbed, he dropped helpless down, and lay stunned for a considerable time by the fall.

When he recovered, the glorious vision had vanished. He was in darkness. He doubted whether it was not a dream that had passed before his sleeping fancy; but gradually his scattered thoughts returned, and with them came remembrance. Yes! he had looked once again upon the gorgeous splendor of nature!

Once again his eyes had trembled beneath their veiled lids at the sun's radiance, and sought repose in the soft verdure of the olive tree, or the gentle swell of undulating waves. Oh, that he were a mariner, exposed upon those waves to the worst fury of storm and tempest; or a very wretch, loathsome with disease, plague-stricken, and his body one leprous contagion from crown to sole, hunted forth to gasp out the remnant of infectious life beneath those verdant trees, so he might shun the destiny upon whose edge he tottered!

Vain thoughts like these would steal over his mind from time to time in spite of himself; but they scarcely moved it from that stupor into which it had sunk, and which kept him, during the whole night, like one who had been drugged with opium. He was equally insensible to the calls of hunger and of thirst, though the third day was now commencing since even a drop of water had passed his lips. He remained on the ground, sometimes sitting, sometimes lying; at intervals, sleeping heavily; and when not sleeping, silently brooding over what was to come, or talking aloud, in disordered speech, of his wrongs, of his friends, of his home, and of those he loved, with a confused mingling of all.

In this pitiable condition the sixth and last morning dawned upon

Vivenzio, if dawn it might be called—the dim obscure light which faintly struggled through the *one* window of his dungeon. He could hardly be said to notice the melancholy token. And yet he did notice it; for as he raised his eyes and saw the portentous sign, there was a slight convulsive distortion of his countenance.

But what did attract his notice, and at the sight of which his agitation was excessive, was the change his iron bed had undergone. It was a bed no longer. It stood before him, the visible semblance of a funeral couch or bier! When he beheld this, he started from the ground, and, in raising himself suddenly struck his head against the roof, which was now so low that he could no longer stand upright. ''God's will be done!'' was all he said, as he crouched his body, and placed his hand upon the bier; for such it was.

The iron bedstead had been so contrived, by the mechanical art of Ludovico Sforza, that as the advancing walls came in contact with its head and feet, a pressure was produced upon concealed springs, which, when made to play, set in motion a very simple though ingeniously contrived machinery that effected the transformation. The object was, of course, to heighten, in the closing scene of this horrible drama, all the feelings of despair and anguish which the preceding ones had aroused. For the same reason the last window was so made as to admit only a shadowy kind of gloom rather than light, that the wretched captive might be surrounded, as it were, with every seeming preparation for approaching death.

Vivenzio seated himself on his bier. Then he knelt and prayed fervently; and sometimes tears would gush from him. The air seemed thick, and he breathed with difficulty; or it might be that he fancied it was so, from the hot and narrow limits of his dungeon, which were now so diminished that he could neither stand up nor lie down at his full length.

But his wasted spirits and oppressed mind no longer struggled within him. He was past hope, and fear shook him no more. Happy if thus revenge had struck its final blow; for he would have fallen beneath it almost unconscious of a pang. But such a lethargy of the soul, after such an excitement of its fiercest passions, had entered into the diabolical calculations of Tolfi; and the fell artificer of his designs had imagined a counteracting device.

The tolling of an enormous bell struck upon the ears of Vivenzio! He started. It beat but once. The sound was so close and stunning that it seemed to shatter his very brain, while it echoed through the rocky passages like reverberating peals of thunder. This was followed by a sudden crash of the roof and walls, as if they were about to fall upon and close around him at once. Vivenzio screamed, and instinctively spread forth his arms, as though he had a giant's strength to hold them back. They had moved nearer to him, and were now motionless.

Vivenzio looked up and saw the roof almost touching his head, even as he sat cowering beneath it; and he felt that a further contraction of but a few inches only must commence the frightful operation. Roused as he had been, he now gasped for breath. His body shook violently—he was bent nearly double. His hands rested upon either wall, and his feet were drawn under him to avoid the pressure in front. Thus he remained for more than an hour, when that deafening bell beat again, and again there came the crash of horrid death. But the concussion was now so great that it struck Vivenzio down.

As he lay gathered up in lessened bulk, the bell beat loud and frequent—crash succeeded crash—and on, and on, and on came the mysterious engine of death, till Vivenzio's smothered groans were heard no more! He was horribly crushed by the ponderous roof and collapsing sides—and the flattened bier was his *Iron Shroud*.

J. Sheridan Le Fanu (1814–1873)

One of the world's greatest horror writers, Joseph Sheridan Le Fanu was born in Dublin of Huguenot stock. At an early age, he began to write poetry. Although he attended Trinity College, beginning in 1833, and was called to the bar in 1837, he never practiced law, to the disappointment of his family.

Instead, he chose to write, His first short story was published in 1838; his first novel, *The Cock and the Anchor*, appeared in 1845, a year after his marriage to Susan Bennet.

From 1839 on he devoted himself to journalism by day, fiction at night, merging three newspapers into the *Evening Mail*. In 1861, he bought the *Dublin University Magazine*. In 1864, he published his most popular work, the psychological thriller, *Uncle Silas*.

After the death of his wife, he slowly withdrew from society, immersing himself in the works of Swedenborg. He brewed strong tea over a spirit lamp and suffered recurring nightmares. Eventually he saw only his family; the people of Dublin dubbed him "The Invisible Prince."

His fiction mirrored his mental state, becoming increasingly weird, featuring characters dogged by guilt, often pursued by evil forces and beings.

On February 7, 1873 he was found dead in his bed, a terrified expression on his face.

While our selection, "Schalken the Painter," is one of his earliest works, it has been called "a superb masterpiece of the horrible."[1]

---

[1]There really was a Dutch painter named Godfried Schalken. Born in Dordrecht in 1643, he was noted for domestic scenes and candlelight effects.

SCHALKEN THE PAINTER

You will no doubt be surprised, my dear friend, at the subject of the following narrative. What had I to do with Schalken, or Schalken with me? He had returned to his native land, and was probably dead and buried before I was born; I never visited Holland, nor spoke with a native of that country. So much I believe you already know. I must, then, give you my authority, and state to you frankly the ground upon which rests the credibility of the strange story which I am about to lay before you.

I was acquainted, in my early days, with a Captain Vandael, whose father had served King William in the Low Countries, and also in my unhappy land during the Irish campaigns. I know not how it happened that I liked this man's society, in spite of his politics and religion: but so it was; and it was by means of the free intercourse to which our intimacy gave rise that I became possessed of the curious tale which you are about to hear.

I had often been struck, while visiting Vandael, by a remarkable picture, in which, though no connoisseur myself, I could not fail to discern some very strong peculiarities, particularly in the distribution of light and shade, as also a certain oddity in the design itself, which interested my curiosity. It represented the interior of what might be a chamber in some antique religious building—the foreground was occupied by a female figure arrayed in a species of white robe, part of which was arrayed so as to form a veil. The dress, however, is not strictly that of any religious order. In its hand the figure bears a lamp, by whose light alone the form and face are illuminated; the features are marked by an arch smile, such as pretty women wear when engaged in successfully practising some roguish trick; in the background, and, excepting where

67

the dim light of an expiring fire serves to define the form, totally in the shade, stands the figure of a man equipped in the old fashion, with doublet and so forth, in the attitude of alarm, his hand being placed upon the hilt of his sword, which he appears to be in the act of drawing.

"There are some pictures," said I to my friend, "which impress one, I know not how, with a conviction that they represent not the mere ideal shapes and combinations which have floated through the imagination of the artist, but scenes, faces, and situations, which have actually existed. When I look upon that picture, something assures me that I behold the representation of a reality."

Vandael smiled, and fixing his eyes upon the painting musingly, he said:

"Your fancy has not deceived you, my good friend, for that picture is the record, and I believe a faithful one, of a remarkable and mysterious occurrence. It was painted by Schalken, and contains, in the face of the female figure which occupies the most prominent place in the design, an accurate portrait of Rose Velderkaust, the niece of Gerard Douw, the first and, I believe, the only love of Godfrey Schalken. My father knew the painter well, and from Schalken himself he learned the story of the mysterious drama, one scene of which the picture has embodied. This painting, which is accounted a fine specimen of Schalken's style, was bequeathed to my father by the artist's will, and, as you have observed, is a very striking and interesting production."

I had only to request Vandael to tell the story of the painting in order to be gratified; and thus it is that I am enabled to submit to you a faithful recital of what I heard myself, leaving you to reject or to allow the evidence upon which the truth of the tradition depends, with this one assurance, that Schalken was an honest, blunt Dutchman, and, I believe, wholly incapable of committing a flight of imagination; and further, that Vandael, from whom I heard the story, appeared firmly convinced of its truth.

There are few forms upon which the mantle of mystery and romance could seem to hang more ungracefully than upon that of the uncouth and clownish Schalken—the Dutch boor—the rude and dogged, but most cunning worker in oils, whose pieces delight the initiated of the present day almost as much as his manners disgusted the refined of his own; and yet this man, so rude, so dogged, so slovenly, I had almost said so savage, in mien and manner, during his after successes, had been selected by the capricious goddess in his early life, to figure as the hero of a romance by no means devoid of interest or of mystery.

Who can tell how meet he may have been in his young days to play the part of the lover or the hero—who can say that in early life he had been the same harsh, unlicked, and rugged boor that, in his maturer age, he proved—or how far the neglected rudeness which afterwards marked his air, and garb, and manners, may not have been the growth of that reckless apathy not infrequently produced by bitter misfortunes and disappointments in early life?

These questions can never be answered.

We must content ourselves, then, with a plain statement of facts, leaving matters of speculation to those who like them.

When Schalken studied under the immortal Gerard Douw, he was a young man; and, in spite of the phlegmatic constitution and excitable manner which he shared, we believe, with his countrymen, he was not incapable of deep and vivid impressions, for it is an established fact that the young painter looked with considerable interest upon the beautiful niece of his wealthy master.

Rose Velderkaust was very young, having, at the period of which we speak, not yet attained her seventeenth year; and, if tradition speaks truth, she possessed all the soft dimpling charms of the fair, light-haired Flemish maidens. Schalken had not studied long in the school of Gerard Douw when he felt this interest deepening into something of a keener and intenser feeling that was quite consistent with that tranquility of his honest Dutch heart; and at the same time he perceived, or thought he perceived, flattering symptoms of a reciprocity of liking, and this was quite sufficient to determine whatever indecision he might have heretofore experienced, and to lead him to devote exclusively to every hope and feeling of his heart. In short, he was as much in love as a Dutchman could be. He was not long in making his passion known to the pretty maiden herself, and his declaration was followed by a corresponding confession upon her part.

Schalken, however, was a poor man, and he possessed no counterbalancing advantage of birth or position to induce the old man to consent to a union which must involve his niece and ward in the strugglings and difficulties of a young and nearly friendless artist. He was, therefore, to wait until time had furnished him with the opportunity, and accident with success; and then, if his labors were found sufficiently lucrative, it was to be hoped that his proposals might at least be listened to by her jealous guardian. Months passed away, and, cheered by the smiles of the little Rose, Schalken's labors were redoubled, and with such effect and improvement as reasonably to promise the realization of his hopes, and no contemptible eminence in his art, before many years should have elapsed.

The even course of this cheering prosperity was, unfortunately, designed to experience a sudden and formidable interruption and that, too, in a manner so strange and mysterious, as to baffle all investigation, and throw upon the events themselves a shadow of almost supernatural horror.

Schalken had one evening remained in the master's studio considerably longer than his more volatile companions, who had gladly availed themselves of the excuse which the dusk of evening afforded to withdraw from their several tasks, in order to finish a day of labor in the jollity and conviviality of the tavern.

But Schalken worked for improvement, or rather for love. Besides, he was now engaged merely in sketching a design, an operation which, unlike that of coloring, might be continued as long as there was light sufficient to distinguish between canvas and charcoal. He had not then, nor, indeed, until long after, discovered the peculiar powers of his pencil; and he was engaged in composing a group of extremely roguish-looking and grotesque imps and demons, who were inflicting various ingenious torments upon a perspiring and pot-bellied St. Anthony, who reclined in the midst of them, apparently in the last stage of drunkenness.

The young artist, however, though incapable of executing, or even of appreciating, anything of true sublimity, had nevertheless discernment enough to prevent his being by any means satisfied with his work; and many were the patient erasures and corrections which the limbs and features of saint and devil underwent, yet all without producing in their arrangement anything of improvement or increased effect.

The large, old-fashioned room was silent, and, with the exception of himself, quite deserted by its usual inmates. An hour had passed—nearly two—without any improved result. Daylight had already declined, and twilight was fast giving away to the darkness of night. The patience of the young man was exhausted, and he stood before his unfinished production, absorbed in no very pleasing ruminations, one hand buried in the folds of his long dark hair, and the other holding the piece of charcoal which had so ill executed his office, and which he now rubbed without much regard to the sable streaks which it produced, with irritable pressure upon his ample Flemish inexpressibles.

"Pshaw!" said the young man aloud, "would that picture, devils, saints, and all, were where they should be—in hell!"

A short, sudden laugh, uttered startlingly close to his ear, instantly responded to the ejaculation.

The artist turned sharply round, and now for the first time became aware that his labors had been overlooked by a stranger.

Within about a yard and a half, and rather behind him, there stood what was, or appeared to be, the figure of an elderly man: he wore a short cloak, and broad-brimmed hat with a conical crown, and in his hand, which was protected by a heavy, gauntlet-shaped glove, he carried a long ebony walking stick, surmounted by what appeared, as it glittered dimly in the twilight, to be a massive head of gold; and upon his breast, through the folds of the cloak, there shone the links of a rich chain of the same metal.

The room was so obscure that nothing further of the appearance of the figure could be ascertained, and the face was altogether over-shadowed by the heavy flap of the beaver which overhung it, so that no feature could be clearly discerned. A quantity of dark hair escaped from beneath this somber hat, a circumstance which, connected with the firm, upright carriage of the intruder, proved that his years could not yet exceed threescore or thereabouts.

There was an air of gravity and importance about the garb of this person, and something indescribably odd—I might say awful—in the perfect, stone-like movelessness of the figure, that effectively checked the testy comment which had at once risen to the lips of the irritated artist. He therefore, as soon as he had sufficiently recovered from his surprise, asked the stranger, civilly, to be seated, and desired to know if he had any message to leave for his master.

"Tell Gerard Douw," said the unknown, without altering his attitude in the smallest degree, "that Mynher Vanderhausen, of Rotterdam, desires to speak with him tomorrow evening at this hour, and if he please, in this room, upon matters of weight; that is all. Good-night."

The stranger, having finished this message, turned abruptly, and, with a quick but silent step quitted the room before Schalken had time to say a word in reply.

The young man felt a curiosity to see in what direction the burgher of Rotterdam would turn on quitting the studio, and for that purpose he went directly to the window which commanded the door.

A lobby of considerable extent intervened between the inner door of the painter's room and the street entrance, so that Schalken occupied the post of observation before the old man could possibly have reached the street.

He watched in vain, however. There was no other mode of exit.

Had the old man vanished, or was he lurking about the recesses of the lobby for some bad purpose? This last suggestion filled the mind of Schalken with a vague horror, which was so unaccountably intense as to make him alike afraid to remain in the room alone and reluctant to pass through the lobby.

However, with an effort which appeared very disproportioned to the occasion, he summoned resolution to leave the room, and, having double-locked the door, and thrust the key in his pocket, without looking to the right or left, he traversed the passage which had so recently, perhaps still, contained the person of his mysterious visitant, scarcely venturing to breathe till he had arrived in the open street.

"Mynher Vanderhausen," said Gerard Douw, within himself, as the appointed hour approached; "Mynher Vanderhausen, of Rotterdam! I never heard of the man till yesterday. What can he want of me? A portrait, perhaps, to be painted; or a younger son or a poor relation to be apprenticed; or a collection to be valued; or—pshaw! there's no one in Rotterdam to leave me a legacy. Well, whatever the business may be, we shall soon know it all."

It was now the close of day, and every easel except that of Schalken was deserted. Gerard Douw was pacing the apartment with the restless step of impatient expectation, every now and then humming a passage from a piece of music which he was himself composing for, though no great proficient, he admired the art—sometimes pausing to glance over the work of one of his absent pupils, but more frequently placing himself at the window, from whence he might observe the passengers who threaded the obscure street in which his studio was placed.

"Said you not, Godfrey," exclaimed Douw, after a long and fruitless gaze from his post of observation, and turning to Schalken— "said you not the hour of appointment was about seven by the clock of the Stadhouse?"

"It had just tolled seven when I first saw him, sir," answered the student.

"The hour is close at hand, then," said the master, consulting a horolage as large and as round as a full-grown orange. "Mynher Vanderhausen from Rotterdam—is it not so?"

"Such was the name."

"And an elderly man, richly clad?" continued Douw.

"As well as I might see," replied his pupil. "He could not be young, nor yet very old neither, and his dress was rich and grave, as might become a citizen of wealth and consideration."

At this moment the sonorous boom of the Stadhouse clock tolled, stroke after stroke, the hour of seven; the eyes of both master and student were directed to the door; and it was not until the last peal of the bell had ceased to vibrate that Douw exclaimed:

"So, so; we shall have his worship presently—that is, if he means to keep his hour; if not, thou mayest wait for him, Godfrey, if you court the acquaintance of a capricious burgomaster. As for me, I think our old Leyden contains a sufficiency of such commodities without an importation from Rotterdam."

Schalken laughed, as if in duty bound; and, after a pause of some minutes, Douw suddenly exclaimed:

"What if it should all prove a jest, a piece of mummery got up by Vankarp, or some such worthy! I wish you had run all risks and cudgeled the old burgomaster, stadholder, or whatever else he may be, soundly. I would wager a dozen of Rhenish, his worship would have pleaded old acquaintance before the third application."

"Here he comes, sir," said Schalken, in a low, admonitory tone; and instantly, upon turning toward the door, Gerard Douw observed the same figure which had, on the day before, so unexpectedly greeted the vision of his pupil Schalken.

There was something in the air and mien of the figure which at once satisfied the painter that there was no mummery in the case, and that he really stood in the presence of a man of worship; and so, without hesitation, he doffed his cap, and courteously saluting the stranger, requested him to be seated.

The visitor waved his hand slightly, as if in acknowledgment of the courtesy, but remained standing.

"I have the honor to see Mynher Vanderhausen, of Rotterdam?" said Gerard Douw.

"The same," was the laconic reply.

"I understand your worship desires to speak with me," continued Douw, "and I am here by appointment to wait your commands."

"Is that a man of trust?" said Vanderhausen, turning toward Schalken, who stood at a little distance behind his master.

"Certainly," replied Gerard.

"Then let him take this box and get the nearest jeweler or goldsmith to value its contents, and let him return hither with a certificate of the valuation."

At the same time he placed a small case, about nine inches square, in the hands of Gerard Douw, who was as much amazed at its weight as at the strange abruptness with which it was handed to him.

In accordance with the wishes of the stranger, he delivered it into the hands of Schalken, and repeating his directions, despatched him upon the mission.

Schalken disposed his precious charge securely beneath the folds of his cloak, and rapidly traversing two or three narrow streets, he stopped at a corner house, the lower part of which was then occupied by the shop of a Jewish goldsmith.

Schalken entered the shop and calling the little Hebrew into the obscurity of its back recesses, he proceeded to lay before him Vanderhausen's packet.

On being examined by the light of a lamp, it appeared entirely encased with lead, the outer surface of which was much scraped and soiled, and nearly white with age. This was with difficulty partially removed, and disclosed beneath a box of some dark and singularly hard wood; this, too, was forced, and after the removal of two or three folds of linen, its contents proved to be a mass of golden ingots, close packed, and, as the Jew declared, of the most perfect quality.

Every ingot underwent the scrutiny of the little Jew, who seemed to feel an epicurean delight in touching and testing these morsels of the glorious metal, and each one of them was replaced in the box with the exclamation:

"Mein Gott, how very perfect! not one grain of alloy—beautiful, beautiful!"

The task was at length finished, and the Jew certified under his hand the value of the ingots submitted to his examination to amount to many thousand rix-dollars.

With his desired document in his bosom, and the rich box of gold carefully pressed under his arm, and concealed by his cloak, he retraced his way, and entering the studio, found his master and the stranger in close conference.

Schalken had no sooner left the room, in order to execute the commission he had taken in charge than Vanderhausen addressed Gerard Douw in the following terms:

"I may not tarry with you tonight more than a few minutes, and so I shall briefly tell you the matter upon which I come. You visited the town of Rotterdam some four months ago, and then I saw in the church of St. Lawrence your niece, Rose Velderkaust. I desire to marry her, and if I satisfy you as to the fact that I am very wealthy—more wealthy than any husband you could dream of for her—I expect that you will forward my views to the utmost of your authority. If you approve my proposal, you must close with it at once, for I cannot command time enough to wait for calculations and delays."

Gerard Douw was, perhaps, as much astonished as anyone could be by the very unexpected nature of Mynher Vanderhausen's communication; but he did not give vent to any unseemly expression of surprise, for, besides the motives supplied by prudence and politeness, the painter experienced a kind of chill and oppressive sensation, something like that which is supposed to affect a man who is placed unconsciously in immediate contact with something to which he has a natural antipathy— an undefined horror and dread while standing in the presence of the eccentric stranger, which made him very unwilling to say anything which might reasonably prove offensive.

"I have no doubt," said Gerard, after two or three prefatory hems, "that the connection which you propose would prove alike advantageous and honorable to my niece; but you must be aware that she has a will of her own, and may not acquiesce in what *we* may design for her advantage."

"Do not seek to deceive me, Sir Painter," said Vanderhausen; "you are her guardian—she is your ward. She is mine if *you* like to make her so."

The man of Rotterdam moved forward a little as he spoke, and Gerard Douw, he scarce knew why, inwardly prayed for the speedy return of Schalken.

"I desire," said the mysterious gentleman, "to place in your hands at once an evidence of my wealth, and a security for my liberal dealings with your niece. The lad will return in a minute or two with a sum in value five times the fortune which she has a right to expect from a husband. This shall be in your hands, together with her dowry, and you may apply the united sum as suits her interest best; it shall be all exclusively hers while she lives. Is that liberal?''

Douw assented, and inwardly thought that fortune had been extraordinarily kind to his niece. The stranger, he thought, must be both wealthy and generous, and such an offer was not to be despised, though made by a humorist, and one of no very prepossessing presence.

Rose had no very high pretensions, for she was almost without dowry; indeed, altogether so, excepting so far as the deficiency had been supplied by the generosity of her uncle. Neither had she any right to raise any scruples against the match on the score of birth, for her own origin was by no means elevated, and as to other objections, Gerard resolved, and, indeed, by the usages of the time was warranted in resolving, not to listen to them for a moment.

''Sir,'' said he, addressing the stranger, ''your offer is most liberal, and whatever hesitation I may feel in closing with it immediately, arises solely from not having the honor of knowing anything of your family or station. Upon these points you can, of course, satisfy me without difficulty?''

''As to my respectability,'' said the stranger, drily, ''you must take that for granted at present, pester me with no inquiries; you can discover nothing more about me than I choose to make known. You shall have sufficient security for my respectability—my word, if you are honorable; if you are sordid, my gold.''

''A testy old gentleman,'' thought Douw; ''he must have his own way. But, all things considered, I am justifed in giving my niece to him. Were she my own daughter, I would do the like by her. I will not pledge myself unnecessarily, however.''

''You will not pledge yourself unnecessarily,'' said Vanderhausen, strangely uttering the very words which had just floated through the mind of his companion, ''but you will do so if it *is* necessary, I presume; and I will show you that I consider it indispensable. If the gold I mean to leave in your hands satisfies you, and if you desire that my proposal shall not be at once withdrawn, you must, before I leave this room, write your name to this engagement.''

Having thus spoken, he placed a paper in the hands of Gerard, the contents of which expressed an engagement entered into by Gerard

Douw, to give to Wilken Vanderhausen, of Rotterdam, in marriage Rose Velderkaust, and so forth, within one week of the date hereof.

While the painter was employed in reading this covenant, Schalken, as we have stated, entered the studio, and having delivered the box and the valuation of the Jew into the hands of the stranger, he was about to retire, when Vanderhausen called to him to wait; and presenting the case and the certificate to Gerard Douw, he waited in silence until he had satisfied himself by an inspection of both as to the value of the pledge left in his hands. At length he said:

"Are you content?"

The painter said he would fain have another day to consider.

"Not an hour," said the suitor, coolly.

"Well, then," said Douw. "I am content; it is a bargain."

"Then sign at once," said Vanderhausen; "I am weary."

At the same time he produced a small case of writing materials, and Gerard signed the important document.

"Let this youth witness the covenant," said the old man; and Godfrey Schalken unconsciously signed the instrument which bestowed upon another that hand which he had so long regarded as the object and reward of all his labors.

The compact being thus completed, the strange visitor folded up the paper, and stowed it safely in an inner pocket.

"I will visit you tomorrow night, at nine of the clock, at your house, Gerard Douw, and you will see the subject of our contract. Farewell." And so saying, Wilken Vanderhausen moved stiffly, but rapidly, out of the room.

Schalken, eager to resolve his doubts, had placed himself by the window in order to watch the street entrance; but the experiment served only to support his suspicions, for the old man did not issue from the door. This was very strange, very odd, very fearful. He and his master returned together, and talked but little on the way, for each had his own subjects of reflection, of anxiety, and of hope.

Schalken, however, did not know the ruin which threatened his cherished schemes.

Gerard Douw knew nothing of the attachment which had sprung up between his pupil and his niece; and even if he had, it is doubtful whether he would have regarded its existence as any serious obstruction to the wishes of Mynher Vanderhausen.

Marriages were then and there matters of traffic and calculation; and it would have appeared as absurd in the eye of the guardian to make a mutual attachment an essential element in a contract of marriage, as it would have been to draw up his bond and receipts in the language of chivalrous romance.

The painter, however, did not communicate to his niece the important step which he had taken on her behalf, and his resolution arose not from any anticipation of opposition on her part, but solely from a ludicrous consciousness that if his ward were, as she very naturally might do, to ask him to describe the appearance of the bridegroom whom he destined for her, he would be forced to confess that he had not seen his face, and, if called upon, would find it impossible to identify him.

Upon the next day, Gerard Douw, having dined, called his niece to him, and having scanned her person with an air of satisfaction, he took her hand, and looking upon her pretty, innocent face with a smile of kindness, he said:

"Rose, my girl, that face of yours will make your fortune." Rose blushed and smiled. "Such faces and such tempers seldom go together, and, when they do, the compound is a love potion which few heads or hearts can resist. Trust me, thou will soon be a bride, girl. But this is trifling, and I am pressed for time, so make ready the large room by eight o'clock tonight, and give directions for supper at nine. I expect a friend tonight; and, observe me, child, do thou trick thyself out handsomely. I would not have him think us poor or sluttish."

With these words he left the chamber and took his way to the room to which we have already had occasion to introduce our readers—that in which his pupils worked.

When evening closed in, Gerard called Schalken, who was about to take his departure to his obscure and comfortless lodgings, and asked him to come home and sup with Rose and Vanderhausen.

The invitation was of course accepted and Gerard Douw and his pupil soon found themselves in the handsome and somewhat antique-looking room which had been prepared for the reception of the stranger.

A cheerful wood fire blazed in the capacious hearth; a little at one side an old-fashioned table, with richly-carved legs was placed—destined, no doubt, to receive the supper, for which preparations were going forward; and ranged with exact regularity, stood the tall-backed chairs, whose ungracefulness was more than counterbalanced by their comfort.

The little party, consisting of Rose, her uncle, and the artist, awaited the arrival of the expected visitor with considerable impatience.

Nine o'clock at length came, and with it a summons at the street door, which, being speedily answered, was followed by a slow and emphatic tread upon the staircase; the steps moved heavily across the lobby, the door of the room in which the party which we have described were assembled slowly opened, and there entered a figure which startled, almost appalled, the phlegmatic Dutchmen, and nearly made Rose scream with affright; it was the form, and arrayed in the garb, of Mynher Vanderhausen; the air, the gait, the height was the same, but the features had never been seen by any of the party before.

The stranger stopped at the door of the room, and displayed his form and face completely. He wore a dark-colored cloak, which was short and full, not falling quite to his knees; his legs were cased in dark purple stockings, and his shoes were adorned with roses of the same color. The opening of the cloak in front showed the under-suit to consist of some very dark, perhaps sable material, and his hands were enclosed in a pair of heavy leather gloves which ran up considerably above the wrist, in the manner of a gauntlet. In one hand he carried his walking stick and his hat, which he had removed, and the other hung heavily by his side. A quantity of grizzled hair descended in long tresses from his head, and its folds rested upon the plaits of a stiff ruff, which effectually concealed his neck.

So far all was well; but the face! All the flesh of the face was colored with the bluish leaden hue which is sometimes produced by the operation of metallic medicines administered in excessive quantities; the eyes were enormous, and the white appeared both above and below the iris, which gave to them an expression of insanity, which was heightened by the glassy fixedness; the nose was well enough, but the mouth was writhed considerably to one side, where it opened in order to give egress to two long, discolored fangs, which projected from the upper jaw, far below the lower lip; the hue of the lips themselves bore the usual relation to that of the face, and was consequently nearly black. The character of the face was malignant, even satanic to the last degree; and indeed, such a combination of horror could hardly be accounted for, except by supposing the corpse of some atrocious malefactor, which had long hung blackening upon the gibbet, to have at length become the habitation of a demon—the frightful sport of satanic possession.

It was remarkable that the worshipful stranger suffered as little as possible of his flesh to appear, and that during his visit he did not once remove his gloves.

Having stood for some moments at the door, Gerard Douw at length found breath and collectedness to bid him welcome and, with a mute inclination of the head, the stranger stepped forward into the room.

There was something indescribably odd, even horrible, about all his motions, something undefinable, that was unnatural, unhuman—it was as if the limbs were guided and directed by a spirit unused to the management of bodily machinery.

The stranger hardly said anything during his visit, which did not exceed half an hour; and the host himself could scarcely muster courage enough to utter the few necessary salutations and courtesies; and, indeed, such was the nervous tension which the presence of Vanderhausen inspired, that very little would have made all his entertainers fly bellowing from the room.

They had not so far lost all self-possession, however, as to fail to observe two strange peculiarities of their visitor.

During his stay he did not once suffer his eyelids to close, nor even to move in the slightest degree; and further, there was a deathlike stillness in his whole person, owing to the total absence of the heaving motion of the chest, caused by the process of respiration.

These two peculiarities, though when told they may appear trifling, produced a very striking and unpleasant effect when seen and observed. Vanderhausen at length relieved the painter of Leyden of his inauspicious presence; and with no small gratification the little party heard the street-door close after him.

"Dear uncle," said Rose, "what a frightful man! I would not see him again for the wealth of the States!"

"Tush, foolish girl!" said Douw, whose sensations were anything but comfortable. "A man may be as ugly as the devil, and yet if his heart and actions are good, he is worth all the pretty-faced, perfumed puppies that walk the Mall. Rose, my girl, it is very true he has not thy pretty face, but I know him to be wealthy and liberal; and were he ten times more ugly—"

"Which is inconceivable," observed Rose.

"These two virtues would be sufficient," continued her uncle, "to counterbalance all his deformity; and if not of power sufficient actually to alter the shape of his features, at least of efficacy enough to prevent one thinking them amiss."

"Do you know, uncle," said Rose, "when I saw him standing at the door, I could not get out of my head that I saw the old, painted, wooden figure that used to frighten me so much in the church of St. Laurence of Rotterdam."

Gerard laughed, though he could not help inwardly acknowledging the justness of the comparison. He was resolved, however, as far as he could, to check his niece's inclination to ridicule the ugliness of her intended bridegroom, although he was not a little pleased to observe that she appeared totally exempt from that mysterious dread of the stranger which, he could not disguise it from himself, considerably affected him as also his pupil Godfrey Schalken.

Early on the next day there arrived, from various quarters of the town, rich presents of silks, velvets, jewelry, and so forth, for Rose; and also a packet directed to Gerard Douw, which, on being opened, was found to contain a contract of marriage, formally drawn up, between Wilken Vanderhausen of the Boom-quay, in Rotterdam, and Rose Velderkaust of Leyden, niece to Gerard Douw, master in the art of painting, also of the same city; and containing engagements on the part of Vanderhausen to make settlements upon his bride, for more splendor than he had before led her guardian to believe likely, and which were to be secured to her use in the most exceptional manner possible—the money being placed in the hands of Gerard Douw himself.

I have no sentimental scenes to describe, no cruelty of guardians, or magnanimity of wards, or agonies of lovers. The record I have to make is one of sordidness, levity and interest. In less than a week after the first interview which we have just described the contract of marriage was fulfilled and Schalken saw the prize which he would have risked anything to secure, carried off triumphantly by his formidable rival.

For two or three days he absented himself from the school; he then returned and worked, if with less cheerfulness, with far more dogged determination than before; the dream of love had given place to that of ambition.

Months passed away and, contrary to his expectations, and, indeed, to the direct promise of the parties, Gerard Douw heard nothing of his niece, or her worshipful spouse. The interest of the money, which was to have been demanded in quarterly sums lay unclaimed in his hands. He began to grow extremely uneasy.

Mynher Vanderhausen's direction in Rotterdam he was full possessed of. After some irresolution he finally determined to journey thither—a trifling undertaking and easily accomplished—and thus to satisfy himself of the safety and comfort of his ward, for whom he entertained an honest and strong affection.

His search was in vain, however. No one in Rotterdam had ever heard of Mynher Vanderhausen.

Gerard Douw left not a house on the Boom-quay untried; but all in vain. No one could give him any confirmation whatever touching the object of his inquiry, and he was obliged to return to Leyden, nothing wiser than when he left it.

On his arrival he hastened to the establishment from which Vanderhausen had hired the lumbering though, considering the times, most luxurious vehicle which the bridal party had employed to convey them to Rotterdam. From the driver of this machine he learned that, having proceeded by slow stages, they had late in the evening approached Rotterdam; but that before they entered the city, and while yet nearly a mile from it, a small party of men, soberly clad, and after the old fashion, with peaked beards and moustaches, standing in the center of the road, obstructed the further progress of the carriage. The driver reined in his horses, much fearing, from the obscurity of the hour and the loneliness of the road, that some mischief was intended.

His fears were, however, somewhat allayed by him observing that these strange men carried a large litter of an antique shape, which they immediately set down upon the pavement, whereupon the bridegroom, having opened the coach-door from within, descended, and having assisted his bride to do likewise, led her, weeping bitterly and wringing her hands, to the litter, which they both entered. It was then raised by the men and speedily carried toward the city, and before it had proceeded many yards the darkness concealed it from the view of the Dutch charioteer.

In the insides of the vehicle he found a purse, whose contents more than thrice paid the hire of the carriage and man. He saw and could tell nothing more of Mynher Vanderhausen and the beautiful lady. This mystery was a source of deep anxiety and almost of grief to Gerard Douw.

There was evidently fraud in the dealing of Vanderhausen with him, though for what purpose committed he could not imagine. He greatly doubted how far it was possible for a man possessing in his countenance so strong an evidence of the presence of the most demoniac feelings, to be in reality anything but a villain, and every day that passed without his hearing from or of his niece, instead of inducing him to forget his fears, on the contrary tended more and more to exasperate them.

The loss of his niece's cheerful society tended also to depress his spirits; and in order to dispel this despondency, which often crept upon his mind after his daily employment was over, he was wont frequently to prevail upon Schalken to accompany him home, and by his presence to dispel, in some degree, the gloom of his otherwise solitary supper.

One evening, the painter and his pupil were sitting by the fire, having accomplished a comfortable supper, and had yielded to that silent pensiveness sometimes induced by the process of digestion, when their reflections were disturbed by a loud sound at the street door, as if occasioned by some person rushing forcibly and repeatedly against it. A domestic had run without delay to ascertain the cause of the disturbance, and they heard him twice or thrice interrogate the applicant for admission, but without producing an answer or any cessation of the sounds.

They heard him then open the hall door, and immediately there followed a light and rapid tread upon the staircase. Schalken laid his hand on his sword, and advanced toward the door. It opened before he reached it, and Rose rushed into the room. She looked wild and haggard, and pale with exhaustion and terror, but her dress surpised them as much even as her unexpected appearance. It consisted of a kind of white woolen wrapper, made close about the neck, and descending to the very ground. It was much deranged and travel soiled. The poor creature had hardly entered the chamber when she fell senseless on the floor. With some difficulty they succeeded in reviving her, and on recovering her senses she instantly exclaimed, in a tone of eager, terrified impatience:

"Wine, wine, quickly, or I'm lost!"

Much alarmed at the strange agitation in which the call was made, they at once administered to her wishes, and she drank some wine with a haste and eagerness which surprised them. She had hardly swallowed it, when she exclaimed, with the same urgency:

"Food, food, at once, or I perish!"

A considerable fragment of a roast joint was upon the table, and Schalken immediately proceeded to cut some, but he was anticipated; for no sooner had she become aware of its presence than she darted at it with the rapacity of a vulture, and, seizing it in her hands she tore off the flesh with her teeth and swallowed it.

When the paroxysm of hunger had been a little appeased, she

appeared suddenly to become aware how strange her conduct had been, or it may have been that other more agitating thoughts recurred to her mind, for she began to weep bitterly, and to wring her hands.

"Oh, send for a minister of God," said she; "I am not safe till he comes; send for him speedily."

Gerard Douw despatched a messenger instantly, and prevailed on his niece to allow him to surrender his bedchamber to her use; he also persuaded her to retire to it at once and rest; her consent was extracted upon the condition that they would not leave her for a moment.

"Oh, that the holy man were here!" she said; "he can deliver me. The dead and the living can never be one—God has forbidden it."

With these mysterious words she surrendered herself to their guidance, and they proceeded to the chamber which Gerard Douw had assigned to her use.

"Do not—do not leave me for a moment," said she. "I am lost if you do."

Gerard Douw's chamber was approached through a spacious apartment, which they were now about to enter. Gerard Douw and Schalken each carried a wax candle so that a sufficient degree of light was cast upon all surrounding objects. They were now entering the large chamber, which, as I have said, communicated with Douw's apartment, when Rose suddenly stopped, and, in a whisper which seemed to thrill with horror, she said:

"Oh, God! he is here—he is here! See, see—there he goes!"

She pointed toward the door of the inner room, and Schalken thought he saw a shadowy and ill-defined form gliding into that apartment. He drew his sword, and raising the candle so as to throw its light with increased distinction upon the objects in the room, he entered the chamber into which the shadow had glided. No figure was there—nothing but the furniture which belonged to the room, and yet he could not be deceived as to the fact that something had moved before them into the chamber.

A sickening dread came upon him, and the cold perspiration broke out in heavy drops upon his forehead; nor was he more composed when he heard the increased urgency, the agony of entreaty, with which Rose implored them not to leave her for a moment.

"I saw him," said she. "He's here! I cannot be deceived—I know him. He's by me—he's with me—he's in the room. Then, for God's sake, as you would save me, do not stir from beside me!"

They at length prevailed upon her to lie down upon the bed, where she continued to urge them to stay by her. She frequently uttered incoherent sentences, repeating again and again, "The dead and the living cannot be one—God had forbidden it!" and then again, "Rest to the wakeful—sleep to the sleep-walkers."

These and other mysterious and broken sentences she continued to utter until the clergyman arrived.

Gerard Douw began to fear, naturally enough, that the poor girl, owing to terror or ill-treatment, had become deranged; and he half suspected, by the suddenness of her appearance, and the unreasonableness of the hour, and, above all, from the wildness and terror of her manner, that she had made her escape from some place of confinement for lunatics, and was in immediate fear of pursuit. He resolved to summon medical advice as soon as the mind of his niece had been in some measure set at rest by the offices of the clergyman whose attendance she had so earnestly desired; and until this object had been attained, he did not venture to put any questions to her which might possibly, by reviving pitiful or horrible recollections, increase her agitation.

The clergyman soon arrived—a man of ascetic countenance and venerable age—one whom Gerard Douw respected much, forasmuch as he was a veteran polemic, though one, perhaps, more dreaded as a combatant than beloved as a Christian—of pure morality, subtle brain, and frozen heart. He entered the chamber which communicated with that in which Rose reclined, and immediately on his arrival she requested him to pray for her, as for one who lay in the hands of Satan, and who could hope for deliverance only from heaven.

That our readers may distinctly understand all the circumstances of the event which we are about imperfectly to describe, it is necessary to state the relative position of the parties who were engaged in it. The old clergyman and Schalken were in the anteroom of which we have already spoken; Rose lay in the inner chamber, the door of which was open; and by the side of the bed, at her urgent desire, stood her guardian; a candle burned in the bedchamber, and three were lighted in the inner apartment.

The old man now cleared his voice, as if about to commence; but before he had time to begin, a sudden gust of air blew out the candle which served to illuminate the room in which the poor girl lay, and she, with hurried alarm, exclaimed:

"Godfrey, bring in another candle, the darkness is unsafe."

Gerard Douw, forgetting for a moment her repeated injunctions in the immediate impulse, stepped from the bedchamber into the other, in order to supply what she desired.

"O God! do not go, dear uncle!" shrieked the unhappy girl; and at the same time she sprang from the bed and darted after him, in order, by her grasp, to detain him.

But the warning came too late, for scarcely had he passed the threshold, and hardly had his niece had time to utter the startling exclamation, when the door which divided the two rooms closed violently after him, as if swung by a strong blast of wind.

Schalken and he both rushed to the door, but their united and desperate efforts could not avail as much as to shake it.

Shriek after shriek burst forth from the inner chamber, with all the piercing loudness of despairing terror. Schalken and Douw applied every energy and strained every nerve to force open the door, but all in vain.

There was no sound of struggling within, but the screams seemed to increase in loudness, and at the same time they heard the bolts of the lattice window withdrawn, and the window itself grated upon the sill as if thrown open.

One last shriek, so long and piercing and agonized as to be scarcely human, swelled from the room, and suddenly there followed a deathlike silence.

A light step was heard crossing the floor, as if from the bed to the window; and almost at the same instant the door gave way, and, yielding to the pressure of the external applicants, they were nearly precipitated into the room. It was empty. The window was open, and Schalken sprang to a chair and gazed out upon the street and the canal below. He saw no form, but he beheld, or thought he beheld, the waters of the broad canal beneath settling ring after ring in heavy circular ripples, as if a moment before disturbed by the immersion of some large and heavy mass.

No trace of Rose was ever after discovered, nor was anything certain respecting her mysterious wooer detected or even suspected; no clue whereby to trace the intricacies of the labyrinth and to arrive at a distinct conclusion was to be found. But an incident occurred, which, though it will not be received by our rational readers as at all approaching to evidence upon the matter, nevertheless produced a strong and lasting impression upon the mind of Schalken.

Many years after the events which we have detailed, Schalken, then remotely situated, received an intimation of his father's death, and of his intended burial upon a fixed day in the church of Rotterdam. It was necessary that a very considerable journey should be performed by the funeral procession, which, as it will readily be believed, was not very numerously attended. Schalken with difficulty arrived in Rotterdam late in the day upon which the funeral was appointed to take place. The procession had not then arrived. Evening closed in, and still it did not appear.

Schalken strolled down to the church. He found it open and notice of the funeral had been given, and the vault in which the body was to be laid had been opened. The official who corresponds to our sexton, on seeing a well-dressed gentleman whose object was to attend the expected funeral, pacing the aisle of the church, hospitably invited him to share with him the comforts of a blazing wood fire, which, as was his custom in wintertime upon such occasions, he had kindled on the hearth of a chamber which communicated, by a flight of steps, with the vault below.

In this chamber Schalken and his entertainer seated themselves, and the sexton, after some fruitless attempts to engage his guest in conversation, was obliged to apply himself to his tobacco-pipe and can to solace his solitude.

In spite of his grief and cares, the fatigues of a rapid journey of nearly forty hours gradually overcame the mind and body of Godfrey Schalken, and he sank into a deep sleep, from which he was awakened by someone shaking him gently by the shoulder. He first thought that the old sexton had called him, but he was no longer in the room.

He roused himself, and as soon as he could clearly see what was around him, he perceived a female form, clothed in a kind of light robe of muslin, part of which was so disposed to act as a veil, and in her hand she carried a lamp. She was moving rather away from him, and toward the flight of steps which conducted toward the vaults.

Schalken felt a vague alarm at the sight of this figure, and at the same time an irresistible impulse to follow its guidance. He followed it toward the vaults, but when it reached the head of the stairs, he paused; the figure paused also, and, turning gently round, displayed, by the light of the lamp it carried, the face and features of his first love, Rose Velderkaust. There was nothing horrible, or even sad, in the countenance. On the contrary, it wore the same sad smile which used to enchant the artist long before in his happy days.

A feeling of awe and interest, too intense to be resisted, prompted him to follow the spectre, if spectre it were. She descended the stairs— he followed; and, turning to the left, through a narrow passage, she led him, to his infinite surprise, into what appeared to be an old-fashioned Dutch apartment, such as the pictures of Gerard Douw have served to immortalize.

Abundance of costly antique furniture was disposed about the room, and in one corner stood a four-poster bed, with heavy black cloth curtains around it; the figure frequently turned toward him with the same arch smile, and when she came to the side of the bed, she drew the curtains, and, by the light of the lamp which she held toward its contents, she disclosed to the horror-stricken painter, sitting bolt upright in bed, the livid and demoniac form of Vanderhausen. Schalken had hardly seen him when he fell senseless upon the floor, where he lay until discovered, on the next morning, by persons employed in closing the passages into the vaults. He was lying in a cell of considerable size, which had not been disturbed for a long time, and he had fallen beside a large coffin which was supported upon small stone pillars, a security against the attacks of vermin.

To his dying day Schalken was satisfied of the reality of the vision which he had witnessed, and he has left behind him a curious evidence of the impression which it wrought upon his fancy, in a painting executed shortly after the event we have narrated, which is valuable as exhibiting not only the peculiarities which have made Schalken's pictures sought after, but even more so as presenting a portrait, as close and faithful as one taken from memory can be, of his early love, Rose Velderkaust, whose mysterious fate must ever remain a matter of speculation.

The picture represents a chamber of antique masonry, such as might be found in most old cathedrals, and is lighted faintly by a lamp carried in the hand of a female figure, such as we have above attempted to describe; and in the background, and to the left of him who examines the painting, there stands the form of a man apparently roused from sleep, and by his attitude, his hand being laid upon his sword, exhibiting considerable alarm: this last figure is illuminated only by the expiring glare of a wood or charcoal fire.

The whole production exhibits a beautiful specimen of that artful and singular distribution of light and shade which has rendered the name of Schalken immortal among the artists of his country. This tale is traditionary, and the reader will easily perceive, by our studiously omitting to heighten many points of the narrative, when a little additional coloring might have added effect to the recital, that we have desired to lay before him, not a figment of the brain, but a curious tradition connected with, and belonging to, the biography of a famous artist.

Edgar Allan Poe (1809–1849)

Shortly after Poe's birth in Boston, his father ran away; his mother succumbed to consumption three years later. Cared for by the John Allans, to whom he initially brought great joy, he lost favor by behaving disgracefully at the University of Virginia.

After two abortive tries at an army career, Poe began to write full-time. Winning the 1833 Baltimore *Sunday Visitor* short story contest ("Ms Found in a Bottle") brought his first editorial job. But he was invariably fired from such positions because of arrogance, strong views, and antisocial behavior.

He moved to New York, living and writing in abject poverty, as his cousin-bride wasted away. Masterpieces such as "The Raven" and "The Purloined Letter," brought scant funds, or were given away.

Yet he was prolific, producing a short science fiction novel and several volumes worth of poems and short stories in a brief period of time.

In 1849, just as he seemed on the verge of straightening out his life, he disappeared and was discovered dying in a Baltimore gutter.

Horror was probably the field to which Poe contributed the largest number of outstanding works, among them "The Black Cat," "The Cask of Amontillado," "The Facts in the Case of M. Valdeman," "The Fall of the House of Usher," "The Masque of Red Death," "The Pit and the Pendulum," and "The Premature Burial." We have chosen his memorable story of obsession, "The Tell-Tale Heart."

THE TELL-TALE HEART

*T*rue!—*nervous—very, very dreadfully nervous I had been and* am! But why *will* you say that I am mad? The disease had sharpened my senses, not destroyed, not dulled them. Above all was the sense of hearing acute. I heard all things in the heaven and in the earth. I heard many things in hell. How, then, am I mad? Hearken and observe how healthily—how calmly—I can tell you the whole story.

It is impossible to say how first the idea entered my brain; but once conceived, it haunted me day and night. Object there was none. Passion there was none. I loved the old man. He had never wronged me. He had never given me insult. For his gold I had no desire. I think it was his eye! Yes, it was this! One of his eyes resembled that of a vulture—a pale blue eye, with a film over it. Whenever it fell upon me, my blood ran cold; and so by degrees—very gradually—I made up my mind to take the life of the old man, and thus rid myself of the eye forever.

Now this is the point. You fancy me mad. Madmen know nothing. But you should have seen *me*. You should have seen how wisely I proceeded, with what caution, with what foresight, with what dissimulation I went to work!

I was never kinder to the old man during the whole week before I killed him. And every night, about midnight, I turned the latch of his door and opened it—oh, so gently! And then, when I had made an opening sufficient for my head, I put in a dark lantern, all closed, closed, so that no light shone out, and then I thrust in my head. Oh, you would have laughed to see how cunningly I thrust it in! I moved it slowly—very slowly, so that I might not disturb the old man's sleep. It took me an hour to place my whole head within the opening so far that I could see him as he lay upon his bed. Ha! Would a madman have been so wise as this? And then, when my head was well in the room, I undid the lantern cautiously—oh, so cautiously—cautiously (for the hinges creaked)—I undid it just so much that a single thin ray fell upon the vulture eye. And this I did for seven long nights—every night just at midnight—but I found the eye always closed; and so it was impossible to do the work; for it was not the old man who vexed me, but his Evil Eye. And every morning, when the day broke, I went boldly into the chamber, and spoke courageously to him, calling him by name in a hearty tone, and inquiring how he had passed the night. So you see he would have been a very profound old man, indeed, to suspect that every night, just at twelve, I looked in upon him while he slept.

Upon the eighth night I was more than usually cautious in opening the door. A watch's minute hand moves more quickly than did mine. Never before that night had I *felt* the extent of my own powers, of my sagacity. I could scarcely contain my feelings of triumph. To think that there I was, opening the door, little by little, and he not even to dream of my secret deeds or thoughts. I fairly chuckled at the idea; and perhaps he heard me; for he moved on the bed suddenly, as if startled. Now you may think that I drew back—but no. His room was as black as pitch with the thick darkness (for the shutters were close fastened, through fear of robbers) and so I knew that he could not see the opening of the door, and I kept pushing it on steadily, steadily.

I had my head in, and was about to open the lantern, when my thumb slipped upon the tin fastening, and the old man sprang up in bed, crying out: "Who's there?"

I kept quite still and said nothing. For a whole hour I did not move a muscle, and in the meantime I did not hear him lie down. He was still sitting up in the bed listening—just as I have done, night after night, hearkening to the death watches in the wall.

Presently I heard a slight groan, and I knew it was the groan of mortal terror. It was not a groan of pain or of grief—oh no!—it was the low stifled sound that arises from the bottom of the soul when overcharged with awe. I knew the sound well. Many a night, just at midnight, when all the world slept, it has welled up from my own bosom, deepening, with its dreadful echo, the terrors that distracted me. I say I knew it well. I knew what the old man felt, and pitied him, although I chuckled at heart. I knew that he had been lying awake ever since the first slight noise, when he had turned in the bed. His fears had been ever since growing upon him. He had been trying to fancy them causeless, but could not. He had been saying to himself, " It is nothing but the wind in the chimney—it is only a mouse crossing the floor," or, "It is merely a cricket which has made a single chirp." Yes, he has been trying to comfort himself with these suppositions; but he had found all in vain. *All in vain;* because Death, in approaching him, had stalked with his black shadow before him, and enveloped the victim. And it was the mournful influence of the unperceived shadow that caused him to feel—although he neither saw nor heard—to *feel* the presence of my head within the room.

When I had waited a long time, very patiently, without hearing him lie down, I resolved to open a little—a very, very little—crevice in the lantern. So I opened it—you cannot imagine how stealthily, stealthily— until, at length, a single dim ray, like the thread of the spider, shot from out the crevice and full upon the vulture eye.

It was open—wide, wide open—and I grew furious as I gazed upon it. I saw it with perfect distinctness, all a dull blue, with a hideous evil veil over it that chilled the very marrow in my bones, but I could see nothing else of the old man's face or person: for I had directed the ray as if by instinct, precisely upon the damned spot.

And now have I not told you that what you mistake for madness is but over-acuteness of the senses? Now, I say, there came to my ears a low, dull, quick sound, such as a watch makes when enveloped in cotton. I knew *that* sound well too. It was the beating of the old man's heart. It increased my fury, as the beating of a drum stimulates the soldier into courage.

But even yet I refrained and kept still. I scarcely breathed. I held the lantern motionless. I tried how steadily I could maintain the ray upon the eye. Meantime the hellish tattoo of the heart increased. It grew quicker and quicker, and louder and louder every instant. The old man's terror *must* have been extreme! It grew louder, I say, louder every moment! Do you mark me well? I have told you that I am nervous: so I am. And now at the dead hour of the night, amid the dreadful silence of that old house, so strange a noise as this excited me to uncontrollable terror. Yet, for some minutes longer I refrained and stood still. But the beating grew louder, louder! I thought the heart must burst. And now a new anxiety seized me—the sound would be heard by a neighbor! The old man's hour had come! With a loud yell, I threw open the lantern and leaped into the room. He shrieked once, once only. In an instant I dragged him to the floor, and pulled the heavy bed over him. I then smiled gaily, to find the deed so far done. But, for many minutes, the heart beat on with a muffled sound. This, however, did not vex me; it would not be heard through the wall. At length it ceased. The old man was dead. I removed the bed and examined the corpse. Yes, he was stone, stone dead. I placed my hand upon the heart and held it there many minutes. There was no pulsation. He was stone dead. His eye would trouble me no more.

If still you think me mad, you will think so no longer when I describe the wise precautions I took for the concealment of the body. The night waned, and I worked hastily, but in silence. First of all I dismembered the corpse. I cut off the head and the arms and the legs.

I then took up three planks from the flooring of the chamber, and deposited all between the scantlings. I then replaced the boards so cleverly, so cunningly, that no human eye—not even *his*—could have detected anything wrong. There was nothing to wash out—no stain of any kind—no blood-spot whatever. I had been too wary for that. A tub had caught all—ha! ha!

When I had made an end of these labors, it was four o'clock—still dark as midnight. As the bell sounded the hour, there came a knocking at the street door. I went down to open it with a light heart, for what had I *now* to fear? There entered three men, who introduced themselves, with perfect suavity, as officers of the police. A shriek had been heard by a neighbor during the night; suspicion of foul play had been aroused; information had been lodged at the police station and they (the officers) had been deputed to search the premises.

I smiled, for *what* had I to fear? I bade the gentlemen welcome. The shriek, I said, was my own in a dream. The old man, I mentioned, was absent in the country. I took my visitors all over the house. I bade them search—search *well*. I led them, at length, to *his* chamber. I showed them his treasures, secure, undisturbed. In the enthusiasm of my confidence, I brought chairs into the room, and desired them *here* to rest from their fatigue, while I myself, in the wild audacity of my perfect triumph, placed my own seat upon the very spot beneath which reposed the corpse of the victim.

The officers were satisfied. My *manner* had convinced them. I was singularly at ease. They sat, and while I answered cheerily, they chatted familiar things. But, ere long, I felt myself getting pale and wished them gone. My head ached, and I fancied a ringing in my ears: but still they sat and still chatted. The ringing became more distinct: it continued and became more distinct. I talked more freely to get rid of the feeling: but it continued and gained definitiveness—until at length, I found that the noise was *not* within my ears.

No doubt I now grew *very* pale—but I talked more fluently, and with a heightened voice. Yet the sound increased, and what could I do? It was *a low, dull, quick sound—much such a sound as a watch makes when enveloped in cotton*. I gasped for breath, and yet the officers heard it not. I talked more quickly—more vehemently; but the noise steadily increased. I arose and argued about trifles, in a high key and with violent gesticulations, but the noise steadily increased. Why *would* they not be gone? I paced the floor to and fro with heavy strides, as if excited to fury by the observation of the men—but the noise steadily increased. Oh God! What *could* I do? I foamed—I raved—I swore! I swung the chair upon which I had been sitting, and grated it upon the boards, but the noise arose over all and continually increased. It grew louder—louder— *louder!* And still the men chatted pleasantly, and smiled. Was it possible they heard not? Almighty God, no, no! They heard! They suspected! They *knew!* They were making a *mockery* of my horror! This I thought, and this I think. But anything was better than this agony! Anything was more tolerable than this derision! I could bear those hypocritical smiles no longer! I felt that I must scream or die, and now—again—hark! Louder, louder, louder, *louder!*

"Villains," I shrieked, "dissemble no more! I admit the deed! Tear up the planks! Here, here! It is the beating of his hideous heart!"

Mrs. Gaskell (1810–1865)

The eighth child of William Stevenson, a Unitarian minister, Elizabeth Cleghorn Stevenson was born in London. After her mother died, her aunt, who lived in Knutsford, took on the duties of raising her.

In her early twenties, she visited Manchester to avoid a cholera epidemic and met William Gaskell, a young Unitarian minister. They married in 1832.

Interested in literature, Mr. Gaskell encouraged his wife to begin writing, but her serious efforts seem to have been triggered by the tragic death of her son from scarlet fever in 1845. Charles Dickens was so impressed by her first novel, *Mary Barton* (1848), that he asked her "to write a ghost story for the first special Christmas issue of *Household Words* in 1852. The result was 'The Old Nurse's Story,' a powerful and atmospheric piece." Several other outstanding horror stories followed and all have recently been brought together in *Mrs. Gaskell's Tales of Mystery and Horror* (1978)

Mrs. Gaskell seemed fascinated by ghosts and enjoyed relating such stories in dramatic fashion.[1] Indeed, she probably would have written several more (three fragments have been found) had she not been struck down by a heart attack.

Our selection, "The Doom of the Griffiths," was begun in the late 1830's and clearly illustrates her major theme of the innocent being drawn to their fate by the inexorable growth of evil.

[1] She claimed to have seen a ghost in 1849.

THE DOOM OF THE GRIFFITHS

CHAPTER I

*W*hen *Sir David Gam, "as black a traitor as if he had been born in* Bluith,'' sought to murder Owen Glendower at Machynlleth, there was one with him whose name Glendwr little dreamed of having associated with his enemies. Rhys ap Gryfydd, his "old familiar friend," his relation, his more than brother had consented unto his blood. Sir David Gam might be forgiven, but one whom he had loved, and who had betrayed him, could never be forgiven. Glendwr was too deeply read in the human heart to kill him. No, he let him live on, the loathing and scorn of his compatriots, and the victim of bitter remorse. The mark of Cain was upon him.

But before he went forth—while he yet stood a prisoner, cowering beneath his conscience before Owain Glendwr—that chieftain passed a doom upon him and his race:

"I doom thee to live, because I know thou wilt pray for death. Thou shalt live on beyond the natural term of the life of man, the scorn of all good men. The very children shall point to thee with hissing tongue, and say, 'There goes one who would have shed a brother's blood!' For I loved thee more than a brother, O Rhys ap Gryfydd! Thou shalt live on to see all of thy house, except the weaklings in arms, perish by the sword. Thy race shall be accursed. Each generation shall see their lands melt away like snow; yea, their wealth shall vanish, though they may labor night and day to heap up gold. And when nine generations have passed from the face of the earth, thy blood shall no longer flow in the veins of any human being. In those days the last male of thy race shall avenge me. The son shall slay the father.''

Such was the traditional account of Owain Glendwr's speech to his once-trusted friend. And it was declared that the doom had been fulfilled in all things; that, live in as miserly a manner as they would, the Griffiths never were wealthy and prosperous—indeed, that their worldly stock diminished without any visible cause.

But the lapse of many years had almost deadened the wonder-inspiring power of the whole curse. It was only brought forth from the hoards of memory when some untoward event happened to the Griffiths family; and in the eighth generation the faith in the prophecy was nearly destroyed, by the marriage of the Griffiths of that day to a Miss Owen, who, unexpectedly, by the death of a brother, became an heiress—to no considerable amount, to be sure, but enough to make the prophecy appear reversed. The heiress and her husband removed from his small patrimonial estate in Merionethshire, to her heritage in Caernarvonshire, and for a time the prophecy lay dormant.

If you go from Tremadoc to Criccaeth, you pass by the parochial church of Ynysynhanarn, situated in a boggy valley running from the mountains, which shoulder up to the Rivals, down to the Cardigan Bay. This trace of land has every appearance of having been redeemed at no distant period of time from the sea, and has all the desolate rankness often attended upon such marshes. But the valley beyond, similar in character, had yet more of gloom at the time of which I write. In the higher part there were large plantations of firs, set too closely to attain any size, and remaining stunted in height and scrubby in appearance. Indeed, many of the smaller and more weakly had died, and the bark had fallen down on the brown soil neglected and unnoticed. These trees had a ghastly appearance, with their white trunks, seen by the dim light which struggled through the thick boughs above. Nearer to the sea, the valley assumed a more open, though hardly a more cheerful character; it looked dark and was overhung by sea-fog through the greater part of the year; and even a farmhouse, which usually imparts something of cheerfulness to a landscape, failed to do so here. This valley formed the greater part of the estate to which Owen Griffiths became entitled by right of his wife. In the higher part of the valley was situated the family mansion, or rather dwelling-house; for "mansion" is too grand a word to apply to the clumsy, but substantially-built Bodowen. It was square and heavy-looking, with just that much pretension to ornament necessary to distinguish it from the mere farmhouse.

In this dwelling Mrs. Owen Griffiths bore her husband two sons—

Llewellyn, the future squire, and Robert, who was early destined for the Church. The only difference in their situation, up to the time when Robert was entered at Jesus College, was that the elder was invariably indulged by all around him, while Robert was thwarted and indulged by turns; that Llewellyn never learned anything from the poor Welsh parson, who was nominally his private tutor; while occasionally Squire Griffiths made a great point of enforcing Robert's diligence, telling him that, as he had his bread to earn, he must pay attention to his learning. There is no knowing how far the very irregular education he had received would have carried Robert through his college examinations; but, luckily for him in this respect, before such a trial of his learning came round, he heard of the death of his elder brother, after a short illness, brought on by a hard drinking-bout. Of course, Robert was summoned home; and it seemed quite as much of course, now that there was no necessity for him to "earn his bread by his learning," that he should not return to Oxford. So the half-educated, but not unintelligent young man continued at home, during the short remainder of his parents' lifetime.

His was not an uncommon character. In general he was mild, indolent, and easily managed; but once thoroughly roused, his passions were vehement and fearful. He seemed, indeed, almost afraid of himself, and in common hardly dared to give way to justifiable anger—so much did he dread losing his self-control. Had he been judiciously educated, he would, probably, have distinguished himself in those branches of literature which call for taste and imagination, rather than for any exertion of reflection or judgement. As it was, his literary taste showed itself in making collections of Cambrian antiquities of every description, till his stock of Welsh manuscripts would have excited the envy of Dr. Pugh himself, had he been alive at the time.

There is one characteristic of Robert Griffiths which I have omitted to note, and which was peculiar among his class. He was no hard drinker; whether it was that his head was easily affected, or that his partially-refined taste led him to dislike intoxication and its attendant circumstances, I cannot say; but at five-and-twenty Robert Griffiths was habitually sober—a thing so rare in Llyn, that he was almost shunned as a churlish, unsociable being, and passed most of his time in solitude.

About this time, he had to appear in some case that was tried at the Caenarvon assizes and, while there, was a guest at the house of his agent, a shrewd, sensible Welsh attorney, with one daughter, who had charms enough to captivate Robert Griffiths. Though he remained only a few days at her father's house, they were sufficient to decide his affections and short was the period allowed to elapse before he brought home a mistress to Bodowen. The new Mrs. Griffiths was a gentle, yielding person, full of love toward her husband, of whom, nevertheless, she stood something in awe, partly arising from the differences in their ages, partly from his devoting much time to studies of which she could understand nothing.

She soon made him the father of a blooming little daughter, called Augharad after her mother. Then there came several uneventful years in the household of Bodowen; and, when the old women had one and all declared that the cradle would not rock again, Mrs. Griffiths bore the son and heir. His birth was soon followed by his mother's death; she had been ailing and low-spirited during her pregnancy, and she seemed to lack the buoyance of body and mind requisite to bring her round after her time of trial. Her husband, who loved her all the more from having few other claims on his affections, was deeply grieved by her early death, and his only comforter was the sweet little boy whom she had left behind. That part of the squire's character, which was so tender, and almost feminine, seemed called forth by the helpless situation of the little infant, who stretched out his arms to his father with the same earnest cooing that happier children make use of to their mother alone. Augharad was almost neglected, while the little Owen was king of the house; still, next to his father, none tended him so lovingly as his sister. She was so accustomed to give way to him that it was no longer hardship. By night and by day Owen was the constant companion of his father, and increasing years seemed only to confirm the custom. It was an unnatural life for the child, seeing no bright little faces peering into his own (for Augharad was, as I said before, five or six years older, and her face, poor motherless girl! was often anything but bright), hearing no din of clear ringing voices, but day after day sharing the otherwise solitary hours of his father, whether in the dim room surrounded by wizardlike antiquities, or pattering his little feet to keep up with his "tada" in his mountain rambles or shooting excursions. When the pair came to some little foaming brook, where the stepping-stones were far and wide, the father carried his little boy across with the tenderest of care; when the lad was weary, they rested, he cradled in his father's arms, or the squire would lift him up and carry him to his home again. The boy was indulged (for his father felt flattered by the desire) in his wish of sharing meals and keeping the same hours. All this indulgence did not render Owen unamiable, but it made him wilful, and not a happy child. He had a thoughtful look, not common to the face of a young boy. He knew no games, no merry sports; his information was of an imaginative and speculative character. His father delighted to interest him in his own studies, without considering how far they were healthy for so young a mind.

Of course Squire Griffiths was not unaware of the prophecy which was to be fulfilled in his generation. He would occasionally refer to it when among his friends, with special levity; but in truth it lay nearer to his heart than he chose to acknowledge. His strong imagination rendered him peculiarly impressionable on such subjects; while his judgement, seldom exercised or fortified by severe thought, could not prevent his continually recurring to it. He used to gaze on the half-sad countenance of the child, who sat looking up into his face with his large dark eyes, so fondly yet so inquiringly, till the old legend swelled around his heart, and became too painful for him not to require sympathy. Besides, the overpowering love he bore to the child seemed to demand fuller vent than tender words; it made him like, yet dread, to upbraid its object for the fearful contrast foretold. Still Squire Griffiths told the legend, in a half-jesting manner, to his little son, when they were roaming over the wild heaths in the autumn days, "the saddest of the year," or while they sat in the oak-wainscoted room, surrounded by mysterious relics that gleamed strangely forth by the flickering firelight. The legend was wrought into the boy's mind, and he would crave, yet tremble, to hear it told over and over again, while the words were intermingled with caresses and questions as to his love. Occasionally his loving words and actions were cut short by his father's light yet bitter speech—"Get thee away, my lad; thou knowest not what is to come of all this love."

When Augharad was seventeen, and Owen eleven or twelve, the rector in the parish in which Bodowen was situated endeavored to prevail on Squire Griffiths to send the boy to school. Now, this rector had many tastes in common with his parishioner, and was his only intimate; and, by repeated arguments, he succeeded in convincing the squire that the unnatural life Owen was leading was in every way injurious. Unwillingly was the father brought to part from his son; but he did at length send him to the grammar school at Bangor, then under the management of an excellent classic. Here Owen showed that he had more talents than

the rector had given him credit for, when he affirmed that the lad had
been completely stupefied by the life he led at Bodowen. He bade fair to
do credit to the school in the peculiar branch of learning for which it was
famous. But he was not popular among his schoolfellows. He was
wayward, though, to a certain degree, generous and unselfish; he was
reserved but gentle, except when the tremendous bursts of passion
(similar in character to those of his father) forced their way.

On his return from school one Christmas time, when he had been a
year or so at Bangor, he was stunned by hearing that the undervalued
Augharad was about to be married to a gentleman of South Wales,
residing near Aberystwith. Boys seldom appreciate their sisters; but
Owen thought of the many slights with which he had requited the patient
Augharad, and he gave way to bitter regrets, which, with a selfish want
of control over his words, he kept expressing to his father, until the
squire was thoroughly hurt and chagrined at the repeated exclamations of
"What shall we do when Augharad is gone?" "How dull we shall be
when Augharad is married!" Owen's holidays were prolonged a few
weeks in order that he might be present at the wedding; and when all the
festivities were over, and the bride and bridegroom had left Bodowen,
the boy and his father really felt how much they missed the quiet, loving
Augharad. She had performed so many thoughtful noiseless little offices, on which their daily comfort depended; and now she was gone, the
household seemed to miss the spirit that peacefully kept it in order; the
servants roamed about in search of commands and directions; the rooms
had no longer the unobtrusive ordering of taste to make them cheerful;
the very fires burned dim, and were always sinking down into the dull
heaps of grey ashes. Altogether Owen did not regret his return to Bangor,
and this also the mortified parent perceived. Squire Griffiths was a
selfish parent.

Letters in those days were a rare occurrence. Owen usually received
one during his half-yearly absences from home, and occasionally his
father paid him a visit. This half-year the boy had no visit, nor even a
letter, till very near the time of his leaving school, and then he was
astounded by the intelligence that his father was married again.

Then came one of his paroxysms of rage; the more disastrous in
effects upon his character because it could find no vent in action.
Independently of slight to the memory of his first wife, which children
are so apt to fancy such an action implies, Owen had hitherto considered

himself (and with justice) the first object of his father's life. They had been so much to each other; and now a shapeless, but too real, something had come between him and his father for ever. He felt as if his permission should have been asked, as if he should have been consulted. Certainly he ought to have been told of the intended event. So the squire felt, and hence his constrained letter, which had so much increased the bitterness of Owen's feelings.

With all this anger, when Owen saw his stepmother, he thought he had never seen so beautiful a woman for her age; for she was no longer in the bloom of youth, being a widow when his father married her. Her manners, to the Welsh lad, who had seen little of female grace among the families of the few antiquarians with whom his father visited, were so fascinating that he watched her with a sort of breathless admiration. Her measured grace, her faultless movements, her tones of voice, sweet, till the ear was sated with their sweetness, made Owen less angry at his father's marriage. Yet he felt, more than ever, that the cloud was between him and his father; that the hasty letter he had sent in answer to the announcement of his wedding was not forgotten, although no allusion was ever made to it. He was no longer his father's confidant— hardly ever his father's companion; for the newly-married wife was all in all to the squire, and his son felt himself almost a cipher, where he had so long been everything. The lady herself had ever the softest consideration for her stepson; almost too obtrusive was the attention paid to his wishes; but still he fancied that the heart had no part in the winning advances. There was a watchful glance of the eye that Owen once or twice caught when she had imagined herself unobserved, and many other nameless little circumstances, that gave him a strong feeling of want of sincerity in his stepmother. Mrs. Griffiths brought with her into the family her little child by her first husband, a boy nearly three years old. He was one of those selfish, observant, mocking children, over whose feelings you seem to have no control: agile and mischievous, his little practical jokes, at first performed in ignorance of the pain he gave, but afterwards proceeding to a malicious pleasure in suffering, really seemed to afford some ground to the superstitious notion of some of the common people that he was a fairy changeling.

Years passed on; and as Owen grew older he became more observant. He saw, even in his occasional visits at home (for from school he had passed on to college), that a great change had taken place in the outward manifestations of his father's character; and, by degrees, Owen traced this change to the influence of his stepmother; so slight, so imperceptible to the common observer, yet so resistless in its effects. Squire Griffiths caught up his wife's humbly advanced opinions, and, unawares to himself, adopted them as his own, defying all argument and opposition. It was the same with her wishes; they met their fulfilment, from the extreme and delicate art with which she insinuated them into her husband's mind as his own. She sacrificed the show of authority for the power. At last, when Owen perceived some oppressive act in his father's conduct toward his dependants, or some unaccountable thwarting of his own wishes, he fancied he saw his stepmother's secret influence thus displayed, however much she might regret the injustice of his father's actions in her conversations with him when they were alone. His father was fast losing his temperate habits, and frequent intoxication soon took its usual effect upon the temper. Yet even here was the spell of his wife upon him. Before her he placed a restraint upon his passion, yet she was perfectly aware of his irritable disposition, and directed it hither and thither with the same apparent ignorance of the tendency of her words.

Meanwhile Owen's situation became peculiarly mortifying to a youth whose early remembrances afforded such a contrast to his present state. As a child, he had been elevated to the consequence of a man before his years gave any mental check to the selfishness which such conduct was likely to engender; he could remember when his will was law to the servants and dependants, and his sympathy necessary to his father: now he was a cipher in his father's house; and the squire, estranged in the first instance by a feeling of the injury he had done his son in not sooner acquainting him with his purposed marriage, seemed rather to avoid than to seek him as a companion, and too frequently showed the most utter indifference to the feelings and wishes which a young man of a high and independent spirit might be supposed to indulge.

Perhaps Owen was not fully aware of the force of all these circumstances; for an actor in a family drama is seldom unimpassioned enough to be perfectly observant. But he became moody and soured; brooding over his unloved existence, and craving with a human heart after sympathy.

This feeling took more full possession of his mind when he had left college, and returned home to lead an idle and purposeless life. As the heir, there was no worldly necessity for exertion: his father was too much of a Welsh squire to dream of the moral necessity; and he himself had not sufficient strength of mind to decide at once upon abandoning a place and mode of life which abounded in daily mortifications. Yet to this course his judgement was slowly tending, when some circumstances occurred to detain him at Bodowen.

It was not to be expected that harmony would long be preserved, even in appearance, between an unguarded and soured young man, such as Owen, and his wary stepmother, when he had once left college, and come, not as a visitor, but as the heir, to his father's house. Some cause of difference occurred, where the woman subdued her hidden anger sufficiently to become convinced that Owen was not entirely the dupe she had believed him to be. Henceforward there was no peace between them. Not in vulgar altercations did this show itself; but in moody reserve on Owen's part, and in undisguised and contemptuous pursuance of her own plans by his stepmother. Bodowen was no longer a place where, if Owen was not loved or attended to, he could at least find peace and care for himself; he was thwarted at every step, and in every wish, by his father's desire, apparently, while the wife sat by with a smile of triumph on her beautiful lips.

So Owen went forth at the early day-dawn, sometimes roaming about on the shore or the upland, shooting or fishing, as the season might be, but oftener ''stretched in indolent repose'' on the short, sweet grass, indulging in gloomy and morbid reveries. He would fancy that this mortified state of existence was a dream, a horrible dream, from which he should awake and find himself again the sole object and darling of his father. And then he would start up and strive to shake off the incubus. There was the molten sunset of his childish memory; the gorgeous. crimson piles of glory in the west, fading away into the cold calm light of the rising moon, while here and there a cloud floated across the western heaven, like a seraph's wing, in its flaming beauty; the earth was the same as in his childhood's days, full of gentle evening sounds, and the harmonies of twilight—the breeze came sweeping low over the heather and bluebells by his side, and the turf was sending up its evening incense of perfume. But life, and heart, and hope were changed forever since those bygone days!

Or he would seat himself in a favorite niche of the rocks on Moel Gêst, hidden by a stunted growth of the whitty, or mountain ash, from general observation, with a rich-tinted cushion of stonecrop for his feet, and a straight precipice of rock rising above. Here would he sit for hours, gazing idly at the bay below with its background of purple hills, and the little fishing sail on its bosom, showing white in the sunbeam, and gliding on in such harmony with the quiet beauty of the glassy sea; or he would pull out an old school volume, his companion for years, and in morbid accordance with the dark legend that still lurked in the recesses of his mind—a shape of gloom in those innermost haunts awaiting its time to come forth in distinct outline—would he turn to the old Greek dramas which treat of a family foredoomed by an avenging Fate. The worn page opened of itself at the play of the Œdipus Tyrannus, and Owen dwelt with the craving disease upon the prophecy so nearly resembling that which concerned himself. With his consciousness of neglect, there was a sort of self-flattery in the consequence which the legend gave him. He almost wondered how they durst, with slights and insults, thus provoke the Avenger.

The days drifted onward. Often he would vehemently pursue some sylvan sport, till thought and feeling were lost in the violence of bodily exertion. Occasionally his evenings were spent at a small public house, such as stood by the unfrequented wayside, where the welcome— hearty, though bought—seemed so strongly to contrast with the gloomy negligence of home—unsympathizing home.

One evening (Owen might be four or five-and-twenty), wearied with a days's shooting on the Glenneny Moors, he passed by the open door of The Goat at Penmorfa. The light and the cheeriness within tempted him, poor self-exhausted man! as it has done many a one more wretched in worldly circumstances, to step in, and take his evening meal where at least his presence was of some consequence. It was a busy day in that little hostel. A flock of sheep, amounting to some hundreds, had arrived at Penmorfa, on their road to England, and thronged the space before the house. Inside was the shrewd, kind-hearted hostess, bustling to and fro, with merry greetings for every tired drover who was to pass the night in her house, while the sheep were penned in a field close by. Ever and anon, she kept attending to the second crowd of guests, who were celebrating a rural wedding in her house. It was busy work to Martha Thomas, yet her smile never flagged; and when Owen Griffiths had finished his evening meal she was there, ready with a hope that it had done him good, and was to his mind, and a word of intelligence that the wedding-folk were about to dance in the kitchen, and the harper was the famous Edward of Corwen.

Owen, partly from good-natured compliance with his hostess's implied wish, and partly from curiosity, lounged to the passage which led to the kitchen—not the everyday, working, cooking kitchen, which was behind, but a good-sized room, where the mistress sat when her work was done, and where the country people were commonly entertained at such merrymakings as the present. The lintels of the door formed a frame for the animated picture which Owen saw within, as he leaned against the wall in the dark passage. The red light of the fire, with every now and then a falling piece of turf sending forth a fresh blaze, shone full upon four young men who were dancing a measure something like a Scotch reel, keeping admirable time in their rapid movements to the capital tune the harper was playing. They had their hats on when Owen first took his stand, but as they grew more and more animated they flung them away, and presently their shoes were kicked off with like disregard to the spot where they might happen to alight. Shouts of applause followed any remarkable exertion of agility, in which each seemed to try to excel his companions. At length, wearied and exhausted, they sat down, and the harper gradually changed to one of those wild, inspiring national airs for which he was so famous. The thronged audience sat earnest and breathless, and you might have heard a pin drop, except when some maiden passed hurriedly, with flaring candle and busy look, through to the real kitchen beyond. When he had finished his beautiful theme of "The March of the Men of Harlech," he changed the measure again to *Tri chant o' bunnan* (Three hundred pounds), and immediately a most unmusical-looking man began chanting "Pennillion," or a sort of recitative stanzas, which were soon taken up by another; and this amusement lasted so long that Owen grew weary, and was thinking of retreating from his post by the door, when some little bustle was occasioned, on the opposite side of the room, by the entrance of a middle-aged man, and a young girl, apparently his daughter. The man advanced to the bench occupied by the seniors of the party, who welcomed him with the usual pretty Welsh greeting, *"Pa sut mae dy galon?"* ("How is thy heart?") and drinking his health passed on to him the cup of excellent *cwrw*. The girl, evidently a village belle, was as warmly greeted by the young men, while the girls eyed her rather askance with a half-jealous look, which Owen set down to the score of her extreme prettiness. Like most Welsh women, she was of middle size as to height, but beautifully made, with the most perfect yet delicate roundness in every limb. Her little mob-cap was carefully adjusted to a face which was excessively pretty, though it never could be called handsome. It also was round, with the slightest tendency to the oval shape, richly colored, though somewhat olive in complexion, with dimples in cheek and chin, and the most scarlet lips Owen had ever seen, that were too short to meet over the small pearly teeth. The nose was the most defective feature; but the eyes were splendid. They were so long, so lustrous, yet at times so very soft under their thick fringe of eyelash! The nut-brown hair was carefully braided beneath the border of delicate lace: it was evident the little village beauty knew how to make the most of all her attractions, for the gay colors which were displayed in her neck-erchief were in complete harmony with the complexion.

Owen was much attracted, while yet he was amused, by the evident coquetry the girl displayed, collecting around her a whole bevy of young fellows, for each of whom she seemed to have some gay speech, some attractive look or action. In a few minutes young Griffiths of Bodowen was at her side, brought thither by a variety of idle motives, and as her undivided attention was given to the Welsh heir, her admirers, one by one, dropped off, to seat themselves by some less fascinating but more attentive fair one. The more Owen conversed with the girl, the more he was taken; she had more wit and talent than he had fancied possible; a self-abandon and thoughtfulness, to boot, that seemed full of charms; and then her voice was so clear and sweet, and her actions so full of grace, that Owen was fascinated before he was well aware, and kept looking into her bright blushing face, till her uplifted flashing eye fell beneath his earnest gaze.

While it thus happened that they were silent—she from confusion at the unexpected warmth of his admiration, he from an unconsciousness of anything but the beautiful changes in her flexile countenance—the man whom Owen took for her father came up and addressed some observation to his daughter, from whence he glided into some common-place though respectful remark to Owen; and at length, engaging him in some slight, local conversation, he led the way to the account of a spot on the peninsula of Penthryn, where teal abounded, and concluded with begging Owen to allow him to show him the exact place, saying that whenever the young squire felt so inclined, if he would honor him by a

call at his house, he would take him across in his boat. While Owen
listened, his attention was not so much absorbed as to be unaware that the
little beauty at his side was refusing one or two who endeavored to draw
her from her place by invitations to dance. Flattered by his own construction of her refusals, he again directed all his attention to her, till she was
called away by her father, who was leaving the scene of festivity. Before
he left he reminded Owen of his promise, and added:

"Perhaps, sir, you do not know me. My name is Ellis Pritchard,
and I live at Ty Glas, on this side of the Moel Gêst; anyone can point it
out to you."

When the father and daughter had left, Owen slowly prepared for
his ride home; but, encountering the hostess, he could not resist asking a
few questions relative to Ellis Pritchard and his pretty daughter. She
answered shortly but respectfully, and then said, rather hesitatingly:

"Master Griffiths, you know the triad, *'Tri pheth tebyg y naill i'r
llall, ysgnbwr heb yd, mail deg heb ddiawd, a merch deg heb ei geirda'*
(Three things are alike: a fine barn without corn, a fine cup without
drink, a fine woman without her reputation)." She hastily quitted him,
and Owen rode slowly to his unhappy home.

Ellis Pritchard, half farmer and half fisherman, was shrewd, and
keen, and worldly; yet he was good natured, and sufficiently generous to
have become rather a popular man among his equals. He had been struck
with the young squire's attention to his pretty daughter, and was not
insensible to the advantages to be derived from it. Nest would not be the
first peasant girl, by any means, who had been transplanted to a Welsh
manor house as its mistress; and, accordingly, her father had shrewdly
given the admiring young man some pretext for further opportunities of
seeing her.

As for Nest herself, she had somewhat of her father's worldliness,
and was fully alive to the superior station of her new admirer, and quite
prepared to slight all her old sweethearts on his account. But then she had
something more of feeling in her reckoning; she had not been insensible
to the earnest yet comparatively refined homage which Owen paid her;
she had noticed his expressive and occasionally handsome countenance
with admiration and was flattered by his so immediately singling her out
from her companions. As to the hint which Martha Thomas had thrown
out, it is enough to say that Nest was very giddy, and that she was
motherless. She had high spirits and a great love of admiration, or, to use

a softer term, she loved to please; men, women, and children, all, she delighted to gladden with her smile and voice. She coquetted, and flirted, and went to the extreme lengths of Welsh courtship, till the seniors of the village shook their heads, and cautioned their daughters against her acquaintance. If not absolutely guilty, she had too frequently been on the verge of guilt.

Even at the time, Martha Thomas's hint made but little impression on Owen, for his senses were otherwise occupied; but in a few days the recollection thereof had wholly died away, and one warm glorious summer's day he bent his steps toward Ellis Pritchard's with a beating heart; for, except some very slight flirtations at Oxford, Owen had never been touched; his thoughts, his fancy, had been otherwise engaged.

Ty Glas was built against one of the lower rocks of Moel Gêst, which, indeed, formed a side to the low, lengthy house. The materials of the cottage were the shingly stones which had fallen from above, plastered rudely together, with deep recesses for the small oblong windows. Altogether, the exterior was much ruder than Owen had expected; but inside there seemed no lack of comforts. The house was divided into two apartments, one large, roomy, and dark, into which Owen entered immediately; and, before the blushing Nest came from the inner chamber (for she had seen the young squire coming, and hastily gone to make some alteration in her dress), he had had time to look around him, and note the various little particulars of the room. Beneath the window (which commanded a magnificent view) was an oaken dresser, replete with drawers and cupboards, and brightly polished to a rich dark color. In the farther part of the room, Owen could at first distinguish little, entering as he did from the glaring sunlight; but he soon saw that there were two oaken beds, closed up after the manner of the Welsh: in fact, the dormitories of Ellis Pritchard and the man who served under him, both on sea and on land. There was the large wheel used for spinning wool, left standing on the middle of the floor, as if in use only a few minutes before; and around the ample chimney hung flitches of bacon, dried kids'-flesh, and the fish, that was in process of smoking for winter's store.

Before Nest had shyly dared to enter, her father, who had been mending his nets down below, and seen Owen winding up to the house, came in and gave him a hearty yet respectful welcome; and then Nest, downcast and blushing, full of the consciousness which her father's advice and conversation had not failed to inspire, ventured to join them. To Owen's mind this reserve and shyness gave her new charms.

It was too bright, too hot, too anything to think of going to shoot teal till later in the day, and Owen was delighted to accept a hesitating invitation to share the noonday meal. Some ewe-milk cheese, very hard and dry, oat-cake, slips of the dried kid's-flesh broiled, after having been previously soaked in water for a few minutes, delicious butter and fresh buttermilk, with a liquor called *"diod griafol"* (made from the berries of the *Sorbus aucuparia,* infused in water and then fermented), composed the frugal repast; but there was something so clean and neat, and withal such a true welcome, that Owen had seldom enjoyed a meal so much. Indeed, at that time of the day the Welsh squires differed from the farmers more in the plenty and rough abundance of their manner of living than in the refinements of style of their table.

At the present day, down in Llyn, the Welsh gentry are not a wit behind their Saxon equals in the expensive elegances of life; but then (where there was but one pewter service in all Northumberland) there was nothing in Ellis Pritchard's mode of living that grated on the young squire's sense of refinement.

Little was said by that young pair of wooers during the meal; the father had all the conversation to himself, apparently heedless of the ardent looks and inattentive mien of his guest. As Owen became more serious in his feelings, he grew more timid in their expression, and at night, when they returned from their shooting excursion, the caress he gave Nest was almost as bashfully offered as received.

This was but the first of a series of days devoted to Nest in reality, though at first he thought some little disguise of his object was necessary. The past, the future, was all forgotten in those happy days of love.

And every worldly plan, every womanly wile was put in practice by Ellis Pritchard and his daughter, to render his visits agreeable and alluring. Indeed, the very circumstances of his being welcome was enough to attract the poor young man, to whom the feeling so produced was new and full of charms. He left a home where the certainty of being thwarted made him chary in expressing his wishes; where no tones of love ever fell on his ear, save those addressed to others; where his presence or absence was a matter of utter indifference; and when he entered Ty Glas, all, down to the little cur which, with clamorous barkings, claimed a part of his attention, seemed to rejoice. His account of his day's employment found a willing listener in Ellis; and when he passed on to Nest, busy at her wheel or at her churn, the deepening color, the conscious eyes, and the gradual yielding of herself up to his lover-like caress, had worlds of charm.

Ellis Pritchard was a tenant on the Bodowen estate, and therefore had reasons in plenty for wishing to keep the young squire's visits secret; and Owen, unwilling to disturb the sunny calm of these halcyon days by any storm at home, was ready to use all the artifice which Ellis suggested as to the mode of his calls at Ty Glas. Nor was he unaware of the probable, nay, the hoped-for termination of these repeated days of happiness. He was quite conscious that the father wished for nothing better than the marriage of his daughter to the heir of Bodowen; and when Nest had hidden her face in his neck, which was encircled by her clasping arms, and murmured into his ear her acknowledgement of love, he felt only too desirous of finding someone to love him for ever. Though not highly principled, he would not have tried to obtain Nest on other terms save those of marriage: he did so pine after enduring love, and fancied he should have bound her heart for evermore to his, when they had taken the solemn oaths of matrimony.

There was no great difficulty attending a secret marriage at such a place and at such a time. One gusty autumn day, Ellis ferried them round Penthryn to Llandutrwyn, and there saw his little Nest become future Lady of Bodowen.

How often do we see giddy, coquetting, restless girls become sobered by marriage? A great object in life is decided, one on which their thoughts have been running in all their vagaries; and they seem to verify the beautiful fable of Undine. A new soul beams out in the gentleness and repose of their future lives. An indescribable softness and tenderness takes the place of the wearying vanity of their former endeavors to attract admiration. Something of this sort happened to Nest Pritchard. If at first she had been anxious to attract the young Squire of Bodowen, long before her marriage this feeling had merged into a truer love than she had ever felt before; and now that he was her own, her husband, her whole soul was bent toward making him amends, as far as in her lay, for the misery which, with a woman's tact, she saw that he had to endure at his home. Her greetings were abounding in delicately expressed love; her study of his tastes unwearying, in the arrangement of her dress, her time, her very thoughts.

No wonder that he looked back on his wedding day with a thankful-ness which is seldom the result of unequal marriages. No wonder that his heart beat aloud as formerly when he wound up the little path to Ty Glas, and saw—keen though the winter's wind might be—that Nest was standing out at the door to watch for his dimly-seen approach, while the candle flared in the little window as a beacon to guide him aright.

The angry words and unkind actions of home fell deadened on his heart; he thought of the love that was surely his, and of the new promise of love that a short time would bring forth; and he could almost have smiled at the impotent efforts to disturb his peace.

A few more months, and the young father was greeted by a feeble little cry, when he hastily entered Ty Glas, one morning early, in consequence of a summons conveyed mysteriously to Bodowen; and the pale mother, smiling, and feebly holding up her babe to its father's kiss, seemed to him even more lovely than the bright, gay Nest who had won his heart at the little inn of Penmorfa.

But the curse was at work! The fulfilment of the prophecy was nigh at hand!

Chapter II

It was the autumn after the birth of their boy; it had been a glorious summer, with bright, hot sunny weather and now the year was fading away as seasonally into mellow days with mornings of silver mists and clear frosty nights. The blooming look of the time of flowers was past and gone; but instead there were even richer tints abroad in the sun colored leaves, the lichens, the golden-blossomed furze; if it was the time of fading, there was a glory in the decay.

Nest, in her loving anxiety to surround her dwelling with every charm for her husband's sake, had turned gardener, and the little corners of the rude court before the house were filled with many a delicate mountain-flower, transplanted more for its beauty than its rarity. The sweetbrier bush may even yet be seen, old and grey, which she and Owen planted, a green slipling, beneath the window of her little cham-ber. In those moments Owen forgot all besides the present; all the cares and griefs he had known in the past, and all that might await him of woe and death in the future. The boy, too, was as lovely a child as the fondest parent was ever blessed with, and crowed with delight, and clapped his

little hands, as his mother held him in her arms at the cottage door to
watch his father's ascent up the rough path that led to Ty Glas, one bright
autumnal morning; and, when the three entered the house together, it
was difficult to say which was the happiest. Owen carried his boy, and
tossed and played with him, while Nest sought out some little article of
work and seated herself on the dresser beneath the window, where, now
busily plying the needle, and then again looking at her husband, she
eagerly told him the little pieces of domestic intelligence, the winning
ways of the child, the result of yesterday's fishing, and such of the gossip
of Penmorfa as came to the ears of the now retired Nest. She noticed that,
when she mentioned any little circumstance which bore the slightest
reference to Bodowen, her husband appeared chafed and uneasy, and at
last avoided anything that might in the least remind him of home. In truth
he had been suffering much of late from the irritability of his father,
shown in trifles to be sure, but not the less galling on that account.

While they were thus talking, and caressing each other and the
child, a shadow darkened the room, and before they could catch a
glimpse of the object that had occasioned it, it vanished, and Squire
Griffiths lifted the door-latch, and stood before them. He stood and
looked—first on his son, so different, in his buoyant expression of
content and enjoyment, with his noble child in his arms, like a proud and
happy father, as he was, from the depressed, moody young man he too
often appeared at Bodowen; then on Nest—poor, trembling, sickened
Nest!—who dropped her work, but yet durst not stir from her seat on the
dresser, while she looked to her husband as if for protection from his
father.

The squire was silent, as he glared from one to the other, his
features white with restrained passion. When he spoke, his words come
most distinct in their forced composure. It was to his son he addressed
himself:

"'That woman! Who is she?''

Owen hesitated one moment, and then replied, in a steady, yet quiet
voice:

"Father, that woman is my wife.''

He would have added some apology for the long concealment of his
marriage; have appealed to his father's forgiveness; but the foam flew
from Squire Griffith's lips as he burst forth with invective against Nest:

"You have married her! It is as they told me! Married Nest
Pritchard, *yr buten!* And you stand there as if you had not disgraced

yourself for ever and ever with your accursed wiving! And the fair harlot sits there, in her mocking modesty, practicing the mimming airs that will become her state as future Lady of Bodowen. But I will move heaven and earth before that false woman darkens the doors of my father's house as mistress!''

All this was said with such rapidity that Owen had no time for the words that thronged to his lips. ''Father!'' (he burst forth at length) ''Father, whosoever told you that Nest Pritchard was a harlot told you a lie as false as hell! Ay! A lie as false as hell!'' he added, in a voice of thunder, while he advanced a step or two nearer to the squire. And then, in a lower tone, he said:

''She is as pure as your own wife; nay, God help me! as the dear, precious mother who brought me forth, and then left me—with no refuge in a mother's heart—to struggle on through life alone. I tell you Nest is as pure as that dear, dead mother!''

''Fool!—Poor fool!''

At this moment the child—the little Owen—who had kept gazing from one countenance to the other, and with earnest look, trying to understand what had brought the fierce glare into the face where till now he had read nothing but love, in some way attracted the squire's attention, and increased his wrath.

''Yes,'' he continued, ''poor, weak fool that you are, hugging the child of another as if it were your own offspring!'' Owen involuntarily caressed the affrighted child, and half smiled at the implication of his father's words. This the squire perceived, and raising his voice to a scream of rage, he went on:

''I bid you, if you call yourself my son, to cast away that miserable, shameless woman's offspring; cast it away this instant—this instant!''

In this ungovernable rage, seeing that Owen was far from complying with his command, he snatched the poor infant from the loving arms that held it, and throwing it to his mother, left the house inarticulate with fury.

Nest—who had been pale and still as marble during this terrible dialogue, looking on and listening as if fascinated by the words that smote her heart—opened her arms to receive and cherish her precious babe; but the boy was not destined to reach the white refuge of her breast. The furious action of the squire had been almost without aim, and the infant fell against the sharp edge of the dresser down on to the stone floor.

Owen sprang up to take the child, but he lay so still, so motionless, that the awe of death came over the father, and he stooped down to gaze more closely. At that moment, the upturned, filmy eyes rolled convulsively—a spasm passed along the body—and the lips, yet warm with kissing, quivered into everlasting rest.

A word from her husband told Nest all. She slid down from her seat, and lay by her little son as corpse-like as he, unheeding all the agonizing endearments and passionate adjurations of her husband. And that poor, desolate husband and father! Scarce one little quarter of an hour, and he had been so blessed in his consciousness of love! The bright promise of many years on his infant's face, and the new, fresh soul beaming forth in its awakened intelligence. And there it was the little clay image, that would never more gladden up at the sight of him, nor stretch forth to meet his embrace; whose inarticulate, yet most eloquent cooings might haunt him in his dreams, but would never more be heard in waking life again! And by the dead babe, almost as utterly insensate, the poor mother had fallen in a merciful faint—the slandered, heart-pierced Nest! Owen struggled against the sickness that came over him, and busied himself in vain attempts at her restoration.

It was now near noonday, and Ellis Pritchard came home, little dreaming of the sight that awaited him; but, though stunned, he was able to take more effectual measures for his poor daughter's recovery than Owen had done.

By-and-by she showed symptoms of returning sense, and was placed in her own little bed in a darkened room, where, without ever waking to complete consciouness, she fell asleep. Then it was that her husband, suffocated by pressure of miserable thought, gently drew his hand from her tightened clasp and, printing one long soft kiss on her white waxen forehead, hastily stole out of the room, and out of the house.

Near the base of Moel Gêst—it might be a quarter of a mile from Ty Glas—was a little neglected solitary copse, wild and tangled with the trailing branches of the dog rose and the tendrils of the white bryony. Toward the middle of this thicket lay a deep crystal pool—a clear mirror for the blue heavens above—and round the margin floated the broad green leaves of the waterlily; and, when the regal sun shone down in his noonday glory, the flowers arose from their cool depths to welcome and greet him. The copse was musical with many sounds; the warbling of birds rejoicing in its shades, the ceaseless hum of the insects that hovered over the pool, the chime of the distant waterfall, the occasional bleating of the sheep from the mountaintop where all blended into delicious harmony of nature.

It had been one of Owen's favorite resorts when he had been a lonely wanderer—a pilgrim in search of love in the years gone by. And hither he went, as if by instinct, when he left Ty Glas quelling the uprising agony till he should reach that little solitary spot.

It was the time of day when a change in the aspect of the weather so frequently takes place, and the little pool was no longer the reflection of a blue and sunny sky; it sent back the dark and slaty clouds above; and, every now and then, a rough gust shook the painted autumn leaves from their branches, and all other music was lost in the sound of the wild winds piping down from the moorlands, which lay up and beyond the clefts in the mountainside. Presently the rain came on and beat down in torrents.

But Owen heeded it not. He sat on the dank ground, his face buried in his hands, and his whole strength, physical and mental, employed in quelling the rush of blood which rose and boiled and gurgled in his brain, as if it would madden him.

The phantom of his dead child rose ever before him, and seemed to cry aloud for vengeance. And, when the poor young man thought upon the victim whom he required in his wild longing for revenge, he shuddered, for it was his father!

Again and again he tried not to think; but still the circle of thought came round, eddying through his brain. At length he mastered his passions, and they were calm; then he forced himself to arrange some plan for the future.

He had not, in the passionate hurry of the moment, seen that his father had left the cottage before he was aware of the fatal accident that befell the child. Owen thought he had seen all! and once he planned to go to the squire and tell him of the anguish of heart he had wrought, and awe him, as it were, by the dignity of grief. But then again he durst not—he distrusted his self-control—the old prophecy rose up in its horror—he dreaded his doom.

At last he determined to leave his father forever; to take Nest to some distant country where he himself might gain a livelihood by his own exertions.

But when he tried to descend to the various little arrangements which were involved in the execution of this plan, he remembered that all his money (and in this respect Squire Griffiths was no niggard) was locked up in his escritoire at Bodowen. In vain he tried to do away with this matter-of-fact difficulty; go to Bodowen he must; and his only hope—nay, his determination—was to avoid his father.

He rose and took a by-path to Bodowen. The house looked even more gloomy and desolate than usual in the heavy down-pouring rain; yet Owen gazed on it with something of regret—for, sorrowful as his days in it had been, he was about to leave it for many years, if not for ever. He entered by a side door opening into a passage that led to his own room, where he kept his books, his guns, his fishing-tackle, his writing materials, *et cetera*.

Here he hurriedly began to select the few articles he intended to take; for, besides the dread of interruption, he was feverishly anxious to travel far that very night, if only Nest was capable of performing the journey. As he was thus employed, he tried to conjecture what his father's feelings would be on finding that his once-loved son was gone away for ever. Would he then awaken to regret for the conduct which had driven him from home, and bitterly think on the loving and caressing boy who haunted his footsteps in former days? Or, alas! would he only feel that an obstacle to his daily happiness—to his contentment with his wife, and his strange, doting affection for the child—was taken away? Would they make merry over the heir's departure? Then he thought of Nest— the young childless mother, whose heart had not yet realized her fulness of desolation. Poor Nest! so loving as she was, so devoted to her child—how should he console her? He pictured her away in a strange land, pining for her native mountains, and refusing to be comforted because her child was not.

Even this thought of the homesickness that might possibly beset Nest hardly made him hesitate in his determination; so strongly had the idea taken possession of him, that only by putting miles and leagues between him and his father could he avert the doom which seemed blending itself with the very purposes of his life, as long as he stayed in proximity with the slayer of his child.

He had not nearly completed his hasty work of preparation, and was full of tender thoughts of his wife, when the door opened, and the elfish Robert peered in, in search of some of his brother's possessions. On seeing Owen he hesitated, but then came boldly forward, and laid his hand on Owen's arm, saying:

"Nesta yr butten! How is Nest *yr buten?"*

He looked maliciously into Owen's face to mark the effect of his words, but was terrified at the expression he read there. He started off and ran to the door, while Owen tried to check himself, saying continually. "He is but a child. He does not understand the meaning of what he says. He is but a child!" Still Robert, now in fancied security, kept calling out his insulting words, and Owen's hand was on his gun, grasping it as if to restrain his rising fury.

But, when Robert passed on daringly to mocking words relating to the poor dead child, Owen could bear it no longer; and, before the boy was well aware, Owen was fiercely holding him in an iron clasp with one hand, while he struck him hard with the other.

In a minute he checked himself. He paused, relaxed his grasp, and, to his horror, he saw Robert sink to the ground; in fact the lad was half-stunned, half-frightened, and thought it best to assume insensibility.

Owen—miserable Owen—seeing him lie there prostrate, was bitterly repentant, and would have dragged him to the carved settle, and done all he could to restore him to his sense but at this instant the squire came in.

Probably, when the household at Bodowen rose that morning, there was but one among them ignorant of the heir's relation to Nest Pritchard and her child; for, secret as he tried to make his visits to Ty Glas, they had been too frequent not to be noticed, and Nest's altered conduct—no longer frequenting dances and merrymaking—was a strongly corroborative circumstance. But Mrs. Griffiths' influence reigned paramount, if unacknowledged, at Bodowen; and, till she sanctioned the disclosure, none would dare to tell the squire.

Now, however, the time drew near when it suited her to make her husband aware of the connection his son had formed; so, with many tears, and much seeming reluctance, she broke the intelligence to him— taking good care, at the same time, to inform him of the light character Nest had borne. She did not confine this evil reputation to her conduct before her marriage, but insinuated that even to this day she was a "woman of the grove and brake"—for centuries the Welsh term of opprobrium for the loosest female characters.

Squire Griffiths easily tracked Owen to Ty Glas and, without any aim but the gratification of his furious anger, followed him to upbraid him as we have seen. But he left the cottage even more enraged against

his son than he had entered it, and returned home to hear the evil
suggestions of the stepmother. He had heard a slight scuffle in which he
caught the tones of Robert's voice, as he passed along the hall, and an
instant afterwards he saw the apparently lifeless body of his little favorite
dragged along by the culprit Owen—the marks of strong passion yet
visible on his face. Not loud, but bitter and deep, were the evil words
which the father bestowed on the son; and, as Owen stood proudly and
sullenly silent, disdaining all exculpation of himself in the presence of
one who had wrought him so much graver—so fatal an injury—Robert's
mother entered the room. At sight of her natural emotion the wrath of the
squire was redoubled, and his wild suspicions that this violence of
Owen's to Robert was a premeditated act appeared like the proven truth
through the mists of rage. He summoned domestics, as if to guard his
own and his wife's life from the attempts of his son; and the servants
stood wondering around—now gazing at Mrs. Griffiths, alternately
scolding and sobbing, while she tried to restore the lad from his really
bruised and half-unconscious state; now at the fierce and angry squire;
and now at the sad and silent Owen. And he—he was hardly aware of
their looks of wonder and terror; his father's words fell on a deadened
ear; for before his eyes there rose a pale dead babe, and in that lady's
violent sounds of grief he heard the wailing of a more sad, more hopeless
mother. For by this time the lad Robert had opened his eyes, and, though
evidently suffering a good deal from the effects of Owen's blows, was
fully conscious of all that was passing around him.

Had Owen been left to his own nature, his heart would have worked
itself to love doubly the boy whom he had injured; but he was stubborn
from injustice, and hardened by suffering. He refused to vindicate
himself; he made no effort to resist the imprisonment the squire had
decreed, until a surgeon's opinion of the real extent of Robert's injuries
were made known. It was not until the door was locked and barred, as if
upon some wild and furious beast, that the recollection of poor Nest,
without his comforting presence, came to his mind. Oh! thought he, how
she would be wearying, pining for his tender sympathy; if, indeed, she
had recovered from the shock of mind sufficiently to be sensible of
consolation! What would she think of his absence? Could she imagine he
believed his father's words, and had left her in this her sore trouble and
bereavement? The thought maddened him, and he looked around for
some mode of escape.

He had been confined in a small unfurnished room on the first floor, wainscoted, and carved all round, with a massy door, calculated to resist the attempts of a dozen strong men, even had he afterward been able to escape from the house unseen, unheard. The window was placed (as is common in old Welsh houses) over the fireplace; with branching chimneys on either hand, forming a sort of projection on the outside. By this outlet his escape was easy, even had he been less determined and desperate than he was. And when he had descended, with a little care, a little winding, he might elude all observation and pursue his original intention of going to Ty Glas.

The storm had abated, and watery sunbeams were gilding the bay, as Owen descended from the window, and, stealing along in the broad afternoon shadows, made his way to the little plateau of green turf in the garden at the top of a steep precipitous rock, down the abrupt face of which he had often dropped, by means of a well-secured rope, into the small sailing-boat (his father's present, alas! in days gone by) which lay moored in the deep sea-water below. He had always kept his boat there, because it was the nearest available spot to the house; but before he could reach the place—unless, indeed, he crossed a broad sun-lighted piece of ground in full view of the windows on that side of the house, and without the shadow of a single sheltering tree or shrub—he had to skirt round a rude semicircle of underwood, which would have been considered as a shrubbery, had any one taken pains with it. Step by step he stealthily moved along—hearing voices now; again seeing his father and stepmother in no distant walk, the squire evidently caressing and consoling his wife, who seemed to be urging some point with great vehemence; again forced to crouch down to avoid being seen by the cook, returning from the rude kitchen-garden with a handful of herbs. This was the way the doomed heir of Bodowen left his ancestral house for ever, and hoped to leave behind him his doom. At length he reached the plateau—he breathed more freely. He stooped to discover the hidden coil of rope, kept safe and dry in a hold under a great round flat piece of rock; his head was bent down; did not see his father approach, nor did he hear his footsteps for the rush of blood to his head in the stooping effort of lifting the stone. The squire had grappled with him before he rose up again, before he fully knew whose hands detained him, now, when his liberty of person and action seemed secure. He made a vigorous struggle to free himself; he wrestled with his father for a moment—he pushed him hard, and drove him on to the great displaced stone, all unsteady in its balance.

Down went the squire, down into the deep waters below—down after him went Owen, half consciously, half unconsciously; partly compelled by the sudden cessation of any opposing body, partly from a vehement irrepressible impulse to rescue his father. But he had instinctively chosen a safer place in the deep sea-water pool than that into which his push had sent his father. The squire had hit his head with much violence against the side of the boat, in his fall; it is, indeed, doubtful whether he was not killed before ever he sank into the sea. But Owen knew nothing save that the awful doom seemed even now present. He plunged down; he dived below the water in search of the body, which had none of the elasticity of life to buoy it up; he saw his father in those depths; he clutched at him; he brought him up and cast him, a dead weight, into the boat; and exhausted by the effort, he had begun himself to sink again before he instinctively strove to rise and climb into the rocking boat. There lay his father with a deep dent in the side of his head where the skull had been fractured by his fall; his face blackened by the arrested course of the blood. Owen felt his pulse, his heart—all was still. He called him by his name.

"Father, father!" he cried, "come back! come back! You never knew how I loved you! how I could love you still—if—Oh, God!"

And the thought of his little child rose before him. "Yes, father," he cried afresh, "you never knew how he fell—how he died! Oh, if I had but had patience to tell you! If you would but have borne with me and listened! And now it is over! Oh, father! father!"

Whether she had heard his wild wailing voice, or whether it was only that she missed her husband and wanted him for some little everyday question, or, as was perhaps more likely, she had discovered Owen's escape, and come to inform her husband of it, I do not know—but on the rock, right above his head, as it seemed, Owen heard his stepmother calling her husband.

He was silent, and softly pushed the boat right under the rock till the sides grated against the stones; and the overhanging branches concealed him and it from all on a level with the water. Wet as he was, he lay down by his dead father, the better to conceal himself and, somehow, the action recalled those early days of childhood—the first in the squire's widowhood—when Owen had shared his father's bed, and used to waken him in the morning in order to hear one of the old Welsh legends.

How long he lay thus—body chilled, and brain hard-working through the heavy pressure of a reality as terrible as a nightmare—he never knew; but at length he roused himself up to think of Nest.

Drawing out a great sail, he covered up the body of his father with it where he lay in the bottom of the boat. Then with his numbed hands he took the oars, and pulled out into the more open sea toward Criccaeth. He skirted along the coast until he found a shadowed cleft in the dark rocks; to that point he rowed, and anchored his boat close inland. Then he mounted, staggering, half longing to fall into the dark waters and be at rest—half instinctively finding out the surest footrests on that precipit-ous face of rock, till he was high up, safe landed on the turfy summit. He ran off, as if pursued, toward Penmorfa; he ran with maddened energy. Suddenly he paused, turned, ran again with the same speed, and threw himself prone on the summit, looking down into his boat with straining eyes to see if there had been any movement of life—any displacement of a fold of sailcloth. It was all quite deep down below, but as he gazed the shifting light gave the appearance of a slight movement. Owen ran to the lower part of the rock, stripped, plunged into the water and swam to the boat. When there, all was still—awfully still! For a minute or two, he dared not lift up the cloth. Then, reflecting the same terror night beset him again—of leaving his father unaided while yet a spark of life lingered—he removed the shrouding cover. The eyes looked into his with a dead stare! He closed the lids and bound up the jaw. Again he looked. This time, he raised himself out of the water and kissed the brow.

"It was my doom, father! It would have been better if I had died at my birth!"

Daylight was fading away. Precious daylight! He swam back, dressed, and set off afresh for Penmorfa. When he opened the door of Ty Glas, Ellis Pritchard looked at him reproachfully from his seat in the darkly-shadowed chimney corner.

"You're come at last," said he. "One of our kind" (i.e., station) "would not have left his wife to mourn by herself over her dead child; nor would one of our kind have let his father kill his own true son. I have a good mind to take her from you forever."

"I did not tell him," cried Nest, looking piteously at her husband; "he made me tell him part, and guessed the rest."

She was nursing her babe on her knee as if it was alive. Owen stood before Ellis Pritchard.

"Be silent," said he quietly. "Neither words nor deeds but what are decreed can come to pass. I was set to do my work, this hundred years and more. The time waited for me, and the man waited for me. I have done what was foretold of me for generations!"

Ellis Pritchard knew the old tale of the prophecy, and believed in it in a dull, dead kind of way, but somehow never thought it would come to pass in his time. Now, however, he understood it all in a moment, though he mistook Owen's nature so much as to believe that the deed was intentionally done, out of revenge for the death of his boy; and, viewing it in this light, Ellis thought it little more than a just punishment for the cause of all the wild despairing sorrow he had seen his only child suffer during the hours of this long afternoon. But he knew the law would not so regard it. Even the lax Welsh law of those days could not fail to examine into the death of a man of Squire Griffiths' standing. So the acute Ellis thought how he could conceal the culprit for a time.

"Come," said he; "don't look so scared! It was your doom, not your fault"; and he laid a hand on Owen's shoulder.

"You're wet," said he suddenly. "Where have you been? Nest, your husband is dripping, drookit wet. That's what makes him look so blue and wan."

Nest softly laid her baby in its cradle; she was half stupefied with crying, and had not understood to what Owen alluded, when he spoke of his doom being fulfilled, if indeed she had heard the words.

Her touch thawed Owen's miserable heart.

"Oh, Nest!" said he, clasping her in his arms; "do you love me still—can you love me, my own darling?"

"Why not?" asked she, her eyes filling with tears. "I only love you more than ever, for you were my poor baby's father!"

"But, Nest—Oh, tell her, Ellis! *You* know."

"No need, no need!" said Ellis. "She's had enough to think on. Bustle, my girl, and get out my Sunday clothes."

"I don't understand," said Nest, putting her hand up to her head. "What is to tell? And why are you so wet? God help me for a poor crazed thing; for I cannot guess at the meaning of your words and your strange looks! I only know my baby is dead!" and she burst into tears.

"Come, Nest! Go and fetch him a change, quick!" and, as she meekly obeyed, too languid to strive further to understand, Ellis said rapidly to Owen, in a low, hurried voice:

"Are you meaning that the squire is dead? Speak low lest she hear. Well, well, no need to talk about how he died. It was sudden, I see; and we must all of us die; and he'll have to be buried. It's well the night is near. And I should not wonder now if you'd like to travel for a bit; it would do Nest a power of good; and then—there's many a one goes out of his own house and never comes back again; and—I trust he's not lying in his own house—and there's a stir for a bit, and a search, and a wonder—and, by-and-by, the heir just steps in, as quiet as can be. And that's what you'll do, and bring Nest to Bodowen after all. Nay, child, better stockings nor those; find the blue woolens I bought at Llanrwst fair. Only don't lose heart. It's done now and can't be helped. It was the piece of work set you to do from the days of the Tudors, they say. And he deserved it. Look in yon cradle. So tell us where he is, and I'll take heart of grace and see what can be done for him."

But Owen sat wet and haggard, looking into the peat fire as if for visions of the past, and never heeding a word Ellis said. Nor did he move when Nest brought the armful of dry clothes.

"Come, rouse up, man!" said Ellis, growing impatient.

But he neither spoke nor moved.

"What is the matter, father?" asked Nest, bewildered.

Ellis kept on watching Owen for a minute or two, till on his daughter's repetition of the question, he said:

"Ask him yourself, Nest."

"Oh, husband, what is it?" said she, kneeling down and bringing her face to a level with his.

"Don't you know?" said he heavily. "You won't love me when you know. And yet it was not my doing: it was my doom."

"What does he mean, father?" asked Nest, looking up; but she caught a gesture from Ellis urging her to go on questioning her husband.

"I will love you, husband, whatever has happened. Only let me know the worst."

A pause, during which Nest and Ellis hung breathless.

"My father is dead, Nest."

Nest caught her breath with a sharp gasp.

"God forgive him!" said she, thinking on her babe.

"God forgive *me*!" said Owen.

"You did not—" Nest stopped.

"Yes, I did. Now you know it. It was my doom. How could I help it? The devil helped me—he placed the stone so that my father fell. I jumped into the water to save him. I did, indeed, Nest. I was nearly drowned myself. But he was dead—dead—killed by the fall!''

''Then he is safe at the bottom of the sea?'' said Ellis with hungry eagerness.

''No, he is not; he lies in my boat,'' said Owen, shivering a little, more at the thought of his last glimpse at his father's face than from cold.

''Oh, husband, change your wet clothes!'' pleaded Nest, to whom the death of the old man was simply a horror with which she had nothing to do, while her husband's discomfort was a present trouble.

While she helped him to take off the wet garments which he would never have had energy enough to remove of himself, Ellis was busy preparing food, and mixing a great tumbler of spirits and hot water. He stood over the unfortunate young man and compelled him to eat and drink, and made Nest, too, taste some mouthfuls—all the while planning in his own mind how best to conceal what had been done, and who had done it; not altogether without a certain feeling of vulgar triumph in the reflection that Nest, as she stood there, carelessly dressed, dishevelled in her grief, was in reality the mistress of Bodowen, than which Ellis Pritchard had never seen a grander house, though he believed such might exist.

By dint of a few dexterous questions he found out all he wanted to know from Owen, as he ate and drank. In fact, it was almost a relief to Owen to dilute the horror by talking about it. Before the meal was done, if meal it could be called, Ellis knew all he cared to know.

''Now, Nest, on with your cloak and haps. Pack up what needs to go with you, for both you and your husband must be halfway to Liverpool by tomorrow's morn. I'll take you past Rhyl Sands in my fishing boat, with yours in tow; and once over the dangerous part, I'll return with my cargo of fish, and learn how much stir there is at Bodowen. Once safe hidden in Liverpool, no one will know where you are, and you may stay quiet till your time comes for returning.''

''I will never come home again,'' said Owen doggedly. ''The place is accursed!''

''Hoot! be guided by me, man. Why, it was by an accident, after all! And we'll land at the Holy Island, at the Point of Llyn; there is an old cousin of mine, the parson, there—for the Pritchards have known better days, Squire—and we'll bury him there. It was but an accident, man.

Hold up your head! You and Nest will come home yet and fill Bodowen with children, and I'll live to see it.''

"Never!" said Owen. "I am the last male of my race, and the son has murdered his father!"

Nest came in laden and cloaked. Ellis was for hurrying them off. The fire was extinguished, the door was locked.

"Here, Nest, my darling, let me take your bundle while I guide you down the steps." But her husband bent his head and spoke never a word. Nest gave her father the bundle (already loaded with such things as he himself had seen fit to take), but clasped another softly and tighter.

"No one shall help me with this," said she, in a low voice.

Her father did not understand her; her husband did and placed his strong helping arm round her waist, and blessed her.

"We will all go together, Nest," said he. "But where?" and he looked up at the storm-tossed clouds coming up from windward.

"It is a dirty night," said Ellis, turning his head round to speak to his companions at last. "But never fear, we'll weather it." And he made for the place where his vessel was moored. Then he stopped and thought for a moment.

"Stay here!" said he, addressing his companions. "I may meet folk, and I shall, maybe, have to hear and to speak. You wait here till I come back for you." So they sat down close together in a corner of the path.

"Let me look at him, Nest!" said Owen.

She took her little dead son out from under her shawl; they looked at his waxen face long and tenderly; kissed it, and covered it up reverently and softly.

"Nest," said Owen, at last, "I feel as though my father's spirit had been near us, and as if it had bent over our poor little one. A strange, chilly air met me as I stooped over him. I could fancy the spirit of our pure, blameless child guiding my father safe over the paths of the sky to the gates of heaven, and escaping those accursed dogs of hell that were darting up from the north in pursuit of souls not five minutes since."

"Don't talk so, Owen," said Nest, curling up to him in the darkness of the copse. "Who knows what may be listening?"

The pair were silent, in a kind of nameless terror, till they heard Ellis Pritchard's loud whisper. "Where are ye? Come along, soft and steady. There were folk about even now, and the squire is missed, and madam in a fright."

They went swiftly down to the little harbor, and embarked on board Ellis's boat. The sea heaved and rocked there; the torn clouds went hurrying overhead in a wild tumultuous manner.

They put out into the bay; still in silence, except when some word of command was spoken by Ellis, who took the management of the vessel. They made for the rocky shore, where Owen's boat had been moored. It was not there. It had broken loose and disappeared.

Owen sat down and covered his face. This last event, so simple and natural in itself, struck on his excited and superstitious mind in an extraordinary manner. He had hoped for a certain reconciliation, so to say, by laying his father and his child both in one grave. But now it appeared to him as if there was to be no forgiveness; as if his father revolted even in death against any such peaceful union. Ellis took a practical view of the case. If the squire's body was found drifting about in a boat known to belong to his son, it would create terrible suspicion as to the manner of his death. At one time in the evening, Ellis had thought of persuading Owen to let him bury the squire in a sailor's grave; or, in other words, to sew him up in a spare sail, and, weighting it well, sink it forever. He had not broached the subject, for a certain fear of Owen's passionate repugnance to the plan; otherwise, if he had consented, they might have returned to Penmorfa, and passively awaited the course of events, secure of Owen's succession to Bodowen, sooner or later; or, if Owen was too much overwhelmed by what had happened, Ellis would have advised him to go away for a short time, and return when the buzz and the talk was over.

Now it was different. It was absolutely necessary that they should leave the country for a time. Through those stormy waters they must plough their way that very night. Ellis had no fear—would have had no fear, at any rate, with Owen as he had been a week, a day ago; but with Owen wild, despairing, helpless, fate-pursued, what could he do?

They sailed into the tossing darkness, and were never more seen of men.

The house of Bodowen has sunk into damp, dark ruins; and a Saxon stranger holds the lands of the Griffiths.

Harriet Prescott Spofford (1835–1921)

Born in Calais, Maine, Harriet Elizabeth Prescott was the daughter of a merchant. When her father traveled westward to seek his fortune, she and her mother moved to Newburyport, Massachussets. During three years at the Putnam Free School, she met, and was encouraged in her literary attempts by, Thomas Wentworth Higgins.

To help support her family, she began "sending small-pay contributions to newspapers and periodicals." Then in 1859 she scored a major breakthrough when *Atlantic Monthly* published her mystery story "In a Cellar."

In 1865 she married Richard Smith Spofford, Jr., a lawyer. The two of them spent some time living in Washington, D.C., and traveling abroad. Throughout the time, Mrs. Spofford kept writing, and for four decades placed a steady stream of stories, poems, and critical pieces in all the leading magazines of the day.

Although both Edgar Allan Poe and Charles Reade influenced her as a writer, she went beyond them to pioneer a stream of consciousness techinique. Unfortunately, however, she never really mastered this approach and, as a result, many of her really interesting ideas are buried by overwritten monologues.

Works of interest to science fiction, fantasy, and horror fans include "The Ray of Displacement," "The Amber Gods," and "The Strathsays." For this collection, we have chosen an edited version of "Circumstances." It is a compelling story of a young woman's attempt to fend off attack and prolong her life by lulling a hungry wildcat with song.[1]

[1]"Circumstance" is based on a real experience undergone by Mrs. Spofford's maternal grandmother, Mrs. Sarah Hitchings.

CIRCUMSTANCE

S*he had remained, all that day, with a sick neighbor*—those eastern wilds of Maine in that epoch making neighbors and miles synonymous—and so busy had she been that she did not at first observe the approaching night. But finally the level rays threw their gleam upon the wall, and, hastily donning cloak and hood, she bade her friend farewell and sallied forth. Home lay some three miles distant, across a copse, a meadow, and a piece of woods—the woods being a fringe of the great forests that stretch far away into the North. Home was one of a dozen log-houses lying a few furlongs apart, with half-cleared demesnes separating them at the rear from wilderness untrodden save by stealthy native or deadly panther tribes.

She was in a nowise exalted frame of spirit—on the contrary, rather depressed by the pain she had witnessed and the fatigue she had endured; but in certain temperaments such a condition throws open the mental pores and renders one receptive of every influence. Through the little copse she walked slowly, with her cloak folded about her; the sunset filtered purple through the mist of woven spray and twig. Just on the edge of the evening she emerged and began to cross the meadowland. At one hand lay the forest to which her path wound; at the other the evening star hung over a tide of failing orange that slowly slipped down the earth's broad side. Walking rapidly now, and with her eyes wide-open, she distinctly saw in the air before her a winding sheet—cold, white, and ghastly, waved by the likeness of four wan hands, while a voice, spectral and melancholy, sighed, "The Lord have mercy on the people! The Lord have mercy on the people!" Three times the sheet with its corpse-covering outline waved beneath the pale hands, and the voice, awful in its solemn and mysterious depth, sighed, ''The Lord have mercy on the people!'' Then all was gone, the place was clear again; she looked about her, shook her shoulders decidedly, and, pulling on her hood, went forward once more.

She might have been frightened by such an apparition if she had led a life of less reality than frontier settlers are apt to lead; but dealing with hard fact does not engender a flimsy habit of mind. She did not even believe herself subject to an hallucination, but smiled simply, a little vexed that her thought could have framed such a glamour from the day's occurrences, and not sorry to lift the bough of the warder of the woods and enter the path. If she had been imaginative, she would have hesitated; but I suppose that the thought of a little child at home would conquer that propensity in the most habituated. So, biting a bit of spicy birch, she went along. Suddenly, a swift shadow, like the fabulous flying-dragon, writhed through the air before her, and she felt herself instantly seized and borne aloft. It was that wild beast—the most savage and subtle and fearless of our latitudes—known as the Indian Devil, and he held her in his clutches on the broad floor of a swinging fir-bough. His long sharp claws were caught in her clothing, he worried them a little, then, finding that ineffectual to free them, he commenced licking her bare arm with his rasping tongue and pouring over her wide streams of hot, fetid breath. So quick had this flashing action been that the woman had had no time for alarm, moreover, she was not of the screaming kind; but now, as she felt him endeavoring to disentangle his claws, and the horrid sense of her fate smote her, and she saw instinctively the fierce plunge of those weapons, the long strips of living flesh torn from her bones, the agony, while by her side and holding her in his great lithe embrace the monster crouched, his white tusks whetting and gnashing, his eyes glaring through the darkness like balls of fire—a shriek that startled every winter-housed thing tore through her lips. The beast left the arm, once white, now crimson, and looked up alertly.

She did not think at this instant to call upon God. She called upon her husband. It seemed to her that she had but one friend in the world— that was he; and again the cry echoed through the woods. It was not the shriek that disturbed the creature; he was not born in the woods to be scared of an owl. It must have been the echo, most musical, most resonant, repeated and yet repeated, dying with long sighs of sweet sound, vibrated from rock to river and back again. Her thought flew after it; she knew that, even if her husband heard, he could not reach her in time; she saw that while the beast listened he would not gnaw—and this she *felt* directly, when the rough, sharp, and multiplied stings of his tongue retouched her arm. Again her lips opened by instinct, but the sound that issued came by reason. She had heard that music charmed wild beasts—this point between life and death intensified every faculty —and when she opened her lips the third time it was not for shrieking, but for singing.

A little thread of melody stole out; it was the cradlesong with which she rocked her baby. Then she remembered the baby sleeping on the long settee before the fire; the father cleaning his gun, with one foot on the green wooden rundle; the merry light from the chimney dancing out through the room and lingering on the baby, with his fringed gentian eyes, his chubby fists, and his fine hair. All this struck her, and made a sob of her breath, and she ceased.

Immediately the long red tongue was thrust forth again. A song sprang to her lips, a wild sea-song, such as some sailor might be singing far out on blue water that night—a song with the wind in its burden and the spray in its chorus. The monster raised his head, then fretted the imprisoned claws a moment and was quiet; only the breath like the vapor from some hell-pit still swathed her. Her voice, at first faint and fearful, gradually lost its quaver, grew under her control; it rose on long swells, it fell in subtle cadences, now and then pealed out like bells from distant belfries on fresh sonorous mornings. She sung the song through, and, wondering if he would detect her, she repeated it. Once or twice the beast stirred uneasily, turned, and made the bough sway at his movement. As she ended, he snapped his jaws together, and tore away the fettered member, curling it under him with a snarl—when she burst into the gayest reel that ever answered a fiddle bow. How many a time she had heard her husband play it on the homely fiddle; how many a time she had seen it danced on the floor of their one room; how many a time she had danced it herself? Did she not remember once, as they joined clasps for right-hands-round, how it had lent its gay, bright measure to her life? And here she was singing it alone, in the forest, at midnight, to a wild beast! As she sent her voice trilling up and down, the creature who grasped her uncurled his paw and scratched the bark from the bough; she must vary the spell, and her voice spun leaping along the projecting points of a hornpipe. She felt herself twisted about with a low growl and a lifting of the red lip from the glittering teeth; she broke the hornpipe's thread, and commenced unraveling a lighter, livelier thing, an Irish jig.

Up and down and round about her voice flew, the beast threw back his head so that the diabolical face fronted hers, and the torrent of his breath prepared her for his feast as the anaconda slimes his prey. Frantically she darted from tune to tune; his restless movements followed her. She tired herself with dancing and vivid national airs, growing feverish and singing spasmodically as she felt her horrid tomb yawning wider. The beast moved again, but only to lay the disengaged paw across her with heavy satisfaction. She did not dare to pause; through the clear cold air, the frosty starlight, she sang. If there were yet any tremor in the tone, it was not fear—she had learned the secret of sound at last; nor could it be chill—far too high a fervor throbbed her pulses; it was nothing but the thought of the log house and of what might be passing within it. She fancied the baby stirring in his sleep and moving his pretty lips—her husband rising and opening the door, looking out after her, and wondering at her absence. She fancied the light pouring through the chink and then shut in again with all the safety and comfort and joy, her husband taking down the fiddle and playing lightly with his head inclined, playing while she sang, while she sang for her life to an Indian Devil.

Suddenly she woke with the daggered tooth penetrating her flesh—dreaming of safety, she had ceased singing and lost it. The beast had regained the use of all his limbs, and now, standing and raising his back, bristling and foaming, with sounds that would have been like hisses but for their deep and fearful sonority, he withdrew step by step toward the trunk of the tree. She was free, on one end of the bough, twenty feet from the ground. She did not measure the distance, but rose to drop herself down, careless of any death, so that it were not this. Instantly, as if he scanned her thoughts, the creature bounded forward with a yell and caught her again in his dreadful hold. It might be that he was not greatly famished; for, as she suddenly flung up her voice again, he settled himself composedly on the bough, still clasping her to his rough, ravenous breast, and listening in a fascination to the sad, strange U-la-lu that now moaned forth in loud, hollow tones above him. He half closed his eyes, and sleepily reopened and shut them again.

What rending pains were close at hand! Death! And what a death! Worse than any other that is to be named! Water, be it cold or warm, kisses as it kills, and draws you down gently through darkening fathoms to its heart. Death at the sword is the festival of trumpet and bugle and banner, with glory ringing out around you. No gnawing disease can bring such hideous end as this; for that is a fiend bred of your own flesh. What dread comes with the thought of perishing in flames! But fire, as it devours, arouses neither hatred nor disgust; does not drip our blood into our faces from foaming mouth nor snarl above us with vitality. Let us be ended by wild beasts, and the base, cursed thing howls with us forever through the forest. All this she felt as she charmed him, and what force it lent to her song God knows. If her voice should fail! If the damp and cold should give her any fatal hoarseness! If all the silent powers of the forest did not conspire to help her! The dark, hollow night rose indifferently over her; the wide cold air breathed rudely past her, lifted her wet hair and blew it down again; the great boughs swung with a ponderous strength, now and then clashed their iron lengths together and shook off a sparkle of icy spears or some long-lain weight of snow from their heavy shadows. The green depths were utterly cold and silent and stern. These beautiful haunts that all the summer were hers and rejoiced to share with her their bounty, all these friends of three moons ago forgot her now and knew her no longer.

Feeling her desolation, wild, melancholy, forsaken songs rose thereon from that frightful aerie—weeping, wailing tunes, that overflow with unexpressed sadness, and that rise and fall like the wind and tide—sailor songs, to be heard only in lone mid-watches beneath the moon and stars.

Still the beast lay with closed eyes, yet never relaxing his grasp. Once a half-whine of enjoyment escaped him—he fawned his fearful head upon her; once he scored her cheek with his tongue: savage caresses that hurt like wounds. How weary she was! and yet how terribly awake! How fuller and fuller of dismay grew the knowledge that she was only prolonging her anguish and playing with death! How appalling the thought that with her voice ceased her existence! Yet she could not sing forever; her throat was dry and hard, her very breath was a pain, her mouth was hotter than any desert-worn pilgrim's—if she could but drop upon her burning tongue one atom of the ice that glittered about her!— but both of her arms were pinioned in the giant's vise. She remembered the winding-sheet, and for the first time in her life shivered with spiritual fear. Was it hers? She asked herself, as she sang, what sins she had committed, what life she had led, to find her punishment so soon and in these pangs, and then she sought eagerly for some reason why her husband was not up and abroad to find her. He failed her—her one sole hope in life—and without being aware of it her voice forsook the songs of suffering and sorrow for old Covenanting hymns—hymns with which her mother had lulled her—grand and sweet Methodist hymns, brimming with melody and fantastic involutions of tune to suit that ecstatic worship, hymns full of the beauty of holiness, sanctified by the salvation had lent to those in worse extremity than hers, for they had found themselves in the grasp of hell, while she was but in the jaws of death. Out of this strange music, peculiar to one character of faith, her voice soared into the glorified chants of churches. What to her was death by cold or famine or wild beasts? "Though He slay me, yet will I trust in Him," she sang. High and clear through the night, the moonbeams splintering in the wood, those sacred anthems rose as a hope from despair. Was she not in God's hands? Did not the world swing at His will? If this were in His great plan of Providence, was it not best, and should she not accept it?

"He is the Lord our God; His judgments are in all the earth."

Never ceasing in the rhythm of her thoughts, articulated in music as they thronged, the memory of her first communion flashed over her. Again she was in that distant place on that sweet spring morning. Again the congregation rustled out, and the few remained, and she trembled to find herself among them. How well she remembered the devout, quiet faces, the snowy linen at the altar, the silver vessels slowly and silently shifting as the cup approached. She had seemed, looking up through the windows where the sky soared blue in constant freshness, to feel all heaven's balms dripping from the portals, and to scent the lilies of eternal peace! "And does it need the walls of a church to renew my communion?" she asked. "Does not every moment stand a temple four-square to God? And in that morning, with its buoyant sunlight, was I any dearer to the Heart of the World than now?" "My beloved is mine, and I am his," she sang over and over again, with all varied inflection and profuse tune. How gently all the winter-wrapt things bent toward her then! Into what relation with her had they grown! How this common dependence was the spell of their intimacy! How at one with Nature had she become! How all the night and the silence and the forest seemed to hold its breath, and to send its soul up to God in her singing! It was no longer despondency, that singing. It was neither prayer nor petition. She had left imploring "How long wilt Thou forget me, O Lord?" She cried rather, "Yea, though I walk through the valley of the shadow of death, I will fear no evil, for Thou art with me; Thy rod and Thy staff, they comfort me''; and lingered, and repeated, and sang again, ''I shall be satisfied, when I awake, with Thy likeness.''

She had no comfort or consolation such as sustained the Christian martyrs in the amphitheatre. She was not dying for her faith, there were no palms in heaven for her to wave—but how many a time had she declared, ''I had rather be a doorkeeper in the house of my God, than to dwell in the tents of wickedness!'' As the broad rays here and there broke through the dense covert of shade and lay in rivers of lustre on crystal sheathing and frozen fretting of trunk and limb, she sang ''And there shall be no night there, for the Lord God giveth them light.''

How the night was passing! And still the beast crouched upon the bough, changing only the posture of his head that again he might command her with those charmed eyes. Half their fire was gone—she could almost have released herself from his custody—yet, had she stirred, no one knows what malevolent instinct might have dominated anew. But of that she did not dream; long ago stripped of any expectation, she was experiencing in her divine rapture how mystically true it is that ''he that dwelleth in the secret place of the Most High shall abide under the shadow of the Almighty.''

Slow clarion cries now wound from the distance as the cocks caught the intelligence of day and reechoed it faintly from farm to farm. Still she chanted on. A remote crash of brushwood told of some other beast, or some night-belated traveller groping his way through the narrow path. Still she chanted on. The far, faint echoes of the chanticleers died into distance, the crashing of the branches grew nearer. No wild beast that, but a man's step, a man's form in the moonlight, stalwart and strong, on one arm slept a little child, in the other hand he held his gun. Still she chanted on.

Perhaps, when her husband last looked forth, he was half ashamed to find what a fear he felt for her. He knew she would never leave the child so long but for some direct need—and yet he may have laughed at himself, as he lifted and wrapped it with awkward care, and, loading his gun and strapping on his horn, opened the door again and closed it behind him, plunging into the darkness and dangers of the forest. He was more alarmed than he would have been willing to acknowledge; as he sat with his bow hovering over the strings, he had half believed to hear her voice mingling gayly with the instrument, till he paused and listened if she were not about to lift the latch and enter. As he drew nearer the heart of the forest, that intimation of melody seemed to grow more actual, to take body and breath, to come and go on long swells and ebbs of the night-breeze, to increase with tune and words, till a strange, shrill singing grew ever clearer, and, as he stepped into an open space of moonbeams, far up in the branches, rocked by the wind, and singing, he saw his wife—his wife—but, great God in heaven! how? Some mad exclamation escaped him, but without diverting her. The child knew the singing voice, though never heard before in that unearthly key, and turned toward it through the veiling dreams. With a celerity almost instantaneous, it lay, in the twinkling of an eye, on the ground at the father's feet, while his gun was raised to his shoulder and levelled at the monster covering his wife with shaggy form and flaming gaze—his wife so ghastly white, so rigid, so stained with blood, her eyes so fixedly bent above, and her lips, the chiselled pallor of marble, parted only with that flood of song.

I do not know if it were the mother-instinct that for a moment lowered her eyes—those eyes, so lately riveted on heaven, now suddenly seeing all lifelong bliss possible. A thrill of joy pierced and shivered through her like a weapon, her voice trembled in its course, her glance lost it steady strength, fever-flushes chased each other over her face, yet she never once ceased chanting. She was quite aware that if her husband shot now the ball must pierce her body before reaching any vital part of the beast—and yet better death, by his hand, than the other. But her husband remained motionless, just covering the creature with the sight. He dared not fire lest some wound not mortal should break the spell exercised by her voice, and the beast, enraged with pain, should rend her in atoms; moreover, the light was too uncertain for his aim. So he waited. Now and then he examined his gun to see if the damp were injuring its charge, now and then he wiped the great drops from his forehead. Again the cocks crowed with the passing hour—the last time they were heard on that night. Cheerful home sound then, how full of safety and all comfort and rest it seemed! What sweet morning incidents of sparkling fire and sunshine, of gay household bustle and cooing baby, of steaming cattle in the yard, and brimming milk-pails at the door! What pleasant voices, what laughter, what security! And here . . .

Now as she sang on in the slow, endless, infinite moments, the fervent vision of God's peace was gone. Just as the grave had lost its sting, she was snatched back again into the arms of earthly hope. Her eyes trembled on her husband's, and she could think only of him, and of the child, and of happiness that yet might be. But what a dreadful gulf of doubt between! She shuddered now in the suspense; all calm forsook her; her face contracted, growing small and pinched; her voice was hoarse and sharp—every tone cut like a knife—the notes became heavy to lift—impossible. One gasp, a convulsive effort, and there was silence —she had lost her voice.

The beast made a sluggish movement—stretched and fawned like one awakening—then, as if he would have yet more of the enchantment, stirred her slightly with his muzzle. As he did so a sidelong hint of the man standing below with the raised gun smote him; he sprung round furiously, and, seizing his prey, was about to leap into some unknown airy den of the topmost branches now waving to the slow dawn. The woman, suspended in mid-air an instant, cast only one agonized glance beneath, but across and through it, ere the lids could fall, shot a withering sheet of flame—a rifle-crack was lost in the terrible yell of desperation that bounded after it, and in the wide arc of some eternal descent she was falling—but the beast fell under her.

I think that the moment following must have been too sacred for us, and perhaps the three have no special interest again till they issue from the shadows of the wilderness upon the white hills that skirt their home. The father carries the child hushed into slumber, the mother follows with no such feeble step as might be anticipated; and as they slowly climb the steep under the clear gray sky and the paling morning star, she stops to gather a spray of the red-rose berries or a feathery tuft of dead grasses for the chimney piece of the log-house—and of these quiet, happy folk you would scarcely dream how lately they had stolen from under the banner and encampment of the great King Death. The husband proceeds a step or two in advance; the wife lingers over a footprint in the snow, stoops and examines it, then looks up with a hurried word. Her husband stands alone on the hill, his arms folded across the babe, his gun fallen—stands defined against the pallid sky like a bronze. What is there in their home, lying below, to fix him with such a stare? She springs to his side. There is no home. The log-house, the barns, the neighboring farms, the fences, are all blotted out and mingled in one smoking ruin. Desolation and death were indeed there, and beneficence and life in the forest. Tomahawk and scalping-knife, descending during that night, had left behind them only this and one subtle footprint in the snow.

For the rest—the world was all before them where to choose.

Villiers de L'Isle-Adam (1838–1889)

Born in Saint-Brieuc, France, Count Jean-Marie Philippe Auguste Mathias de Villiers de L'Isle-Adam was a descendent of the last Grand-Master of the Knights of Malta. As a young man, he began his writing career with *Premières Poésies* (1859), a collection of romantic poems. Later he helped found the symbolist movement, in which abstract "ideas, qualities, emotions, and values" were indirectly represented through symbols.

Many of his works, which included novels, plays, and short stories, received critical praise and profoundly influenced younger writers. His satirical science fiction novel, *L'Eve Future* (1886); was acclaimed a masterpiece. His play *La Révolte* (1870) and was called as worthy as Henrik Ibsen's *Doll's House*. And his two collections of Conte Cruels (1883 and 1889) were referred to as "one of the peaks of the French story." Unfortunately, however, these works did not bring in a great deal of money, and since his family was impoverished, he spent most of his life as an impecunious Parisian Bohemian, a penniless man, eventually dying from cancer.

Under such circumstances it is perhaps understandable that he developed an inordinate pride in his heritage; a contempt for money, science, and progress; a longing to return to medieval heroism; and a certain fascination with death.

A close friend of Huysman, Villiers de L'Isle-Adam was at once both ferverntly Catholic and intensely interested in satanism and the occult. His frequent excursions into fantasy or horror include the books *Axel* (1860), *Iris* (1862), and his famous story of the Spanish Inquisition, "Torture by Hope."

TORTURE BY HOPE

A Sardonic Tale

*M**any years ago, as evening was closing in, the venerable Pedro* Arbuez d'Espila, sixth prior of the Dominicans of Segovia, and third Grand Inquisitor of Spain, followed by a *fra redemptor*, and preceded by two familiars of the Holy Office, carrying lanterns, made their way to a subterranean dungeon. The bolt of a massive door creaked, and they entered a mephitic *in pace*, where the dim light revealed between rings fastened to the wall a bloodstained rack, a brazier, and a jug. On a pile of straw, loaded with fetters and with his neck encircled by an iron collar, sat a haggard man, of uncertain age, clothed in rags.

This prisoner was no other than Rabbi Aser Abarbanel, a Jew of Aragon, who, accused of usury and pitiless scorn for the poor for more than a year, had been daily subjected to torture. Yet "his blindness was as dense as his hide," and he had refused to abjure his faith.

Proud of a filiation dating back thousands of years, proud of his ancestors—for all Jews worthy of the name are vain of their blood—he descended Talmudically from Othoniel and consequently from Ipsiboa, the wife of the last judge of Israel, a circumstance which had sustained his courage under incessant torture. With tears in his eyes at the thought of this resolute soul rejecting salvation, the venerable Pedro Arbuez d'Espila, approaching the shuddering rabbi, addressed him as follows:

"My son, rejoice: your trials here below are to end. If in the presence of such obstinacy I was forced to permit, with deep regret, the use of great severity, my task of fraternal correction has its limits. You are the fig tree which, having failed so many times to bear fruit, at last withered, but God alone can judge your soul. Perhaps Infinte Mercy will shine upon you at the last moment! We must hope so. There are

147

examples. So sleep in peace tonight. Tomorrow you will be included in the *auto-da-fé:* that is, you will be exposed to the *quémadero,* the symbolical flames of the Everlasting Fire: it burns, as you know, only at a distance, my son; and Death is at least two hours (often three) in coming, on account of the wet, iced bandages with which we protect the heads and hearts of the condemned. There will be forty-three of you. Placed in the last row, you will have time to invoke God and offer to Him this baptism of fire, which is of the Holy Spirit. Hope in the Light, and rest.''

With these words, having signed to his companions to unchain the prisoner, the prior tenderly embraced him. Then came the turn of the *fra redemptor,* who, in a low tone, entreated the Jew's forgiveness for what he had made him suffer for the purpose of redeeming him; then the two familiars silently kissed him. This ceremony over, the captive was left, solitary and bewildered, in the darkness.

Rabbi Aser Abarbanel, with parched lips and visage worn by suffering, at first gazed at the closed door with vacant eyes. Closed? The word unconsciously roused a vague fancy in his mind, the fancy that he had seen for an instant the light of the lanterns through the chink between the door and the wall. A morbid idea of hope, due to the weakness of his brain, stirred his whole being. He dragged himself toward the strange *appearance*. Then, very gently and cautiously, slipping one finger into the crevice, he drew the door toward him. Marvelous! By an extraordinary accident the familiar who closed it had turned the huge key an instant before it struck the stone casing, so that the rusty bolt not having entered the hold, the door again rolled on its hinges.

The rabbi ventured to glance outside. By the aid of a sort of luminous dusk he distinguished at first a semicircle of walls surrounding winding stairs; and opposite him, at the top of five or six stone steps, a sort of black portal, opening into an immense corridor, whose first arches only were visible from below.

Stretching himself flat he crept to the threshold. Yes, it was really a corridor, but endless in length. A wan light illumined it: lamps suspended from the vaulted ceiling lightened at intervals the dull hue of the atmosphere—the distance was veiled in shadow. Not a single door appeared in the whole extent! Only on one side, the left, heavily grated loopholes, sunk in the walls, admitted a light which must be that of evening, for crimson bars rested at intervals on the flags of the pavement. What a terrible silence! Yet, yonder, at the far end of the passage there might be a doorway of escape! The Jew's vacillating hope was tenacious, for it was *the last*.

Without hesitating, he ventured out on the flags, keeping close under the loopholes, trying to make himself part of the blackness of the long walls. He advanced slowly, dragging himself along on his breast, forcing back the cry of pain when some raw wound sent a sharp pang through his whole body.

Suddenly the sound of a sandaled foot approaching reached his ears. He trembled violently, fear stifled him, his sight grew dim. Well, it was over, no doubt. He pressed himself into a niche and, half-lifeless with terror, waited.

It was a familiar hurrying along. He passed swiftly by, holding in his clenched hand an instrument of torture—a frightful figure—and vanished. The suspense which the rabbi had endured seemed to have suspended the functions of life, and he lay nearly an hour unable to move. Fearing an increase of tortures if he were captured, he thought of returning to his dungeon. But the old hope whispered in his soul that divine *perhaps*, which comforts us in our sorest tirals. A miracle had happened. He could doubt no longer. He began to crawl toward the chance of escape. Exhausted by suffering and hunger, trembling with pain, he pressed onward. The sepulchral corridor seemed to lengthen mysteriously, while he, still advancing, gazed into the gloom where there *must* be some avenue of escape.

Oh! Oh! He again heard footsteps, but this time they were slower, more heavy. The white and black forms of two inquisitors appeared, emerging from the obscurity beyond. They were conversing in low tones, and seemed to be discussing some important subject, for they were gesticulating vehemently.

At this spectacle Rabbi Aser Abarbanel closed his eyes: his heart beat so violently that it almost suffocated him; his rags were damp with the cold sweat of agony; he lay motionless by the wall, his mouth wide open, under the rays of a lamp, praying to the God of David.

Just opposite to him the two inquisitors paused under the light of the lamp—doubtless owing to some accident due to the course of their argument. One, while listening to his companion, gazed at the rabbi! And, beneath the look—whose absence of expression the hapless man did not at first notice—he fancied he again felt the burning pincers scorch his flesh, he was to be once more a living wound. Fainting, breathless, with fluttering eyelids, he shivered at the touch of the monk's floating robe. But—strange yet natural fact—the inquisitor's gaze was evidently that of a man deeply absorbed in his intended reply, engrossed by what he was hearing; his eyes were fixed—and seemed to look at the Jew *without seeing him.*

In fact, after the lapse of a few minutes, the two gloomy figures slowly pursued their way, still conversing in low tones, toward the place whence the prisoner had come; HE HAD NOT BEEN SEEN! Amid the horrible confusion of the rabbi's thoughts, the idea darted through his brain: "Can I be already dead that they did not see me?" A hideous impression roused him from his lethargy: in looking at the wall against which his face was pressed, he imagined he beheld two fierce eyes watching him! He flung his head back in a sudden frenzy of fright, his hair fairly bristling! No! No! His hand groped over the stones: it was the *reflection* of the inquisitor's eyes, still retained in his own, which had been refracted from two spots on the wall.

Forward! He must hasten toward that goal which he fancied (absurdly, no doubt) to be deliverance, toward the darkness from which he was now barely thirty paces distant. He pressed forward faster on his knees, his hands, at full length, dragging himself painfully along, and soon entered the dark portion of this terrible corridor.

Suddenly the poor wretch felt a gust of cold air on the hands resting upon the flags; it came from under the little door to which the two walls led.

Oh, Heaven, if that door should open outward. Every nerve in the miserable fugitive's body thrilled with hope. He examined it from top to bottom, though scarcely able to distinguish its outlines in the surrounding darkness. He passed his hand over it: no bolt, no lock! A latch! He started up, the latch yielded to the pressure of his thumb: the door silently swung open before him.

"Hallelujah!" murmured the rabbi in a transport of gratitude as, standing on the threshold, he beheld the scene before him.

The door had opened into the gardens, above which arched a starlit sky, into spring, liberty, life! It revealed the neighboring fields, stretching toward the sierras, whose sinuous blue lines were relieved against the horizon. Yonder lay freedom! Oh, to escape! He would journey all night through the lemon groves, whose fragrance reached him. Once in the mountains he was safe! He inhaled the delicious air; the breeze revived him, his lungs expanded! He felt in his swelling heart the *Veni foras* of Lazarus! And to thank once more the God who had bestowed this mercy upon him, he extended his arms, raising his eyes toward Heaven. It was an ecstasy of joy!

Then he fancied he saw the shadow of his arms approach him—fancied that he felt these shadowy arms inclose, embrace him—and that he was pressed tenderly to someone's breast. A tall figure actually did stand directly before him. He lowered his eyes—and remained motionless, gasping for breath, dazed, with fixed eyes, fairly driveling with terror.

Horror! He was in the clasp of the Grand Inquisitor himself, the venerable Pedro Arbuez d'Espila, who gazed at him with tearful eyes, like a good shepherd who had found his stray lamb.

The dark-robed priest pressed the hapless Jew to his heart with so fervent an outburst of love, that the edges of the hair shirt, under the robe, galled the Dominican's breast. And while Aser Abarbanel with protruding eyes gasped in agony in the ascetic's embrace, vaguely comprehending that *all the phases of this fatal evening were only a prearranged torture, that of* HOPE, the Grand Inquisitor, with an accent of touching reproach and a look of consternation, murmured in his ear, his breath parched and burning from long fasting:

"What, my son! On the eve, perchance, of salvation—you wished to leave us?"

Guy de Maupassant (1850–1893)

Of noble heritage, de Maupassant was born in Normandy and spent much of his youth in coastal Etretat.

In 1867, he found a writing instructor and enrolled in Caen University. After obtaining his bachelor's degree in 1879, he traveled to Paris to read law. There, Gustave Flaubert assumed the role of de Maupassant's writing instructor, mentor, and surrogate father.

In 1880, *Des Vers*, a book of poems, appeared without fanfare. However, the applause that followed his publication of "Ball of Fat" later that year convinced him that he had found his forte.

Approximately three hundred short stories brought him world fame. Conciseness of style, precision of imagery, and fate-crossed characters hallmark his work, which grew increasingly pessimistic as his health declined.

Progressively worsening headaches evoked memories of his family's long history of mental problems. More and more he turned to drugs and wine for temporary relief. His once-athletic constitution ravaged by debauchery and pain, de Maupassant attempted suicide, was confined to a Parisian nursing home, lapsed into complete insanity and expired at the age of forty-three.

Much of his work is horrific, with his characters trying to deny fate, yet being crushed in the end. Fantastic examples appear in *Tales of Supernatural Terror* (1872), but he was also at home with realistic horror as seen in "A Piece of String" or "The Diamond Necklace."

THE DIAMOND NECKLACE

*T*he girl was one of those pretty and charming young creatures who sometimes are born, as if by a slip of fate, into a family of clerks. She had no dowry, no expectation, no way of being known, understood, loved, married by any rich and distinguished man; so she let herself be married to a little clerk of the Ministry of Public Instruction.

She dressed plainly because she could not dress well, but she was unhappy as if she had really fallen from a higher station; since with women there is neither caste nor rank, for beauty, grace, and charm take the place of family and birth. Natural ingenuity, instinct for what is elegant, a supple mind are their sole hierarchy, and often make of women of the people the equals of the very greatest ladies.

Mathilde suffered ceaselessly, feeling herself born to enjoy all delicacies and all luxuries. She was distressed at the poverty of her dwelling, at the bareness of the walls, at the shabby chairs, the ugliness of the curtains. All those things, of which another woman of her rank would never even have been conscious, tortured her and made her angry. The sight of the little Breton peasant who did her humble housework aroused in her despairing regrets and bewildering dreams. She thought of silent antechambers hung with Oriental tapestry, illumined by tall bronze candelabra, and of two great footmen in knee breeches who sleep in the big armchairs, made drowsy by the oppressive heat of the stove. She thought of long reception halls hung with ancient silk, of the dainty cabinets containing priceless curiosities and of the little coquettish perfumed reception rooms made for chatting at five o'clock with intimate friends, with men famous and sought after, whom all women envy and whose attention they all desire.

When she sat down to dinner, before the round table covered with a tablecloth in use three days, opposite her husband, who uncovered the soup tureen and declared with a delighted air, ''Ah, the good soup! I don't know anything better than that,'' she thought of dainty dinners, of shining silverware, of tapestry that people the walls with ancient personages and with strange birds flying in the midst of a fairy forest; and she thought of delicious dishes served on marvellous plates and of the whispered gallantries to which you listen with a sphinxlike smile while you are eating the pink meat of a trout or the wings of a quail.

She had no gowns, no jewels, nothing. And she loved nothing but that. She felt made for that. She would have liked so much to please, to be envied, to be charming, to be sought after.

She had a friend, a former schoolmate at the convent, who was rich, and whom she did not like to go to see any more because she felt so sad when she came home.

But one evening her husband reached home with a triumphant air and holding a large envelope in his hand.

''There,'' said he, ''there is something for you.''

She tore the paper quickly and drew out a printed card which bore these words:

The Minister of Public Instruction and Madame Georges Ramponneau request the honor of M. and Madame Loisel's company at the palace of the Ministry on Monday evening, January 18th.

Instead of being delighted, as her husband had hoped, she threw the invitation on the table crossly, muttering:

''What do you wish me to do with that?''

''Why, my dear, I thought you would be glad. You never go out, and this is such a fine opportunity. I had great trouble to get it. Every one wants to go; it is very select, and they are not giving many invitations to clerks. The whole official world will be there.''

She looked at him with an irritated glance and said impatiently:

''And what do you wish me to put on my back?''

He had not thought of that. He stammered:

''Why, the gown you go to the theater in. It looks very well to me.''

He stopped, distracted, seeing that his wife was weeping. Two great tears ran slowly from the corners of her eyes toward the corners of her mouth.

"What's the matter? What's the matter?" he answered.

By a violent effort she conquered her grief and replied in a calm voice, while she wiped her wet cheeks:

"Nothing. Only I have no gown, and, therefore, I can't go to this ball. Give your card to some colleague whose wife is better equipped than I am."

He was in despair. He resumed:

"Come, let us see, Mathilde. How much would it cost, a suitable gown, which you could use on other occasions—something very simple?"

She reflected several seconds, making her calculations and wondering also what sum she could ask without drawing on herself an immediate refusal and a frightened exclamation from the economical clerk.

Finally she replied hesitatingly:

"I don't know exactly, but I think I could manage it with four hundred francs."

He grew a little pale, because he was laying aside just that amount to buy a gun and treat himself to a little shooting next summer on the plain of Nanterre, with several friends who went to shoot larks there of a Sunday.

But he said:

"Very well. I will give you four hundred francs. And try to have a pretty gown."

The day of the ball drew near and Madame Loisel seemed sad, uneasy, anxious. Her frock was ready, however. Her husband said to her one evening:

"What is the matter? Come, you have seemed very queer these last three days."

And she answered:

"It annoys me not to have a single piece of jewelry, not a single ornament, nothing to put on. I shall look poverty-stricken. I would almost rather not go at all."

"You might wear natural flowers," said her husband. "They're very stylish at this time of year. For ten francs you can get two or three magnificent roses."

She was not convinced.

"No; there's nothing more humiliating than to look poor among other women who are rich."

"How stupid you are!" her husband cried. "Go look up your

friend, Madame Forestier, and ask her to lend you some jewels. You're intimate enough with her to do that.''

She uttered a cry of joy:

"True! I never thought of it.''

The next day she went to her friend and told her of her distress.

Madame Forestier went to a wardrobe with a mirror, took out a large jewel box, brought it back, opened it and said to Madame Loisel:

"Choose, my dear.''

She saw first some bracelets, then a pearl necklace, then a Venetian gold cross set with precious stones, of admirable workmanship. She tried on the ornaments before the mirror, hesitated and could not make up her mind to part with them, to give them back. She kept asking:

"Haven't you any more?''

"Why, yes. Look further; I don't know what you like.''

Suddenly she discovered, in a black satin box, a superb diamond necklace, and her heart throbbed with an immoderate desire. Her hands trembled as she took it. She fastened it round her throat, outside her high-necked waist, and was lost in ecstasy at her reflection in the mirror.

Then she asked, hesitating, filled with anxious doubt:

"Will you lend me this, only this?''

"Why, yes, certainly.''

She threw her arms round her friend's neck, kissed her passionately, then fled with her treasure.

The night of the ball arrived. Madame Loisel was a great success. She was prettier than any other woman present, elegant, graceful, smiling and wild with joy. All the men looked at her, asked her name, sought to be introduced. All the attachés of the cabinet wished to waltz with her. She was remarked by the minister himself.

She danced with rapture, with passion, intoxicated by pleasure, forgetting all in the triumph of her beauty, in the glory of her success, in a sort of cloud of happiness composed of all this homage, admiration, these awakened desires and of that sense of triumph which is so sweet to woman's heart.

She left the ball about four o'clock in the morning. Her husband had been sleeping since midnight in a little deserted anteroom with three other gentlemen whose wives were enjoying the ball.

He threw over her shoulders the wraps he had brought, the modest wraps of common life, the poverty of which contrasted with the elegance of the ball dress. She felt this and wished to escape so as not to be remarked by the other women, who were enveloping themselves in costly furs.

Loisel held her back, saying: "Wait a bit. You will catch cold outside. I will call a cab."

But she did not listen to him and rapidly descended the stairs. When they reached the street they could not find a carriage and began to look for one, shouting after the cabmen passing at a distance.

They went toward the Seine in despair, shivering with cold. At last they found on the quay one of those ancient night cabs which, as though they were ashamed to show their shabbiness during the day, are never seen round Paris until after dark.

It took them to their dwelling in the Rue des Martyrs, and sadly they mounted the stairs to their flat. All was ended for her. As to him, he reflected that he must be at the ministry at ten o'clock that morning.

She removed her wraps before the glass so as to see herself once more in all her glory. But suddenly she uttered a cry. She no longer had the necklace round her neck!

"What is the matter with you?" demanded her husband, already half undressed.

She turned distractedly toward him.

"I have—I have—I've lost Madame Forestier's necklace," she cried.

He stood up, bewildered.

"What!—how? Impossible!"

They looked among the folds of her skirt, of her cloak, in her pockets, everywhere, but did not find it.

"You're sure you had it on when you left the ball?" he asked.

"Yes, I felt it in the vestibule of the minister's house."

"But if you had lost it in the street we should have heard it fall. It must be in the cab."

"Yes, probably. Did you take his number?"

"No. And you—didn't notice it?"

"No."

They looked, thunderstruck, at each other. At last Loisel put on his clothes.

"I shall go back on foot," said he, "over the whole route, to see whether I can find it."

He went out. She sat waiting on a chair in her ball dress, without strength to go to bed, overwhelmed, without any fire, without any thought.

Her husband returned about seven o'clock. He had found nothing.

He went to the police headquarters, to the newspaper offices to offer a reward; he went to the cab companies—everywhere, in fact, whither he was urged by the least spark of hope.

She waited all day, in the same condition of mad fear before this terrible calamity.

Loisel returned at night with a hollow, pale face. He had discovered nothing.

"You must write to your friend," said he, "that you have broken the clasp of her necklace and that you are having it mended. That will give us time to turn round."

She wrote at his dictation.

At the end of the week they had lost all hope. Loisel, who had aged five years, declared:

"We must consider how to replace that ornament."

The next day they took the box that had contained it and went to the jeweler whose name was found within. He consulted his books.

"It was not I, madame, who sold that necklace; I must simply have furnished the case."

Then they went from jeweler to jeweler, searching for a necklace like the other, trying to recall it, both sick with chagrin and grief.

They found, in a shop at the Palais Royal, a string of diamonds that seemed to them exactly like the one they had lost. It was worth forty thousand francs. They could have it for thirty-six.

So they begged the jeweler not to sell it for three days yet. And they made a bargain that he should buy it back for thirty-four thousand francs, in case they should find the lost necklace before the end of February.

Loisel possessed eighteen thousand francs which his father had left him. He would borrow the rest.

He did borrow, asking a thousand francs of one, five hundred of another, five louis here, three louis there. He gave notes, took up ruinous obligations, dealt with usurers and all the race of lenders. He compromised all the rest of his life, risked signing a note without even knowing whether he could meet it; and, frightened by the trouble yet to come, by the black misery that was about to fall upon him, by the prospect of all the physical privations and moral tortures that he was to suffer, he went to get the new necklace, laying upon the jeweler's counter thirty-six thousand francs.

When Madame Loisel took back the necklace, Madame Forestier said to her with a chilly manner;

"You should have returned it sooner; I might have needed it."

She did not open the case, as her friend had so much feared. If she had detected the substitution, what would she have thought, what would she have said? Would she not have taken Madame Loisel for a thief?

Thereafter Madame Loisel knew the horrible existence of the needy. She bore her part, however, with sudden heroism. That dreadful debt must be paid. She would pay it. They dismissed their servant; they changed their lodgings; they rented a garret under the roof.

She came to know what heavy housework meant and the odious cares of the kitchen. She washed the dishes, using her dainty fingers and rosy nails on greasy pots and pans. She washed the soiled linen, the shirts and the dishcloths, which she dried upon a line; she carried the slops down to the street every morning and carried up the water, stopping for breath at every landing. And dressed like a woman of the people, she went to the fruiterer, the grocer, the butcher, a basket on her arm, bargaining, meeting with impertinence, defending her miserable money, sou by sou.

Every month they had to meet some notes, renew others, obtain more time.

Her husband worked evenings, making up a tradesman's accounts, and late at night he often copied manuscript for five sous a page.

This life lasted ten years.

At the end of ten years they had paid everything, everything, with the rates of usury and the accumulations of the compound interest.

Madame Loisel looked old now. She had become the woman of impoverished households—strong and hard and rough. With frowsy hair, skirts askew and red hands, she talked loud while washing the floor with great swishes of water. But sometimes, when her husband was at the office, she sat down near the window and she thought of that gay evening of long ago, of that ball where she had been so beautiful and so admired.

What would have happened if she had not lost that necklace? Who knows? Who knows? How strange and changeful is life! How small a thing is needed to make or ruin us!

But one Sunday, having gone to take a walk in the Champs Elysées to refresh herself after the labors of the week, she suddenly perceived a woman who was leading a child. It was Madame Forestier, still young, still beautiful, still charming.

Madame Loisel felt moved. Should she speak to her? Yes, certainly. And now that she had paid, she would tell her all about it. Why not?

She went up.

"Good-day, Jeanne."

The other, astonished to be familiarly addressed by this plain goodwife, did not recognize her at all and stammered:

"But—madame!—I do not know—You must have mistaken."

"No. I am Mathilde Loisel."

Her friend uttered a cry.

"Oh, my poor Mathilde! How you are changed!"

"Yes, I have had a pretty hard life, since I last saw you, and great poverty—and that because of you!"

"Of me! How so?"

"Do you remember that diamond necklace you lent me to wear at the ministerial ball?"

"Yes. Well?"

"Well, I lost it."

"What do you mean? You brought it back."

"I brought you back another exactly like it. And it has taken us ten years to pay for it. You can understand that it was not easy for us, for us who had nothing. At last it is ended, and I am very glad."

Madame Forestier had stopped.

"You say that you bought a necklace of diamonds to replace mine?"

"Yes. You never noticed it, then! They were very similar."

And she smiled with a joy that was at once proud and ingenuous.

Madame Forestier, deeply moved, took her hands.

"Oh, my poor Mathilde! Why, my necklace was paste! It was worth at most only five hundred francs!"

Rudyard Kipling (1865–1936)

Born in Bombay, India, Rudyard Kipling absorbed Hindustani and the Indian spirit concurrently with the English language. At the age of six, because he was a delicate child, he was sent back to England to be looked after by an elderly relative. It was not a wise decision and he remained unhappy until enrolling in a public school for Anglo-Indians.

In 1883, he returned to India to work for the *Lehore Civil and Military Gazette*. The short stories he began contributing to his paper made his reputation when collected in *Plain Tales from the Hills* (1888).

In 1889, the Allahabad *Pioneer* returned him to London as a correspondent. He settled in Fleet Street and married American Caroline Balestier three years later. During the next decade he was at the height of his powers, traveling frequently and publishing such classics as *Barrack-Room Ballads* (1892), *The Jungle Books* (1894–1895), *Captains Courageous* (1897), and *Kim* (1901) before planting himself in the Sussex countryside.

Awarded the Nobel Prize in 1907, he found his literary popularity declining in later years because of the public's growing unhappiness with war, imperialism, and chauvinism.

At his best, however, he was a persuasive advocate for patriotism, camaraderie, courage, and duty. A master of setting and language, he was capable of emotions ranging from whimsy to horror.

For this volume we have selected "The Strange Ride of Morrowbie Jukes," a story Kipling published when just twenty. Strong and haunting, its inappropriate ending is its only flaw.

THE STRANGE RIDE OF
MORROWBIE JUKES

Alive or dead—there is no other way. —*Native Proverb*.

There is, as the conjurers say, no deception about this tale. Jukes by accident stumbled upon a village that is well-known to exist, though he is the only Englishman who has been there. A somewhat similar institution used to flourish on the outskirts of Calcutta, and there is a story that if you go into the heart of Bikanir, which is in the heart of the Great Indian Desert, you shall come across not a village but a town where the Dead who did not die but may not live have established their headquarters. And, since it is perfectly true that in the same Desert is a wonderful city where all the rich moneylenders retreat after they have made their fortunes (fortunes so vast that the owners cannot trust even the strong hand of the government to protect them, but take refuge in the waterless sands), and drive sumptuous C-spring barouches, and buy beautiful girls and decorate their palaces with gold and ivory and Minton tiles and mother-o'-pearl, I do not see why Jukes's tale should not be true. He is a civil engineer, with a head for plans and distances and things of that kind, and he certainly would not take the trouble to invent imaginary traps. He could earn more by doing his legitimate work. He never varies the tale in the telling, and grows very hot and indignant when he thinks of the disrespectful treatment he received. He wrote this quite straightforwardly at first, but he has since touched it up in places and introduced moral reflections, thus:

In the beginning it all arose from a slight attack of fever. My work necessitated my being in camp for some months between Pakpattan and Mubarakpur—a desolate sandy stretch of country as every one who has had the misfortune to go there may know. My coolies were neither more

nor less exasperating than other gangs, and my work demanded sufficient attention to keep me from moping, had I been inclined to so
unmanly a weakness.

On December 23, 1884, I felt a little feverish. There was a full
moon at the time, and, in consequence, every dog near my tent was
baying it. The brutes assembled in twos and threes and drove me frantic.
A few days previously I had shot one loud-mouthed singer and suspended his carcass *in terrorem* about fifty yards from my tent door. But his
friends fell upon, fought for, and ultimately devoured the body; and, as it
seemed to me, sang their hymns of thanksgiving afterward with renewed
energy.

The lightheartedness which accompanies fever acts differently on
different men. My irritation gave way, after a short time, to a fixed
determination to slaughter one huge black and white beast who had been
foremost in song and first in flight throughout the evening. Thanks to a
shaking hand and a giddy head I had already missed him twice with both
barrels of my shotgun, when it struck me that my best plan would be to
ride him down in the open and finish him off with a hog-spear. This, of
course, was merely the semi-delirious notion of a fever patient; but I
remember that it struck me at the time as being eminently practical and
feasible.

I therefore ordered my groom to saddle Pornic and bring him round
quietly to the rear of my tent. When the pony was ready, I stood at his
head prepared to mount and dash out as soon as the dog should again lift
up his voice. Pornic, by the way, had not been out of his pickets for a
couple of days; the night air was crisp and chilly; and I was armed with a
specially long and sharp pair of persuaders with which I had been rousing
a sluggish cob that afternoon. You will easily believe, then, that when he
was let go he went quickly. In one moment, for the brute bolted as
straight as a die, the tent was left far behind, and we were flying over the
smooth sandy soil at racing speed. In another we had passed the wretched
dog, and I had almost forgotten why it was that I had taken the horse and
hog-spear.

The delirium of fever and the excitement of rapid motion through
the air must have taken away the remnant of my senses. I have a faint
recollection of standing upright in my stirrups, and of brandishing my
hog-spear at the great white moon that looked down so calmly on my
mad gallop; and of shouting challenges to the camel-thorn bushes as they

whizzed past. Once or twice, I believe, I swayed forward on Pornic's neck, and literally hung on by my spurs—as the marks next morning showed.

The wretched beast went forward like a thing possessed, over what seemed to be a limitless expanse of moonlit sand. Next, I remember, the ground rose suddenly in front of us, and as we topped the ascent I saw the waters of the Sutlej shining like a silver bar below. Then Pornic blundered heavily on his nose, and we rolled together down some unseen slope.

I must have lost consciousness, for when I recovered I was lying on my stomach in a heap of soft white sand, and the dawn was beginning to break dimly over the edge of the slope down which I had fallen. As the light grew stronger I saw that I was at the bottom of a horse shoe-shaped crater of sand, opening on one side directly on to the shoals of the Sutlej. My fever had altogether left me, and, with the exception of a slight dizziness in the head, I felt no bad effects from the fall over night.

Pornic, who was standing a few yards away, was naturally a good deal exhausted, but had not hurt himself in the least. His saddle, a favorite polo one, was much knocked about, and had been twisted under his belly. It took me some time to put him to rights, and in the meantime I had ample opportunities of observing the spot into which I had so foolishly dropped.

At the risk of being considered tedious, I must describe it at length; inasmuch as an accurate mental picture of its peculiarities will be of material assistance in enabling the reader to understand what follows.

Imagine then, as I have said before, a horseshoe-shaped crater of sand with steeply graded sand walls about thirty-five feet high. (The slope, I fancy, must have been about 65°.) This crater enclosed a level piece of ground about fifty yards long by thirty at its broadest part, with a crude well in the center. Round the bottom of the crater, about three feet from the level of the ground proper, ran a series of eighty-three semicircular, ovoid, square, and multilateral holes, all about three feet at the mouth. Each hole on inspection showed that it was carefully shored internally with driftwood and bamboos, and over the mouth a wooden dripboard projected, like the peak of a jockey's cap, for two feet. No sign of life was visible in these tunnels, but a most sickening stench pervaded the entire amphitheatre—a stench fouler than any which my wanderings in Indian villages have introduced me to.

Having remounted Pornic, who was as anxious as I to get back to camp, I rode round the base of the horseshoe to find some place whence an exit would be practicable. The inhabitants, whoever they might be, had not thought fit to put in an appearance, so I was left to my own devices. My first attempt to "rush" Pornic up the steep sandbanks showed me that I had fallen into a trap exactly on the same model as that which the ant-lion sets for its prey. At each step the shifting sand poured down from above in tons, and rattled on the dripboards of the holes like small shot. A couple of ineffectual charges sent us both rolling down to the bottom, half-choked with the torrents of sand; and I was constrained to turn my attention to the riverbank.

Here everything seemed easy enough. The sand hills ran down to the river edge, it is true, but there were plenty of shoals and shallows across which I could gallop Pornic, and find my way back to *terra firma* by turning sharply to the right or left. As I led Pornic over the sands I was startled by the faint pop of a rifle across the river; and at the same moment a bullet dropped with a sharp *"whit"* close to Pornic's head.

There was no mistaking the nature of the missile—a regulation Martini-Henry "picket." About five hundred yards away a country-boat was anchored in midstream; and a jet of smoke drifting away from its bows in the still morning air showed me whence the delicate attention had come. Was ever a respectable gentleman in such an *impasse*? The treacherous sand slope allowed no escape from a spot which I had visited most involuntarily, and a promenade on the river frontage was the signal for a bombardment from some insane native in a boat. I'm afraid that I lost my temper very much indeed.

Another bullet reminded me that I had better save my breath to cool my porridge; and I retreated hastily up the sands and back to the horseshoe, where I saw that the noise of the rifle had drawn sixty-five human beings from the badger holes which I had up till that point supposed to be untenanted. I found myself in the midst of a crowd of spectators—about forty men, twenty women, and one child who could not have been more than five years old. They were all scantily clothed in that salmon-colored cloth which one associates with Hindu mendicants, and, at first sight, gave me the impression of a band of loathsome *fakirs*. The filth and repulsiveness of the assembly were beyond all description, and I shuddered to think what their life in the badger holes must be.

Even in these days, when local self-government has destroyed the greater part of a native's respect for a Sahib, I have been accustomed to a certain amount of civility from my inferiors, and on approaching the crowd naturally expected that there would be some recognition of my presence. As a matter of fact there was; but it was by no means what I had looked for.

The ragged crew actually laughed at me—such laughter I hope I may never hear again. They cackled, yelled, whistled, and howled as I walked into their midst; some of them literally throwing themselves down on the ground in convulsions of unholy mirth. In a moment I had let go Pornic's head, and, irritated beyond expression at the morning's adventure, commenced cuffing those nearest to me with all the force I could. The wretches dropped under my blows like ninepins, and the laughter gave place to wails for mercy; while those yet untouched clasped me round the knees, imploring me in all sorts of uncouth tongues to spare them.

In the tumult, and just when I was feeling very much ashamed of myself for having thus easily given way to my temper, a thin, high voice murmured in English from behind my shoulder, ''Sahib! Sahib! Do you not know me? Sahib, it is Gunga Dass, the telegraph-master.''

I spun round quickly and faced the speaker.

Gunga Dass (I have, of course, no hesitation in mentioning the man's real name) I had known four years before as a Deccanee Brahmin loaned by the Punjab Government to one of the Khalsia States. He was in charge of a branch telegraph office there, and when I had last met him was a jovial, full-stomached, portly Government servant with a marvelous capacity for making bad puns in English—a peculiarity which made me remember him long after I had forgotten his services to me in his official capacity. It is seldom that a Hindu makes English puns.

Now, however, the man was changed beyond all recognition. Caste-mark, stomach, slate-colored continuations, and unctuous speech were all gone. I looked at a withered skeleton, turbanless and almost naked, with long matted hair and deep-set codfish-eyes. But for a crescent-shaped scar on the left cheek—the result of an accident for which I was responsible—I should never have known him. But it was indubitably Gunga Dass, and—for this I was thankful—an English-speaking native who might at least tell me the meaning of all that I had gone through that day.

The crowd retreated to some distance as I turned toward the miserable figure, and ordered him to show me some method of escaping from the crater. He held a freshly plucked crow in his hand, and in reply to my question climbed slowly on a platform of sand which ran in front of the holes, and commenced lighting a fire there in silence. Dried bents, sand-poppies, and driftwood burn quickly; and I derived much consolation from the fact that he lit them with an ordinary sulphur-match. When they were in a bright glow, and the crow was nearly spitted in front thereof, Gunga Dass began without a word of preamble:

"There are only two kinds of men, Sar. The alive and the dead. When you are dead you are dead, but when you are alive you live." (Here the crow demanded his attention for an instant as it twirled before the fire in danger of being burned to a cinder.) "If you die at home and do not die when you come to the ghât to be burned you come here."

The nature of the reeking village was made plain now, and all that I had known or read of the grotesque and the horrible paled before the fact just communicated by the ex-Brahmin. Sixteen years ago, when I first landed in Bombay, I had been told by a wandering Armenian of the existence, somewhere in India, of a place to which such Hindus as had the misfortune to recover from trance or catalepsy were conveyed and kept, and I recollect laughing heartily at what I was then pleased to consider a traveler's tale. Sitting at the bottom of the sandtrap, the memory of Watson's Hotel, with its swinging punkahs, white-robed attendants, and the sallow-faced Armenian, rose up in my mind as vividly as a photograph, and I burst into a loud fit of laughter. The contrast was too absurd!

Gunga Dass, as he bent over the unclean bird, watched me curiously. Hindus seldom laugh, and his surroundings were not such as to move Gunga Dass to any undue excess of hilarity. He removed the crow solemnly from the wooden spit and as solemnly devoured it. Then he continued his story, which I give in his own words:

"In epidemics of the cholera you are carried to be burned almost before you are dead. When you come to the riverside the cold air, perhaps, makes you alive, and then, if you are only little alive, mud is put on your nose and mouth and you die conclusively. If you are rather more alive, more mud is put; but if you are too lively they let you go and take you away. I was too lively, and made protestation with anger against the indignities that they endeavored to press upon me. In those days I was Brahmin and proud man. Now I am dead man and eat"—here he eyed the well-gnawed breast bone with the first sign of emotion that I had seen in him since we met—''crows, and other things. They took me from my sheets when they saw that I was too lively and gave me medicines for one week, and I survived successfully. Then they sent me by rail from my place to Okara Station, with a man to take care of me; and at Okara Station we met two other men, and they conducted we three on camels, in the night, from Okara Station to this place, and they propelled me from the top to the bottom, and the other two succeeded, and I have been here ever since two and a half years. Once I was Brahmin and proud man, and now I eat crows.''

''There is no way of getting out?''

''None of what kind at all. When I first came I made experiments frequently and all the others also, but we have always succumbed to the sand which is precipitated upon our heads.''

''But surely,'' I broke in at this point, ''the river front is open and it is worthwhile dodging the bullets; while at night''—

I had already matured a rough plan of escape which a natural instinct of selfishness forbade me sharing with Gunga Dass. He, however, divined my unspoken thought almost as soon as it was formed; and, to my intense astonishment, gave vent to a long low chuckle of derision—the laughter, be it understood, of a superior or at least of an equal.

''You will not''—he had dropped the Sir completley after his opening sentence—''make any escape that way. But you can try. I have tried. Once only.''

The sensation of nameless terror and abject fear which I had in vain attempted to strive against overmastered me completely. My long fast—it was now close upon ten o'clock, and I had eaten nothing since tiffin on the previous day—combined with the violent and unnatural agitation of the ride had exhausted me, and I verily believe that, for a few minutes, I acted as one mad. I hurled myself against the pitiless sandslope. I ran round the base of the crater, blaspheming and praying by turns. I crawled out among the sedges of the river front, only to be driven back each time in an agony of nervous dread by the rifle-bullets which cut up the sand round me—for I dared not face the death of a mad dog among that hideous crowd—and finally fell, spent and raving at the curb of the well. No one had taken the slightest notion of an exhibition which makes me blush hotly even when I think of it now.

Two or three men trod on my panting body as they drew water, but

they were evidently used to this sort of thing, and had no time to waste
upon me. The situation was humiliating. Gunga Dass, indeed, when he
had banked the embers of his fire with sand, was at some pains to throw
half a cupful of fetid water over my head, an attention for which I could
have fallen on my knees and thanked him, but he was laughing all the
while in the same mirthless, wheezy key that greeted me on my first
attempt to force the shoals. And so, in a semi-comatose condition, I lay
till noon. Then, being only a man after all, I felt hungry, and intimated as
much to Gunga Dass, whom I had begun to regard as my natural
protector. Following the impulse of the outer world when dealing with
natives, I put my hand into my pocket and drew out four annas. The
absurdity of the gift struck me at once, and I was about to replace the
money.

Gunga Dass, however, was of a different opinion. "Give me the
money," said he; "all you have, or I will get help, and we will kill you!"
All this as if it were the most natural thing in the world!

A Briton's first impulse, I believe, is to guard the contents of his
pockets; but a moment's reflection convinced me of the futility of
differing with the one man who had it in his power to make me comfortable; and with whose help it was possible that I might eventually escape
from the crater. I gave him all the money in my possession, Rs. 9-8-5—
nine rupees, eight annas, and five pie—for I always keep small change
as *bakshish* when I am in camp. Gunga Dass clutched the coins, and hid
them at once in his ragged loin cloth, his expression changing to something diabolical as he looked round to assure himself that no one had
observed us.

"*Now* I will give you something to eat," said he.

What pleasure the possession of my money could have afforded
him I am unable to say; but inasmuch as it did give him evident delight I
was not sorry that I had parted with it so readily, for I had no doubt that he
would have had me killed if I had refused. One does not protest against
the vagaries of a den of wild beasts; and my companions were lower than
any beasts. While I devoured what Gunga Dass had provided, a coarse
chapatti and a cupful of the foul well-water, the people showed not the
faintest sign of curiosity—that curiosity which is so rampant, as a rule in
an Indian village.

I could even fancy that they despised me. At all events they treated
me with the most chilling indifference, and Gunga Dass was nearly as

bad. I plied him with questions about the terrible village, and received extremely unsatisfactory answers. So far as I could gather, it had been in existence from time immemorial—whence I concluded that it was at least a century old—and during that time no one had ever been known to escape from it. [I had to control myself here with both hands, lest the blind terror should lay hold of me a second time and drive me raving round the crater.] Gunga Dass took a malicious pleasure in emphasizing this point and in watching me wince. Nothing that I could do would induce him to tell me who the mysterious "They" were.

"It is so ordered," he would reply, "and I do not yet know any one who has disobeyed the orders."

"Only wait till my servants find that I am missing," I retorted, "and I promise you that this place shall be cleared off the face of the earth, and I'll give you a lesson in civility, too, my friend."

"Your servants would be torn in pieces before they came near this place; and, besides, you are dead, my dear friend. It is not your fault, of course, but none the less you are dead *and* buried."

At irregular intervals supplies of food, I was told, were dropped down from the land side into the amphitheatre, and the inhabitants fought for them like wild beasts. When a man felt his death coming on he retreated to his lair and died there. The body was sometimes dragged out of the hole and thrown onto the sand, or allowed to rot where it lay.

The phrase "thrown onto the sand" caught my attention, and I asked Gunga Dass whether this sort of thing was not likely to breed pestilence.

"That," said he, with another of his wheezy chuckles, "you may see for yourself subsequently. You will have much time to make observations."

Whereat, to his great delight, I winced once more and hastily continued the conversation. "And how do you live here from day to day? What do you do?" The question elicited exactly the same answer as before—coupled with the information that "this place is like your European heaven; there is neither marrying nor giving in marriage."

Gunga Dass had been educated at a Mission School, and, as he himself admitted, had he only changed his religion "like a wise man," might have avoided the living grave which was now his portion. But as long as I was with him I fancy he was happy.

Here was a Sahib, a representative of the dominant race, helpless as a child and completely at the mercy of his native neighbors. In a deliberate lazy way he set himself to torture me as a schoolboy would devote a rapturous half-hour to watching the agonies of an impaled beetle, or as a ferret in a blind burrow might glue himself comfortably to the neck of a rabbit. The burden of his conversation was that there was no escape "of no kind whatever," and that I should stay here till I died and was "thrown onto the sand." If it were possible to forejudge the conversation of the damned on the advent of a new soul in their abode, I should say that they would speak as Gunga Dass did to me throughout that long afternoon. I was powerless to protest or answer; all my energies being devoted to a struggle against the inexplicable terror that threatened to overwhelm me again and again. I can compare the feeling to nothing except the struggles of a man against the overpowering nausea of the Channel passage—only my agony was of the spirit and infinitely more terrible.

As the day wore on, the inhabitants began to appear in full strength to catch the rays of the afternoon sun, which were now sloping in at the mouth of the crater. They assembled in little knots, and talked among themselves without even throwing a glance in my direction. About four o'clock, as far as I could judge Gunga Dass rose and dived into his lair for a moment, emerging with a live crow in his hands. The wretched bird was in a most draggled and deplorable condition, but seemed to be in no way afraid of its master. Advancing cautiously to the river front, Gunga Dass stepped from tussock to tussock until he had reached a smooth patch of sand directly in the line of the boat's fire. The occupants of the boat took no notice. Here he stopped, and, with a couple of dexterous turns of the wrist, pegged the bird on its back with outstretched wings. As was only natural, the crow began to shriek at once and beat the air with its claws. In a few seconds the clamor had attracted the attention of a bevy of wild crows on a shoal a few hundred yards away, where they were discussing something that looked like a corpse. Half a dozen crows flew over at once to see what was going on, and also, as it proved, to attack the pinioned bird. Gunga Dass, who had lain down on a tussock, motioned to me to be quiet, though I fancy this was a needless precaution. In a moment, and before I could see how it happened, a wild crow, who had grappled with the shrieking and helpless bird, was entangled in the latter's claws, swiftly disengaged by Gunga Dass, and pegged down beside its companion in adversity. Curiosity, it seemed, overpowered the rest of the flock, and almost before Gunga Dass and I had time to withdraw to the tussock, two more captives were struggling in the upturned claws of the decoys. So the chase—if I can give it so dignified a name—continued until Gunga Dass had captured seven crows. Five of them he throttled at once, reserving two for further operations another day. I was a good deal impressed by this, to me, novel method of securing food, and complimented Gunga Dass on his skill.

"It is nothing to do," said he. "Tomorrow you must do it for me. You are stronger than I am."

This calm assumption of superiority upset me not a little, and I answered peremptorily;—"Indeed, you old ruffian! What do you think I have given you money for?"

"Very well," was the unmoved reply. "Perhaps not tomorrow, nor the day after, nor subsequently; but in the end, and for many years, you will catch crows and eat crows, and you will thank your European God that you have crows to catch and eat."

I could have cheerfully strangled him for this; but judged it best under the circumstances to smother my resentment. An hour later I was eating one of the crows; and, as Gunga Dass had said, thanking my God that I had a crow to eat. Never as long as I live shall I forget that evening meal. The whole population were squatting on the hard sand platform opposite their dens, huddled over tiny fires of refuse and dried rushes. Death, having once laid his hand upon these men and forborne to strike, seemed to stand aloof from them now; for most of our company were old men, bent and worn and twisted with years, and women aged to all appearance as the Fates themselves. They sat together in knots and talked—God only knows what they found to discuss—in low equable tones, curiously in contrast to the strident babble with which natives are accustomed to make day hideous. Now and then an access of that sudden fury which had possessed me in the morning would lay hold on a man or woman; and with yells and imprecations the sufferer would attack the steep slope until, baffled and bleeding, he fell back on the platform incapable of moving a limb. The others would never even raise their eyes when this happened, as men too well aware of the futility of their fellows' attempts and wearied with their useless repetition. I saw four such outbursts in the course of the evening.

Gunga Dass took an eminently businesslike view of my situation, and while we were dining—I can afford to laugh at the recollection now, but it was painful enough at the time—propounded the terms on which he would consent to "do" for me. My nine rupees, eight annas, he argued, at the rate of three annas a day, would provide me with food for fifty-one days, or about seven weeks; that is to say, he would be willing to cater for me for that length of time. At the end of it I was to look after myself. For a further consideration—*videlicet* my boots—he would be willing to allow me to occupy the den next to his own, and would supply me with as much dried grass for bedding as he could spare.

"Very well, Gunga Dass," I replied; "to the first terms I cheerfully agree, but, as there is nothing on earth to prevent my killing you as you sit here and taking everything that you have," (I thought of the two invaluable crows at the time) "I flatly refuse to give you my boots and shall take whichever den I please."

The stroke was a bold one, and I was glad when I saw that it had succeeded. Gunga Dass changed his tone immediately, and disavowed all intention of asking for my boots. At the time it did not strike me as at all strange that I, a civil engineer, a man of thirteen years' standing in the service, and, I trust, an average Englishman, should thus calmly threaten murder and violence against the man who had, for a consideration it is true, taken me under his wing. I had left the world, it seemed, for centuries. I was as certain then as I am now of my own existence, that in the accursed settlement there was no law save that of the strongest; that the living dead men had thrown behind them every canon of the world which had cast them out; and that I had to depend for my own life on my strength and vigilance alone. The crew of the ill-fated Mignonette are the only men who would understand my frame of mind. "At present," I argued to myself, "I am strong and a match for six of these wretches. It is imperatively necessary that I should, for my own sake, keep both health and strength until the hour of my release comes—if it ever does."

Fortified with these resolutions, I ate and drank as much as I could, and made Gunga Dass understand that I intended to be his master, and that the least sign of insubordination on his part would be visited with the only punishment I had it in my power to inflict—sudden and violent death. Shortly after this I went to bed. That is to say, Gunga Dass gave me a double armful of dried bents which I thrust down the mouth of the lair to the right of his, and followed myself, feet foremost; the hole running about nine feet into the sand with a slight downward inclination, and being neatly shored with timbers. From my den, which faced the river front, I was able to watch the waters of the Sutlej flowing past under the light of a young moon and compose myself to sleep as best I might.

The horrors of that night I shall never forget. My den was nearly as narrow as a coffin, and the sides had been worn smooth and greasy by the contact of innumerable naked bodies, added to which it smelled abominably. Sleep was altogether out of question to one in my excited frame of mind. As the night wore on, it seemed that the entire amphitheatre was filled with legions of unclean devils that, trooping up from the shoals below, mocked the unfortunates in their lairs.

Personally I am not of an imaginative temperament—very few Engineers are—but on that occasion I was as completely prostrated with nervous terror as any woman. After half an hour or so, however, I was able once more to calmly review my chances of escape. Any exit by the steep sand walls was, of course, impracticable. I had been thoroughly convinced of this some time before. It was possible, just possible, that I might, in the uncertain moonlight, safely run the gauntlet of the rifle shots. The place was so full of terror for me that I was prepared to undergo any risk in leaving it. Imagine my delight, then, when after creeping stealthily to the river front I found that the infernal boat was not there. My freedom lay before me in the next few steps!

By walking out to the first shallow pool that lay at the foot of the projecting left horn of the horseshoe, I could wade across, turn the flank of the crater, and make my way inland. Without a moment's hesitation I marched briskly past the tussocks where Gunga Dass had snared the crows, and out in the direction of the smooth white sand beyond. My first step from the tufts of dried grass showed me how utterly futile was any hope of escape; for, as I put my foot down, I felt an indescribable drawing, sucking motion of the sand below. Another moment and my leg was swallowed up nearly to the knee. In the moonlight the whole surface of the sand seemed to be shaken with devilish delight at my disappointment. I struggled clear, sweating with terror and exertion, back to the tussocks behind me and fell on my face.

My only means of escape from the semicircle was protected with a quicksand!

How long I lay I have not the faintest idea; but I was roused at last by the malevolent chuckle of Gunga Dass at my ear. "I would advise you, Protector of the Poor" (the ruffian was speaking English) "to return to your house. It is unhealthy to lie down here. Moreover, when the boat returns, you will most certainly be rifled at.'' He stood over me in the dim light of the dawn, chuckling and laughing to himself. Suppressing my first impulse to catch the man by the neck and throw him onto the quicksand, I rose sullenly and followed him to the platform below the burrows.

Suddenly, and futilely as I thought while I spoke, I asked, ''Gunga Dass, what is the good of the boat if I can't get out *anyhow*?'' I recollect that even in my deepest trouble I had been speculating vaguely on the waste of ammunition in guarding an already well protected foreshore.

Gunga Dass laughed again and made answer, ''They have the boat only in daytime. It is for the reason that *there is a way*. I hope we shall have the pleasure of your company for much longer time. It is a pleasant spot when you have been here some years and eaten roast crow long enough.''

I staggered, numbed and helpless, toward the fetid burrow allotted to me, and fell asleep. An hour or so later I was awakened by a piercing scream—the shrill, high-pitched scream of a horse in pain. Those who have once heard that will never forget the sound. I found some little difficulty in scrambling out of the burrow. When I was in the open, I saw Pornic, my poor old Pornic, lying dead on the sandy soil. How they had killed him I cannot guess. Gunga Dass explained that horse was better than crow, and ''greatest good of greatest number is political maxim. We are now Republic, Mister Jukes, and you are entitled to a fair share of the beast. If you like, we will pass a vote of thanks. Shall I propose?''

Yes, we were a Republic indeed! A Republic of wild beasts penned at the bottom of a pit, to eat and fight and sleep until we died. I attempted no protest of any kind, but sat down and stared at the hideous sight in front of me. In less time almost than it takes me to write this, Pornic's body was divided, in some unclean way or other; the men and women had dragged the fragments onto the platform and were preparing their normal meal. Gunga Dass cooked mine. The almost irresistible impulse to fly at the sand walls until I was wearied laid hold of me afresh, and I had to struggle against it with all my might. Gunga Dass was offensively jocular till I told him that if he addressed another remark of any kind whatever to me I should strangle him where he sat. This silenced him till silence became insupportable, and I bade him say something.

''You will live here till you die like the other Feringhi,'' he said, coolly, watching me over the fragment of gristle that he was gnawing.

"What other Sahib, you swine? Speak at once, and don't stop to tell me a lie."

"He is over there," answered Gunga Dass, pointing to a burrow mouth about four doors to the left of my own. "You can see for yourself. He died in the burrow as you will die, and I will die, and as all these men and women and the one child will also die."

"For pity's sake tell me all you know about him. Who was he? When did he come, and when did he die?"

This appeal was a weak step on my part. Gunga Dass only leered and replied, "I will not—unless you give me something first."

Then I recollected where I was, and struck the man between the eyes, partially stunning him. He stepped down from the platform at once, and, cringing and fawning and weeping and attempting to embrace my feet, led me round to the burrow which he had indicated.

"I know nothing whatever about the gentleman. Your God be my witness that I do not. He was as anxious to escape as you were, and he was shot from the boat, though we all did all things to prevent him from attempting. He was shot here." Gunga Dass laid his hand on his lean stomach and bowed to the earth.

"Well, and what then? Go on!"

"And then—and then, Your Honor, we carried him to his house and gave him water, and put wet cloths on the wound, and he laid down in his house and gave up the ghost."

"In how long? In how long?"

"About half an hour, after he received his wound. I call Vishnu to witness," yelled the wretched man, "that I did everything for him. Everything which was possible, that I did!"

He threw himself down on the ground and clasped my ankles. But I had my doubts about Gunga Dass's benevolence, and kicked him off as he lay protesting.

"I believe you robbed him of everything he had. But I can find out in a minute or two. How long was the Sahib here?"

"Nearly a year and a half. I think he must have gone mad. But hear me swear, Protector of the Poor! Won't Your Honor hear me swear that I never touched an article that belonged to him? What is Your Worship going to do?"

I had taken Gunga Dass by the waist and had hauled him to the platform opposite the deserted burrow. As I did so I thought of my wretched fellow-prisoner's unspeakable misery among all these horrors for eighteen months, and the final agony of dying like a rat in a hole, with a bullet-wound in the stomach. Gunga Dass fancied I was going to kill him and howled pitifully. The rest of the population, in the plethora that follows a full flesh meal, watched us without stirring.

"Go inside, Gunga Dass," said I, "and fetch it out."

I was feeling sick and faint with horror now. Gunga Dass nearly rolled off the platform and howled aloud.

"But I am Brahmin, Sahib—a high-caste Brahmin. By your soul, by your father's soul, do not make me do this thing!"

"Brahmin or no Brahmin, by my soul and my father's soul, in you go!" I said, and, seizing him by the shoulders, I crammed his head into the mouth of the burrow, kicked the rest of him in, and, sitting down, covered my face with my hands.

At the end of a few minutes I heard a rustle and a creak; then Gunga Dass in a sobbing, choking whisper speaking to himself; then a soft thud—and I uncovered my eyes.

The dry sand had turned the corpse entrusted to its keeping into a yellow-brown mummy. I told Gunga Dass to stand off while I examined it. The body—clad in an olive-green hunting suit much stained and worn, with leather pads on the shoulders—was that of a man between thirty and forty, above middle height, with light, sandy hair, long mustache, and a rough unkempt beard. The left canine of the upper jaw was missing, and a portion of the lobe of the right ear was gone. On the second finger of the left hand was a ring—a shield-shaped bloodstone set in gold, with a monogram that might have been either "B.K." or "B.L." On the third finger of the right hand was a silver ring in the shape of a coiled cobra, much worn and tarnished. Gunga Dass deposited a handful of trifles he had picked out of the burrow at my feet, and, covering the face of the body with my handkerchief, I turned to examine these. I give the full list in the hope that it may lead to the identification of the unfortunate man:

1. Bowl of a briarwood pipe, serrated at the edge; much worn and blackened; bound with string at the screw.

2. Two patent-lever keys; wards of both broken.

3. Tortoiseshell-handled penknife, silver or nickel name-plate, marked with monogram "B.K."

4. Envelope, postmark undecipherable, bearing a Victorian

stamp, addressed to "Miss Mon—" (rest illegible)—"ham"—"nt."

5. Imitation crocodile-skin notebook with pencil. First forty-five pages blank; four and a half illegible; fifteen others filled with private memoranda relating chiefly to three persons—a Mrs. L. Singleton, abbreviated several times to "Lot Single," "Mrs. S. May," and "Garmison," referred to in places as "Jerry" or "Jack."

6. Handle of small-sized hunting knife. Blade snapped short. Buck's horn, diamond cut, with swivel and ring on the butt; fragment of cotton cord attached.

It must not be supposed that I inventoried all these things on the spot as fully as I have here written them down. The notebook first attracted my attention, and I put it in my pocket with a view of studying it later on. The rest of the articles I conveyed to my burrow for safety's sake, and there being a methodical man, I inventoried them. I then returned to the corpse and ordered Gunga Dass to help me to carry it out to the river front. While we were engaged in this, the exploded shell of an old brown cartridge dropped out of one of the pockets and rolled at my feet. Gunga Dass had not seen it; and I fell to thinking that a man does not carry exploded cartridge-cases, especially "browns," which will not bear loading twice, about with him when shooting. In other words, that cartridge-case had been fired inside the crater. Consequently there must be a gun somewhere. I was on the verge of asking Gunga Dass, but checked myself, knowing that he would lie. We laid the body down on the edge of the quicksand by the tussocks. It was my intention to push it out and let it be swallowed up—the only possible mode of burial that I could think of. I ordered Gunga Dass to go away.

Then I gingerly put the corpse on the quicksand. In doing so, it was lying face downward, I tore the frail and rotten khaki shooting-coat open, disclosing a hideous cavity in the back. I have already told you that the dry sand had, as it were, mummified the body. A moment's glance showed that the gaping hole had been caused by a gunshot wound; the gun must have been fired with the muzzle almost touching the back. The shooting-coat, being intact, had been drawn over the body after death, which must have been instantaneous. The secret of the poor wretch's death was plain to me in a flash. Some one of the crater, presumably Gunga Dass, must have shot him with his own gun—the gun that fitted the brown cartridges. He had never attempted to escape in the face of the rifle-fire from the boat.

I pushed the corpse out hastily and saw it sink from sight literally in a few seconds. I shuddered as I watched. In a dazed, half-conscious way I turned to peruse the notebook. A stained and discolored slip of paper had been inserted between the binding and the back, and dropped out as I opened the pages. This is what it contained:—*"Four out from crow-clump: three left; nine out; two right; three back; two left; fourteen out; two left; seven out; one left; nine back; two right; six back; four right; seven back."* The paper had been burned and charred at the edges. What it meant I could not understand. I sat down on the dried bents turning it over and over between my fingers, until I was aware of Gunga Dass standing immediately behind me with glowing eyes and outstretched hands.

"Have you got it?" he panted. "Will you not let me look at it also? I swear that I will return it."

"Got what? Return what?" I asked.

"That which you have in your hands. It will help us both." He stretched out his long, bird-like talons, trembling with eagerness.

"I could never find it," he continued. "He had secreted it about his person. Therefore I shot him, but nevertheless I was unable to obtain it."

Gunga Dass had quite forgotten his little fiction about the rifle-bullet. I received the information perfectly calmly. Morality is blunted by consorting with the dead who are alive.

"What on earth are you raving about? What is it you want me to give you?"

"The piece of paper in the notebook. It will help us both. Oh, you fool! You fool! Can you not see what it will do for us? We shall escape!"

His voice rose almost to a scream, and he danced with excitement before me. I own I was moved at the chance of my getting away.

"Don't skip! Explain yourself. Do you mean to say that this slip of paper will help us? What does it mean?"

"Read it aloud! Read it aloud! I beg and I pray you to read it aloud."

I did so. Gunga Dass listened delightedly, and drew an irregular line in the sand with his fingers.

"See now! It was the length of his gun-barrels without the stock. I have those barrels. Four gun-barrels out from the place where I caught crows. Straight out; do you follow me? Then three left—Ah! how well I remember when that man worked it out night after night. Then nine out, and so on. Out is always straight before you across the quicksand. He told me so before I killed him.''

''But if you knew all this why didn't you get out before?''

''I did *not* know it. He told me that he was working it out a year and a half ago, and how he was working it out night after night when the boat had gone away, and he could get out near the quicksand safely. Then he said that we would get away together. But I was afraid that he would leave me behind one night when he had worked it all out, and so I shot him. Besides, it is not advisable that the men who once get in here should escape. Only I, and *I* am a Brahmin.''

The prospect of escape had brought Gunga Dass's caste back to him. He stood up, walked about, and gesticulated violently. Eventually I managed to make him talk soberly, and he told me how this Englishman had spent six months night after night in exploring, inch by inch, the passage across the quicksand; how he had declared it to be simplicity itself up to within about twenty yards of the river bank after turning the flank of the left horn of the horseshoe. This much he had evidently not completed when Gunga Dass shot him with his own gun.

In my frenzy of delight at the possibilities of escape I recollect shaking hands effusively with Gunga Dass, after we had decided that we were to make an attempt to get away that very night. It was weary work waiting throughout the afternoon.

About ten o'clock, as far as I could judge, when the Moon had just risen above the lip of the crater, Gunga Dass made a move for his burrow to bring out the gun-barrels whereby to measure our path. All the other wretched inhabitants had retired to their lairs long ago. The guardian boat drifted downstream some hours before, and we were utterly alone by the crow clump. Gunga Dass, while carrying the gun-barrels, let slip the piece of paper which was to be our guide. I stooped down hastily to recover it, and, as I did so, I was aware that the diabolical Brahmin was aiming a violent blow at the back of my head with the gun barrels. It was too late to turn round. I must have received the blow somewhere on the nape of my neck. A hundred thousand fiery stars danced before my eyes, and I fell forwards senseless at the edge of the quicksand.

When I recovered consciousness, the Moon was going down, and I was sensible of intolerable pain in the back of my head. Gunga Dass had disappeared and my mouth was full of blood. I lay down again and prayed that I might die without more ado. Then the unreasoning fury which I had before mentioned, laid hold upon me, and I staggered inland toward the walls of the crater. It seemed that someone was calling to me in a whisper, "Sahib! Sahib! Sahib!" exactly as my bearer used to call me in the morning. I fancied that I was delirious until a handful of sand fell at my feet. Then I looked up and saw a head peering down into the amphitheatre—the head of Dunnoo, my dog-boy, who attended to my collies. As soon as he had attracted my attention, he held up his hand and showed a rope. I motioned, staggering to and fro for the while, that he should throw it down. It was a couple of leather punkah ropes knotted together, with a loop at one end. I slipped the loop over my head and under my arms; heard Dunnoo urge something forward; was conscious that I was being dragged, face downward, up the steep sand slope, and the next instant found myself choked and half fainting on the sand hills overlooking the crater. Dunnoo, with his face ashy grey in the moonlight, implored me not to stay but to get back to my tent at once.

It seemed that he had tracked Pornic's footprints fourteen miles across the sands to the crater; had returned and told my servants, who flatly refused to meddle with any one, white or black, once fallen into the hideous Village of the Dead; whereupon Dunnoo had taken one of my ponies and a couple of punkah ropes, returned to the crater, and hauled me out as I have described.

To cut a long story short, Dunnoo is now my personal servant on a gold mohur a month—a sum which I still think far too little for the services he has rendered. Nothing on earth will induce me to go near that devilish spot again, or to reveal its whereabouts more clearly than I have done. Of Gunga Dass I have never found a trace, nor do I wish to do. My sole motive in giving this to be published is the hope that someone may possibly identify, from the details and the inventory which I have given above, the corpse of the man in the olive-green hunting suit.

Robert Louis Stevenson (1850–1894)

Robert Louis Stevenson always wanted to write. In time he became one of the world's most widely-read authors, despite his father's desire that the boy follow paternal footsteps and become a civil engineer.

Born in Edinburgh, Scotland, an only child, Stevenson had a happy childhood, except for chronic health problems, which eventually developed into tuberculosis.

In 1867 he attended the University of Edinburgh, but left in 1871 to read law at an Edinburgh firm in an attempt to compromise his ideas with those of his father. In his free time he wrote.

Four years later, he passed his bar exam, but never practiced. His writing was beginning to be published.

His first book (*An Inland Voyage*) appeared in 1867, the same year the he met his future wife, Fanny Osbourne. She was ten years older than he, with two children. After she secured a divorce in California, they married in 1880, made peace with Stevenson's parents, and began a search for a healthful climate in which to live.

Literary fame and domestic happiness grew as his health declined. Stevenson returned to California in 1888 and hired a yacht to cruise the South Seas, eventually settling down in Samoa. Here is power grew. When he died there of a cerebral hemorrhage in 1894 he was working on the novel *Weir of Hemiston*, which critics called his masterpiece.

His major contributions to horror are *The Strange Case of Dr. Jekyll and Mr. Hyde* (a science fictional tale of multiple personalities), "The Body Snatchers" (a ghost story), and our selection, "Markheim" (an hallucinatory story of murder).

MARKHEIM

"*Y*es," said the dealer, "*our windfalls are of various kinds.* Some customers are ignorant, and then I touch a dividend on my superior knowledge. Some are dishonest," and here he held up the candle, so that the light fell strongly on his visitor, "and in that case," he continued, "I profit by my virtue."

Markheim had but just entered from the daylight streets, and his eyes had not yet grown familiar with the mingled shine and darkness in the shop. At these pointed words, and before the near presence of the flame, he blinked painfully and looked aside.

The dealer chuckled. "You come to me on Christmas Day," he resumed, "when you know that I am alone in my house, put up my shutters, and make a point of refusing business. Well, you will have to pay for that; you will have to pay for my loss of time, when I should be balancing my books; you will have to pay, besides, for a kind of manner that I remark in you today very strongly. I am the essence of discretion, and ask no awkward questions; but when a customer cannot look me in the eye, he has to pay for it." The dealer once more chuckled; and then, changing to his usual business voice, though still with a note of irony, "You can give, as usual, a clear account of how you came into the possession of the object?" he continued. "Still your uncle's cabinet? A remarkable collector, sir!"

And the little pale, round-shouldered dealer stood almost on tiptoe, looking over the top of his gold spectacles, and nodding his head with every mark of disbelief. Markheim returned his gaze with one of infinite pity, and a touch of horror.

"This time," said he, "you are in error. I have not come to sell, but to buy. I have no curios to dispose of; my uncle's cabinet is bare to the wainscot; even were it still intact, I have done well on the Stock Exchange, and should more likely add to it than otherwise, and my errand today is simplicity itself. I seek a Christmas present for a lady,'' he continued, waxing more fluent as he struck into the speech he had prepared; ''and certainly I owe you every excuse for thus disturbing you upon so small a matter. But the thing was neglected yesterday; I must produce my little compliment at dinner; and, as you very well know, a rich marriage is not a thing to be neglected.''

There followed a pause, during which the dealer seemed to weigh this statement incredulously. The ticking of many clocks among the curious lumber of the shop, and the faint rushing of the cabs in a near thoroughfare, filled up the interval of silence.

''Well, sir,'' said the dealer, ''be it so. You are an old customer after all; and if, as you say, you have the chance of a good marriage, far be it from me to be an obstacle. Here is a nice thing for a lady now,'' he went on, ''this hand glass—fifteenth century, warranted; comes from a good collection, too; but I reserve the name, in the interests of my customer, who was just like yourself, my dear sir, the nephew and sole heir of a remarkable collector.''

The dealer, while he thus ran on in his dry and biting voice, had stooped to take the object from its place; and, as he had done so, a shock had passed through Markheim, a start both of hand and foot, a sudden leap of many tumultuous passions to the face. It passed as swiftly as it came, and left no trace beyond a certain trembling of the hand that now received the glass.

''A glass,'' he said hoarsely, and then paused, and repeated it more clearly. ''A glass? For Christmas? Surely not?''

''And why not?'' cried the dealer. ''Why not a glass?''

Markheim was looking upon him with an indefinable expression. ''You ask me why not?'' he said. ''Why, look here—look in it—look at yourself! Do you like to see it? No! nor I—nor any man.''

The little man had jumped back when Markheim had so suddenly confronted him with the mirror; but now, perceiving there was nothing worse on hand, he chuckled. ''Your future lady, sir, must be pretty hard favored,'' said he.

''I ask you,'' said Markheim, ''for a Christmas present, and you give me this—this damned reminder of years, and sins and follies—this hand-conscience! Did you mean it? Had you a thought in your mind? Tell me. It will be better for you if you do. Come, tell me about yourself. I hazard a guess now, that you are in secret a very charitable man?

The dealer looked closely at his companion. It was very odd, Markheim did not appear to be laughing; there was something in his face like an eager sparkle of hope, but nothing of mirth.

"What are you driving at?" the dealer asked.

"Not charitable?" returned the other, gloomily. "Not charitable; not pious; not scrupulous; unloving, unbeloved; a hand to get money, a safe to keep it. Is that all? Dear God, man, is that all?"

"I will tell you what it is," began the dealer, with some sharpness, and then broke off again into a chuckle. "But I see this is a love match of yours, and you have been drinking the lady's health."

"Ah!" cried Markheim, with a strange curiosity. "Ah, have you been in love? Tell me about that."

"I," cried the dealer. "I in love! I never had the time, nor have I the time today for all this nonsense. Will you take the glass?"

"Where is the hurry?" returned Markheim. "It is very pleasant to stand here talking; and life is so short and insecure that I would not hurry away from any pleasure—no, not even from so mild a one as this. We should rather cling, cling to what little we can get, like a man at a cliff's edge. Every second is a cliff, if you think upon it—a cliff a mile high—high enough, if we fall, to dash us out of every feature of humanity. Hence it is best to talk pleasantly. Let us talk of each other; why should we wear this mask? Let us be confidential. Who knows, we might become friends?"

"I have just one word to say to you," said the dealer. "Either make your purchase, or walk out of my shop."

"True, true," said Markheim. "Enough fooling. To business. Show me something else."

The dealer stooped once more, this time to replace the glass upon the shelf, his thin blond hair falling over his eyes as he did so. Markheim moved a little nearer, with one hand in the pocket of his greatcoat; he drew himself up and filled his lungs; at the same time many different emotions were depicted together on his face—terror, horror, and resolve, fascination and a physical repulsion; and through a haggard lift of his upper lip, his teeth looked out.

"This, perhaps, may suit," observed the dealer; and then, as he began to re-arise, Markheim bounded from behind upon his victim. The long, skewerlike dagger flashed and fell. The dealer struggled like a hen, striking his temple on the shelf, and then tumbled on the floor in a heap.

Time had some score of small voices in that shop, some stately and slow as was becoming to their great age; others garrulous and hurried. All these tolled out the seconds in an intricate chorus of tickings. Then the passage of a lad's feet, heavily running on the pavement, broke in upon these smaller voices and startled Markheim into the consciousness of his surroundings. He looked about him. The candle stood on the counter, its flame solemnly wagging in a draught; and by that inconsiderable movement, the whole room was filled with noiseless bustle and kept heaving like a sea: the tall shadows nodding, the gross blots of darkness swelling and dwindling as with respiration, the faces of the portraits and the china gods changing and wavering like images in water. The inner door stood ajar and peered into the leaguer of shadows with a long slit of daylight like a pointing finger.

From these fearstricken rovings, Markheim's eyes returned to the body of his victim, where it lay both humped and sprawling, incredibly small and strangely meaner than in life. In these poor, miserly clothes, in that ungainly attitude, the dealer lay like so much sawdust. Markheim had feared to see it, and, lo! it was nothing. And yet, as he gazed, this bundle of old clothes and pool of blood began to find eloquent voices. There it must lie; there was none to work the cunning hinges or direct the miracle of locomotion—there it must lie till it was found. Found! ay, and then? Then would this dead flesh lift up a cry that would ring over England, and fill the world with the echoes of pursuit. Ay, dead or not, this was still the enemy. "Time was that when the brains were out," he thought; and the first word struck into his mind. Time, now that the deed was accomplished—time, which had closed for the victim, had become instant and momentous for the slayer.

The thought was yet in his mind, when, first one and then another, with every variety of pace and voice—one deep as the bell from a cathedral turret, another ringing on its treble notes the prelude of a waltz—the clocks began to strike the hour of three in the afternoon.

The sudden outbreak of so many tongues in that dumb chamber staggered him. He began to bestir himself, going to and fro with the candle, beleaguered by moving shadows, and startled to the soul by chance reflections. In many rich mirrors, some of home designs, some from Venice or Amsterdam, he saw his face repeated and repeated, as it were an army of spies; his own eyes met and detected him; and the sound of his own steps, lightly as they fell, vexed the surrounding quiet. And still as he continued to fill his pockets, his mind accused him, with a sickening iteration, of the thousand faults of his design. He should have chosen a more quiet hour; he should have prepared an alibi; he should not have used a knife; he should have been more cautious, and only bound and gagged the dealer, and not killed him; he should have been more bold, and killed the servant also; he should have done all things otherwise; poignant regrets, weary incessant toiling of the mind to change what was unchangeable, to plan what was now useless, to be the architect of the irrevocable past. Meanwhile, and behind all this activity, brute terrors, like the scurrying of rats in a deserted attic, filled the more remote chambers of his brain with riot; the hand of the constable would fall heavy on his shoulder, and his nerves would jerk like a hooked fish; or he beheld, in galloping defile, the dock, the prison, the gallows, and the black coffin.

Terror of the people in the street sat down before his mind like a besieging army. It was impossible, he thought, but that some rumor of the struggle must have reached their ears and set on edge their curiosity; and now, in all the neighboring houses, he divined them sitting motionless and with uplifted ear—solitary people, condemned to spend Christmas dwelling alone on memories of the past, and now startlingly recalled from that tender exercise; happy family parties, struck into silence round the table, the mother still with raised finger: every degree and age and humor, but all, by their own hearts, prying and hearkening and weaving the rope that was to hang him. Sometimes it seemed to him he could not move too swiftly; the clink of the tall Bohemian goblets rang out loudly like a bell; and alarmed by the bigness of the ticking, he was tempted to stop the clocks. And then, again, with a swift transition of his terrors, the very silence of the place appeared a source of peril, and a thing to strike and freeze the passerby; and he would step more boldly, and bustle aloud among the contents of the shop, and imitate, with elaborate bravado, the movements of a busy man at ease in his own house.

But he was now so pulled about by different alarms that, while one portion of his mind was still alert and cunning, another trembled on the brink of lunacy. One hallucination in particular took a strong hold on his credulity. The neighbor hearkening with white face beside his window, the passerby arrested by a horrible surmise on the pavement—these could at worst suspect, they could not know; through the brick walls and shuttered windows only sounds could penetrate. But here, within the house, was he alone? he knew he was; he had watched the servant set forth sweethearting, in her poor best, "out for the day" written in every ribbon and smile. Yes, he was alone, of course; and yet, in the bulk of empty house above him, he could surely hear a stir of delicate footing— he was surely conscious, inexplicably conscious of some presence. Ay, surely; to every room and corner of the house his imagination followed it; and now it was a faceless thing, and yet had eyes to see with; and again it was a shadow of himself; and yet again behold the image of the dead dealer, reinspired with cunning and hatred.

At times, with a strong effort, he would glance at the open door which still seemed to repel his eyes. The house was tall, the skylight small and dirty, the day blind with fog; and the light that filtered down to the ground story was exceedingly faint, and showed dimly on the threshold of the shop. And yet, in that strip of doubtful brightness, did there not hang wavering a shadow?

Suddenly, from the street outside, a very jovial gentleman began to beat with a staff on the shop door, accompanying his blows with shouts and railleries in which the dealer was continually called upon by name. Markheim, smitten into ice glanced at the dead man. But no! he lay quite still; he was fled away far beyond earshot of these blows and shoutings; he was sunk beneath seas of silence; and his name, which would once have caught his notice above the howling of a storm, had become an empty sound. And presently the jovial gentleman desisted from his knocking and departed.

Here was a broad hint to hurry what remained to be done, to get forth from this accusing neighborhood, to plunge into a bath of London multitudes, and to reach, on the other side of day, that haven of safety and apparent innocence—his bed. One visitor had come; at any moment another might follow and be more obstinate. To have done the deed, and yet not to reap the profit, would be too abhorrent a failure. The money, that was now Markheim's concern; and as a means to that, the keys.

He glanced over his shoulder at the open door, where the shadow was still lingering and shivering; and with no conscious repugnance of the mind, yet with a tremor of the belly, he drew near the body of his victim. The human character had quite departed. Like a suit half-stuffed with bran, the limbs lay scattered, the trunk doubled on the floor; and yet the thing repelled him. Although so dingy and inconsiderable to the eye, he feared it might have more significance to the touch. He took the body by the shoulders, and turned it on its back. It was strangely light and supple, and the limbs, as if they had been broken, fell into the oddest postures. The face was robbed of all expression; but it was as pale as wax, and shockingly smeared with blood about one temple. That was, for Markheim, the one displeasing circumstance. It carried him back, upon the instant, to a certain fair day in a fishers' village: a gray day, a piping wind, a crowd upon the street, the blare of brasses, the booming of drums, the nasal voice of a ballad singer; and a boy going to and fro, buried overhead in the crowd and divided between interest and fear, until, coming upon the chief place of concourse, he beheld a booth and a great screen with pictures, dismally designed, garishly colored: Brown-rigg with her apprentice; the Mannings with their murdered guest; Weare in the death-grip of Thurtell; and a score besides of famous crimes. The thing was as clear as an illusion; he was once again that little boy; he was looking once again, and with the same sense of physical revolt, at these vile pictures; he was still stunned by the thumping of the drums. A bar of that day's music returned upon his memory; and at that, for the first time, a qualm came over him, a breath of nausea, a sudden weakness of the joints, which he must instantly resist and conquer.

He judged it more prudent to confront than to flee from these considerations; looking the more hardily in the dead face, bending his mind to realize the nature and greatness of his crime. So little a while ago that face had moved with every change of sentiment, that pale mouth had spoken, that body had been all on fire with governable energies; and now, and by his act, that piece of life had been arrested, as the horologist, with interjected finger, arrests the beating of the clock. So he reasoned in vain; he could rise to no more remorseful consciousness; the same heart which had shuddered before the painted effigies of crime, looked on its reality unmoved. At best, he felt a gleam of pity for one who had been endowed in vain with all those faculties that can make the world a garden of enchantment, one who had never lived and who was now dead. But of penitence, no, not a tremor.

With that, shaking himself clear of these considerations, he found the keys and advanced toward the open door of the shop. Outside, it had begun to rain smartly; and the sound of the shower upon the roof had banished silence. Like some dripping cavern, the chambers of the house were haunted by an incessant echoing, which filled the ear and mingled with the ticking of the clocks. And, as Markheim approached the door, he seemed to hear, in answer to his own cautious tread, the steps of another foot withdrawing up the stair. The shadow still palpitated loosely on the threshold. He threw a ton's weight of resolve upon his muscles, and drew back the door.

The faint, foggy daylight glimmered dimly on the bare floor and stairs; on the bright suit of armor posted, halbert in hand, upon the landing; and on the dark wood carvings, and framed pictures that hung against the yellow panels of the wainscot. So loud was the beating of the rain through all the house that, in Markheim's ears, it began to be distinguished into many different sounds. Footsteps and sighs, the tread of regiments marching in the distance, the chink of money in the counting, and the creaking of doors held stealthily ajar, appeared to mingle with the patter of the drops upon the cupola and the gushing of the water in the pipes. The sense that he was not alone grew upon him to the verge of madness. On every side he was haunted and begirt by presences. He heard them moving in the upper chambers; from the shop, he heard the dead man getting to his legs; and as he began with a great effort to mount the stairs, feet fled quietly before him and followed stealthily behind. If he were but deaf, he thought, how tranquilly he would possess his soul! And then again, and hearkening with ever fresh attention, he blessed himself for that unresting sense which held the outposts and stood a trusty sentinel upon his life. His head turned continually on his neck; his eyes, which seemed starting from their orbits, scouted on every side, and on every side were half-rewarded as with the tail of something nameless vanishing. The four-and-twenty steps to the first floor were four-and-twenty agonies.

On that first story, the doors stood ajar, three of them like three ambushes, shaking his nerves like the throats of cannon. He could never again, he felt, be sufficiently immured and fortified from men's observing eyes; he longed to be home, girt in by walls, buried among bedclothes, and invisible to all but God. And at that thought he wondered a little, recollecting tales of other murderers and the fear they were said to entertain of heavenly avengers. It was not so, at least, with him. He feared the laws of nature, lest, in their callous and immutable procedure, they should preserve some damning evidence of his crime. He feared tenfold more, with a slavish, superstitious terror, some scission in the continuity of man's experience, some wilful illegality of nature. He played a game of skill, depending on the rules, calculating consequence from cause; and what if nature, as the defeated tyrant overthrew the chessboard, should break the mold of their succession? The like had befallen Napoleon (so writers said) when the winter changed the time of its appearance. The like might befall Markheim: the solid walls might become transparent and reveal his doings like those of bees in a glass hive; the stout planks might yield under his foot like quicksands and detain him in their clutch; ay, and there were soberer accidents that might destroy him: if, for instance, the house should fall and imprison him beside the body of his victim; or the house next door should fly on fire, and the firemen invade him from all sides These things he feared; and, in a sense, these things might be called the hands of God reached forth against sin. But about God himself he was at ease; his act was doubtless exceptional, but so were his excuses, which God knew; it was there, and not among men, that he felt sure of justice.

When he had got safe into the drawing room, and shut the door behind him, he was aware of a respite from alarms. The room was quite dismantled, uncarpeted besides, and strewn with packing cases and incongruous furniture; several great pier glasses, in which he beheld himself at various angles, like an actor on a stage; many pictures, framed and unframed, standing, with their faces to the wall; a fine Sheraton sideboard, a cabinet of marquetry, and a great old bed, with tapestry hangings. The windows opened to the floor; but by great good fortune the lower part of the shutters had been closed, and this concealed him from the neighbors. Here, then, Markheim drew in a packing case before the cabinet, and began to search among the keys. It was a long business, for there were many; and it was irksome, besides; for, after all, there might be nothing in the cabinet, and time was on the wing. But the closeness of the occupation sobered him. With the tail of his eye he saw the door—even glanced at it from time to time directly, like a besieged commander pleased to verify the good estate of his defenses. But in truth he was at peace. The rain falling in the street sounded natural and pleasant. Presently, on the other side, the notes of a piano were wakened to the music of a hymn, and the voices of many children took up the air and words. How stately, how comfortable was the melody! How fresh the youthful voices! Markheim gave ear to it smilingly, as he sorted out the keys; and his mind was thronged with answerable ideas and images; churchgoing children and the pealing of the high organ; children afield, bathers by the brookside, ramblers on the brambly common, kite-fliers in the windy and cloud-navigated sky; and then, at another cadence of the hymn, back again to church, and the somnolence of summer Sundays, and the high genteel voice of the parson (which he smiled a little to recall) and the painted Jacobean tombs, and the dim lettering of the Ten Commandments in the chancel.

And as he sat thus, at once busy and absent, he was startled to his feet. A flash of ice, a flash of fire, a bursting gush of blood, went over him, and then he stood transfixed and thrilling. A step mounted the stair slowly and steadily, and presently a hand was laid upon the knob, and the lock clicked, and the door opened.

Fear held Markheim in a vise. What to expect he knew not, whether the dead man walking, or the official ministers of human justice, or some chance witness blindly stumbling in to consign him to the gallows. But when a face was thrust into the aperture, glanced round the room, looked at him, nodded and smiled as if in friendly recognition, and then withdrew again, and the door closed behind it, his fear broke loose from his control in a hoarse cry. At the sound of this the visitant returned.

"Did you call me?" he asked, pleasantly, and with that he entered the room and closed the door behind him.

Markheim stood and gazed at him with all his eyes. Perhaps there was a film upon his sight, but the outlines of the newcomer seemed to change and waver like those of the idols in the wavering candlelight of the shop; and at times he thought he knew him; and at times he thought he bore a likeness to himself; and always, like a lump of living terror, there lay in his bosom the conviction that this thing was not of the earth and not of God.

And yet the creature had a strange air of the commonplace, as he stood looking on Markheim with a smile; and when he added: "You are looking for the money, I believe?" it was in the tones of everyday politeness.

Markheim made no answer.

"I should warn you," resumed the other, "that the maid has left her sweetheart earlier than usual and will soon be here. If Mr. Markheim be found in this house, I need not describe to him the consequences."

"You know me?" cried the murderer.

The visitor smiled. "You have long been a favorite of mine," he said; "and I have long observed and often sought to help you."

"What are you?" cried Markheim: "the devil?"

"What I may be," returned the other, "cannot affect the service I propose to render you."

"It can," cried Markheim, "it does! Be helped by you? No, never; not by you! You do not know me yet; thank God, you do not know me!"

"I know you," replied the visitant, with a sort of kind severity or rather firmness. "I know you to the soul."

"Know me!" cried Markheim. "Who can do so? My life is but a travesty and slander on myself. I have lived to belie my nature. All men do; all men are better than this disguise that grows about and stifles them. You see each dragged away by life, like one whom bravos have seized and muffled in a cloak. If they had their own control—if you could see their faces, they would be altogether different, they would shine out for heroes and saints! I am worse than most; my self is more overlaid; my excuse is known to me and God. But, had I the time, I could disclose myself."

"To me?" inquired the visitant.

"To you before all," returned the murderer. "I supposed you were intelligent. I thought—since you exist—you would prove a reader of the heart. And yet you would propose to judge me by my acts! Think of it; my acts! I was born and I have lived in a land of giants; giants have dragged me by the wrists since I was born out of my mother—the giants of circumstance. And you would judge me by my acts! But can you not look within? Can you not understand that evil is hateful to me? Can you not see within me the clear writing of conscience, never blurred by any wilful sophistry, although too often disregarded? Can you not read me for a thing that surely must be common as humanity—the unwilling sinner?"

"All this is very feelingly expressed," was the reply, "but it regards me not. These points of consistency are beyond my province, and I care not in the least by what compulsion you may have been dragged away, so as you are but carried in the right direction. But time flies; the servant delays, looking in the faces of the crowd and at the pictures on the hoardings, but still she keeps moving nearer; and remember, it is as if the gallows itself was striding toward you through the Christmas streets! Shall I help you; I, who know all? Shall I tell you where to find the money?"

"For what price?" asked Markheim.

"I offer you the service of a Christmas gift," returned the other.

Markheim could not refrain from smiling with a kind of bitter triumph. "No," said he, "I will take nothing at your hands; if I were dying of thirst, and it was your hand that put the pitcher to my lips, I should find the courage to refuse. It may be credulous, but I will do nothing to commit myself to evil."

"I have no objection to a deathbed repentance," observed the visitant.

"Because you disbelieve their efficacy!" Markheim cried.

"I do not say so," returned the other; "but I look on these things from a different side, and when the life is done my interest falls. The man has lived to serve me, to spread black looks under color of religion, or to sow tares in the wheat field, as you do, in a course of weak compliance with desire. Now that he draws so near to his deliverance, he can add but one act of service—to repent, to die smiling, and thus to build up in confidence and hope the more timorous of my surviving followers. I am not so hard a master. Try me. Accept my help. Please yourself in life as you have done hitherto; please yourself more amply, spread your elbows at the board; and when the night begins to fall and the curtains to be drawn, I tell you, for your greater comfort, that you will find it even easy to compound your quarrel with your conscience, and to make a truckling peace with God. I came but now from such a deathbed, and the room was full of sincere mourners, listening to the man's last words: and when I looked into that face, which had been set as a flint against mercy, I found it smiling with hope."

"And do you, then, suppose me such a creature?" asked Markheim. "Do you think I have no more generous aspirations than to sin, and sin, and sin, and, at last, sneak into heaven? My heart rises at the thought. Is this, then, your experience of mankind? or is it because you find me with red hands that you presume such baseness? and is this crime of murder indeed so impious as to dry up the very springs of good?"

"Murder is to me no special category," replied the other. "All sins are murder, even as all life is war. I behold your race, like starving mariners on a raft, plucking crusts out of the hands of famine and feeding on each other's lives. I follow sins beyond the moment of their acting; I find in all that the last consequence is death; and to my eyes, the pretty maid who thwarts her mother with such taking graces on a question of a ball, drips no less visibly with human gore than such a murderer as yourself. Do I say I follow sins? I follow virtues also; they differ not by the thickness of a nail, they are both scythes for the reaping Angel of Death. Evil, for which I live, consists not in action but in character. The bad man is dear to me; not the bad act, whose fruits, if we could follow them far enough down the hurtling cataract of the ages, might yet be found more blessed than those of the rarest virtues. And it is not because you have killed a dealer, but because you are Markheim, that I offered to forward your escape.''

"I will lay my heart open to you," answered Markheim. "This crime on which you find me is my last. On my way to it I have learned many lessons; itself is a lesson, a momentous lesson. Hitherto I have been driven with revolt to what I would not; I was a bond-slave to poverty, driven and scourged. There are robust virtues that can stand in these temptations; mine was not so: I had a thirst of pleasure. But today, and out of this deed, I pluck both warning and riches—both the power and a fresh resolve to be myself. I become in all things a free actor in the world; I begin to see myself all changed, these hands the agents of good, this heart at peace. Something comes over me out of the past; something of what I have dreamed on Sabbath evenings to the sound of the church organ, of what I forecast when I shed tears over noble books, or talked, an innocent child, with my mother. There lies my life; I have wandered a few years, but now I see once more my city of destination.''

"You are to use this money on the Stock Exchange, I think?" remarked the visitor; "and there, if I mistake not, you have already lost some thousands?''

"Ah," said Markheim, "but this time I have a sure thing."

"This time, again, you will lose," replied the visitor quietly.

"Ah, but I keep back the half!" cried Markheim.

"That also you will lose," said the other.

The sweat started upon Markheim's brow. "Well, then, what matter?" he exclaimed. "Say it be lost, say I am plunged again in poverty, shall one part of me, and that the worst, continue until the end to override the better? Evil and good run strong in me, halving me both ways. I do not love the one thing, I love all. I can conceive great deeds, renunciations, martyrdoms; and though I be fallen to such a crime as murder, pity is no stranger to my thoughts. I pity the poor; who knows their trials better than myself? I pity and help them; I prize love, I love honest laughter; there is no good thing nor true thing on earth but I love it from my heart. And are my vices only to direct my life, and my virtues to lie without effect, like some passive lumber of the mind? Not so; good, also, is a spring of acts.''

But the visitant raised his finger. ''For six-and-thirty years that you have been in this world,'' said he, ''through many changes of fortune and varieties of humor, I have watched you steadily fall. Fifteen years ago you would have started at a theft. Three years back you would have blanched at the name of murder. Is there any crime, is there any cruelty or meanness, from which you still recoil?—five years from now I shall detect you in the fact! Downward, downward, lies your way; nor can anything but death avail to stop you.''

''It is true,'' Markheim said huskily, ''I have in some degree complied with evil. But it is so with all: the very saints, in the mere exercise of living, grow less dainty, and take on the tone of their surroundings.''

''I will propound to you one simple question,'' said the other; ''and as you answer, I shall read to you your moral horoscope. You have grown in many things more lax; possibly you do right to be so; and at any account, it is the same with all men. But granting that, are you in any one particular, however trifling, more difficult to please with your own conduct, or do you go in all things with a looser rein?''

''In any one?'' repeated Markheim, with an anguish of consideration. ''No,'' he added, with despair, ''in none! I have gone down in all.''

''Then,'' said the visitor, ''content yourself with what you are, for you will never change; and the words of your part on this stage are irrevocably written down.''

Markheim stood for a long while silent, and indeed it was the visitor who first broke the silence. ''That being so,'' he said, ''shall I show you the money?''

''And grace?'' cried Markheim.

''Have you not tried it?'' returned the other. ''Two or three years ago, did I not see you on the platform of revival meetings, and was not your voice the loudest in the hymn?''

''It is true,'' said Markheim; ''and I see clearly what remains for me by way of duty. I thank you for these lessons from my soul; my eyes are opened, and I behold myself at last for what I am.''

At this moment, the sharp note of the doorbell rang through the house; and the visitant, as though this were some concerted signal for which he had been waiting, change at once in his demeanor.

"The maid!" he cried. "She has returned, as I forewarned you, and there is now before you one more difficult passage. Her master, you must say, is ill; you must let her in, with an assured but rather serious countenance—no smiles, no overacting, and I promise you success! Once the girl within, and the door closed, the same dexterity that has already rid you of the dealer will relieve you of this last danger in your path. Thenceforward you have the whole evening—the whole night, if needful—to ransack the treasures of the house and to make good your safety. This is help that comes to you with the mask of danger. Up!" he cried: "up, friend; your life hangs trembling in the scales: up, and act!"

Markheim steadily regarded his counsellor. "If I be condemned to evil acts," he said, "there is still one door of freedom open—I can cease from action. If my life be an ill thing, I can lay it down. Though I be, as you say truly, at the beck of every small temptation, I can yet, by one decisive gesture, place myself beyond the reach of all. My love of good is damned to barrenness; it may, and let it be! But I have still my hatred of evil; and from that, to your galling disappointment, you shall see that I can draw both energy and courage."

The features of the visitor began to undergo a wonderful and lovely change: they brightened and softened with a tender triumph; and, even as they brightened, faded and dislimned. But Markheim did not pause to watch or understand the transformation. He opened the door and went downstairs very slowly, thinking to himself. His past went soberly before him; he beheld it as it was, ugly and strenuous like a dream, random as chance-medley—a scene of defeat. Life, as he thus reviewed it, tempted him no longer; but on the further side he perceived a quiet haven for his bark. He paused in the passage, and looked into the shop, where the candle still burned by the dead body. It was strangely silent. Thoughts of the dealer swarmed into his mind, as he stood gazing. And then the bell once more broke out into impatient clamor.

He confronted the maid upon the threshold with something like a smile.

"You had better go for the police," said he: "I have killed your master."

Anton Chekov (1860–1904)

A major playwright and short story writer, Anton Pavlovich Chekov was born in Taganrog, Russia, the son of an unsuccessful shopkeeper. While studying to be a doctor at the University of Moscow, he began selling sketches to comic papers, becoming so successful that he rarely practiced medicine after graduation.

Until 1886, he never spent more than twenty-four hours on a story, yet his first collection of humor-filled tales (*Motley Stories*, 1886) was extremely well received. As he grew older, however, his production dropped and his views about the everyday lives of ordinary people seemed to darken into tragedy.[1] People are portrayed as communicating ineffectively with each other and as being overwhelmed by futility, boredom, and loneliness; mood and symbolism dominate these plots.

In 1892 he purchased a country estate fifty miles south of Moscow. Here he produced many of his best short stories until 1897, when a lung hemorrhage forced him to seek the warmer climate of the Crimea.

At Yalta, he met Konstanin Stanislavsky, the famous director of the Moscow Art Theater. Stanislavsky loved Chekov's plays, staging *The Sea Gull* in 1898, *Uncle Vanya* in 1899, *The Three Sisters* in 1901, and *The Cherry Orchard* in 1904. But unfortunately, death from tuberculosis claimed Chekov just as he was reaching the height of his talent and popularity.

Most of his mature work emphasized quiet desperation rather than active horror. Still, he did produce the shocking stories, "A Terrible Night," "Woe," and our selection of frenzy, "Sleepyhead."

---

[1]Ironically, Chekov continued to insist that even his later works were farces and comedies.

SLEEPYHEAD

I

*N**ight. Varka, the little nurse, a girl of thirteen, is rocking the* cradle in which the baby is lying, and humming hardly audibly:

> Hush-a-bye, my baby wee,
> While I sing a song for thee.

A little green lamp is burning before the icon; there is a string stretched from one end of the room to the other, on which baby clothes and a pair of big black trousers are hanging. There is a big patch of green on the ceiling from the icon lamp, and the baby clothes and the trousers throw long shadows on the stove, on the cradle, and on Varka. . . . When the lamp begins to flicker, the green patch and the shadows come to life, and are set in motion, as though by the wind. It is stuffy. There is a smell of cabbage soup, and of the inside of a boot shop.

The baby is crying. For a long while he has been hoarse and exhausted with crying; but he still goes on screaming, and there is no knowing when he will stop. And Varka is sleepy. Her eyes are glued together, her head droops, her neck aches. She cannot move her eyelids or her lips, and she feels as though her face is dried and wooden, as though her head has become as small as the head of a pin.

"Hush-a-bye, my baby wee," she hums, "while I cook the groats for thee. . . ."

A cricket is churring in the stove. Through the door in the next room the master and the apprentice Afanasy are snoring. . . . The cradle creaks plaintively, Varka murmurs—and it all blends into that soothing music of the night to which it is so sweet to listen, when one is lying in bed.

Now that music is merely irritating and oppressive, because it goads her to sleep, and she must not sleep; if Varka—God forbid!—should fall asleep, her master and mistress would beat her.

The lamp flickers. The patch of green and the shadows are set in motion, forcing themselves on Varka's fixed, half-open eyes, and in her half-slumbering brain are fashioned into misty visions. She sees dark clouds chasing one another over the sky, and screaming like the baby. But then the wind blows, the clouds are gone, and Varka sees a broad highroad covered with liquid mud; along the highroad stretch files of wagons, while people with wallets on their backs are trudging along and shadows flit backward and forward; on both sides she can see forests through the cold harsh mist. All at once the people with their wallets and their shadows fall on the ground in the liquid mud. "What is that for?" Varka asks. "To sleep, to sleep!" they answer her. And they fall sound asleep, and sleep sweetly, while crows and magpies sit on the telegraph wires, scream like the baby, and try to wake them.

"Hush-a-bye, my baby wee, and I will sing a song to thee," murmurs Varka, and now she sees herself in a dark stuffy hut.

Her dead father, Yefim Stepanov, is tossing from side to side on the floor. She does not see him, but she hears him moaning and rolling on the floor from pain. His guts have burst, as he says; the pain is so violent that he cannot utter a single word, and can only draw in his breath and clack his teeth like the rattling of a drum:

"Boo—boo—boo—boo."

Her mother, Pelageya, has run to the master's house to say that Yefim is dying. She has been gone a long time, and ought to be back. Varka lies awake on the stove, and hears her father's "boo—boo—boo." And then she hears someone has driven up to the hut. It is a young doctor from the town, who has been sent from the big house where he is staying on a visit. The doctor comes into the hut; he cannot be seen in the darkness, but he can be heard coughing and rattling the door.

"Light a candle," he says.

"Boo—boo—boo," answers Yefim.

Pelageya rushes to the stove and begins looking for the broken pot with the matches. A minute passes in silence. The doctor, feeling in his pocket, lights a match.

"In a minute, sir, in a minute," says Pelageya. She rushes out of the hut, and soon afterward comes back with a bit of candle.

Yefim's cheeks are rosy and his eyes are shining, and there is a peculiar keenness in his glance, as though he were seeing right through the hut and the doctor.

"Come, what is it? What are you thinking about?" says the doctor, bending down to him. "Aha! have you had this long?"

"What? Dying, your honor, my hour has come. I am not to stay among the living."

"Don't talk nonsense! We will cure you!"

"That's as you please, your honor, we humbly thank you, only we understand. Since death has come, there it is."

The doctor spends a quarter of an hour over Yefim, then he gets up and says:

"I can do nothing. You must go into the hospital, there they will operate on you. Go at once. . . . You must go! It's rather late, they will all be asleep in the hospital, but that doesn't matter. I will give you a note. Do you hear?"

"Kind sir, but what can he go in?" says Pelageya. "We have no horse."

"Never mind. I'll ask your master, he'll let you have a horse."

The doctor goes away, the candle goes out, and again there is the sound of "boo—boo—boo." Half an hour later someone drives up to the hut. A cart has been sent to take Yefim to the hospital. He gets ready and goes.

But now it is a clear bright morning. Pelageya is not at home; she has gone to the hospital to find what is being done to Yefim. Somewhere there is a baby crying, and Varka hears someone singing with her own voice:

"Hush-a-bye, my baby wee, I will sing a song to thee."

Pelageya comes back; she crosses herself and whispers:

"They put him to rights in the night, but toward morning he gave up his soul to God. The Kingdom of Heaven be his and peace everlasting. . . .They say he was taken too late. . . .He ought to have gone sooner. . . ."

Varka goes out into the road and cries there, but all at once someone hits her on the back of her head so hard that her forehead knocks against a birch tree. She raises her eyes, and sees facing her, her master, the shoemaker.

"What are you about, you scabby slut?" he says. "The child is crying, and you are asleep!"

He gives her a sharp slap behind the ear, and she shakes her head, rocks the cradle, and murmurs her song. The green patch and the shadows from the trousers and the baby clothes move up and down, nod to her, and soon take possession of her brain again. Again she sees the highroad covered with liquid mud. The people with wallets on their backs and the shadows have lain down and are fast asleep. Looking at them, Varka has a passionate longing for sleep; she would lie down with enjoyment, but her mother Pelageya is walking beside her, hurrying her on. They are hastening together to the town to find situations.

"Give alms, for Christ's sake!" her mother begs of the people they meet. "Show us the Divine Mercy, kind-hearted gentlefolk!"

"Give the baby here!" a familiar voice answers. "Give the baby here!" the same voice repeats, this time harshly and angrily. "Are you asleep, you wretched girl?"

Varka jumps up, and looking round grasps what is the matter: there is no highroad, no Pelageya, no people meeting them, there is only her mistress, who has come to feed the baby, and is standing in the middle of the room. While the stout, broad-shouldered woman nurses the child and soothes it, Varka stands looking at her and waiting till she has done. And outside the windows the air is already turning blue, the shadows and the green patch on the ceiling are visibly growing pale, it will soon be morning.

"Take him," says her mistress, buttoning up her chemise over her bosom; "he is crying. He must be bewitched."

Varka takes the baby, puts him in the cradle, and begins rocking it again. The green patch and the shadows gradually disappear, and now there is nothing to force itself on her eyes and cloud her brain. But she is as sleepy as before, fearfully sleepy! Varka lays her head on the edge of the cradle, and rocks her whole body to overcome her sleepiness, but yet her eyes are glued together, and her head is heavy.

"Varka, heat the stove!" she hears the master's voice through the door.

So it is time to get up and set to work. Varka leaves the cradle, and runs to the shed for firewood. She is glad. When one moves and runs about, one is not so sleepy as when one is sitting down. She brings the wood, heats the stove, and feels that her wooden face is getting supple again, and that her thoughts are growing clearer.

"Varka, set the samovar!" shouts her mistress.

Varka splits a piece of wood, but has scarcely time to light the splinters and put them in the samovar, when she hears a fresh order:

"Varka, clean the master's galoshes!"

She sits down on the floor, cleans the galoshes, and thinks how nice it would be to put her head into a big deep galosh, and have a little nap in it. And all at once the galosh grows, swells, fills up the whole room. Varka drops the brush, but at once shakes her head, opens her eyes wide, and tries to look at things so that they may not grow big and move before her eyes.

"Varka, wash the steps outside; I am ashamed for the customers to see them!"

Varka washes the steps, sweeps and dusts the rooms, then heats another stove and runs to the shop. There is a great deal of work: she hasn't one minute free.

But nothing is so hard as standing in the same place at the kitchen table peeling potatoes. Her head droops over the table, the potatoes dance before her eyes, the knife tumbles out of her hand while her fat, angry mistress is moving about near her with her sleeves tucked up, talking so loud that it makes a ringing in Varka's ears. It is agonizing, too, to wait at dinner, to wash, to sew; there are minutes when she longs to flop on to the floor regardless of everything, and to sleep.

The day passes. Seeing the windows getting dark, Varka presses her temples that feel as though they were made of wood, and smiles, though she does not know why. The dusk of evening caresses her eyes that will hardly keep open, and promises her sound sleep soon. In the evening visitors come.

"Varka, set the samovar!" shouts her mistress.

The samovar is a little one, and before the visitors have drunk all the tea they want, she has to heat it five times. After tea Varka stands for a whole hour on the same spot, looking at the visitors, and waiting for orders.

"Varka, run and buy three bottles of beer!"

She starts off, and tries to run as quickly as she can, to drive away sleep.

"Varka, fetch some vodka! Varka, where's the corkscrew? Varka, clean a herring!"

But now, at last, the visitors have gone; the lights are put out, the master and mistress go to bed.

"Varka, rock the baby!" she hears the last order.

The cricket shurrs in the stove; the green patch on the ceiling and the shadows from the trousers and baby clothes force themselves on Varka's half-opened eyes again, wink at her and cloud her mind.

"Hush-a-bye, my baby wee," she murmurs, "and I will sing a song to thee."

And the baby screams, and is worn out with screaming. Again Varka sees the muddy highroad, the people with wallets, her mother Pelageya, her father Yefim. She understands everything, she recognizes everyone, but through her half sleep she cannot understand the force which binds her, hand and foot, weighs upon her, and prevents her from living. She looks round, searches for that force that she may escape from it, but she cannot find it. At last, tired to death, she does her very utmost, strains her eyes, looks up at the flickering green patch, and listening to the screaming, finds the foe who will not let her live.

That foe is the baby.

She laughs. It seems strange to her that she has failed to grasp such a simple thing before. The green patch, the shadows, and the cricket seem to laugh and wonder too.

The hallucination takes possession of Varka. She gets up from her stool, and with a broad smile on her face and wide unblinking eyes, she walks up and down the room. She feels pleased and tickled at the thought that she will be rid directly of the baby that binds her hand and foot. Kill the baby and then sleep, sleep, sleep. . . .

Laughing and winking and shaking her finger at the green patch, Varka steals up to the cradle and bends over the baby. When she has strangled him, she quickly lies down on the floor, laughs with delight that she can sleep, and in a minute is sleeping as sound as the dead.

W.C. Morrow (1853–1923)

Born the son of a Baptist minister in Selma, Alabama, William Chambers Morrow II grew up to be a tall, handsome man with an impressive presence. He attended the University of Alabama and Howard College, temporarily withdrawing in 1876 to help support his family during his father's illness. Morrow managed family hotels in Mobile, Alabama, and Meridan, Mississippi, then finished his degree after his father's death in 1879.

He traveled West to San Francisco, settled in Oakland, and began writing. E.H. Clough, a newsman he met, introduced Morrow to the local publishers. Late in 1979 Morrow's first story, "Punishing a 'Shocker'," appeared in *Argonaut*.

His gruesome, but ingenious, stories quickly gained acclaim. Gertrude Atherton said he was "A dramatic and interesting storyteller,' with a clean, forcible style." Even the influential Ambrose Bierce praised—and may have been influenced by—Morrow's tales.

Later, Morrow produced works as varied as *Bohemian Paris of Today* (1900), *Lentala of the South-Seas* (1908), and *The Logic of Punctuation for All Who Have to Do With Written English* (1926). But his fame still rests on his early horror stories, some of which were collected in *The Ape, The Idiot,* and *Other People* (1897). Others, still uncollected, were "The Bloodhounds" and "A Night in New Orleans."

Our selection for this volume is Morrow's most famous horror story, "His Unconquerable Enemy." It describes a feud to the death between a Rajah and a slave who is a quandruamputee.

HIS UNCONQUERABLE ENEMY

I *was summoned from Calcutta to the heart of India to perform a* difficult surgical operation on one of the women of a great rajah's household. I found the rajah a man of a noble character, but possessed, as I afterward discovered, of a sense of cruelty purely Oriental and in contrast to the indolence of his disposition. He was so grateful for the success that attended my mission that he urged me to remain a guest at the palace as long as it might please me to stay, and I thankfully accepted the invitation.

One of the male servants attracted my notice for his marvelous capacity of malice. His name was Neranya, and I am certain that there must have been a large proportion of Malay blood in his veins, for, unlike the Indians (from whom he differed also in complexion), he was extremely alert, active, nervous, and sensitive. A redeeming circumstance was his love for his master. Once his violent temper led him to the commission of an atrocious crime—the fatal stabbing of a dwarf. In punishment for this the rajah ordered that Neranya's right arm (the offending one) be severed from his body. The sentence was executed in a bungling fashion by a stupid fellow armed with an axe, and I, being a surgeon, was compelled, in order to save Neranya's life, to perform an amputation of the stump, leaving not a vestige of the limb remaining.

After this he developed an augmented fiendishness. His love for the rajah was changed to hate, and in his mad anger he flung discretion to the winds. Driven once to frenzy by the rajah's scornful treatment, he sprang upon the rajah with a knife, but, fortunately, was seized and disarmed. To his unspeakable dismay the rajah sentenced him for this offense to suffer amputation of the remaining arm. It was done as in the former instance. This had the effect of putting a temporary curb on Neranya's spirit, or, rather, of changing the outward manifestations of his diabolism. Being armless, he was at first largely at the mercy of those who ministered to his needs—a duty which I undertook to see was properly discharged, for I felt an interest in this strangely distorted nature. His sense of helplessness, combined with a damnable scheme for revenge which he had secretly formed, caused Neranya to change his fierce, impetuous, and unruly conduct into a smooth, quiet, insinuating bearing, which he carried so artfully as to deceive those with whom he was brought in contact, including the rajah himself.

Neranya, being exceedingly quick, intelligent, and dexterous, and having an unconquerable will, turned his attention to the cultivating of an enlarged usefulness of his legs, feet, and toes, with so excellent effect that in time he was able to perform wonderful feats with those members. Thus his capability, especially for destructive mischief, was considerably restored.

One morning the rajah's only son, a young man of an uncommonly amiable and noble disposition, was found dead in bed. His murder was a most atrocious one, his body being mutilated in a shocking manner, but in my eyes the most significant of all the mutilations was the entire removal and disappearance of the young prince's arms.

The death of the young man nearly brought the rajah to the grave. It was not, therefore, until I had nursed him back to health that I began a systematic inquiry into the murder. I said nothing of my own discoveries and conclusions until after the rajah and his officers had failed and my work had been done; then I submitted to him a written report, making a close analysis of all the circumstances, and closing by charging the crime to Neranya. The rajah, convinced by my proof and argument, at once ordered Neranya to be put to death, this to be accomplished slowly and with frightful tortures. The sentence was so cruel and revolting that it filled me with horror, and I implored that the wretch be shot. Finally, through a sense of gratitude to me, the rajah relaxed. When Neranya was charged with the crime he denied it, of course, but, seeing that the rajah was convinced, he threw aside all restraint, and, dancing, laughing, and shrieking in the most horrible manner, confessed his guilt, gloated over it, and reviled the rajah to his teeth—this, knowing that some fearful death awaited him.

The rajah decided upon the details of the matter that night, and in the morning he informed me of his decision. It was that Neranya's life should be spared, but that both of his legs should be broken with hammers, and that then I should amputate the limbs at the trunk! Appended to this horrible sentence was a provision that the maimed wretch should be kept and tortured at regular intervals by such means as afterward might be devised.

Sickened to the heart by the awful duty set out for me, I nevertheless performed it with success, and I care to say nothing more about that part of the tragedy. Neranya escaped death very narrowly and was a long time in recovering his wonted vitality. During all these weeks the rajah neither saw him nor made inquiries concerning him, but when, as in duty bound, I made official report that the man had recovered his strength, the rajah's eyes brightened, and he emerged with deadly activity from the stupor into which he so long had been plunged.

The rajah's palace was a noble structure, but it is necessary here to describe only the grand hall. It was an immense chamber, with a floor of polished, inlaid stone and a lofty, arched ceiling. A soft light stole into it through stained glass set in the roof and in high windows on one side. In the middle of the room was a rich fountain, which threw up a tall, slender column of water, with smaller and shorter jets grouped around it. Across one end of the hall, halfway to the ceiling, was a balcony, which communicated with the upper story of a wing, and from which a flight of stone stairs descended to the floor of the hall. During the hot summers this room was delightfully cool; it was the rajah's favorite lounging place, and when the nights were hot he had his cot taken thither, and there he slept.

This hall was chosen for Neranya's permanent prison; here he was to stay so long as he might live, with never a glimpse of the shining world or the glorious heavens. To one of his nervous, discontented nature such confinement was worse than death. At the rajah's order there was constructed for him a small pen of open ironwork, circular, and about four feet in diameter, elevated on four slender iron posts, ten feet above the floor, and placed between the balcony and the fountain. Such was Neranya's prison. The pen was about four feet in depth, and the pen top was left open for the convenience of the servants whose duty it should be to care for him. These precautions for his safe confinement were taken at my suggestion, for, although the man was now deprived of all four of his limbs, I still feared that he might develop some extraordinary, unheard-

of power for mischief. It was provided that the attendants should reach
his cage by means of a movable ladder.

All these arrangements having been made, and Neranya hoisted
into his cage, the rajah emerged upon the balcony to see him for the first
time since the last amputation. Neranya had been lying panting and
helpless on the floor of his cage, but when his quick ear caught the sound
of the rajah's footfall he squirmed about until he had brought the back of
his head against the railing elevating his eyes above his chest, and
enabling him to peer through the openwork of the cage. Thus the two
deadly enemies faced each other. The rajah's stern face paled at sight of
the hideous, shapeless thing which met his gaze; but he soon recovered,
and the old hard, cruel, sinister look returned. Neranya's black hair and
beard had grown long, and they added to the natural ferocity of his
aspect. His eyes blazed upon the rajah with a terrible light, his lips
parted, and he gasped for breath; his face was ashen with rage and
despair, and his thin, distended nostrils quivered.

The rajah folded his arms and gazed down from the balcony upon
the frightful wreck that he had made. Oh, the dreadful pathos of that
picture; the inhumanity of it; the deep and dismal tragedy of it! Who
might look into the wild, despairing heart of the prisoner and see and
understand the frightful turmoil there; the surging, choking passion;
unbridled but impotent ferocity; frantic thirst for a vengeance that should
be deeper than hell! Neranya gazed, his shapeless body heaving, his eyes
aflame; and then, in a strong, clear voice, which rang throughout the
great hall, with rapid speech he hurled at the rajah the most insulting
defiance, the most awful curses. He cursed the womb that had conceived
him, the food that should nourish him, the wealth that had brought him
power; cursed him in the name of Buddha and all the wise men; cursed by
the sun, the moon and the stars; by the continents, mountains, oceans,
and rivers; by all things living; cursed his head, his heart, his entrails;
cursed in a whirlwind of unmentionable words; heaped unimaginable
insults and contumely upon him; called him a knave, a beast, a fool, a
liar, an infamous and unspeakable coward.

The rajah heard it all calmly, without the movement of a muscle,
without the slightest change of countenance; and when the poor wretch
had exhausted his strength and fallen helpless and silent to the floor, the
rajah, with a grim, cold smile, turned and strode away.

The days passed. The rajah, not deterred by Neranya's curses often heaped upon him, spent even more time than formerly in the great hall, and slept there oftener at night; and finally Nernaya wearied of cursing and defying him, and fell into a sullen silence. The man was a study for me, and I observed every change in his fleeting moods. Generally his condition was that of miserable despair, which he attempted bravely to conceal. Even the boon of suicide had been denied him, for when he would wriggle into an erect position the rail of his pen was a foot above his head, so that he could not clamber over and break his skull on the stone floor beneath; and when he had tried to starve himself the attendants forced food down his throat; so that he abandoned such attempts. At times his eyes would blaze and his breath would come in gasps, for imaginary vengeance was working within him; but steadily he became quieter and more tractable, and was pleasant and responsive when I would converse with him. Whatever might have been the tortures which the rajah had decided on, none as yet had been ordered; and although Neranya knew that they were in contemplation, he never referred to them or complained of his lot.

The awful climax of this situation was reached one night, and even after this lapse of years I cannot approach its description without a shudder.

It was a hot night, and the rajah had gone to sleep in the great hall, lying on a high cot placed on the main floor just underneath the edge of the balcony. I had been unable to sleep in my own apartment, and so I had stolen into the great hall through the heavily curtained entrance at the end farthest from the balcony. As I entered I heard a peculiar, soft sound above the patter of the fountain. Neranya's cage was partly concealed from my view by the spraying water, but I suspected that the unusual sound came from him. Stealing a little to one side, and crouching against the dark hangings of the wall, I could see him in the faint light which dimly illuminated the hall, and then I discovered that my surmise was correct—Neranya was quietly at work. Curious to learn more, and knowing that only mischief could have been inspiring him, I sank into a thick robe on the floor and watched him.

To my great astonishment Neranya was tearing off with his teeth the bag which served as his outer garment. He did it cautiously, casting sharp glances frequently at the rajah, who, sleeping soundly on his cot below, breathed heavily. After starting a strip with his teeth, Neranya, by the same means, would attach it to the railing of his cage and then wriggle away, much after the manner of a caterpillar's crawling, and this would cause the strip to be torn out the full length of his garment. He repeated this operation with incredible patience and skill until his entire garment had been torn into strips. Two or three of these he tied end to end with his teeth, lips, and tongue, tightening the knots by placing one end of the strip under his body and drawing the other taut with his teeth. In this way he made a line several feet long, one end of which he made fast to the rail with his mouth. It then began to dawn upon me that he was going to make an insane attempt—impossible of achievement without hands, feet, arms, or legs—to escape from his cage! For what purpose? The rajah was asleep in the hall—ah! I caught my breath. Oh, the desperate, insane thirst for revenge which could have unhinged so clear and firm a mind! Even though he should accomplish the impossible feat of climbing over the railing of his cage that he might fall to the floor below (for how could he slide down the rope?), he would be in all probability killed or stunned; and even if he should escape these dangers, it would be impossible for him to clamber upon the cot without rousing the rajah, and impossible even though the rajah were dead! Amazed at the man's daring, and convinced that his sufferings and brooding had destroyed his reason, nevertheless I watched him with breathless interest.

With other strips tied together he made a short swing across one side of his cage. He caught the long line in his teeth at a point not far from the rail; then, wriggling with great effort to an upright position, his back braced against the rail, he put his chin over the swing and worked toward one end. He tightened the grasp of his chin on the swing, and with tremendous exertion, working the lower end of his spine against the railing, he began gradually to ascent the side of his cage. The labor was so great that he was compelled to pause at intevals, and his breathing was hard and painful; and even while thus resting he was in a position of terrible strain, and his pushing against the swing caused it to press hard against his windpipe and nearly strangle him.

After amazing effort he had elevated the lower end of his body until it protruded above the railing, the top of which was now across the lower end of his abdomen. Gradually he worked his body over, going backward, until there was sufficient excess of weight on the outer side of the rail; and then, with a quick lurch, he raised his head and shoulders and swung into a horizontal position on top of the rail. Of course, he would have fallen to the floor below had it not been for the line which he held in his teeth. With so great nicety had he estimated the distance between his mouth and the point where the rope was fastened to the rail, that the line tightened and checked him just as he reached the horizontal position on the rail. If one had told me beforehand that such a feat as I had just seen this man accomplish was possible, I should have thought him a fool.

Neranya was now balanced on his stomach across the top of the rail, and he eased his position by bending his spine and hanging down on either side as much as possible. Having rested thus for some minutes, he began cautiously to slide off backward, slowly paying out the line through his teeth, finding almost a fatal difficulty in passing the knots. Now, it is quite possible that the line would have escaped altogether from his teeth laterally when he would slightly relax his hold to let it slip, had it not been for a very ingenious plan to which he had resorted. This consisted in his having made a turn of the line around his neck before he attacked the wing, thus securing a threefold control of the line—one by his teeth, another by friction against his neck, and a third by his ability to compress it between his cheek and shoulder. It was quite evident now that the minutest details of a most elaborate plan had been carefully worked out by him before beginning the task, and that possibly weeks of difficult theoretical study had been consumed in the mental preparation. As I observed him I was reminded of certain hitherto unaccountable things which he had been doing for some weeks past—going through certain hitherto inexplicable motions, undoubtedly for the purpose of training his muscles for the immeasurably arduous labor which he was now performing.

A stupendous and seemingly impossible part of his task had been accomplished. Could he reach the floor in safety? Gradually he worked himself backward over the rail, in imminent danger of falling; but his nerve never wavered, and I could see a wonderful light in his eyes. With something of a lurch, his body fell against the outer side of the railing, to which he was hanging by his chin, the line still held firmly in his teeth. Slowly he slipped his chin from the rail, and then hung suspended by the line in his teeth. By almost imperceptible degrees, with infinite caution, he descended the line, and, finally, his unwieldy body rolled upon the floor, safe and unhurt!

What miracle would this superhuman monster next accomplish? I was quick and strong, and was ready and able to intercept any dangerous act; but not until danger appeared would I interfere with this extraordinary scene.

I must confess to astonishment upon having observed that Neranya, instead of proceeding directly toward the sleeping rajah, took quite another direction. Then it was only escape, after all, that the wretch contemplated, and not the murder of the rajah. But how could he escape? The only possible way to reach the outer air without great risk was by ascending the stairs to the balcony and leaving by the corridor which opened upon it, and thus fall into the hands of some British soldiers, quartered thereabout, who might conceive the idea of hiding him; but surely it was impossible for Neranya to ascend that long flight of stairs! Nevertheless, he made directly for them, his method of progression this: He lay upon his back, with the lower end of his body toward the stairs; then bowed his spine upward, thus drawing his head and shoulders a little forward; straightened, and then pushed the lower end of his body forward a space equal to that through which he had drawn his head; repeating this again and again, each time, while bending his spine, preventing his head from slipping by pressing it against the floor. His progress was laborious and slow, but sensible; and, finally, he arrived at the foot of the stairs.

It was manifest that his insane purpose was to ascend them. The desire for freedom must have been strong within him! Wriggling to an upright position against the newel-post, he looked up at the great height which he had to climb, and sighed; but there was no dimming of the light in his eyes. How could he accomplish the impossible task?

His solution of the problem was very simple, though daring and perilous as all the rest. While leaning against the newel-post he let himself fall diagonally upon the bottom step, where he lay partly hanging over, but safe, on his side. Turning upon his back, he wriggled forward along the step to the rail and raised himself to an upright position against it as he had against the newel-post, fell as before, and landed on the second step. In this manner, with inconceivable labor, he accomplished the ascent of the entire flight of stairs.

It being apparent to me that the rajah was not the object of Neranya's movements, the anxiety which I had felt on that account was now entirely dissipated. The things which already he had accomplished were entirely beyond the nimblest imagination. The sympathy which I had always felt for the wretched man was now greatly quickened; and as infinitesimally small as I knew his chances for escape to be, I nevertheless hoped that he would succeed. Any assistance from me, however, was out of the question; and it never should be known that I had witnessed the escape.

Neranya was now upon the balcony, and I could dimly see him wriggling along toward the door which led out upon the balcony. Finally, he stopped and wriggled to an upright position against the rail, which had wide openings between the balusters. His back was toward me, but he slowly turned and faced me and the hall. At that great distance I could not distinguish his features, but the slowness with which he had worked, even before he had fully accomplished the ascent of the stairs, was evidence all too eloquent of his extreme exhaustion. Nothing but a most desperate resolution could have sustained him thus far, but he had drawn upon the last remnant of his strength. He looked around the hall with a sweeping glance, and then down upon the rajah, who was sleeping immediately beneath him, over twenty feet below. He looked long and earnestly, sinking lower, and lower, and lower upon the rail. Suddenly, to my inconceivable astonishment and dismay, he toppled through and shot downward from his lofty height! I held my breath, expecting to see him crushed upon the stone floor beneath; but instead of that he fell upon the rajah's breast, driving him through the cot to the floor. I sprang forward with a loud cry for help, and was instantly at the scene of the catastrophe. With indescribable horror I saw that Neranya's teeth were buried in the rajah's throat! I tore the wretch away, but the blood was pouring from the rajah's arteries, his chest was crushed in, and he was gasping in the agony of death. People came running in, terrified. I turned to Neranya. He lay upon his back, his face hideously smeared with blood. Murder, and not escape, had been his intention from the beginning; and he had employed the only method by which there was ever a possibility of accomplishing it. I knelt beside him, and saw that he, too, was dying; his back had been broken by the fall. He smiled sweetly into my face, and a triumphant look of accomplished revenge sat upon his face even in death.

Léopold von Sacher-Masoch (1836–1895)

Count Léopold von Sacher-Masoch was born at Lemberg in Galicia. Coming from a multinational background (his ancestors were Slavs, Spaniards and Bohemians; his grandparents were functionaries of the Austro-Hungarian Empire), his work was influenced by the problems of minorities, nationalities, and revolutionary movements in the Empire. The son of the chief of police at Lemberg, he witnessed in childhood scenes of prison and riot which affected him profoundly.

While a history professor at Gräz, he began his literary career by writing historical novels and achieved a rapid success. Influenced by Panslavism, he was called "the Turgenev of Little Russia," and wrote Galician, Jewish, Hungarian, and Prussian stories.

The Divorced Woman (1870), one of his first genre novels, received wide distribution, even to America. His folk and historic novels fared well. He was a celebrated and honored author.

Eventually, nineteenth century censure worked against him. Oblique and diffuse sexual references were tolerated, but Sacher-Masoch combined folklore, history, politics, eroticism, the rational, and the perverse, mixing them sharply. Predilections for whips and corpulent women in furs helped to make his name synonymous with sexual perversion.

Although he was decorated in 1886, celebrated by *Le Figaro* and *La Revue des Deux Mondes*, his literary oeuvre is now almost unknown. He died in 1895, suffering from the oblivion into which his work had fallen.

For this volume we have chosen his story "The Gravedigger's Daughter," a grim tale of orders and love.[1]

---

[1] Information on Sacher-Masoch is hard to come by. So far we have traced an English translation of this story back to 1891, but the original version probably appeared earlier.

THE GRAVEDIGGER'S DAUGHTER

There was shooting in the village. The old gravedigger awoke and lay listening. Yes, surely mustketry, some heavier fire. He called his daughter.

"Milena," he said, "there seems to be a battle in our village."

"I'll see," said Milena.

She went out almost as she was when she got up from her straw pallet. Tall, powerful, only half-clad in her shift, she merely wrapped a short sheepskin coat about her, in nowise concealing her amazonian hips and magnificent shoulders.

The gravedigger's hut was at the gate of the graveyard, on a hill which gave a view of the village. The snow was deep, the cold bitter. Milena rubbed her face and hands and knees with the snow and huddled into the coat. It was curiously profoundly peaceful here in the graveyard while the battle raged below. But as the firing ceased a wolf came right up to her and looked at her with glowing eyes. She seized a spade which was leaning against the house wall, and darted at the beast so energetically that it leaped over the fence.

She went down the hill toward the village. At the first of the huts she met a peasant woman who was assisting a wounded man, her husband, as well as she could, with her shoulders; every staggering step leaving a pool of blood on the snow. Milena picked him up like a sack of grain and carried him into the hut. "What has happened?" she asked.

"The old feud," said the wounded man. "Our baron against Mikulov, with us folk doing the fighting. Your father will have much work."

"My father is ill," said Milena, "and unable to work at present."

225

She assisted the woman to bind up his wounds then went to assure her father that the skirmish was over.

A short time after her return there was a violent knocking at the gate of the graveyard. "Open up, old mole!" said an authoritative voice. "We bring you paying guests."

Milena opened the door of the hut and saw many horse-drawn sleds covered with motionless human forms. Gunbarrels and scythes gleamed in the moonlight.

"Father," she said, "they have brought here those killed in the battle."

She admitted the man who had spoken. "They must be buried at once," he said.

"I am ill," said the gravedigger. "They will have to wait."

"They cannot!" said the spokesman. "They will be eaten by wolves. Would you have that on your soul?"

"Bury them yourselves."

"We must get away, quickly."

"I will bury them," said Milena. The spokesman nodded. "That is what I expected." They counted the bodies and he gave her the customary amount per interment. He handed her a pint of brandy, promised that as soon as he could return he would bring her a new sheepskin coat. Then the bodies were deposited on the snow-covered mound and the squad moved on.

Milena took a good swig of the brandy. Her beautiful face showed not the slightest expression of compassion, but there was a strange eagerness in her beautiful eyes. She dug and drank, dug and drank. She smiled at the despairing cries of the cheated wolves and ravens in the not-far distance. When she had made a trench of adequate length and depth and professional symmetry, she looked critically at the corpses. "You," she addressed one of them, "must have been a leader. You shall be first."

She held him in her arms and gently, tenderly, laid him to rest. Then, indifferently, she put away strangers, acquaintances. One head, almost severed from the body, arrested her attention. "The Squire of Kamienecz! Skinflint, robber of widows and orphans, slave-driver of peasants!" she gave the head a mighty swipe with the shovel. The head rolled into the trench and she flung the body after it.

Now the moon had come out in full brilliance. Suddenly even

stouthearted Milena was startled. She heard a groan. Then she saw that one of the prostrate figures was attempting to rise. She went to him. "Valerian!"

"Yes," he said feebly. "Save me, Milena; I implore you by the wounds of the Savior."

She shook her head. "God has given you into my hands," she said with a tranquility that was more terrible than wrath or the triumph of repressed vengeance. "You betrayed me, but now you belong to me. Pray to God; maybe He will be merciful. From me you can expect no forgiveness."

"Milena! Have you forgotten how I loved you?"

"No, but *you* forgot. In spite of your vows to me you left me for another. I cannot spare you."

"Will you kill me?"

"Ah no. You have already been killed."

"What in the name of God are you going to do?"

"The task I have undertaken: to bury those killed in this battle."

"Bury me alive?" he shrieked.

"Why not?" she said, with a brutal laugh. "I have been paid in advance, but I have still to earn a sheepskin coat which has been promised me on completion of the task."

"Have mercy, Milena!"

"Have you had mercy on me?"

She seized him by the shoulders. He attempted to struggle, but he was so faint from loss of blood that she had no difficulty dragging him into his grave. There for a moment, her right hand in the grip of the shovel handle, her left hand on her hip, she contemplated him, listened avidly to his groans, with an expression of voluptuous cruelty.

"Now you belong to me!" she said.

She spat on her hands and began to fill the grave. For a time, as she was packing down the earth she heard his death rattle. A last pat with the shovel and the night's work was ended. She took a long drink of the brandy.

In the east appeared the first streaks of morning gray, cold and pale as Milena's face.

Ambrose Bierce (1842–1914)

Satirist, editor, story writer, and poet, Ambrose Bierce was born in Ohio. He was the youngest child of a poverty-stricken, pious, eccentric farmer, whom he hated. At the age of 17, he received his only year of formal schooling at the Kentucky Military Institute.

In 1861 he volunteered for the Union Army, was wounded twice, and rose from drummer boy to lieutenant with brevet title of major.

After the war Bierce traveled West to San Francisco. There his satirical cartoons led to newspaper work; biting political pieces became his forte. He was appointed editor of the San Francisco *News Letter* in 1868 and published his first short story three years later.

During the next twenty years he was the literary lion of the West Coast: encouraging young authors such as Emma Dawson and Robert Duncan Milne, writing powerful stories, and promoting old San Francisco's science fiction and fantasy movement.[1]

Ironically, the collection *Tales of Soldiers and Civilians* (1891), which helped launch his national reputation, was published as his personal decline began. In 1889, one son was killed in a senseless duel. His wife left him in 1891, divorcing him in 1904. In 1901, his other son, Leigh, died of alcoholism. He disappeared in Mexico in 1914, never to be heard from again.

Many of his sixty-eight short stories are horrific; all but two deal with death. For this volume we have chosen the famous *tour de force*, "An Occurrence at Owl Creek Bridge."

[1]See Sam Moskowitz, *Science Fiction in Old San Francisco Volume I: History of the Movement, From 1854 to 1890* (Rhode Island: Donald M. Grant, Publisher, 1980).

AN OCCURRENCE AT
OWL CREEK BRIDGE

A man stood upon a railroad bridge in northern Alabama, looking down into the swift water twenty feet below. The man's hands were behind his back, the wrists bound with a cord. A rope closely encircled his neck. It was attached to a stout cross-timber above his head and the slack fell to the level of his knees. Some loose boards laid upon the sleepers supporting the metals of the railway supplied a footing for him and his executioners—two private soldiers of the Federal army, directed by a sergeant who in civil life may have been a deputy sheriff. At a short remove upon the same temporary platform was an officer in the uniform of his rank, armed. He was a captain. A sentinel at each end of the bridge stood with his rifle in the position known as "support," that is to say, vertical in front of the left shoulder, the hammer resting on the forearm thrown straight across the chest—a formal and unnatural position, enforcing an erect carriage of the body. It did not appear to be the duty of these two men to know what was occurring at the center of the bridge; they merely blockaded the two ends of the foot planking that traversed it.

Beyond one of the sentinels nobody was in sight; the railroad ran straight away into a forest for a hundred yards, then curving, was lost to view. Doubtless there was an outpost farther along. The other bank of the stream was open ground—a gentle acclivity topped with a stockade of vertical tree trunks, loopholed for rifles, with a single embrasure through which protruded the muzzle of a brass cannon commanding the bridge. Midway on the slope between bridge and fort were the spectators—a single company of infantry in line, at "parade rest," the butts of the rifles on the ground, the barrels inclining slightly backward against the right shoulder, the hands crossed upon the stock. A lieutenant stood at the right of the line, the point of his sword upon the ground, his left hand resting upon his right. Excepting the group of four at the center of the bridge, not a man moved. The company faced the bridge, staring stonily, motionless. The sentinels, facing the banks of the stream, might have been statues to adorn the bridge. The captain stood with folded arms, silent, observing the work of his subordinates, but making no sign. Death is a dignitary who when he comes announced is to be received with formal manifestations of respect, even by those most familiar with him. In the code of military etiquette silence and fixity are forms of deference.

The man who was engaged in being hanged was apparently about thirty-five years of age. He was a civilian, if one might judge from his habit, which was that of a planter. His features were good—a straight nose, firm mouth, broad forehead, from which his long, dark hair was combed straight back, falling behind his ears to the collar of his well-fitting frock coat. He wore a mustache and pointed beard, but no whiskers; his eyes were large and dark gray, and had a kindly expression which one would hardly have expected in one whose neck was in the hemp. Evidently this was no vulgar assassin. The liberal military code makes provision for hanging many kinds of persons, and gentlemen are not excluded.

The preparations being complete, the two private soldiers stepped aside and each drew away the plank upon which he had been standing. The sergeant turned to the captain, saluted and placed himself immediately behind that officer, who in turn moved apart one pace. These movements left the condemned man and the sergeant standing on the two ends of the same plank, which spanned three of the crossties of the bridge. The end upon which the civilian stood almost, but not quite, reached a fourth. This plank had been held in place by the weight of the captain; it was now held by that of the sergeant. At a signal from the former the latter would step aside, the plank would tilt and the condemned man go down between two ties. The arrangement commended itself to his judgment as simple and effective. His face had not been covered nor his eyes bandaged. He looked a moment at his "unsteadfast footing," then let his gaze wander to the swirling water of the stream racing madly beneath his feet. A piece of dancing driftwood caught his attention and his eyes followed it down the current. How slowly it appeared to move! What a sluggish stream!

He closed his eyes in order to fix his last thoughts upon his wife and children. The water, touched to gold by the early sun, the brooding mists under the banks at some distance down the stream, the fort, the soldiers, the piece of drift—all had distracted him. And now he became conscious of a new disturbance. Striking through the thought of his dear ones was a sound which he could neither ignore nor understand, a sharp, distinct, metallic percussion like the stroke of a blacksmith's hammer upon the anvil; it had the same ringing quality. He wondered what it was, and whether immeasurably distant or nearby—it seemed both. Its recurrence was regular, but as slow as the tolling of a death knell. He awaited each stroke with impatience and—he knew not why—apprehension. The intervals of silence grew progressively longer; the delays became maddening. With their great infrequency the sounds increased in strength and sharpness. They hurt his ear like the thrust of a knife; he feared he would shriek. What he heard was the ticking of his watch.

He unclosed his eyes and saw again the water below him. "If I could free my hands," he thought, "I might throw off the noose and spring into the stream. By diving I could evade the bullets and, swimming vigorously, reach the bank, take to the woods and get away home. My home, thank God, is as yet outside their lines; my wife and little ones are still beyond the invader's farthest advance."

As these thoughts, which have here to be set down in words, were flashed into the doomed man's brain rather than evolved from it, the captain nodded to the sergeant. The sergeant stepped aside.

II

Peyton Farquhar was a well-to-do planter, of an old and highly respected Alabama family. Being a slave owner and like other slave owners a politician he was naturally an original secessionist and ardently devoted to the Southern cause. Circumstances of an imperious nature, which it is unnecessary to relate here, had prevented him from taking service with the gallant army that had fought the disastrous campaigns ending with the fall of Corinth, and he chafed under the inglorious restraint, longing for the release of his energies, the larger life of the soldier, the opportunity for distinction. That opportunity, he felt, would come, as it comes to all in war time. Meanwhile he did what he could. No service was too humble for him to perform in aid of the South, no adventure too perilous for him to undertake if consistent with the charac-

ter of a civilian who was at heart a soldier, and who in good faith and
without too much qualification assented to at least a part of the frankly
villainous dictum that all is fair in love and war.

One evening while Farquhar and his wife were sitting on a rustic
bench near the entrance to his grounds, a gray-clad soldier rode up to the
gate and asked for a drink of water. Mrs. Farquhar was only too happy to
serve him with her own white hands. While she was fetching the water
her husband approached the dusty horseman and inquired eagerly for
news from the front.

"The Yanks are repairing the railroads," said the man, "and are
getting ready for another advance. They have reached the Owl Creek
bridge, put it in order and built a stockade on the north bank. The
commandant has issued an order, which is posted everywhere, declaring
that any civilian caught interfering with the railroad, its bridges, tunnels
or trains will be summarily hanged. I saw the order."

"How far is it to the Owl Creek bridge?" Farquhar asked.

"About thirty miles."

"Is there no force on this side the creek?"

"Only a picket post half a mile out, on the railroad, and a single
sentinel at this end of the bridge."

"Suppose a man—a civilian and student of hanging—should elude
the picket post and perhaps get the better of the sentinel," said Farquhar,
smiling, "what could he accomplish?"

The soldier reflected. "I was there a month ago," he replied. "I
observed that the flood of last winter had lodged a great quantity of
driftwood against the wooden pier at this end of the bridge. It is now dry
and would burn like tow."

The lady had now brought the water, which the soldier drank. He
thanked her ceremoniously, bowed to her husband and rode away. An
hour later, after nightfall, he repassed the plantation, going northward in
the direction from which he had come. He was a Federal scout.

III

As Peyton Farquhar fell straight downward through the bridge he
lost consciousness and was as one already dead. From this state he was
awakened—ages later, it seemed to him—by the pain of a sharp pressure upon his throat, followed by a sense of suffocation. Keen, poignant

agonies seemed to shoot from his neck downward through every fiber of his body and limbs. These pains appeared to flash along well-defined lines of ramification and to beat with an inconceivably rapid periodicity. They seemed like streams of pulsating fire heating him to an intolerable temperature. As to his head, he was conscious of nothing but a feeling of fulness—of congestion. These sensations were unaccompanied by thought. The intellectual part of his nature was already effaced; he had power only to feel, and feeling was torment. He was conscious of motion, encompassed in a luminous cloud, of which he was now merely the fiery heart, without material substance, he swung through unthinkable arcs of oscillation, like a vast pendulum. Then all at once, with terrible suddenness, the light about him shot upward with the noise of a loud splash; a frightful roaring was in his ears, and all was cold and dark. The power of thought was restored; he knew that the rope had broken and he had fallen into the stream. There was no additional strangulation; the noose about his neck was already suffocating him and kept the water from his lungs. To die of hanging at the bottom of a river!—the idea seemed to him ludicrous. He opened his eyes in the darkness and saw about him a gleam of light, but how distant, how inaccessible! He was still sinking, for the light became fainter and fainter until it was a mere glimmer. Then it began to grow and brighten, and he knew that he was rising toward the surface—knew it with reluctance, for he was now very comfortable. "To be hanged and drowned," he thought, "that is not so bad; but I do not wish to be shot. No; I will not be shot; that is not fair."

He was not conscious of an effort, but a sharp pain in his wrist apprised him that he was trying to free his hands. He gave the struggle his attention, as an idler might observe the feat of a juggler, without interest in the outcome. What splendid effort!—what magnificent, what superhuman strength! Ah, that was a fine endeavor! Bravo! The cord fell away; his arms parted and floated upward, the hands dimly seen on each side in the growing light. He watched them with a new interest as first one and then the other pounced upon the noose at his neck. They tore it away and thrust it fiercely aside, its undulations resembling those of a water-snake. "Put it back, put it back!" He thought he shouted these words to his hands, for the undoing of the noose had been succeeded by the direst pang that he had yet experienced. His neck ached horribly; his brain was on fire; his heart, which had been fluttering faintly, gave a great leap, trying to force itself out at his mouth. His whole body was racked and wrenched with an insupportable anguish! But his disobedient hands gave no heed to the command. They beat the water vigorously with quick, downward strokes, forcing him to the surface. He felt his head emerge; his eyes were blinded by the sunlight; his chest expanded convulsively, and with a supreme and crowning agony his lungs engulfed a great draught of air, which instantly he expelled in a shriek!

He was now in full possession of his physical senses. They were, indeed, preternaturally keen and alert. Something in the awful disturbance of his organic system had so exalted and refined them that they made record of things never before perceived. He felt the ripples upon his face and heard their separate sounds as they struck. He looked at the forest on the bank of the stream, saw the individual trees, the leaves and the veining of each leaf—saw the very insects upon them: the locusts, the brilliant-bodied flies, the gray spiders stretching their webs from twig to twig. He noted the prismatic colors in all the dewdrops upon a million blades of grass. The humming of the gnats that danced above the eddies of the stream, the beating of the dragonflies' wings, the strokes of the water spiders' legs, like oars which had lifted their boat—all these made audible music. A fish slid along beneath his eyes and he heard the rush of its body parting the water.

He had come to the surface facing down the stream; in a moment the visible world seemed to wheel slowly round, himself the pivotal point, and he saw the bridge, the fort, the soldiers upon the bridge, the captain, the sergeant, the two privates, his executioners. They were in sihouette against the blue sky. They shouted and gesticulated, pointing at him. The captain had drawn his pistol, but did not fire; the others were unarmed. Their movements were grotesque and horrible, their forms gigantic.

Suddenly he heard a sharp report and something struck the water smartly within a few inches of his head, spattering his face with spray. He heard a second report, and saw one of the sentinels with his rifle at his shoulder, a light cloud of blue smoke rising from the muzzle. The man in the water saw the eye of the man on the bridge gazing into his own through the sights of the rifle. He observed that it was a gray eye and remembered having read that gray eyes were keenest, and that all famous marksmen had them. Nevertheless, this one had missed.

A counterswirl had caught Farquhar and turned him half round; he was again looking into the forest on the bank opposite the fort. The sound of a clear, high voice in a monotonous singsong now rang out behind him and came across the water with a distinctness that pierced and subdued all other sounds, even the beating of the ripples in his ears. Although no soldier, he had frequented camps enough to know the dread significance of that deliberate, drawling, aspirated chant; the lieutenant on shore was taking a part in the morning's work. How coldly and pitilessly—with what an even, calm intonation, presaging, and enforcing tranquility in the men—with what accurately measured intervals fell those cruel words:

"Attention, company! . . . Shoulder arms! . . . Ready! . . . Aim! . . . Fire!"

Farquhar dived—dived as deeply as he could. The water roared in his ears like the voice of Niagara, yet he heard the dulled thunder of the volley and, rising again toward the surface, met shining bits of metal, singularly flattened, oscillating slowly downward. Some of them touched him on the face and hands, then fell away, continuing their descent. One lodged between his collar and neck; it was uncomfortably warm and he snatched it out.

As he rose to the surface, gasping for breath, he saw that he had been a long time under water; he was perceptibly farther down stream— nearer to safety. The soldiers had almost finished reloading; the metal ramrods flashed all at once in the sunshine as they were drawn from the barrels, turned in the air, and thrust into their sockets. The two sentinels fired again, independently and ineffectually.

The hunted man saw all this over his shoulder; he was now swimming vigorously with the current. His brain was as energetic as his arms and legs; he thought with the rapidity of lightning.

"The officer," he reasoned, "will not make that martinet's error a second time. It is as easy to dodge a volley as a single shot. He has probably already given the command to fire at will. God help me, I cannot dodge them all!"

An appalling plash within two yards of him was followed by a loud, rushing sound, *diminuendo,* which seemed to travel back through the air to the fort and died in an explosion which stirred the very river to its deeps! A rising sheet of water curved over him, fell down upon him, blinded him, strangled him! The cannon had taken a hand in the game. As he shook his head free from the commotion of the smitten water he heard the deflected shot humming through the air ahead, and in an instant it was cracking and smashing the branches in the forest beyond.

''They will not do that again,'' he thought; ''the next time they will use a charge of grape. I must keep my eye upon the gun; the smoke will apprise me—the report arrives too late; it lags behind the missile. That is a good gun.''

Suddenly, he felt himself whirled round and round—spinning like a top. The water, the banks, the forests, the now distant bridge, fort and men—all were commingled and blurred. Objects were represented by their colors only; circular horizontal streaks of color—that was all he saw. He had been caught in a vortex and was being whirled on with a velocity of advance and gyration that made him giddy and sick. In a few moments he was flung upon the gravel at the foot of the left bank of the stream—the southern bank—and behind a projecting point which concealed him from his enemies. The sudden arrest of his motion, the abrasion of one of his hands on the gravel, restored him, and he wept with delight. He dug his fingers into the sand, threw it over himself in handfuls and audibly blessed it. It looked like diamonds, rubies, emeralds; he could think of nothing beautiful which it did not resemble. The trees upon the bank were giant garden plants; he noted a definite order in their arrangement, inhaled the fragrance of their blooms. A strange, roseate light shone through the spaces among their trunks and the wind made in their branches the music of aeolian harps. He had no wish to perfect his escape—was content to remain in that enchanting spot until retaken.

A whiz and rattle of grapeshot among the branches high above his head roused him from his dream. The baffled cannoneer had fired him a random farewell. He sprang to his feet, rushed up the sloping bank, and plunged into the forest.

All that day he traveled, laying his course by the rounding sun. The forest seemed interminable; nowhere did he discover a break in it, not even a woodman's road. He had not known that he lived in so wild a region. There was something uncanny in the revelation.

By nightfall he was fatigued, footsore, famishing. The thought of his wife and children urged him on. At last he found a road which led him in what he knew to be the right direction. It was as wide and straight as a city street, yet it seemed untraveled. No fields bordered it, no dwelling anywhere. Not so much as the barking of a dog suggested human habitation. The black bodies of the trees formed a straight wall on both sides, terminating on the horizon in a point, like a diagram in a lesson in perspective. Overhead, as he looked up through this rift in the wood, shone great golden stars looking unfamiliar and grouped in strange constellations. He was sure they were arranged in some order which had a secret and malign significance. The wood on either side was full of singular noises, among which—once, twice, and again—he distinctly heard whispers in an unknown tongue.

His neck was in pain and lifting his hand to it he found it horribly swollen. He knew that it had a circle of black where the rope had bruised it. His eyes felt congested; he could no longer close them. His tongue was swollen with thirst; he relieved its fever by thrusting it forward from between his teeth into the cold air. How softly the turf had carpeted the untraveled avenue—he could no longer feel the roadway beneath his feet!

Doubtless, despite his suffering, he had fallen asleep while walking for now he sees another scene—perhaps he has merely recovered from a delirium. He stands at the gate of his own home. All is as he left it, and all bright and beautiful in the morning sunshine. He must have traveled the entire night. As he pushes open the gate and passes up the wide white walk, he sees a flutter of female garments; his wife, looking fresh and cool and sweet, steps down from the veranda to meet him. At the bottom of the steps she stands waiting, with a smile of ineffable joy, an attitude of matchless grace and dignity. Ah, how beautiful she is! He springs forward with extended arms. As he is about to clasp her he feels a stunning blow upon the back of the neck; a blinding white light blazes all about him with a sound like the shock of a cannon—then all is darkness and silence!

Peyton Farquhar was dead; his body, with a broken neck, swung gently from side to side beneath the timbers of the Owl Creek bridge.

Lorimer Stoddard (1864–1901)

Born in New York City, Lorimer Stoddard was the only surviving son of famous parents. His father was Richard Henry Stoddard, a noted literary critic, poet, editor, and biographer. A friend of Nathaniel Hawthorne, Richard eventually became one of New York City's most influential critics, serving as reviewer for, and literary editor of, several New York newspapers and magazines.

Lorimer Stoddard's mother was Elizabeth Drew Stoddard, a talented poet and novelist who Amy Lowell once praised highly as "the best writer of blank verse in America."

For the last three decades of the nineteenth century, his parents' house "was a leading gathering place for writers and artists." Growing up in this environment, Lorimer received encouragement for his literary endeavors and established contacts that were to help him in his career.

As a playwright he achieved his greatest fame. Several promising one-act plays were followed by *The Emperor Napoleon*, a flop. But his work had impressed actress Minnie Maddern Fiske, and she hired him to adapt Thomas Hardy's *Tess of the D'Urbervilles*. Stoddard wrote the play in five days. Produced in 1897, critics judged it the year's best drama. He went on to dramatize works by William Makepeace Thackeray, Alphonse Daudet, and F. Marion Crawford.

His only published story appears to be "Vengeance," a dramatic study of a woman's anguish.[1]

---

[1]The original title of the story was "The Indian's Hand." It was changed so that the content of the story would not be revealed.

241

VENGEANCE

*T*he men had driven away. Their carts and horses disappeared behind the roll of the low hills. They appeared now and then, like boats on the crest of a wave, further each time. And their laughter and singing and shouts grew fainter as the bushes hid them from sight.

The women and children remained, with two old men to protect them. They might have gone too, the hunters said. "What harm could come in the broad daylight?—the bears and panthers were far away. They'd be back by night, with only two carts to fill."

Then Jim, the crack shot of the settlement, said, "We'll drive home the bears in the carts."

The children shouted and danced as they thought of the sport to come, of the hunters' return with their game, of the bonfires they always built.

One pale woman clung to her husband's arm. "But the Indians!" she said.

That made the men all laugh. "Indians!" they cried; "why there've been none here for twenty years! We drove them away, down there"—pointing across the plain—"to a hotter place than this, where the sand burns their feet and they ride for days for water."

The pale woman murmured, "Ah, but they returned."

"Yes," cried her big husband, whose brown beard covered his chest, "and burned two cabins. Small harm they did, the curs!"

"Hush," said the pale woman, pressing her husband's arm; and the men around were quiet, pretending to fix their saddles, as they glanced at another woman, dressed in black, who turned and went into her house.

"I forgot her boy," said the bearded man, as he gravely picked up his gun.

They started off in the morning cool, toward the mountains where the trees grew. And the long shadows lessened as the sun crept up the sky.

The woman in black stood silent by her door. No one bade her good-by. The other women went back to their houses to work. The children played in the dust; clouds rose as they shouted and ran. A day's freedom lay before them.

But the woman in black still stood by her door, like a spectre in the sunshine, her thin hands clasped together as she gazed away over the plain toward Mexico.

Her face was parched and drawn, as if the sun from the sand had burned into the bone. Her eyes alone seemed to live; they were hard and bright.

Her house was a little away from the rest, on the crest of a hill facing the desert plain.

She had heard the words of the bearded man: "Small harm the Indians did." Had he forgotten her boy? How could he forget, while she was there to remind them of the dead? Near her house was a small rock roughly marked. The rude letters "Will, gone, '69," she had cut on it with her own hands. It marked the last place where her boy had played. She remembered how she went away softly—so he should not cry to follow her—without a word, without a kiss.

Here her hands beat the side of the house.

"Oh, to have that kiss now and die!" But she had gone, unthinking, up the road where the pale woman lived, then a rosy-cheeked happy bride, not a widow like herself. They laughed and discussed the new-comers at the settlement. It was a holiday, for the men were away over the hills, cutting down trees to build their houses with.

As they talked there idly, they heard what they thought was the shrill bark of dogs running up the hill. Startled, they went to the window. Round the curve of the road came horses wildly galloping, and upon their backs. . . . Here the pale woman shrieked and fled. They were Indians, beating their horses with their bare legs, their black hair streaming in the wind.

Like a flash, she had bolted the door and barred the shutters as they galloped up. She turned then. Through the open back door she saw the women run screaming up the hill, their children in their arms.

Their children! Where was hers! She stopped as if turned to stone, then undid the door.

They dragged her out by the wrists, by the hair. She fought with them stronger than ten men. But there were twenty; she was alone. The little street was empty. They strangled her, bent down her face, dragged her upon a horse, and, with her crosswise on the saddle, galloped up and down, as they fired the cabins and the sheds. Her hands were shackled, and her eyes blind with blood, but she thought only of her child. "Where could he be?"

There were gunshots. Down the hills like mad came the white men for their wives and children.

Then the Indians turned back toward the plain. They rode past her house.

There, where she had left him, stood the child, dazed with surprise. She held out her arms tied together and called to him to come.

"Fool! fool!" Here the woman in black struck her temples with her hands. "Fool!" Why had she not galloped by and never noticed him?

But she begged, caught at the horse's head, struggled to get to him; and the Indian stopped for a moment in his flight and caught up the child and went on.

Then the thought came to her of the end of that ride—what was to come—after. And she tried to drop the boy, to let him slide gently to the ground; but the Indian held them fast.

Behind, nearer, came the following men, louder the guns. The horse she was on snorted, staggered under the weight of the three, and as they reached the plain the child was torn from her, she was pushed away. But she rose and staggered after them amid the blinding dust. They must take her too. Sobbing, she called to them as she stumbled on. Many times she fell. Then she could go no more.

That was all. Her story ended there, with the thundering of horses' hoofs and the taste of dust in her mouth. They found her there unconscious. Her friends tended her. When she came back to life she asked no questions but left her neighbor's house and came to her door, where she was standing now, and gazed away over the sand where *he* had gone, down toward Mexico.

The years went by, and she was still alone in the house where *two* should have been. And now far off she saw the dust blowing in a long, rolling, pinkish line. But the dust blew so often, and nothing came of it—not even the Indians.

The boy she knew was dead, but they—his murderers—remained, somewhere.

If she could have one now in her power!

The woman in black pondered, as she had so many times, how she should torture him. No pain could be too horrible. She looked at the fire in the stove, and piled on the logs—the logs that were brought with such trouble from the mountains where the trees grew. She could not make it hot enough. She dropped on her knees and watched the iron grow red. And the letters of the maker's name stamped on it grew distinct, and the word "Congress," half-defaced, and the figures "64." Ah, those letters! she could have kissed the spot, for her child had touched it. Charmed by the glow, when left alone, he laid his baby hand flat on it, and burned deep into the palm were those letters, "SS, 64."

She would know him among a million by that mark. But he was dead. The Indians remained.

The woman in black stood up. Why should she not go to them? There were pools in the plain where she could drink. That would be enough.

The men were away; the women were at work. Who could stop her?

She put on her bonnet and started off down the hill through the green bushes. The air was still crisp, though the sun was hot.

The desert must have an end. She would keep on to Mexico. She walked quickly, and her dress grew gray with dust, and the air scorching, as she reached the plain. But she kept on, and only looked back once at the house on the hill and at the window where the pale woman sat.

The dust choked her, and she stumbled, and the sole of one shoe came half off, and slapped, and banged, and delayed her as she walked. She tore it off and went on, but the sand cut and burned her so that she sat down and wept, and wanted to go back for her other pair, the ones she wore on Sundays. The hill, though, looked so distant that she wearily got up and went on, on, till she could go no more, and crept under the shadow of a rock. There was no water near. Her throat was parched, and her temples beat wildly. She must go back and start again, strengthened, fortified. She would start tomorrow, or at night, when the cool would let her get too far to return.

By slow degrees she dragged herself up the hill. The pale woman came out of her house, and nodded, but the woman in black did not smile in return. She closed her door, and went up to her bed, and fell on it, and slept, amid the buzzing of the flies and the fitful flapping of the window shade in the breeze.

The pale woman sighed and glanced across the plain. The roll of blowing dust was larger, and more regular, and nearer. The woman shuddered as she watched it creep slowly along behind the sand mounds. "It always blows," she said to herself, "but not like that, so steadily, so even." She strained her eyes, but there was only dust to be seen. Then she thought of a telescope that belonged to the minister's wife, who came from a seaport town, and ran to fetch it. The two women came out with it together, the minister's wife laughing at her friend, she was such a timid thing!

But the pale woman was paler than ever, and trembled so she could not steady it. The laughing one looked through it, and laughed no more.

"I see a head over the mound there," she said.

The pale woman shrieked.

"They are miles away. We may have time."

"For what?"

"To get away."

"They may be friends—"

"They are Indians! White men would not live through that sand. We must go to the woods. Help me. Warn the women. Gather the children. Come."

She rushed into her house. The other still stood and looked.

The dust cloud was a little nearer. In a moment all was wild confusion, names were called, but not loudly, girls sobbed, some carried their little treasures, mothers held their children. All gathered together, hidden from the plain by a house.

The pale woman led out her father, then ran to her neighbor's door. She opened it, and called clearly, but softly, "Mary, Mary." There was no answer. The woman in black, on her bed, slept on. Her neighbor hesitated, then hurried after the others, as they ran up the low hills toward the mountains, where their men had gone.

The dust cloud grew nearer. Now and then a head could be seen. But all was as still as the grave. The woman in black slept heavily and dreamed that revenge had come at last—that in her hand she held an Indian's head.

The window shade flapped loudly, and she woke with an apprehension crushing her. She went to the window and looked out. There was no blowing dust upon the plains, and the street was empty. The doors of the houses stood open; a shawl lay in the middle of the road. The woman leaned out and looked toward the woods.

She saw on the crest of a hill the white skirts of the flying women, and then, below, down the road, her ears sharpened, her heart tightening, she heard the soft, regular thumping of horses' feet.

Then she *knew*.

She sat on the edge of the bed. This was what she had waited for! Was it her turn now?—or theirs again?

She could kill *one*.

Where was her gun?

She had loaned it to the men.

But her axe—that was below.

As she started for it, there was a burst of war cries.

She ran down the narrow stairs, and took the axe from its place on the wall.

They were passing her door. The room grew lighter. She turned. One stood in the open doorway, black against the sunshine. She set her teeth hard, hid the axe behind her skirts, watched him motionless.

He stretched out his hand clawlike, and laughed, his eyes gleaming, as catlike he moved nearer. A terror seized her: with a hoarse cry, she sprang up the stairs, flinging down a chair as he followed panting.

Quickly she climbed up the ladder to the loft, threw down the trapdoor, fell on it, bolted it, waited. All was still. Outside she heard the distant yells. She stooped noiselessly and put her ear upon the floor. There was soft breathing underneath, and through a crack in the floor she saw an eye peering up at her.

She stood a long time, motionless, axe in hand, ready.

Her back was to the bolt, but suddenly she *felt* that there was something there. She turned softly. A slim brown hand was almost through a crevice in the floor.

She raised her axe. The slender fingers touched the bolt and gently drew it back.

Then with the force of all her hatred fell the axe upon the wrist. The hand sprang up at her. With a howl of agony the creature fell bumping beneath.

Then all again was still.

Her face was wet and warm with the spattered blood.

Outside she heard the crackling of a burning house, then gunshots far away, and distant shouts. On tiptoe she went to the garret window, and peeped round its edge. Over the hills, quite near, she saw the men returning. One house was blazing—the minister's. The Indians were retreating. Near her door, grazing, stood a riderless horse. *She* knew its owner. As they rode past, they caught at it, but were stopped by a shout from her door. An Indian rushed out, handsome, young, holding aloft a bare right arm without a hand. In his language he shrieked to them for revenge, pointing up with his red wrist to the attic where she stood.

The eyes of the woman shot fire. She leaned far out and shook her fist from the garret window.

"One Indian at least!"

She hurled the axe at them. It fell far short. They fired as they passed, but none hit her. Nearer came the men.

The wounded man leaped to his horse and with a curse rode on. The woman laughed as he passed beneath, then sat down in the dusky loft with a red pool at her feet.

Shortly the men returned. Some went by down the hill, after the Indians. Others put out the fire. All was confusion, bustle, shouts.

Then the women and the children came and added to the din, and the men who had followed returned. But the woman in black sat alone in the loft, till she heard the crowd at her door below, and the voice of the pale woman say:

"Where is Mary?"

She rose and lifted the trap door—it was unbolted—and went down.

The pale woman came to her, but she pushed her aside, and wiped her face with her sleeve.

"Are they killed? Any of them?" she said. Her friend answered, "No, Mary, not one." "No harm this time," said the bearded man. "Except my house, it is burned," said the minister's wife. "We'll soon have another."

"I don't mean *you!*" cried the woman in black. "I mean them— red devils. Have you got any?—killed any? *You*"—this to Jim, who never missed a shot—"you"—this to the bearded man—"have *you* killed any?"

And the men answered, "No."

And one man said, "Their horses were faster than ours."

"Not one!" The woman in black drew herself up proudly. "Yes, one; better than killed. Wait." The women shrunk from her as she darted up the stair. They looked at each other wonderingly. The woman returned with something in her grasp. She flung it on the table. "It is an

Indian's hand. His arm will shrivel to the bone. They will leave him some day to die in the sand." The women shuddered and drew back; the men crowded round, but they did not touch the hand.

"Are you afraid?" said the woman in black. "Afraid of that thing!"

She bent back the fingers and looked in it with a smile of contempt. Her face took an ashen hue: the hand struck the table edge and fell upon the floor. She seemed to be trying to think for a second, then she gave one awful cry, and leaned her face against the wall, with her hands hanging at her side.

The pale woman tried to go to her, but her husband drew her back, and, with a silent crowd around, slowly picked up the hand.

For a second he hesitated, then did as she had done, but gently. He bent back the fingers of the severed hand and read its history written there, "SS,64," in white letters on the palm.

He remembered then how, twenty years ago, when she brought the child to him, he had tied its little hand in cooling salve.

It was larger now.

The whisper went around, "It is her boy's hand," and they crept toward the door.

The pale woman took a flower from her dress, one she had put there hours before, and placed it in the brown fingers on the table and went out.

The woman did not stir from the wall. "Leave the hand," she said.

"It is there," and the bearded man closed the door gently behind him.

The woman in black turned. Her hard eyes were dim now. She took the hand from the table and undid her dress and placed it in her breast, and went to the window, and watched, far off, a cloud of dust made golden by the sun, as it rolled away across the plain, down toward Mexico.

Kate Chopin (1851–1904)

Katherine O'Flaherty was born in St. Louis, Missouri. Her father was a prosperous Irish immigrant. Her mother was of French extraction.

An omnivorous reader and a devout, liberal-minded Catholic, she graduated from the Sacred Heart Convent in 1868. Two years later, she married Oscar Chopin, of Lousiana, and moved to New Orleans.

When his business failed, they moved to Cloutierville, Louisiana, to manage his sister's plantation. There Chopin met the Creole and Cajun people; she would later become famous writing about them. In 1884, two years after Oscar had died from swamp fever, she took her six children and returned to St. Louis, where she began to write and be published in periodicals.

The family physician, Dr. Frederick Kolhenheyer, a witty and learned radical, encouraged her in her endeavors, and under his influence she ceased practicing Catholicism and began studying Darwin, Huxley, and Spencer.

Though her first book appeared in 1890, it was her first collection of stories, *Bayou Folk* (1894), which brought her success and acclaim as a local colorist. But like her beloved de Maupassant, her primary interest lay in the examination of human nature. For example, Chopin's novel *The Awakening* (1899) was a thoughtful and talented presentation of a married woman's emancipation as a result of her seduction by a rake.

However, this last work led to such a firestorm of personal and professional rejection that she became despondent and gave up writing.

Our selection for this volume is "Désirée's Baby." It deals with misplaced pride and has been called one of the greatest short stories ever written.

251

DÉSIRÉE'S BABY

*A*s *the day was pleasant, Madame Valmondé drove over to L'Abri* to see Désirée and the baby.

It made her laugh to think of Désirée with a baby. Why, it seemed but yesterday that Désirée was little more than a baby herself; when Monsieur, in riding through the gateway of Valmondé, had found her lying asleep in the shadow of the big stone pillar.

The little one awoke in his arms and began to cry for "Dada." That was as much as she could do or say. Some people thought she might have strayed there of her own accord, for she was of the toddling age. The prevailing belief was that she had been purposely left by a party of Texans, whose canvas-covered wagon, late in the day, had crossed the ferry that Coton Maïs kept, just below the plantation. In time Madame Valmondé abandoned every speculation but the one that Désirée had been sent to her by a beneficent Providence to be the child of her affection, seeing that she was without child of the flesh. For the girl grew to be beautiful and gentle, affectionate and sincere—the idol of Valmondé.

It was no wonder, when she stood one day against the stone pillar in whose shadow she had lain asleep, eighteen years before, that Armand Aubigny riding by and seeing her there, had fallen in love with her. That was the way all the Aubignys fell in love, as if struck by a pistol shot. The wonder was that he had not loved her before; for he had known her since his father brought him home from Paris, a boy of eight, after his mother died there. The passion that awoke in him that day, when he saw her at the gate, swept along like an avalanche, or like a prairie fire, or like anything that drives headlong over all obstacles.

Monsieur Valmondé grew practical and wanted things well-considered: that is, the girl's obscure origin. Armand looked into her eyes and did not care. He was reminded that she was nameless. What did it matter about a name when he could give her one of the oldest and proudest in Louisiana? He ordered the *corbeille* from Paris, and contained himself with what patience he could until it arrived; then they were married.

Madame Valmondé had not seen Désirée and the baby for four weeks. When she reached L'Abri she shuddered at the first sight of it, as she always did. It was a sad looking place, which for many years had not known the gentle presence of a mistress, old Monsieur Aubigny having married and buried his wife in France, and she having loved her own land too well to ever leave it. The roof came down steep and black like a cowl, reaching out beyond the wide galleries that encircled the yellow stuccoed house. Big, solemn oaks grew close to it, and their thick-leaved, far-reaching branches shadowed it like a pall. Young Aubigny's rule was a strict one, too, and under it his negroes had forgotten how to be gay, as they had been during the old master's easy-going and indulgent lifetime.

The young mother was recovering slowly, and lay full length, in her soft white muslins and laces, upon a couch. The baby was beside her, upon her arm, where he had fallen asleep, at her breast. The yellow nurse woman sat beside a window fanning herself.

Madame Valmondé bent her portly figure over Désirée and kissed her, holding her an instant tenderly in her arms. The she turned to the child.

"This is not the baby!" she exclaimed, in startled tones. French was the language spoken at Valmondé in those days.

"I knew you would be astonished," laughed Désirée, "at the way he has grown. The little *cochon de lait!* Look at his legs, mamma, and his hands and fingernails—real fingernails. Zandrine had to cut them this morning. Isn't it true, Zandrine?"

The woman bowed her turbaned head majestically, "Mais si, Madame."

"And the way he cries," went on Désirée, "is deafening. Armand heard him the other day as far away as La Blanche's cabin."

Madame Valmondé had never removed her eyes from the child. She lifted it and walked with it over to the window that was the lightest. She scanned the baby narrowly, then looked as searchingly at Zandrine, whose face was turned to gaze across the fields.

"Yes, the child has grown, has changed," said Madame Valmondé, slowly, as she replaced it beside its mother. "What does Armand say?"

Désirée's face became suffused with a glow that was happiness itself.

"Oh, Armand is the proudest father in the parish, I believe, chiefly because it is a boy, to bear his name; though he says not—that he would have loved a girl as well. But I know it isn't true. I know he says that to please me. And mamma," she added, drawing Madame Valmondé's head down to her, and speaking in a whisper, "he hasn't punished one of them—not one of them—since baby is born. Even Négrillon, who pretended to have burnt his leg that he might rest from work—he only laughed, and said Négrillon was a great scamp. Oh, mamma, I'm so happy; it frightens me."

What Désirée said was true. Marriage, and later the birth of his son, had softened Armand Aubigny's imperious and exacting nature greatly. This was what made the gentle Désirée so happy, for she loved him desperately. When he frowned she trembled, but loved him. When he smiled, she asked no greater blessing of God. But Armand's dark, handsome face had not often been disfigured by frowns since the day he fell in love with her.

When the baby was about three months old, Désirée awoke one day to the conviction that there was something in the air menacing her peace. It was at first too subtle to grasp. It had only been a disquieting suggestion; an air of mystery among the blacks; unexpected visits from far-off neighbors who could hardly account for their coming. Then a strange, an awful change in her husband's manner, which she dared not ask him to explain. When he spoke to her, it was with averted eyes, from which the old love-light seemed to have gone out. He absented himself from home; and when there, avoided her presence and that of her child, without excuse. And the very spirit of Satan seemed suddenly to take hold of him in his dealings with the slaves. Désirée was miserable enough to die.

She sat in her room, one hot afternoon, in her *peignoir,* listlessly drawing through her fingers the strands of her long, silky brown hair that hung about her shoulders. The baby, half naked, lay asleep upon her own great mahogany bed, that was like a sumptuous throne, with its satin-lined half-canopy. One of La Blanche's little quadroon boys—half naked too—stood fanning the child slowly with a fan of peacock feathers. Désirée's eyes had been fixed absently and sadly upon the baby, while she was striving to penetrate the threatening mist that she felt closing about her. She looked from her child to the boy who stood beside him, and back again; over and over. "Ah!" It was a cry that she could not help; which she was not conscious of having uttered. The blood turned like ice in her veins, and a clammy moisture gathered upon her face.

She tried to speak to the little quadroon boy; but no sound would come, at first. When he heard his name uttered, he looked up, and his mistress was pointing to the door. He laid aside the great, soft fan, and obediently stole away, over the polished floor, on his bare tiptoes.

She stayed motionless, with gaze riveted upon her child, and her face the picture of fright.

Presently her husband entered the room, and without noticing her, went to a table and began to search among some papers which covered it.

"Armand," she called to him, in a voice which must have stabbed him, if he was human. But he did not notice. "Armand," she said again. Then she rose and tottered toward him. "Armand," she panted once more, clutching his arm, "look at our child. What does it mean? Tell me."

He coldly but gently loosened her fingers from about his arm and thrust the hand away from him. "Tell me what it means!" she cried despairingly.

"It means," he answered lightly, "that the child is not white; it means that you are not white."

A quick conception of all that this accusation meant for her nerved her with unwonted courage to deny it. "It is a lie; it is not true, I am white! Look at my hair, it is brown; and my eyes are gray, Armand, you know they are gray. And my skin is fair," seizing his wrist. "Look at my hand; whiter than yours, Armand," she laughed hysterically.

"As white as La Blanche's," he returned cruelly; and went away leaving her alone with their child.

When she could hold a pen in her hand, she sent a despairing letter to Madame Valmondé.

"My mother, they tell me I am not white. Armand has told me I am not white. For God's sake tell them it is not true. You must know it is not true. I shall die. I must die. I cannot be so unhappy, and live."

The answer that came was as brief:

"My own Désirée: Come home to Valmondé; back to your mother who loves you. Come with your child."

When the letter reached Désirée she went with it to her husband's study, and laid it open upon the desk before which he sat. She was like a stone image: silent, white, motionless after she had placed it there.

In silence he ran his cold eyes over the written words. He said nothing. "Shall I go, Armand?" she asked in tones sharp with agonized suspense.

"Yes, go."

"Do you want me to go?"

"Yes, I want you to go."

He thought Almighty God had dealt cruelly and unjustly with him; and felt, somehow, that he was paying Him back in kind when he stabbed thus into his wife's soul. Moreover he no longer loved her, because of the unconscious injury she had brought upon his home and his name.

She turned away like one stunned by a blow, and walked slowly toward the door, hoping he would call her back.

"Goodby, Armand," she moaned.

He did not answer her. That was his last blow at fate.

Désirée went in search of her child. Zandrine was pacing the somber gallery with it. She took the little one from the nurse's arms with no word of explanation, and descending the steps, walked away, under the live-oak branches.

It was an October afternoon; the sun was just sinking. Out in the still fields the negroes were picking cotton.

Désirée had not changed the thin white garment nor the slippers which she wore. Her hair was uncovered and the sun's rays brought a golden gleam from its brown meshes. She did not take the broad, beaten road which led to the far-off plantation of Valmondé. She walked across a deserted field, where the stubble bruised her tender feet, so delicately shod, and tore her thin gown to shreds.

She disappeared among the reeds and willows that grew thick along the banks of the deep, sluggish bayou; and she did not come back again.

Some weeks later there was a curious scene enacted at L'Abri. In the center of the smoothly swept back yard was a great bonfire. Armand Aubigny sat in the wide hallway that commanded a view of the spectacle; and it was he who dealt out to a half dozen negroes the material which kept this fire ablaze.

A graceful cradle of willow, with all its dainty furbishings, was laid upon the pyre, which had already been fed with the richness of a priceless *layette*. Then there were silk gowns, and velvet and satin ones added to these; laces, too, and embroideries; bonnets and gloves; for the *corbeille* had been of rare quality.

The last thing to go was a tiny bundle of letters; innocent little scribblings that Désirée had sent to him during the days of their espousal. There was the remnant of one back in the drawer from which he took them. But it was not Désirée's; it was part of an old letter from his mother to his father. He read it. She was thanking God for the blessing of her husband's love:

"But, above all," she wrote, "night and day, I thank the good God for having so arranged our lives that our dear Armand will never know that his mother, who adores him, belongs to the race that is cursed with the brand of slavery."

Bram Stoker (1847–1912)

Abraham Stoker was born in Dublin, Ireland. He was so sickly that he could not stand upright until the age of seven, but he grew into a gifted man, becoming the athletic champion of Dublin University as well as winning medals and honors in pure mathematics.

For the ten years between his twentieth and thirtieth birthdays, he was an Irish civil servant. From November, 1871, he wrote dramatic criticism, without pay, for the *Dublin Mail*. Other jobs included newspaper editor, journalist, short story writer, and serving as a barrister of the Inner Temple.

His chief employment began December 8, 1878, when he became manager of the famous actor, Henry Irving. He remained so until Irving's death in 1905. In this capacity Stoker corresponded voluminously. A pamphlet he wrote as a result of travels with Irving, *A Glimpse of America*, prompted the famous African explorer H.M. Stanley to urge Stoker to write more.

Stoker's novel *Dracula* (1897) brought him international fame. Featuring vampirism, lycanthropy, and hypnotism, it has been called "the most bloodcurdling horror story in English" and perhaps grew from his experiences as an invalid child, a time which he said, made him thoughtful.

After Irving's death, Stoker wrote for the London Telegraph, was manager for David Bispham's opera *The Vicar of Wakefield*, and wrote several books.

A posthumous collection of horrific short stories is *Dracula's Guest* (1914). From it we have chosen "The Squaw," a story of revenge which first appeared in the *Holly Leaves* issued of *Illustrated Sporting News*, December 2, 1893.

THE SQUAW

*N*urnberg *at the time was not so much exploited as it has been* since then. Irving had not been playing *Faust*, and the very name of the old town was hardly known to the great bulk of the traveling public. My wife and I being in the second week of our honeymoon, naturally wanted someone else to join our party, so that when the cheery stranger, Elias P. Hutcheson, hailing from Isthmian City, Bleeding Gulch, Maple Tree County, Neb., turned up at the station at Frankfort, and casually remarked that he was going on to see the most all-fired old Methuselah of a town in Yurrup, and that he guessed that so much traveling alone was enough to send an intelligent, active citizen into the melancholy ward of a daft house, we took the pretty broad hint and suggested that we should join forces. We found, on comparing notes afterward, that we had each intended to speak with some diffidence or hesitation so as not to appear too eager, such not being a good compliment to the success of our married life; but the effect was entirely marred by our both beginning to speak at the same instant—stopping simultaneously and then going on together again. Anyhow, no matter how, it was done; and Elias P. Hutcheson became one of our party. Straightway Amelia and I found the pleasant benefit; instead of quarreling, as we had been doing, we found that the restraining influence of a third party was such that we now took every opportunity of spooning in odd corners. Amelia declares that ever since she has, as the result of that experience, advised all her friends to take a friend on the honeymoon. Well, we "did" Nurnberg together, and much enjoyed the racy remarks of our Transatlantic friend, who, from his quaint speech and his wonderful stock of adventures, might have stepped out of a novel. We kept for the last object of interest in the city to be visited the Burg, and on the day appointed for the visit strolled round the outer wall of the city by the eastern side.

The Burg is seated on a rock dominating the town, and an immensely deep fosse guards it on the northern side. Nurnberg has been happy in that it was never sacked; had it been it would certainly not be so spick and span perfect as it is at present. The ditch has not been used for centuries, and now its base is spread with tea gardens and orchards, of which some of the trees are of quite respectable growth. As we wandered round the wall, dawdling in the hot July sunshine, we often paused to admire the views spread before us, and in especial the great plain covered with towns and villages and bounded with a blue line of hills, like a landscape of Claude Lorraine. From this we always turned with new delight to the city itself, with its myriad of quaint old gables and acre-wide red roofs dotted with dormer windows, tier upon tier. A little to our right rose the towers of the Burg, and nearer still, standing grim, the Torture Tower, which was, and is, perhaps, the most interesting place in the city. For centuries the tradition of the Iron Virgin of Nurnberg has been handed down as an instance of the horrors of cruelty of which man is capable; we had long looked forward to seeing it; and here at last was its home.

In one of our pauses we leaned over the wall of the moat and looked down. The garden seemed quite fifty or sixty feet below us, and the sun pouring into it with an intense, moveless heat like that of an oven. Beyond rose the gray, grim wall seemingly of endless height, and losing itself right and left in the angles of bastion and counterscarp. Trees and bushes crowned the wall, and above again towered the lofty houses on whose massive beauty Time has only set the hand of approval. The sun was hot and we were lazy; time was our own, and we lingered, leaning on the wall. Just below us was a pretty sight—a great black cat lying stretched in the sun, whilst round her gambolled prettily a tiny black kitten. The mother would wave her tail for the kitten to play with, or would raise her feet and push away the little one as an encouragement to further play. They were just at the foot of the wall, and Elias P. Hutcheson, in order to help the play, stopped and took from the walk a moderate sized pebble.

"See!" he said, "I will drop it near the kitten, and they will both wonder where it came from."

"Oh, be careful," said my wife; "you might hit the dear little thing!"

"Not me, ma'am," said Elias P. "Why, I'm as tender as a Maine cherry tree. Lor, bless ye, I wouldn't hurt the poor pooty little critter more'n I'd scalp a baby. An' you may bet your variegated socks on that! See, I'll drop it fur away on the outside so's not to go near her!" Thus saying, he leaned over, and held his arm out at full length and dropped the stone. It may be that there is some attractive force which draws lesser matters to greater; or more probably that the wall was not plumb but sloped to its base—we not noticing the inclination from above; but the stone fell with a sickening thud that came up to us through the hot air, right on the kitten's head, and shattered out its little brains, then and there. The black cat cast a swift upward glance, and we saw her eyes like green fire fixed an instant on Elias P. Hutcheson; and then her attention was given to the kitten, which lay still with just a quiver of her tiny limbs, whilst a thin red stream trickled from a gaping wound. With a muffled cry, such as a human being might give, she bent over the kitten, licking its wound and moaning. Suddenly she seemed to realize that it was dead, and again threw her eyes up at us. I shall never forget the sight, for she looked the perfect incarnation of hate. Her green eyes blazed with lurid fire, and the white, sharp teeth seemed to almost shine through the blood which dabbled her mouth and whiskers. She gnashed her teeth, and her claws stood out stark and at full length on every paw. Then she made a wild rush up the wall as if to reach us, but when the momentum ended fell back, and further added to her horrible appearance for she fell on the kitten, and rose with her back fur smeared with its brains and blood. Amelia turned quite faint, and I had to lift her back from the wall. There was a seat close by in shade of a spreading plane tree, and here I placed her whilst she composed herself. Then I went back to Hutcheson, who stood without moving, looking down on the angry cat below.

As I joined him, he said:

"Wall, I guess that air the savagest beast I ever see—'cept once when an Apache squaw had an edge on a half-breed what they nick-named 'Splinters' 'cos of the way he fixed up her papoose which he stole on a raid just to show that he appreciated the way they had given his mother the fire torture. She got that kinder look so set on her face that it just seemed to grow there. She followed Splinters more'n three year till at last the braves got him and handed him over to her. They did say that no man, white or Injun, had ever been so long a-dying under the tortures of the Apaches. The only time I ever see her smile was when I wiped her out. I kem on the camp just in time to see Splinters pass in his checks, and he wasn't sorry to go either. He was a hard citizen, and though I never could shake with him after that papoose business—for it was bitter bad, and he should have been a white man, for he looked like one—I see he had got paid out in full. Durn me, but I took a piece of his hide from one of his skinnin' posts an' had it made into a pocket-book. It's here now!'' and he slapped the breast pocket of his coat.

Whilst he was speaking the cat was continuing her frantic efforts to get up the wall. She would take a run back and then charge up, some-times reaching an incredible height. She did not seem to mind the heavy fall which she got each time but started with renewed vigor; and at every tumble her appearance became more horrible. Hutcheson was a kind-hearted man—my wife and I had both noticed little acts of kindness to animals as well as to persons—and he seemed concerned at the state of fury to which the cat had wrought herself.

"Wall now!" he said, "I du declare that the poor critter seems quite desperate. There! there! poor thing, it was all an accident—though that won't bring back your little one to you. Say! I wouldn't have had such a thing happen for a thousand! Just shows what a clumsy fool of a man can do when he tries to play! Seems I'm too darned slipperhanded to even play with a cat. Say Colonel!''—it was a pleasant way he had to bestow titles freely—"I hope your wife don't hold no grudge against me on account of this unpleasantness? Why, I wouldn't have had it occur on no account.''

He came over to Amelia and apologized profusely, and she with her usual kindness of heart hastened to assure him that she quite understood that it was an accident. Then we all went again to the wall and looked over.

The cat missing Hutcheson's face had drawn back across the moat, and was sitting on her haunches as though ready to spring. Indeed, the very instant she saw him she did spring, and with a blind unreasoning fury, which would have been grotesque, only that it was so frightfully real. She did not try to run up the wall, but simply launched herself at him as though hate and fury could lend her wings to pass straight through the great distance between them. Amelia, womanlike, got quite concerned, and said to Elias P. in a warning voice:

"Oh! you must be very careful. That animal would try to kill you if she were here; her eyes look like positive murder.''

He laughed out jovially. "Excuse me, ma'am," he said, "but I can't help laughin'. Fancy a man that has fought grizzlies an' Injuns bein' careful of bein' murdered by a cat!"

When the cat heard him laugh, her whole demeanor seemed to change. She no longer tried to jump or run up the wall, but went quietly over, and sitting again beside the dead kitten began to lick and fondle it as though it were alive.

"See!" said I, "the effect of a really strong man. Even that animal in the midst of her fury recognizes the voice of a master, and bows to him!"

"Like a squaw!" was the only comment of Elias P. Hutcheson, as we moved on our way round the city fosse. Every now and then we looked over the wall and each time saw the cat following us. At first she had kept going back to the dead kitten, and then as the distance grew greater took it in her mouth and so followed. After a while, however, she abandoned this, for we saw her following all alone; she had evidently hidden the body somewhere. Amelia's alarm grew at the cat's persistence, and more than once she repeated her warning; but the American always laughed with amusement, till finally, seeing that she was beginning to be worried, he said:

"I say, ma'am, you needn't be skeered over the cat. I go heeled, I du!" Here he slapped his pistol pocket at the back of his lumbar region. "Why sooner'n have you worried, I'll shoot the critter, right here, an' risk the police interferin' with a citizen of the United States for carryin' arms contrairy to reg'lations!" As he spoke he looked over the wall, but the cat, on seeing him, retreated, with a growl, into a bed of tall flowers, and was hidden. He went on: "Blest if that ar critter ain't got more sense of what's good for her than most Christians. I guess we've seen the last of her! You bet, she'll go back now to that busted kitten and have a private funeral of it, all to herself!"

Amelia did not like to say more, lest he might, in mistaken kindness to her, fulfil his threat of shooting the cat: and so we went on and crossed the little wooden bridge leading to the gateway whence ran the steep paved roadway between the Burg and the pentagonal Torture Tower. As we crossed the bridge we saw the cat again down below us. When she saw us her fury seemed to return, and she made frantic efforts to get up the steep wall. Hutcheson laughed as he looked down at her, and said:

"Good-bye, old girl. Sorry I in-jured your feelin's, but you'll get over it in time! So long!'' And then we passed through the long, dim archway and came to the gate of the Burg.

When we came out again after our survey of this most beautiful old place which not even the well-intended efforts of the Gothic restorers of forty years ago have been able to spoil—though their restoration was then glaring white—we seemed to have quite forgotten the unpleasant episode of the morning. The old lime tree with its great trunk gnarled with the passing of nearly nine centuries, the deep well cut through the heart of the rock by those captives of old, and the lovely view from the city wall whence we heard, spread over almost a full quarter of an hour, the multitudinous chimes of the city, had all helped to wipe out from our minds the incident of the slain kitten.

We were the only visitors who had entered the Torture Tower that morning—so at least said the old custodian—and as we had the place all to ourselves were able to make a minute and more satisfactory survey than would have otherwise been possible. The custodian, looking to us as the sole source of his gains for the day, was willing to meet our wishes in any way. The Torture Tower is truly a grim place, even now when many thousands of visitors have sent a stream of life, and the joy that follows life, into the place; but at the time I mention it wore its grimmest and most gruesome aspect. The dust of ages seemed to have settled on it, and the darkness and the horror of its memories seem to have become sentient in a way that would have satisfied the Pantheistic souls of Philo or Spinoza. The lower chamber where we entered was seemingly, in its normal state, filled with incarnate darkness; even the hot sunlight streaming in through the door seemed to be lost in the vast thickness of the walls, and only showed the masonry rough as when the builder's scaffolding had come down, but coated with dust and marked here and there with patches of dark stain which, if walls could speak, could have given their own dread memories of fear and pain. We were glad to pass up the dusty wooden staircase, the custodian leaving the outer door open to light us somewhat on our way; for to our eyes the one long-wick'd, evil-smelling candle stuck in a sconce on the wall gave an inadequate light. When we came up through the open trap in the corner of the chamber overhead, Amelia held on to me so tightly that I could actually feel her heart beat. I must say for my own part that I was not surprised at her fear, for this room was even more gruesome than that below. Here there was certainly more light, but only just sufficient to realize the horrible surroundings of the place. The builders of the tower had evidently intended that only they who should gain the top should have any of the joys of light and prospect. There, as we had noticed from below, were ranges of windows, albeit of medieval smallness, but elsewhere in the tower were only a very few narrow slits such as were habitual in places of medieval defense. A few of these only lit the chamber, and these so high up in the wall that from no part could the sky be seen through the thickness of the walls. In racks, and leaning in disorder against the walls, were a number of headsmen's swords, great double-handed weapons with broad blade and keen edge. Hard by were several blocks whereon the necks of the victims had lain, with here and there deep notches where the steel had bitten through the guard of flesh and shored into the wood. Round the chamber, placed in all sorts of irregular ways, were many implements of torture which made one's heart ache to see—chairs full of spikes which gave instant and excruciating pain; chairs and couches with dull knobs whose torture was seemingly less, but which, though slower, were equally efficacious; racks, belts, boots, gloves, collars, all made for compressing at will; steel baskets in which the head could be slowly crushed into a pulp if necessary; watchmen's hooks with long handle and knife that cut at resistance—this a specialty of the old Nurnberg police system; and many, many other devices for man's injury to man. Amelia grew quite pale with the horror of the things, but fortunately did not faint, for being a little overcome she sat down on a torture chair, but jumped up again with a shriek, all tendency to faint gone. We both pretended that it was the injury done to her dress by the dust of the chair, and the rusty spikes which had upset her, and Mr. Hutcheson acquiesced in accepting the explanation with a kind-hearted laugh.

But the central object in the whole of this chamber of horrors was the engine known as the Iron Virgin, which stood near the center of the room. It was a rudely-shaped figure of a woman, something of the bell order, or, to make a closer comparison, of the figure of Mrs. Noah in the children's Ark, but without that slimness of waist and perfect *rondeur* of hip which marks the aesthetic type of the Noah family. One would hardly have recognized it as intended for a human figure at all had not the founder shaped on the forehead a rude semblance of a woman's face. This machine was coated with rust without, and covered with dust; a rope was fastened to a ring in the front of the figure, about where the waist should have been, and was drawn through a pulley, fastened on the wooden pillar which sustained the flooring above. The custodian pulling this rope showed that a section of the front was hinged like a door at one side; we then saw that the engine was of considerable thickness, leaving just room enough inside for a man to be placed. The door was of equal thickness and of great weight, for it took the custodian all his strength, aided though he was by the contrivance of the pulley, to open it. This weight was partly due to the fact that the door was of manifest purpose hung so as to throw its weight downwards, so that it might shut of its own accord when the strain was released. The inside was honey-combed with rust—nay more, the rust alone that comes through time would hardly have eaten so deep into the iron walls; the rust of the cruel stains was deep indeed! It was only, however, when we came to look at the inside of the door that the diabolical intention was manifest to the full. Here were several long spikes, square and massive, broad at the base and sharp at the points, placed in such a position that when the door should close the upper ones would pierce the eyes of the victim, and the lower ones his heart and vitals. The sight was too much for poor Amelia, and this time she fainted dead off, and I had to carry her down the stairs, and place her on a bench outside till she recovered. That she felt it to the quick was afterward shown by the fact that my eldest son bears to this day a rude birthmark on his breast, which has, by family consent, been accepted as representing the Nurnberg Virgin.

When we got back to the chamber we found Hutcheson still opposite the Iron Virgin; he had been evidently philosophizing, and now gave us the benefit of his thought in the shape of a sort of exordium.

"Wall, I guess I've been learnin' somethin' here while madam has been gettin' over her faint. 'Pears to me that we're a long way behind the times on our side of the big drink. We uster think out on the plains that the Injun could give us points in tryin' to make a man oncomfortable; but I guess your old medieval law-and-order party could raise him every time. Splinters was pretty good in his bluff on the squaw, but this here young miss held a straight flush all high on him. The points of them spikes air sharp enough still, though even the edges air eaten out by what uster be on them. It'd be a good thing for our Indian section to get some specimens of this here play-toy to send round to the Reservations jest to knock the stuffin' out of the bucks, an the squaws too, by showing them as how old civilization lays over them at their best. Guess but I'll get in that box a minute jest to see how it feels!"

"Oh no! no!" said Amelia. "It is too terrible!"

"Guess, ma'am, nothin's too terrible to the explorin' mind. I've been in some queer places in my time. Spent a night inside a dead horse while a prairie fire swept over me in Montana Territory—an' another time slept inside a dead buffler when the Comanches was on the war path an' I didn't keer to leave my kyard on them. I've been two days in a caved-in tunnel in the Billy Broncho gold mine in new Mexico, an' was one of the four shut up for three parts of a day in the caisson what slid over on her side when we was settin' the foundations of the Buffalo Bridge. I've not funked an odd experience yet, an' I don't propose to begin now!"

We saw that he was set on the experiment, so I said: "Well, hurry up, old man, and get through it quick."

"All right, General," said he, "but I calculate we ain't quite ready yet. The gentlemen, my predecessors, what stood in that thar canister, didn't volunteer for the office—not much! And I guess there was some ornamental tyin' up before the big stroke was made. I want to go into this thing fair and square, so I must get fixed up proper first. I dare say this old galoot can rise some string and tie me up accordin' to sample?"

This was said interrogatively to the old custodian, but the latter, who understood the drift of his speech, though perhaps not appreciating to the full the niceties of dialect and imagery, shook his head. His protest was, however, only formal and made to be overcome. The American thrust a gold piece into his hand, saying, "Take it, pard! it's your pot; and don't be skeer'd. This ain't no necktie party that you're asked to assist in!" He produced some thin frayed rope and proceeded to bind our companion, with sufficient strictness for the purpose. When the upper part of his body was bound, Hutcheson said:

"Hold on a moment, Judge. Guess I'm too heavy for you to tote into the canister. You jest let me walk in, and then you can wash up regardin' my legs!"

Whilst speaking he had backed himself into the opening which was just enough to hold him. It was a close fit and no mistake. Amelia looked on with fear in her eyes, but she evidently did not like to say anything. Then the custodian completed his task by tying the American's feet together so that he was now absolutely helpless and fixed in his voluntary prison. He seemed to really enjoy it, and the incipient smile which was habitual to his face blossomed into actuality as he said:

"Guess this here Eve was made out of the rib of a dwarf! There ain't

much room for a full-grown citizen of the United States to bustle. We
uster make our coffins more roomier in Idaho territory. Now, Judge, you
just begin to let this door down, slow, on to me. I want to feel the same
pleasure as the other jays had when those spikes began to move toward
their eyes!''

"Oh no! no! no!'' broke in Amelia hysterically. ''It is too terrible! I
can't bear to see it!—I can't! I can't!''

But the American was obdurate. ''Say, Colonel,'' said he, ''why
not take Madame for a little promenade? I wouldn't hurt her feelin's for
the world; but now that I am here, havin' kem eight thousand miles,
wouldn't it be too hard to give up the very experience I've been pinin'
and pantin' fur? A man can't get to feel like canned goods every time!
Me and the Judge here'll fix up this thing in no time, an' then you'll come
back, an' we'll all laugh together!''

Once more the resolution that is born of curiosity triumphed, and
Amelia stayed holding tight to my arm and shivering whilst the custodian
began to slacken slowly inch by inch the rope that held back the iron
door. Hutcheson's face was positively radiant as his eyes followed the
first movement of the spikes.

''Wall!'' he said. ''I guess I've not had enjoyment like this since I
left Noo York. Bar a scrap with a French sailor at Wapping—an' that
warn't much of a picnic either—I've not had a show fur real pleasure in
this dod-rotted continent, where there ain't no b'ars nor no Injuns, an'
where nary man goes heeled. Slow there, Judge! Don't you rush this
business! I want a show for my money this game—I du!''

The custodian must have had in him some of the blood of his
predecessors in that ghastly tower, for he worked the engine with a
deliberate and excruciating slowness which after five minutes, in which
the outer edge of the door had not moved half as many inches, began to
overcome Amelia. I saw her lips whiten, and felt her hold upon my arm
relax. I looked around an instant for a place whereupon to lay her, and
when I looked at her again found that her eye had become fixed on that
side of the Virgin. Following its direction I saw the black cat crouching
out of sight. Her green eyes shone like danger lamps in the gloom of the
place, and their color was heightened by the blood which still smeared
her coat and reddened her mouth. I cried out:

''The cat! look out for the cat!'' for even then she sprang out before
the engine. At this moment she looked like a triumphant demon. Her

eyes blazed with ferocity, her hair bristled out till she seemed twice her normal size, and her tail lashed about as does a tiger's when the quarry is before it. Elias P. Hutcheson when he saw her was amused, and his eyes positively sparkled with fun as he said:

"Darned if the squaw hain't got on all her war paint! Jest give her a shove off if she comes any of her tricks on me, for I'm so fixed everlastingly by the boss, that durn my skin if I can keep my eyes from her if she wants them! Easy there, Judge! Don't you slack that ar rope or I'm euchered!"

At this moment Amelia completed her faint, and I had to clutch hold of her round the waist or she would have fallen to the floor. Whilst attending to her I saw the black cat crouching for a spring, and jumped up to turn the creature out.

But at that instant, with a sort of hellish scream, she hurled herself, not as we expected at Hutcheson, but straight at the face of the custodian. Her claws seemed to be tearing wildly as one sees in the Chinese drawings of the dragon rampant, and as I looked I saw one of them light on the poor man's eye, and actually tear through it, and down his cheek, leaving a wide band of red where the blood seemed to spurt from every vein.

With a yell of sheer terror which came quicker than even his sense of pain, the man leaped back, dropped as he did so the rope which held back the iron door. I jumped for it, but was too late, for the cord ran like lightning through the pulley-block, and the heavy mass fell forward from its own weight.

As the door closed I caught a glimpse of our poor companion's face. He seemed frozen with terror. His eyes stared with a horrible anguish as if dazed, and no sound came from his lips.

And then the spikes did their work. Happily the end was quick, for when I wrenched open the door they had pierced so deep that they had locked in the bones of the skull through which they had crushed, and actually tore him—it—out of his iron prison till, bound as he was, he fell at full length with a sickly thud upon the floor, the face turning upward as he fell.

I rushed to my wife, lifted her up and carried her out, for I feared for her very reason if she should wake from her faint to such a scene. I laid her on the bench outside and ran back. Leaning against the wooden column was the custodian moaning in pain whilst he held his reddening handkerchief to his eyes. And sitting on the head of the poor American was the cat, purring loudly as she licked the blood which trickled through the gashed sockets of his eyes.

　　I think no one will call me cruel because I seized one of the old executioner's swords and shore her in two as she sat.

Edwin L. Arnold (1857–1935)

The son of the famous British poet, Sir Edwin Arnold (1832–1904), Edwin Lester Arnold was born in Swanscombe, Kent, England. As an infant, he was taken to India where he spent much of his early life. After college he turned to cattle breeding in Scotland, then forest cultivation in India, where a case of malaria forced his return to England. There he began his journalistic career by securing a position on the *London Daily Telegraph*, a paper which was, at that time, edited by his father.

His first novel, *The Wonderful Adverntures of Phra the Phoenician* (1890) was serialized in the *Illustrated London News*. It tells the story of a man who awakens from a death sleep again and again to undergo numerous adventures until his final death in the reign of Queen Elizabeth I, over one thousand year later. A popular success, it passed through many editions, and encouraged Arnold to continue writing.

A second fantasy novel, *Lepidus the Centurion: A Roman of Today* (1901), portrayed the reactions of a Roman soldier to the modern world. A commercial failure, it was followed by *Lieut. Gullivar Jones: His Vacation* (1905). A novel of a young man's Martian escapades, it foreshadoews the John Carter tales by Edgar Rice Burroughs and some feel it may have directly inspired them. Unfortunately, it too was unsuccessful, and Arnold, bitterly discouraged, simply gave up writing.

For this volume we have selected his symbolic horror story, "A Dreadful Night." Despite the geographical misplacement of an anaconda, it packs a powerful punch.

A DREADFUL NIGHT

*O*nly *he who has been haunted by a dream, a black horror of the* night so real and terrible that many days of repugnance and effort are needed to purge the mind of its ugly details, can understand how a dream that was a fact—a horrible waking fantasy, grotesque and weird, a repetition in hard actuality of the ingenious terrors of sleep—clings to him who, with his faculties about him, and all his senses on the alert, has experienced it.

Some five years ago I was hunting in the southwest corner of Colorado, where the great mountain spurs slope down in rocky ravines and gullies from the inland ranges toward the green plains along the course of the Rio San Juan. I had left my camp, late one afternoon, in charge of my trusty comrade, Will Hartland and had wandered off alone into the scrub. Some five or six miles from the tents I stalked and wounded a buck. He was so hard hit that I already smelt venison in the supperpot, and followed the broad trail he had left with the utmost eagerness. He crossed a couple of stony ridges with their deep intervening hollows, and came at last into a wild desolate gorge, full of loose rocks and bushes, and ribboned with game tracks, but otherwise a most desolate and Godforsaken place, where no man had been, or might come for fifty years. Here I sighted my venison staggering down the glen, and dashed after him as fast as I could, through the bushy tangled, and the dry, slippery, summer grass. In a few hundred yards the valley became a pass, and in a score more the steep, bare sides had drawn in until they were walls on either hand, and the way trailed along the bottom of what was little better than a knife-cleft in the hills.

I was a good runner, and the hunter blood was hot within me; my moccasins flashed through the yellow herbage; my cheeks burnt with excitement; I dropped my gun to be the freer—the quarry was plunging along only ten yards ahead, and seemed a certain victim! In front was the outing of that narrow ravine—long reaches of the silver San Juan twining in countless threads through interminable leagues of green pasture and forest—I saw it all like a beautiful picture in the narrow black frame of the rocks; the evening wind was blowing softly up the cañon, and the sky was already gorgeous and livid with the streaks of sunset. Another ten yards and we were flying down the narrowest part of the defile, the beast path under our feet hardly a foot wide, and almost hidden by long, wiry, dead grass.

Suddenly the wounded buck, now within my grasp, staggered up onto its hind legs, in a mad fit of terror, just as, with a shout of triumph, I leapt up to it, and in half a breathing space I and the stag were reeling on the very brink of a horrible funnel—a slippery yellow slope that had opened suddenly before us, leading down to a cavernous mouth gaping dark and dreadful in the heart of the earth. With a scream louder than my shout of triumph I threw up my hands and tried to stop; it was too late; I felt my feet slip from under me, and in a second, shouting and plunging, and clutching at the rotten herbage, I was flying downward. I caught a last glimpse of the San Juan and the blaze of the sky overhead and then I was spinning into darkness, horrible stygian darkness, through which I fell for a giddy, senseless moment or two, and then landed with a thud which ought to have killed me, bruised and nearly senseless, on a soft quaggy mound of something that seemed to sink under me like a feather bed. I passed out.

My first sensation on recovering consciousness was that of an overpowering smell, a sickly, deadly taint in the air that there was no growing accustomed to, and which, after a few gasps, seemed to have run its deadly venom into every corner of my frame, and, turning my blood yellow, to have transformed my constitution into keeping with its own accursed nature. It was a damp, musty, charnel house smell, sickly and wicked, with the breath of the slaughterpit in it—an aroma of blood and corruption. I sat up and glared, gasped about in the gloom, and then I carefully felt my limbs up and down. All were safe and sound, and I was unhurt, though as sore and bruised as if my body had stood a long day's pummelling. Then I groped about me in the pitch dark, and soon touched the still warm body of the dead buck I had shot, and on which indeed I was sitting. Still feeling about, I found on the other side something soft and furry too. I touched and patted it, and in a minute recognized with a start that my fingers were deep in the curly mane of a bull bison. I pulled, and the curly mane came off in stinking tufts. That bull bison had been lying there six months or more. All about me, wherever I felt, was cold, clammy fur and hair and hoofs and bare ribs and bones mixed in wild confusion, and as that wilderness of death unfolded itself in the darkness to me, and the fetid, close atmosphere mounted to my head, my nerves began to tremble like harp strings in a storm, and my heart, that I had always thought terrorproof, to patter like a girl's.

Plunging and slipping I got upon my feet, and then became conscious of a dim circle of twilight far above, representing the hole through which I had fallen. The twilight was fading outside every moment, and it was already so faintly luminous that my hand, held in front of me, looked ghostly and scarcely discernible. I began to explore slowly round the walls of my prison. With a heart that grew sicker and sicker, and sensations that you can imagine better than I can describe, I traced the jagged but unbroken circle of a great chamber in the underground, a hundred feet long, perhaps, by fifty across, with cruel, remorseless walls that rose sloping gently inward from an uneven horrible floor of hides and bones to that narrow neck far overhead, where the stars were already twinkling in a cloudless sky. By this time I was fairly frightened, and the cold perspiration of dread began to stand in beads upon my forehead.

A fancy then seized me that someone might be within hearing distance above. I shouted again and again, and listening acutely each time as the echoes of my shout died away, I could have sworn something like the clash of ghostly teeth on teeth, something like the rattle of jaws in an ague fit, fell on the silence behind. With beating heart, and an unfamiliar dread creeping over me, I crouched down in the gloom and listened. There was water dripping out in the dark, monotonous and dismal, and something like the breath from a husky throat away in the distance of the cavern came fitfully to my ears, though so uncertain that at first I thought it might have been only the rustle of the wind in the grass far overhead.

Again mastering all my resolution, I shouted until the darkness rang, then listened eagerly with every faculty on stretch; and again from the dimness came that tremulous gnashing of teeth, and that wavering, long-drawn breath. Then my hair literally stood on end, and my eyes were fixed with breathless wonder in front of me, for out of the remotest gloom, where the corruption of the floor was already beginning to glow with pale blue wavering phosphorescent light as the night fell, rose glimmering itself with that ghastly lustre, something slim and tall and tremulous. It was full of life and yet was not quite of human form, and reared itself against the dark wall, all agleam, until its top, set with hollow eyes, was nine or ten feet from the ground, and oscillated and wavered, and seemed to feel about, as I had done, for an opening—and then suddenly collapsed in a writhing heap upon the ground, and I distinctly heard the fall of its heavy body as it disappeared into the blue inferno that burnt below.

Again that spectral thing rose laboriously, this time many paces nearer to me, to twice the height of a man, and wavered and felt about, and then sank down with a fall like the fall of heavy draperies, as though the energy that had lifted it suddenly expired. Nearer and nearer it came, traveling round the circuit of the walls in that strange way, and awed and bewildered I crept out into the open to let that dreadful thing go by. And presently, to my infinite relief, it traveled away, still wavering and writhing and I breathed again.

As that luminous shadow faded into the remote corners of the cave, I shouted once more, for the pleasure, it must have been, of hearing my own voice—again there was that gnashing of teeth—and the instant afterward such a hideous chorus of yells from the other side of the cavern, such a commingled howl of spirits, such an infernal moan of sorrow and shame and misery, that rose and fell on the stillness of the night, that, for an instant, lost to everything but that dreadful sound, I leapt to my feet, with the stagnant blood cold as ice within me, my body pulseless for the moment, and mingled my mad shouting with the voices of those unseen devils in a hideous chorus. Then my manhood came back with a rush upon me, and judgment and sense, and I recognized in the trembling echoes a cry that I had often listened to in happier circumstances. That uproar came from the throats of wolves that had been trapped like myself. But, were they alive? I thought in fascinated wonder—how could they be in this horrible pit? and if they were not, picture oneself cornered in such a trap with a pack of wolfish spirits—it would not bear thinking of; already my fancy saw constellations of fierce yellow eyes everywhere, and herds of wicked gray backs racing to and fro in the shadows. With a tremulous hand I felt in my pocket for a match, and found I had two—and two only!

By this time the moon was up and a great band of silver light, broad and bright, was creeping down the walls of our prison, but I would not wait for it. I struck the match with feverish eagerness, and held it overhead. It burnt brightly for a moment, and I saw I was in a great natural crypt, with no outlet anywhere but by the narrow neck above, and all chance of reaching that was impossible, as the walls sloped inwards everywhere as they rose to it. All the floor was piled thigh-deep with a ghastly tangle of animal remains, in every state of return to their native earth, from the bare bones, that would have crumbled at a touch, to the hide, still glossy and sleek, of the stag that had fallen in only a week or two before. Such a carnage place I never saw—such furs, such trophies, such heads and horns there were all round, as raised the envy of my hunter spirit, even in that emergency.

But what held me spellbound and rooted my eyes into the shadows was—twenty paces off, lying full stretch along the glossy, undulating path which the incessant feet of new victims had worn, month after month, over the hill and valley of dead bodies under the walls—a splendid eighteen-foot python. It was this creature's ghostly rambles and ineffectual attempts to scale the walls that had first scared me in that place of horrors. I turned round, for the match was short, and scarcely noticing a score or two of dejected rats, who squeaked and scrambled amongst lesser snakes and strange reptiles, looked hard across the cave.

There, on their haunches, in a huddle against the far wall, staring at me with dull cold eyes, were five of the biggest, ugliest wolves ever mortal saw. I had often seen wolves, but never any like those. All the pluck, grace and savage vigor of their kind had gone from them; their bodies, gorged with carrion, were vast, swollen, and hideous; their shaggy fur was hanging in tatters from their red and mangy skins, the saliva streamed from their jaws in yellow ribbons, their bleary eyes were drowsy and dull, their great throats, as they opened them to howl in sad chorus at the handful of purple night above, were dry and yellow, and there was about them such an air of disgusting misery and woebegoneness, that, with a shudder and a cry I could not suppress, I let the last embers of the burning match fall to the ground.

How long I crouched in the darkness against the wall, with those hideous serenaders grinding their foam-flecked teeth and bemoaning our common fate in hideous unison, I do not know. Nor have I space to tell the wild horrible visions which filled my mind for the next hour or two, but presently the moonlight had come down off the wall, and was spread

at my feet in a silver carpet, and as I sullenly watched the completion of
that arena of light, I was aware that the wolves were moving. Very
slowly they came forward out of the darkness, led by the biggest and
ugliest, until they were all in the silver circle, gaunt, spectral, and vile,
every mangy tuft of loose hair upon their sore-speckled backs clear as
daylight. Then those pot-bellied phosphorescent undertakers began the
strangest movements, and after watching them for a moment or two in
fascinated wonder, I saw they had come to me in their despair to solicit
my companionship and countenance. I could not have believed it possible that dumb brutes could have made their meaning so clear, as those
poor shaggy scoundrels did. They halted ten yards off, and with humble
heads sagged down, and averted eyes, slowly wagged their mud-locked
tails. Then they came a few steps further and whined and fawned, and
then another pace, and lay down upon their stomachs, putting their noses
between their paws like dogs who watch and doze, while they regarded
me steadfastly with sad, great eyes, forlorn and terrible.

Foot by foot, gray and silver in the moonlight, they advanced with
the offer of their dreadful friendship, until at last I was fairly bewitched,
and when the big wolf came forward till he was at my knees, a horrible
epitome of corruption, and licked my hand with his great burning
tongue, I submitted to the caress as readily as though he were my favorite
hound. Henceforth the pack seemed to think the compact was sealed,
and thrust their odious company upon me, trotting at my heels, howling
when I shouted, and muzzling down to me, putting their heavy paws
upon my feet, and their great steaming jaws upon my chest whenever, in
despair and weariness, I tried to snatch a moment's sleep.

But it would be impossible to go step by step through the infinitely
painful hours of that night. Not only was the place full of spectral forms
and strange cries, but presently legions of unclean things of a hundred
kinds, that had lived on those dead beasts when they too were living,
swarmed in thousands and assailed us, adding a new terror to the inferno,
ravaging us who still kept body and soul together, till our flesh seemed
burning on our bones.

There was no rest for man or brute; the light was a mockery and the
silence hideous. Round and round we pattered, I and the gaunt wolves,
over the dim tracks worn by the feet of disappointment and suffering; we
waded knee-deep through a wavering sea of steamy blue flame, that rose
from the remains and bespattered us from head to heel, stumbling and
tripping and groping, and cursing our fates, each in his separate tongue,

while the night waned, the dew fell clammy and cold into our prison, and the stars, who looked down upon us from the free purple sky overhead, made a dim twilight in our cell.

I was blundering and staggering round the walls for the hundredth time, feeling about with my hands in a hopeless search for some cleft or opening, when the grimmest thing of the whole evening happened. In a lonely corner of the den, in a little recess not searched before, pattering about in the dark, I suddenly touched with my hand—think with what a shock it thrilled me—the cloth-clad shoulder of a man! With a gasp and a cry I leapt back, and stood trembling and staring into the shadows, scarcely daring to breathe. Much as I had suffered in that hideous place, nothing affected me half so much as dropping my hand upon that dreadful shoulder. Heaven knows we were all cowards down there, but for a minute I was the biggest coward of us, and felt full of those strange throes of superstitious terror that I had often wondered before to hear weaker men describe.

Then I mustered my wavering spirit, and with the gaunt wolves squatting in a luminous circle around me, went into the recess again and put my hand once more upon my grim companion. The coat upon him was dry and rough with age, and beneath it—I could tell by the touch— there was nothing but bare, rattling bones! I stood still, grimly waiting for the flutter of my physical cowardice to subside, and then I thought of that second match, and in a moment of keen intensity, with such care as you may imagine, struck it against the wall. It lit, and at my feet, in ragged miner's garb, sitting against the wall with his knees drawn up and his chin upon them, was the skeleton of a man so bleached and dry, that it must have been there for fifty years at least. At his side lay his miner's pick and pannikin, an old dusty pocket-Bible, the fragments of a felt hat, and a pair of heavy boots, still neatly side by side, just as the luckless fellow had placed the well-worn things when, for some reason, he last took them off.

And overhead something scratched upon a flat face of the rock. Hastily I snatched a scrap of paper from my pocket and lighting it at the expiring match, read on the stone:

"Monday,"
"Tuesday,"
"Wednesd—"

—there was nothing but that, and even the "Wednesday" was unfinished, dying away in a shaky, uncertain scratch, that spoke infinitely
more plainly than many words would have done, of the growing feeble-
ness of the hand that traced it—and then all was darkness again.

I crept back to my distant corner, and crouched like the dead man
against the wall, with my chin upon my knees, and kept repeating to
myself the horrible simplicity of that diary—"Monday, Tuesday,
Wednesday! Poor nameless Monday, Tuesday, Wednesday! And was
this to be my fate?" I laughed bitterly—I would begin such another
record with the first streak of dawn, and in the meantime I would sleep,
whatever befell, and sleep I did, with those restless blue wolves canter-
ing round the well-worn paths of the charnel house, to their own hideous
music, the silent unknown away in the distance, and the opal eyes of the
great serpent staring at me like baleful planets, cold, sullen, and cruel,
from between the dead man's feet.

It was a shout that woke me next morning, a clear ringing shout,
that jerked me from dreadful dreams. I scrambled to my feet and saw
from the bright light about me that it was day above, and while I still
staggered and wandered stupidly, again came that shout. I stared up
overhead where the sunlight was making the neck of the trap a disc of
intolerable brightness and there, when my eyes grew accustomed to that
shining, was a round something that presently resolved itself into the
blessed face of my steadfast chum, Will Hartland.

There is little need to say more. With the help of his strong
cow-rope, at his saddle-bow, and a round point of earth-embedded rock
as purchase, he had me out of that accursed hole in an incredibly,
ridiculously short space of time. And there I was, leaning on his shoulder, free again, in the first flush of as glorious a morning as you could
wish for, with the San Juan away in the distance, winding in a sapphire
streak through miles of emerald forests, a sweet blue sky above, and
underfoot the earth wet with morning mist, smelling like a wine cooler,
and every bent and twig underfoot gemmed with glittering prismatic
dewdrops. I sat down on a stone, and after a long pull at Will's flask, told
him something like the narrative I have just given. And when the tale was
done I paused a minute, and then said somewhat shyly, "And now I am
going back, Will, old man! back for those poor devils down yonder, who
haven't a chance for their lives unless I do." Will, who had listened to

my narrative with horror and wonder flitting across his honest brown face, started up at this as though he thought the night's adventure had fairly turned my head. But he was a good fellow, chivalrous and tender of heart under his Mexican jacket, and speedily acknowledging that I was right, set to work to help me.

Down I went back into the pit, the very sight and shadow of which now made me sick, and with the noose end of Will's lasso (he holding the other end above) set to work to secure those poor beasts, who whined and crowded round my legs in hideous glee to have me back again amongst them. 'Twas easy work; they were stupid and heavy; and seemed to have some idea of my intentions, and thus I noosed them one at a time, and when a wolf was fast, shouted to Will, who hauled away with scant ceremony, and up the gray ghoul went into that sunshine he had not seen for many weeks, until he and all his comrades were free once more, spinning, and struggling, and yelping—truly a wonderful sight.

But nothing would move the python. I followed him round and round, trying all I knew to get his cruel, cynical head through the noose, and then, when he had refused it a dozen times, I grew angry and cursed him and gathering up all the tortoises, lizards, and lesser beasts I could find into my waistband, ascended into the sweet outer air once more.

A very few hours afterwards a heavy blasting-charge, fetched from a neighboring mine, was dangling by a string just inside the mouth of the detestable trap, with its fuse burning brightly. A few minutes of suspense, a mighty crash, a cloud of white smoke hanging over the green hilltop, and one of the most treacherous places that ever marred the face of nature's sweet earth was a harmless heap of dust and tumbled stones.

Ralph Adams Cram (1863–1942)

Architect, social reformer, and author, Ralph Adams Cram was born in Hampton Falls, New Hampshire. After studying in Boston and Europe, he moved back to Boston in 1889 and opened an architectural office. Later, with Bertram G. Goodhue and C.F. Wentworth, he formed an architectural firm which was to become one of the nation's most famous.

In his work, Cram wanted "to create an environment that would convey spiritual values as a corrective to technological civilization." He strongly advocated the Gothic style, believing it to be "the most pleasing aesthetically, the most compelling logically, and the most satisfying morally."

Gothic churches were one of his specialties. Besides redesigning the Cathedral of St. John the Devine (New York City), he designed the First Baptist Church (Cleveland), and the Washington Cathedral. He also constructed buildings at Princeton, Rice Institute, West Point, and Williams College, and was, to a large extent, responsible for popularizing the "collegiate Gothic" look.

As a social reformer, he called for a return to medieval values, walled towns, and an autocratic government by the "high minded."

As an author, he served as art critic for the *Boston Transcript* and produced volumes on architecture and social philosophy such as *Church Building* (1901), *The Gothic Quest* (1907), *My Life in Architecture* (1936), and *The End of Democracy* (1937). However, horror fans remember him for *Black Spirits and White: A Book of Ghost Stories* (1898) which contains "The Dead Valley," a famous and atmospheric tale.

THE DEAD VALLEY

I have a friend, Olaf Ehrensvärd, a Swede by birth, who yet, by reason of a strange and melancholy mischance of his early boyhood, has thrown his lot with that of the New World. It is a curious story of a headstrong boy and a proud and relentless family: the details do not matter here, but they are sufficient to weave a web of romance around the tall yellow-bearded man with the sad eyes and the voice that gives itself perfectly to plaintive little Swedish songs remembered out of childhood. In the winter evenings we play chess together, he and I, and after some close, fierce battle has been fought to a finish—usually with my own defeat—we fill our pipes again, and Ehrensvärd tells me stories of the far, half-remembered days in the fatherland, before he went to sea: stories that grow very strange and incredible as the night deepens and the fire falls together, but stories that, nevertheless, I fully believe.

One of them made a strong impression on me, so I set it down here, only regretting that I cannot reproduce the curiously perfect English and the delicate accent which to me increased the fascination of the tale. Yet, as best I can remember it, here it is.

"I never told you how Nils and I went over the hills to Hallsberg, and how we found the Dead Valley, did I? Well, this is the way it happened. I must have been about twelve years old, and Nils Sjöberg, whose father's estate joined ours, was a few months younger. We were inseparable just at that time, and whatever we did, we did together.

"Once a week it was market day in Engelholm, and Nils and I went always there to see the strange sights that the market gathered from all the surrounding country. One day we quite lost our hearts, for an old man from across the Elfborg had brought a little dog to sell, that seemed to us the most beautiful dog in all the world. He was a round, wooly puppy, so funny that Nils and I sat down on the ground and laughed at him, until he came and played with us in so jolly a way that we felt that there was only one really desirable thing in life, and that was the little dog of the old man from across the hills. But alas! we had not half money enough wherewith to buy him, so we were forced to beg the old man not to sell him before the next market day, promising that we would bring the money for him then. He gave us his word, and we ran home very fast and implored our mothers to give us money for the little dog.

"We got the money, but we could not wait for the next market day. Suppose the puppy should be sold! The thought frightened us so that we begged and implored that we might be allowed to go over the hills to Hallsberg where the old man lived, and get the little dog ourselves, and at last they told us we might go. By starting early in the morning we should reach Hallsberg by three o'clock, and it was arranged that we should stay there that night with Nils's aunt, and leaving by noon the next day, be home again by sunset.

"Soon after sunrise we were on our way, after having received minute instructions as to just what we should do in all possible and impossible circumstances, and finally a repeated injunction that we should start for home at the same hour the next day, so that we might get safely back before nightfall.

"For us, it was magnificent sport, and we started off with our rifles, full of the sense of our very great importance: yet the journey was simple enough, along a good road, across the big hills we knew so well, for Nils and I had shot over half the territory this side of the dividing ridge of the Elfborg. Back of Engelholm lay a valley, from which rose the low mountains, and we had to cross this, and then follow the road along the side of the hills for three or four miles, before a narrow path branched off to the left, leading up through the pass.

"Nothing occurred of interest on the way over, and we reached Hallsberg in due season, found to our inexpressible joy that the little dog was not sold, secured him, and so went to the house of Nils's aunt to spend the night.

"Why we did not leave early on the following day, I can't quite remember; at all events, I know we stopped at a shooting range just outside of the town, where most attractive paste-board pigs were sliding slowly through painted foliage, serving so as beautiful marks. The result was that we did not get fairly started for home until afternoon, and as we found ourselves at last pushing up the side of the mountain with the sun dangerously near their summits, I think we were a little scared at the prospect of the examination and possible punishment that awaited us when we got home at midnight.

"Therefore we hurried as fast as possible up the mountainside, while the blue dusk closed in about us, and the light died in the purple sky. At first we had talked hilariously, and the little dog had leaped ahead of us with the utmost joy. Latterly, however, a curious oppression came on us; we did not speak or even whistle, while the dog fell behind, following us with hesitation in every muscle.

"We had passed through the foothills and the low spurs of the mountains, and were almost at the top of the main range, when life seemed to go out of everything, leaving the world dead, so suddenly silent the forest became, so stagnant the air. Instinctively we halted to listen.

"Perfect silence—the crushing silence of deep forests at night; and more, for always, even in the most impenetrable fastness of the wooded mountains, is the multitudinous murmur of little lives, awakened by the darkness, exaggerated and intensified by the stillness of the air and the great dark: but here and now the silence seemed unbroken even by the turn of a leaf, the movement of a twig, the note of night bird or insect. I could hear the blood beat through my veins; and the crushing of the grass under our feet as we advanced with hesitating steps sounded like the falling of trees.

"And the air was stagnant—dead. The atmosphere seemed to lie upon my body like the weight of sea on a diver who has ventured too far into its awful depths. What we usually call silence seems so only in relation to the din of ordinary experience. This was silence in the absolute, and it crushed the mind while it intensified the senses, bringing down the awful weight of inextinguishable fear.

"I know that Nils and I stared toward each other in abject terror, listening to our quick, heavy breathing that sounded to our acute senses like the fitful rush of waters. And the poor little dog we were leading justified our terror. The black oppression seemed to crush him even as it did us. He lay close to the ground, moaning feebly, and dragging himself painfully and slowly closer to Nils's feet. I think this exhibition of utter animal fear was the last touch, and must inevitably have blasted our reason—mine anyway; but just then, as we stood quaking on the bounds of madness, came a sound, so awful, so ghastly, so horrible, that it seemed to rouse us from the dead spell that was on us.

"In the depth of the silence came a cry, beginning as a low, sorrowful moan, rising to a tremulous shriek, culminating in a yell that seemed to tear the night in sunder and rend the world as by a cataclysm. So fearful was it that I could not believe it had actual existence: it passed previous experience, the powers of belief, and for a moment I thought it the result of my own animal terror, an hallucination born of tottering reason.

"A glance at Nils dispelled this thought in a flash. In the pale light of the high stars he was the embodiment of all possible human fear, quaking with an ague, his jaw fallen, his tongue out, his eyes protruding like those of a hanged man. Without a word we fled, the panic of fear giving us strength, and together, the little dog caught close in Nils's arms, we sped down the side of the cursed mountains—anywhere, goal was of no account: we had but one impulse—to get away from that place.

"So under the black trees and the far white stars that flashed through the still leaves overhead, we leaped down the mountainside, regardless of path or landmark, straight through the tangled underbrush, across mountain streams, through fens and copses, anywhere, so only that our course was downward.

"How long we ran thus, I have no idea, but by and by the forest fell behind, and we found ourselves among the foothills, and fell exhausted on the dry short grass, panting like tired dogs.

"It was lighter here in the open, and presently we looked around to see where we were, and how we were to strike out in order to find the path that would lead us home. We looked in vain for a familiar sign. Behind us rose the great wall of black forest on the flank of the mountain: before us lay the undulating mounds of low foothills, unbroken by trees or rocks, and beyond, only the fall of black sky bright with multitudinous stars that turned its velvet depth to a luminous gray.

"As I remember, we did not speak to each other once: the terror was too heavy on us for that, but by and by we rose simultaneously and started out across the hills.

"Still the same silence, the same dead, motionless air—air that was at once sultry and chilling: a heavy heat struck through with an icy chill that felt almost like the burning of frozen steel. Still carrying the helpless dog, Nils pressed on through the hills, and I followed close behind. At last, in front of us, rose a slope of moor touching the white stars. We climbed it wearily, reached the top, and found ourselves gazing down into a great, smooth valley, filled halfway to the brim with—what?

"As far as the eye could see stretched a level plain of ashy white, faintly phosphorescent, a sea of velvet fog that lay like motionless water, or rather like a floor of alabaster, so dense did it appear, so seemingly capable of sustaining weight. If it were possible, I think that sea of dead white mist struck even greater terror into my soul than the heavy silence or the deadly cry—so ominous was it, so utterly unreal, so phantasmal, so impossible, as it lay there like a dead ocean under the steady stars. Yet through that mist *we must go!* there seemed no other way home, and, shattered with abject fear, mad with the one desire to get back, we started down the slope to where the sea of milky mist ceased, sharp and distinct around the stems of the rough grass.

"I put one foot into the ghostly fog. A chill as of death struck through me, stopping my heart, and I threw myself backward on the slope. At that instant came again the shriek, close, close, right in our ears, in ourselves, and far out across the damnable sea I saw the cold fog lift like a waterspout and toss itself high in writhing convolutions toward the sky. The stars began to grow dim as thick vapor swept across them, and in the growing dark I saw a great, watery moon lift itself slowly above the palpitating sea, vast and vague in the gathering mist.

"This was enough: we turned and fled along the margin of the white sea that throbbed now with fitful motion below us, rising, rising, slowly and steadily, driving us higher and higher up the side of the foothills.

"It was a race for life; that we knew. How we kept it up I cannot understand, but we did, and at last we saw the white sea fall behind us as we staggered up the end of the valley, and then down into a region that we knew, and so into the old path. The last thing I remember was hearing a strange voice, that of Nils, but horribly changed, stammer brokenly, 'The dog is dead!' and then the whole world turned around twice, slowly and resistlessly, and consciousness went out with a crash.

"It was some three weeks later, as I remember, that I awoke in my own room, and found my mother sitting beside the bed. I could not think very well at first, but as I slowly grew strong again, vague flashes of recollection began to come to me, and little by little the whole sequence of events of that awful night in the Dead Valley came back. All that I could gain from what was told me was that three weeks before I had been found in my own bed, raging sick, and that my illness grew fast into brain fever. I tried to speak of the dread things that had happened to me, but I saw at once that no one looked on them save as the hauntings of a dying frenzy, and so I closed my mouth and kept my own counsel.

"I must see Nils, however, and so I asked for him. My mother told me that he also had been ill with a strange fever, but that he was now quite well again. Presently they brought him in, and when we were alone I began to speak to him of the night on the mountain. I shall never forget the shock that struck me down on my pillow when the boy denied everything: denied having gone with me, ever having heard the cry, having seen the valley, or feeling the deadly chill of the ghostly fog. Nothing would shake his determined ignorance, and in spite of myself I was forced to admit that his denials came from no policy of concealment, but from blank oblivion.

"My weakened brain was in a turmoil. Was it all but the floating phantasm of delirium? Or had the horror of the real thing blotted Nils's mind into blankness so far as the events of the night in the Dead Valley were concerned? The latter explanation seemed the only one, else how explain the sudden illness which in a night had struck us both down? I said nothing more, either to Nils or to my own people, but waited, with a growing determination that, once well again, I would find that valley if it really existed.

"It was some weeks before I was really well enough to go, but finally, late in September, I chose a bright, warm, still day, the last smile of the dying summer, and started early in the morning along the path that led to Hallsberg. I was sure I knew where the trail struck off to the right, down which we had come from the valley of dead water, for a great tree grew by the Hallsberg path at the point where, with a sense of salvation, we had found the home road. Presently I saw it to the right, a little distance ahead.

"I think the bright sunlight and the clear air had worked as a tonic to me, for by the time I came to the foot of the great pine, I had quite lost faith in the verity of the vision that haunted me, believing at last that it was indeed but the nightmare of madness. Nevertheless, I turned sharply to the right, at the base of the tree, into a narrow path that led through a dense thicket. As I did so I tripped over something. A swarm of flies sung into the air around me, and looking down I saw the matted fleece, with the poor little bones thrusting through, of the dog we had bought in Hallsberg.

"Then my courage went out with a puff, and I knew that it all was true, and that now I was frightened. Pride and the desire for adventure urged me on, however, and I pressed into the close thicket that barred my way. The path was hardly visible: merely the worn road of some small beasts, for, though it showed in the crisp grass, the bushes above grew thick and hardly penetrable. The land rose slowly, and rising grew clearer, until at last I came out on a great slope of hill, unbroken by trees or shrubs, very like my memory of that rise of land we had topped in order that we might find the Dead Valley and the icy fog. I looked at the sun; it was bright and clear, and all around insects were humming in the autumn air, and birds were darting to and fro. Surely there was no danger, not until nightfall at least; so I began to whistle, and with a rush mounted the last crest of brown hill.

"There lay the Dead Valley! A great oval basin, almost as smooth and regular as though made by man. On all sides the grass crept over the brink of the encircling hills, dusty green on the crests, then fading into ashy brown, and so to a deadly white, this last color forming a thin ring, running in a long line around the slope. And then? Nothing. Bare, brown, hard earth, glittering with grains of alkali, but otherwise dead and barren. Not a tuft of grass, not a stick of brushwood, not even a stone, but only the vast expanse of beaten clay.

"In the midst of the basin, perhaps a mile and a half away, the level expanse was broken by a great dead tree, rising leafless and gaunt into the air. Without a moment's hesitation I started down into the valley and made for this goal. Every particle of fear seemed to have left me, and even the valley itself did not look so very terrifying. At all events, I was driven by an overwhelming curiosity, and there seemed to be but one thing in the world to do—to get to that tree! As I trudged along over the hard earth, I noticed that the multitudinous voices of birds and insects had died away. No bee or butterfly hovered through the air, no insects leaped or crept over the dull earth. The very air itself was stagnant.

"As I drew near the skeleton tree, I noticed the glint of sunlight on a kind of white mound around its roots, and I wondered curiously. It was not until I had come close that I saw its nature.

"All around the roots and barkless trunk was heaped a wilderness of little bones. Tiny skulls of rodents and of birds, thousands of them, rising about the dead tree and streaming off for several yards in all directions, until the dreadful pile ended in isolated skulls and scattered skeletons. Here and there a larger bone appeared—the thigh of a sheep, the hoofs of a horse, and to one side, grinning slowly, a human skull.

"I stood quite still, staring with all my eyes, when suddenly the dense silence was broken by a faint, forlorn cry high over my head. I looked up and saw a great falcon turning and sailing downward just over the tree. In a moment more she fell motionless on the bleaching bones.

"Horror struck me, and I rushed for home, my brain whirling, a strange numbness growing in me. I ran steadily, on and on. At last I glanced up. Where was the rise of the hill? I looked around wildly. Close before me was the dead tree with its pile of bones. I had circled it round and round, and the valley wall was still a mile and a half away.

"I stood dazed and frozen. The sun was sinking, red and dull, toward the line of hills. In the east the dark was growing fast. Was there still time? *Time!* It was not *that* I wanted, it was *will!* My feet seemed clogged as in a nightmare. I could hardly drag them over the barren earth. And then I felt the slow chill creeping through me. I looked down. Out of the earth a thin mist was rising, collecting in little pools that grew ever larger until they joined here and there, their currents swirling slowly like thin blue smoke. The western hills halved the copper sun. When it was dark I should hear that shriek again, and then I should die. I knew that, and with every remaining atom of will I staggered toward the red west through the writhing mist that crept clammily around my ankles, retarding my steps.

"And as I fought my way off from the tree, the horror grew, until at last I thought I was going to die. The silence pursued me like dumb ghosts, the still air held my breath, the hellish fog caught at my feet like cold hands.

"But I won! though not a moment too soon. As I crawled on my hands and knees up the brown slope, I heard, far away and high in the air, the cry that already had almost bereft me of reason. It was faint and vague, but unmistakable in its horrible intensity. I glanced behind. The fog was dense and pallid, heaving undulously up the brown slope. The sky was gold under the setting sun, but below was the ashy gray of death. I stood for a moment on the brink of this sea of hell, and then leaped down the slope. The sunset opened before me, the night closed behind, and as I crawled home weak and tired, darkness shut down on the Dead Valley."

H.G. Wells (1866–1946)

Herbert George Wells was born to a lower middle-class family in Bromley, England and had to struggle fiercely to rise above his origins.

A small, bright, imaginative man with a large head and chest, darting eyes and a shrill voice, he seemed driven by three desires: to succeed, to satisfy strong sexual appetites, and to save the world.

Alternating apprenticeships with classes he won a scholarship to the Normal School of Science and studied under biologist T.H. Huxley, who greatly influenced him. He left school early to teach, finally graduating from London University in 1888.

After almost dying from a tubercular hemorrhage, he ran away from wife and job "to make one last attempt at authorship before early death." Success was almost immediate with science fiction books such as *The Time Machine* (1895) and *The War of the Worlds* (1898).

As he grew older and his attempts at a political career floundered, his literary works became correspondingly more didactic. But nobody seemed to listen. The world drifted into World War II; he became disillusioned, pessimistic, and eccentric. His last book's message was that "man's scientific advances were totally outdistancing his intellectual and social development."

Though primarily thought of as a science fiction writer, many of his novels evoke considerable horror by focusing on potentially venomous by-products of progress. In addition, he produced several brilliant shorter works of horror, such as "In the Avu Observatory," "The Cone," and the following story of African revenge, "Pollock and the Porroh Man."

POLLOCK AND THE PORROH MAN

*I*t was in a swampy village on the lagoon river behind the Turner Peninsula that Pollock's first encounter with the Porroh man occurred. The women of that country are famous for their good looks—they are Gallinas with a dash of European blood that dates from the days of Vasco da Gama and the English slave-traders, and the Porroh man, too, was possibly inspired by a faint Caucasian taint in his composition. (It's a curious thing to think that some of us may have distant cousins eating men on Sherboro Island or raiding with the Sofas.) At any rate, the Porroh man stabbed the woman to the heart as though he had been a mere low-class Italian, and very narrowly missed Pollock. But Pollock, using his revolver to parry the lightning stab which was aimed at his deltoid muscle, sent the iron dagger flying, and, firing, hit the man in the hand.

He fired again and missed, knocking a sudden window out of the wall of the hut. The Porroh man stooped in the doorway, glancing under his arm at Pollock. Pollock caught a glimpse of his inverted face in the sunlight, and then the Englishman was alone, sick and trembling with the excitement of the affair, in the twilight of the place. It had all happened in less time than it takes to read about it.

The woman was quite dead, and having ascertained this, Pollock went to the entrance of the hut and looked out. Things outside were dazzling bright. Half a dozen of the porters of the expedition were standing up in a group near the green huts they occupied, and staring towards him, wondering what the shots might signify. Behind the little group of men was the broad stretch of black fetid mud by the river, a green carpet of rafts of papyrus and watergrass, and then the leaden water. The mangroves beyond the stream loomed indistinctly through the blue haze. There were no signs of excitement in the squat village, whose fence was just visible above the cane-grass.

Pollock came out of the hut cautiously and walked towards the river, looking over his shoulder at intervals. But the Porroh man had vanished. Pollock clutched his revolver nervously in his hand.

One of his men came to meet him, and as he came, pointed to the bushes behind the hut in which the Porroh man had disappeared. Pollock had an irritating persuasion of having made an absolute fool of himself; he felt bitter, savage, at the turn things had taken. At the same time, he would have to tell Waterhouse—the moral, exemplary, cautious Waterhouse—who would inevitably take the matter seriously. Pollock cursed bitterly at his luck, at Waterhouse, and especially at the West Coast of Africa. He felt consummately sick of the expedition. And in the back of his mind all the time was a speculative doubt where precisely within the visible horizon the Porroh man might be.

It is perhaps rather shocking, but he was not at all upset by the murder that had just happened. He had seen so much brutality during the last three months, so many dead women, burnt huts, drying skeletons, up the Kittam River in the wake of the Sofa cavalry, that his senses were blunted. What disturbed him was the persuasion that this business was only beginning.

He swore savagely at the black, who ventured to ask a question, and went on into the tent under the orange trees where Waterhouse was lying, feeling exasperatingly like a boy going into the headmaster's study.

Waterhouse was still sleeping off the effects of his last dose of chlorodyne, and Pollock sat down on a packing case beside him, and, lighting his pipe, waited for him to awake. About him were scattered the pots and weapons Waterhouse had collected from the Mendi people, and which he had been repacking for the canoe voyage to Sulyma.

Presently Waterhouse woke up, and after judicial stretching, decided he was all right again. Pollock got him some tea. Over the tea the incidents of the afternoon were described by Pollock, after some preliminary beating about the bush. Waterhouse took the matter even more seriously than Pollock had anticipated. He did not simply disapprove, he scolded, he insulted.

"You're one of those infernals who think a black man isn't a human being," he said. "I can't be ill a day without you must get into some dirty scrape or other. This is the third time in a month that you have come crossways-on with a native, and this time you're in for it with a vengeance. Porroh, too! They're down upon you enough as it is, about that idol you wrote your silly name on. And they're the most vindictive devils on earth! You make a man ashamed of civilization. To think you come of a decent family! If ever I cumber myself up with a vicious, stupid young lout like you again—''

"Steady on, now,'' snarled Pollock, in the tone that always exasperated Waterhouse; "steady on.''

At that Waterhouse became speechless. He jumped to his feet.

"Look here, Pollock,'' he said, after a struggle to control his breath. "You must go home. I won't have you any longer. I'm ill enough as it is through you—''

"Keep your hair on,'' said Pollock, staring in front of him. "I'm ready enough to go.''

Waterhouse became calmer again. He sat down on the camp-stool. "Very well,'' he said. "I don't want a row, Pollock, you know; but it's confoundedly annoying to have one's plans put out by this kind of thing. I'll come to Sulyma with you, and see you safe aboard—''

"You needn't,'' said Pollock. "I can go alone. From here.''

"Not far,'' said Waterhouse. "You don't understand this Porroh business.''

"How should *I* know she belonged to a Porroh man?'' said Pollock, bitterly.

"Well, she did,'' said Waterhouse; "and you can't undo the thing. Go alone, indeed! I wonder what they'd do to you. You don't seem to understand that this Porroh hokey-pokey rules this country, is its law, religion, constitution, medicine, magic—They appoint the chiefs. The Inquisition, at its best, couldn't hold a candle to these chaps. He will probably set Awajale, the chief here, onto us. It's lucky our porters are Mendis. We shall have to shift this little settlement of ours—Confound you, Pollock! And, of course, you must go and miss him.''

He thought, and his thoughts seemed disagreeable. Presently he stood up and took his rifle. "I'd keep close for a bit, if I were you,'' he said, over his shoulder, as he went out. "I'm going out to see what I can find out about it.''

Pollock remained sitting in the tent, meditating. "I was meant for a civilized life,'' he said to himself, regretfully, as he filled his pipe. "The sooner I get back to London or Paris the better for me.''

His eye fell on the sealed case in which Waterhouse had put the featherless poisoned arrows they had bought in the Mendi country. "I wish I had hit the beggar somewhere vital," said Pollock, viciously.

Waterhouse came back after a long interval. He was not communicative, though Pollock asked him questions enough. The Porroh man, it seems, was a prominent member of that mystical society. The village was interested, but not threatening. No doubt the witch doctor had gone into the bush. He was a great witch doctor. "Of course, he's up to something," said Waterhouse, and became silent.

"But what can he do?" asked Pollock, unheeded.

"I must get you out of this. There's something brewing, or things would not be so quiet," said Waterhouse, after a gap of silence. Pollock wanted to know what the brew might be. "Dancing in a circle of skulls," said Waterhouse; "brewing a stink in a copper pot." Pollock wanted particulars. Waterhouse was vague, Pollock pressing. At last Waterhouse lost his temper. "How the devil should *I* know?" he said to Pollock's twentieth inquiry what the Porroh man would do. "He tried to kill you offhand in the hut. *Now,* I fancy he will try something more elaborate. But you'll see fast enough. I don't want to help unnerve you. It's probably all nonsense."

That night, as they were sitting at their fire, Pollock again tried to draw Waterhouse out on the subject of Porroh methods. "Better get to sleep," said Waterhouse, when Pollock's bent became apparent; "we start early tomorrow. You may want all your nerve about you."

"But what line will he take?"

"Can't say. They're versatile people. They know a lot of rum dodges. You'd better get that copper devil, Shakespear, to talk."

There was a flash and a heavy bang out of the darkness behind the huts, and a clay bullet came whistling close to Pollock's head. This, at least, was crude enough. The blacks and half-breeds sitting and yarning round their own fire jumped up, and someone fired into the dark.

"Better go into one of the huts," said Waterhouse, quietly, still sitting unmoved.

Pollock stood up by the fire and drew his revolver. Fighting, at least, he was not afraid of. But a man in the dark is in the best of armor. Realizing the wisdom of Waterhouse's advice, Pollock went into the tent and lay down there.

What little sleep he had was disturbed by dreams, variegated dreams, but chiefly of the Porroh man's face, upside down, as he went out of the hut, and looked up under his arm. It was odd that this transitory impression should have stuck so firmly in Pollock's memory. Moreover, he was troubled by queer pains in his limbs.

In the white haze of the early morning, as they were loading the canoes, a barbed arrow suddenly appeared quivering in the ground close to Pollock's foot. The boys made a perfunctory effort to clear out the thicket, but it led to no capture.

After these two occurrences, there was a disposition on the part of the expedition to leave Pollock to himself, and Pollock became, for the first time in his life, anxious to mingle with blacks. Waterhouse took one canoe, and Pollock, in spite of a friendly desire to chat with Waterhouse, had to take the other. He was left all alone in the front part of the canoe, and he had the greatest trouble to make the men—who did not love him—keep to the middle of the river, a clear hundred yards or more from either shore. However, he made Shakespear, the Freetown half-breed, come up to his own end of the canoe and tell him about Porroh, which Shakespear, failing in his attempts to leave Pollock alone, presently did with considerable freedom and gusto.

The day passed. The canoe glided swiftly along the ribbon of lagoon water, between the drift of water figs, fallen trees, papyrus, and palm-wine palms, and with the dark mangrove swamp to the left, through which one could hear now and then the roar of the Atlantic surf. Shakespear told, in his soft blurred English, of how the Porroh could cast spells; how men withered up under their malice; how they could send dreams and devils; how they tormented and killed the sons of Ijibu; how they kidnapped a white trader from Sulyma who had maltreated one of the sect, and how his body looked when it was found. And Pollock after each narrative cursed under his breath at the want of missionary enterprise that allowed such things to be, and at the inert British Government that ruled over this dark heathendom of Sierra Leone. In the evening they came to the Kasi Lake, and sent a score of crocodiles lumbering off the island on which the expedition camped for the night.

The next day they reached Sulyma, and smelt the sea breeze; but Pollock had to put up there for five days before he could get on to Freetown. Waterhouse, considering him to be comparatively safe here, and within the pale of Freetown influence, left him and went back with the expedition to Gbemma, and Pollock became very friendly with

Perera, the only resident white trader at Sulyma—so friendly, indeed, that he went about with him everywhere. Perera was a little Portuguese Jew, who had lived in England, and he appreciated the Englishman's friendliness as a great compliment.

For two days nothing happened out of the ordinary; for the most part Pollock and Perera played Nap—the only game they had in common— and Pollock got into debt. Then, on the second evening, Pollock had a disagreeable intimation of the arrival of the Porroh man in Sulyma by getting a flesh wound in the shoulder from a lump of filed iron. It was a long shot, and the missile had nearly spent its force when it hit him. Still it conveyed its message plainly enough. Pollock sat up in his hammock, revolver in hand, all that night, and next morning confided, to some extent, in the Anglo-Portuguese.

Perera took the matter seriously. He knew the local customs pretty thoroughly. "It is a personal question, you must know. It is revenge. And of course he is hurried by your leaving de country. None of de natives or half-breeds will interfere wid him very much—unless you make it wort deir while. If you come upon him suddenly, you might shoot him. But den he might shoot you.

"Den dere's dis—infernal magic," said Perera. "Of course, I don't believe in it—superstition; but still it's not nice to tink dat wher- ever you are, dere is a black man, who spends a moonlight night now and den a-dancing about a fire to send you bad dreams—Had any bad dreams?"

"Rather," said Pollock. "I keep on seeing the beggar's head upside down grinning at me and showing all his teeth as he did in the hut, and coming close up to me, and then going ever so far off, and coming back. It's nothing to be afraid of, but somehow it simply paralyzes me with terror in my sleep. Queer things—dreams. I know it's a dream all the time, and I can't wake up from it."

"It's probably only fancy," said Perera. "Den my niggers say Porroh men can send snakes. Seen any snakes lately?"

"Only one. I killed him this morning, on the floor near my ham- mock. Almost trod on him as I got up."

"*Ah!*" said Perera, and then, reassuringly, "Of course it is a— coincidence. Still I would keep my eyes open. Den dere's pains in de bones."

"I thought they were due to miasma," said Pollock.

"Probably dey are. When did dey begin?"

Then Pollock remembered that he first noticed them the night after the fight in the hut. "It's my opinion he don't want to kill you," said Perera—"at least not yet. I've heard deir idea is to scare and worry a man wid deir spells, and narrow misses and rheumatic pains, and bad dreams, and all dat, until he's sick of life. Of course, it's all talk, you know. You mustn't worry about it—But I wonder what he'll be up to next."

"*I* shall have to be up to something first," said Pollock, staring gloomily at the greasy cards that Perera was putting on the table. "It don't suit my dignity to be followed about, and shot at, and blighted in this way. I wonder if Porroh hokey-pokey upsets your luck at cards."

He looked at Perera suspiciously.

"Very likely it does," said Perera, warmly, shuffling. "Dey are wonderful people."

That afternoon Pollock killed two snakes in his hammock, and there was also an extraordinary increase in the number of red ants that swarmed over the place; and these annoyances put him in a fit temper to talk over business with a certain Mendi rough he had interviewed before. The Mendi rough showed Pollock a little iron dagger, and demonstrated where one struck in the neck, in a way that made Pollock shiver; and in return for certain considerations Pollock promised him a double-barreled gun with an ornamental lock.

In the evening, as Pollock and Perera were playing cards, the Mendi rough came in through the doorway, carrying something in a blood-soaked piece of native cloth.

"Not here!" said Pollock, very hurriedly. "Not here!"

But he was not quick enough to prevent the man, who was anxious to get to Pollock's side of the bargain, from opening the cloth and throwing the head of the Porroh man upon the table. It bounded from there on to the floor, leaving a red trail on the cards, and rolled into a corner, where it came to rest upside down, but glaring hard at Pollock.

Perera jumped up as the thing fell among the cards, and began in his excitement to gabble in Portuguese. The Mendi was bowing, with the red cloth in his hand. "De gun!" he said. Pollock stared back at the head in the corner. It bore exactly the expression it had in his dreams. Something seemed to snap in his own brain as he looked at it.

Then Perera found his English again.

"You got him killed?" he said. "You did not kill him yourself?"

"Why should I?" said Pollock.

"But he will not be able to take it off now!"

"Take *what* off?" said Pollock.

"And all dese cards are spoiled!"

"*What* do you mean by taking it off?" said Pollock.

"You must send me a new pack from Freetown. You can buy dem dere."

"But—'take it off'?"

"It is only superstition. I forgot. De niggers say dat if de witches—he was a witch—But it is rubbish—You must make de Porroh man take it off, or kill him yourself—It is very silly."

Pollock swore under his breath, still staring hard at the head in the corner.

"I can't stand that glare," he said. Then suddenly he rushed at the thing and kicked it. It rolled some yards or so, and came to rest in the same position as before, upside down, and looking at him.

"He is ugly," said the Anglo-Portuguese. "Very ugly. Dey do it on deir faces with little knives."

Pollock would have kicked the head again, but the Mendi man touched him on the arm. "De gun?" he said, looking nervously at the head.

"Two—if you will take that beastly thing away," said Pollock.

The Mendi man shook his head, and intimated that he only wanted one gun now due to him, and for which he would be obliged. Pollock found neither cajolery nor bullying any good with him. Perera had a gun to sell (at a profit of three hundred percent), and with that the man presently departed. Then Pollock's eyes, against his will, were recalled to the thing on the floor.

"It is funny dat his head keeps upside down," said Perera, with an uneasy laugh. "His brains must be heavy, like de weight in de little images one sees dat keep always upright wid lead in dem. You will take him wiv you when you go presently. You might take him now. De cards are all spoilt. Dere is a man sell dem in Freetown. De room is in a filty mess as it is. You should have killed him yourself."

Pollock pulled himself together, and went and picked up the head. He would hang it up by the lamp-hook in the middle of the ceiling of his room, and dig a grave for it at once. He was under the impression that he hung it up by the hair, but that must have been wrong, for when he returned for it, it was hanging by the neck upside down.

He buried it before sunset on the north side of the shed he occupied, so that he should not have to pass the grave after dark when he was returning from Perera's. He killed two snakes before he went to sleep. In the darkest part of the night he awoke with a start, and heard a pattering sound and something scraping on the floor. He sat up noiselessly, and felt under his pillow for his revolver. A mumbling growl followed, and Pollock fired at the sound. There was a yelp, and something dark passed for a moment across the hazy blue of the doorway. "A dog!" said Pollock, lying down again.

In the early dawn he awoke again with a peculiar sense of unrest. The vague pain in his bones had returned. For some time he lay watching the red ants that were swarming over the ceiling, and then, as the light grew brighter, he looked over the edge of his hammock and saw something dark on the floor. He gave such a violent start that the hammock overset and flung him out.

He found himself lying, perhaps, a yard away from the head of the Porroh man. It had been disinterred by the dog, and the nose was grievously battered. Ants and flies swarmed over it. By an odd coincidence, it was still upside down, and with the same diabolical expression in the inverted eyes.

Pollock sat paralyzed, and stared at the horror for some time. Then he got up and walked round it—giving it a wide berth—and out of the shed. The clear light of the sunrise, the living stir of vegetation before the breath of the dying land breeze, and the empty grave with the marks of the dog's paws, lightened the weight upon his mind a little.

He told Perera of the business as though it was a jest—a jest to be told with white lips. "You should not have frighten de dog," said Perera, with poorly simulated hilarity.

The next two days, until the steamer came, were spent by Pollock in making a more effectual disposition of his possession. Overcoming his aversion to handling the thing, he went down to the river mouth and threw it into the sea water, but by some miracle it escaped the crocodiles, and was cast up by the tide on the mud a little way up the river, to be found by an intelligent Arab half-breed, and offered for sale to Pollock and Perera as a curiosity, just on the edge of night. The native hung about in the brief twilight, making lower and lower offers, and at last, getting scared in some way by the evident dread these wise white men had for the thing, went off, and, passing Pollock's shed, threw his burden in there for Pollock to discover in the morning.

At this Pollock got into a kind of frenzy. He would burn the thing. He went out straightway into the dawn, and had constructed a big pyre of brushwood before the heat of the day. He was interrupted by the hooter of the little paddle steamer from Monrovia to Bathurst, which was coming through the gap in the bar. ''Thank Heaven!'' said Pollock, with infinite piety, when the meaning of the sound dawned upon him. With trembling hands he lit his pile of wood hastily, threw the head upon it, and went away to pack his portmanteau and make his adieux to Perera.

That afternoon, with a sense of infinite relief, Pollock watched the flat swampy foreshore of Sulyma grow small in the distance. The gap in the long line of white surge became narrower and narrower. It seemed to be closing in and cutting him off from his trouble. The feeling of dread and worry began to slip from him bit by bit. At Sulyma belief in Porroh malignity and Porroh magic had been in the air, his sense of Porroh had been vast, pervading, threatening, dreadful. Now manifestly the domain of Porroh was only a little place, a little black band between the sea and the blue cloudy Mendi uplands.

''Good-bye, Porroh!'' said Pollock. ''Good-bye—certainly not *au revoir.*''

The captain of the steamer came and leant over the rail beside him, and wished him good evening, and spat at the froth of the wake in token of friendly ease.

''I picked up a rummy curio on the beach this go,'' said the captain. ''It's a thing I never saw done this side of Indy before.''

''What might that be?'' said Pollock.

''Pickled 'ed,'' said the captain.

''*What?*'' said Pollock.

'''Ed—smoked. 'Ed of one of these Porroh chaps, all ornamented with knife-cuts. Why! What's up? Nothing? I shouldn't have took you for a nervous chap. Green in the face. By gosh! you're a bad sailor. All right, eh? Lord, how funny you went! Well, this 'ed I was telling you of is a bit rum in a way. I've got it, along with some snakes, in a jar of spirit in my cabin what I keeps for such curios, and I'm hanged if it don't float upsy down. Hullo!''

Pollock had given an incoherent cry, and had his hands in his hair.

He ran towards the paddle-boxes with a half-formed idea of jumping into the sea, and then he realized his position and turned back toward the captain.

"Here!" said the captain. "Jack Philips, just keep him off me! Stand off! No nearer, mister! What's the matter with you? Are you mad?"

Pollock put his hand to his head. It was no good explaining. "I believe I am pretty nearly mad at times," he said. "It's a pain I have here. Comes suddenly. You'll excuse me, I hope."

He was white and in a perspiration. He saw suddenly very clearly all the danger he ran of having his sanity doubted. He forced himself to restore the captain's confidence, by answering his sympathetic inquiries, noting suggestions, even trying a spoonful of neat brandy in his cheek, and, that matter settled, asking a number of questions about the captain's private trade in curiosities. The captain described the head in detail. All the while Pollock was struggling to keep under a preposterous persuasion that the ship was as transparent as glass, and that he could distinctly see the inverted face looking at him from the cabin beneath his feet.

Pollock had a worse time almost on the steamer than he had at Sulyma. All day he had to control himself in spite of his intense perception of the imminent presence of that horrible head that was overshadowing his mind. At night his old nightmare returned, until, with a violent effort, he would force himself awake, rigid with the horror of it, and with the ghost of a hoarse scream in his throat.

He left the actual head behind at Bathurst, where he changed ship for Teneriffe, but not his dreams nor the dull ache in his bones. At Teneriffe Pollock transferred to a Cape liner, but the head followed him. He gambled, he tried chess, he even read books; but he knew the danger of drink. Yet whenever a round black shadow, a round black object came into his range, there he looked for the head, and—saw it. He knew clearly enough that his imagination was growing traitor to him, and yet at times it seemed the ship he sailed in, his fellow passengers, the sailors, the wide sea, was all part of a filmy phantasmagoria that hung, scarcely veiling it, between him and a horrible real world. Then the Porroh man, thrusting his diabolical face through that curtain, was the one real and undeniable thing. At that he would get up and touch things, taste something, gnaw something, burn his hand with a match, or run a needle into himself.

So, struggling grimly and silently with his excited imagination, Pollock reached England. He landed at Southampton, and went on straight from Waterloo to his banker's in Cornhill in a cab. There he transacted some business with the manager in a private room; and all the while the head hung like an ornament under the black marble mantel and dripped upon the fender. He could hear the drops fall, and see the red on the fender.

"A pretty fern," said the manager, following his eyes. "But it makes the fender rusty."

"Very," said Pollock; "a *very* pretty fern. And that reminds me. Can you recommend me a physician for mind troubles? I've got a little—what is it?—hallucination."

The head laughed savagely, wildly. Pollock was surprised the manager did not notice it. But the manager only stared at his face.

With the address of a doctor, Pollock presently emerged in Cornhill. There was no cab in sight, and so he went on down to the western end of the street, and essayed the crossing opposite the Mansion House. The crossing is hardly easy even for the expert Londoner; cabs, vans, carriages, mail-carts, omnibuses go by in one incessant stream; to any one fresh from the malarious solitudes of Sierra Leone it is a boiling, maddening confusion. But when an inverted head suddenly comes bouncing, like an india-rubber ball, between your legs, leaving distinct smears of blood every time it touches the ground, you can scarcely hope to avoid an accident. Pollock lifted his feet convulsively to avoid it, and then kicked at the thing furiously. Then something hit him violently in the back, and a hot pain ran up his arm.

He had been hit by the pole of an omnibus, and three of the fingers of his left hand smashed by the hoof of one of the horses—the very fingers, as it happened, that he shot from the Porroh man. They pulled him out from between the horse's legs, and found the address of the physician in his crushed hand.

For a couple of days Pollock's sensations were full of the sweet, pungent smell of chloroform, of painful operations that caused him no pain, of lying still and being given food and drink. Then he had a slight fever, and was very thirsty, and his old nightmare came back. It was only when it returned that he noticed it had left him for a day.

"If my skull had been smashed instead of my fingers, it might have gone altogether," said Pollock, staring thoughtfully at the dark cushion that had taken on for the time the shape of the head.

Pollock at the first opportunity told the physician of his mind trouble. He knew clearly that he must go mad unless something should intervene to save him. He explained that he had witnessed a decapitation in Dahomey, and was haunted by one of the heads. Naturally he did not care to state the facts. The physician looked grave.

Presently he spoke hesitatingly. "As a child, did you get very much religious training?"

"Very little," said Pollock.

A shade passed over the physician's face. "I don't know if you have heard of the miraculous cures—it may be, of course, they are not miraculous—at Lourdes."

"Faith healing will hardly suit me, I am afraid," said Pollock, with his eye on the dark cushion.

The head distorted its scarred features in an abominable grimace. The physician went upon a new track. "It's all imagination," he said, speaking with sudden briskness. "A fair case for faith healing, anyhow. Your nervous system has run down, you're in that twilight state of health when the bogles come easiest. The strong impression was too much for you. I must make you up a little mixture that will strengthen your nervous system—especially your brain. And you must take exercise."

"I'm no good for faith healing," said Pollock.

"And therefore we must restore tone. Go in search of stimulating air—Scotland, the Alps—"

"Jericho, if you like," said Pollock, "where Naaman went."

However, so soon as his fingers would let him, Pollock made a gallant attempt to follow out the doctor's suggestion. It was now November. He tried football; but to Pollock the game consisted in kicking a furious inverted head about a field. He was no good at the game. He kicked blindly, with a kind of horror, and when they put him back into goal, and the ball came swooping down upon him, he suddenly yelled and got out of its way. The discreditable stories that had driven him from England to wander in the tropics shut him off from any but men's society, and now his increasingly strange behavior made even his man friends avoid him. The thing was no longer a thing of the eye merely; it gibbered at him, spoke to him. A horrible fear came upon him that presently, when he took hold of the apparition, it would no longer become some mere article of furniture, but would *feel* like a real dissevered head. Alone, he would curse at the thing, defy it, entreat it; once or twice, in spite of his grim self-control, he addressed it in the presence of others. He felt the growing suspicion in the eyes of the people that watched him—his landlady, the servant, his man.

One day early in December his cousin Arnold—his next of kin—came to see him and draw him out, and watch his sunken, yellow face with narrow, eager eyes. And it seemed to Pollock that the hat his cousin carried in his hand was no hat at all, but a Gorgon head that glared at him upside down, and fought with its eyes against his reason. However, he was still resolute to see the matter out. He got a bicycle, and, riding over the frosty road from Wandsworth to Kingston, found the thing rolling along at his side, and leaving a dark trail behind it. He set his teeth and rode faster. Then suddenly, as he came down the hill toward Richmond Park, the apparition rolled in front of him and under his wheel, so quickly that he had no time for thought, and, turning quickly to avoid it, was flung violently against a heap of stones and broke his left wrist.

The end came on Christmas morning. All night he had been in a fever, the bandages encircling his wrist like a band of fire, his dreams more vivid and terrible than ever. In the cold, colorless, uncertain light that came before the sunrise, he sat up in his bed, and saw the head upon the bracket in the place of the bronze jar that had stood there overnight.

"I know that is a bronze jar," he said, with a chill doubt at his heart. Presently the doubt was irresistible. He got out of bed slowly, shivering, and advanced to the jar with his hand raised. Surely he would see now his imagination had deceived him, recognize the distinctive sheen of bronze. At last, after an age of hesitation, his fingers came down on the patterned cheek of the head. He withdrew them spasmodically. The last stage was reached. His sense of touch had betrayed him.

Trembling, stumbling against the bed, kicking against his shoes with his bare feet, a dark confusion eddying round him, he groped his way to the dressing table, took his razor from the drawer, and sat down on the bed with this in his hand. In the looking glass he saw his own face, colorless, haggard, full of the ultimate bitterness of despair.

He beheld in swift succession the incidents in the brief tale of his experience. His wretched home, his still more wretched schooldays, the years of vicious life he had led since then, one act of selfish dishonor leading to another; it was all clear and pitiless now, all its squalid folly, in the cold light of the dawn. He came to the hut, to the fight with the Porroh man, to the retreat down the river to Sulyma, to the Mendi assassin and his red parcel, to his frantic endeavors to destroy the head, to the growth of his hallucination. It was a hallucination! He *knew* it was. A hallucination merely. For a moment he snatched at hope. He looked away from the glass, and on the bracket, the inverted head grinned and grimaced at him—With the stiff fingers of his bandaged hand he felt at his neck for the throb of his arteries. The morning was very cold, the steel blade felt like ice.

Sir Arthur Conan Doyle (1859–1930)

Born in Edinburgh, Scotland, Doyle was a lover of sports and outdoor life. He had a sturdy build, a plain, honest face, and was courageous and tenacious in temperament. In 1879 he began writing and studying medicine at the University of Edinburgh.

He graduated in 1881, but could not build a successful practice, so he signed on as ship's doctor for an Arctic whaler and African steamer, and continued writing.

In 1891, writing won out. *The Strand Magazine*, impressed by his first Sherlock Holmes novel, *A Study in Scarlet* (1882), commissioned Doyle to write a series of Holmes stories. These tales were wildly popular and provided their creator with financial security.

Thereafter he dabbled in current affairs and nonfiction, with mixed results. His political campaigns—in 1900 and 1906 he stood for Parliament—were unsuccessful. But his two books explaining and justifying the Boer War (*The Great Boer War*, 1900, and *The War in South Africa: Its Cause and Conduct*, 1902) earned him knighthood.

When his son Kingsley died in World War I, Doyle became an avid spiritualist and redirected his talents, spending much of the remainder of his life penning books about psychic phenomena and the existence of an afterlife.

His numerous tales of terror include realistic, science fictional, and fantastic examples. Many can be found in *Tales of Terror and Mystery* (1977), *The Best Science Fiction of Arthur Conan Doyle* (1981), and *The Best Supernatural Stories of Arthur Conan Doyle* (1979). From the first collection comes "The Story of the Brazilian Cat," a graphic depiction of man against beast.

THE STORY OF THE BRAZILIAN CAT

*I*t *is hard luck on a young fellow to have expensive tastes, great* expectations, aristocratic connections, but no actual money in his pocket, and no profession by which he may earn any. The fact was that my father, a good, sanguine, easy-going man, had such confidence in the wealth and benevolence of his bachelor elder brother, Lord Southerton, that he took it for granted that I, his only son, would never be called upon to earn a living for myself. He imagined that if there were not a vacancy for me on the great Southerton Estates, at least there would be found some post in that diplomatic service which still remains the special preserve of our privileged classes. He died too early to realize how false his calculations had been. Neither my uncle nor the State took the slightest notice of me, or showed any interest in my career. An occasional brace of pheasants, or basket of hares, was all that ever reached me to remind me that I was heir to Otwell House and one of the richest estates in the country. In the meantime, I found myself a bachelor and man about town, living in a suite of apartments in Grosvenor Mansions, with no occupation save that of pigeon-shooting and polo-playing at Hurlingham. Month by month I realized that it was more and more difficult to get the brokers to renew my bills, or to cash any further post-obits upon an unentailed property. Ruin lay right across my path, and every day I saw it clearer, nearer, and more absolutely unavoidable.

What made me feel my own poverty the more was that, apart from the great wealth of Lord Southerton, all my other relations were fairly well-to-do. The nearest of these was Everard King, my father's nephew and my own first cousin, who had spent an adventurous life in Brazil, and had now returned to this country to settle down on his fortune. We never knew how he made his money, but he appeared to have plenty of it, for he bought the estate of Greylands, near Clipton-on-the-Marsh, in Suffolk. For the first year of his residence in England he took no more notice of me than my miserly uncle; but at last one summer morning, to my very great relief and joy, I received a letter asking me to come down that very day and spend a short visit at Greylands Court. I was expecting a rather long visit to Bankruptcy Court at the time, and this interruption seemed almost providential. If I could only get on terms with this unknown relative of mine, I might pull through yet. For the family credit he could not let me go entirely to the wall. I ordered my valet to pack my valise, and I set off the same evening for Clipton-on-the-Marsh.

After changing at Ipswich, a little local train deposited me at a small, deserted station lying amidst a rolling grassy country, with a sluggish and winding river curving in and out amidst the valleys, between high, silted banks, which showed that we were within reach of the tide. No carriage was awaiting me (I found afterwards that my telegram had been delayed), so I hired a dogcart at the local inn. The driver, an excellent fellow, was full of my relative's praises, and I learned from him that Mr. Everard King was already a name to conjure with in that part of the country. He had entertained the school-children, he had thrown his grounds open to visitors, he had subscribed to charities—in short, his benevolence had been so universal that my driver could only account for it on the supposition that he had Parliamentary ambitions.

My attention was drawn away from my driver's panegyric by the appearance of a very beautiful bird which settled on a telegraph-post beside the road. At first I thought that it was a jay, but it was larger, with a brighter plumage. The driver accounted for its presence at once by saying that it belonged to the very man whom we were about to visit. It seems that the acclimatization of foreign creatures was one of his hobbies, and that he had brought with him from Brazil a number of birds and beasts which he was endeavoring to rear in England. When once we had passed the gates of Greylands Park we had ample evidence of this taste of his. Some small spotted deer, a curious wild pig known, I believe, as a peccary, a gorgeously feathered oriole, some sort of armadillo, and a singular lumbering intoed beast like a very fat badger, were among the creatures which I observed as we drove along the winding avenue.

Mr. Everard King, my unknown cousin, was standing in person

upon the steps of his house, for he had seen us in the distance, and guessed that it was I. His appearance was very homely and benevolent, short and stout, forty-five years old, perhaps, with a round, good-humored face, burned brown with the tropical sun, and shot with a thousand wrinkles. He wore white linen clothes, in true planter style, with a cigar between his lips, and a large Panama hat upon the back of his head. It was such a figure as one associates with a verandaed bungalow, and it looked curiously out of place in front of this broad, stone English mansion, with its solid wings and its Palladio pillars over the doorway.

"My dear!" he cried, glancing over his shoulder; "my dear, here is our guest! Welcome, welcome to Greylands! I am delighted to make your acquaintance, Cousin Marshall, and I take it as a great compliment that you should honor this sleepy little country place with your presence."

Nothing could be more hearty than his manner, and he set me at my ease in an instant. But it needed all his cordiality to atone for the frigidity and even rudeness of his wife, a tall, haggard woman, who came forward at his summons. She was, I believe, of Brazilian extraction, though she spoke excellent English, and I excused her manners on the score of her ignorance of our customs. She did not attempt to conceal, however, either then or afterward, that I was no very welcome visitor at Greylands Court. Her actual words were, as a rule, courteous, but she was the possessor of a pair of particularly expressive dark eyes, and I read in them very clearly from the first that she heartily wished me back in London once more.

However, my debts were too pressing and my designs upon my wealthy relative were too vital for me to allow them to be upset by the ill-temper of his wife, so I disregarded her coldness and reciprocated the extreme cordiality of his welcome. No pains had been spared by him to make me comfortable. My room was a charming one. He implored me to tell him anything which could add to my happiness. It was on the tip of my tongue to inform him that a blank cheque would materially help toward that end, but I felt that it might be premature in the present state of our acquaintance. The dinner was excellent, and as we sat together afterward over his Havanas and coffee, which later he told me was specially prepared upon his own plantation, it seemed to me that all my driver's eulogies were justified, and that I had never met a more large-hearted and hospitable man.

But, in spite of his cheery good nature, he was a man with a strong will and a fiery temper of his own. Of this I had an example upon the following morning. The curious aversion which Mrs. Everard King had conceived toward me was so strong, that her manner at breakfast was almost offensive. But her meaning became unmistakable when her husband had quitted the room.

"The best train in the day is at twelve-fifteen," said she.

"But I was not thinking of going today," I answered, frankly—perhaps even defiantly, for I was determined not to be driven out by this woman.

"Oh, if it rests with you—" said she, and stopped with a most insolent expression in her eyes.

"I am sure," I answered, "that Mr. Everard King would tell me if I were outstaying my welcome."

"What's this? What's this?" said a voice, and there he was in the room. He had overheard my last words, and a glance at our faces had told him the rest. In an instant his chubby, cheery face set into an expression of absolute ferocity;.

"Might I trouble you to walk outside, Marshall?" said he. (I may mention that my own name is Marshall King.)

He closed the door behind me, and then, for an instant, I heard him talking in a low voice of concentrated passion to his wife. This gross breach of hospitality had evidently hit upon his tenderest point. I am no eavesdropper, so I walked out on to the lawn. Presently I heard a hurried step behind me, and there was the lady, her face pale with excitement, and her eyes red with tears.

"My husband has asked me to apologize to you, Mr. Marshall King," said she, standing with downcast eyes before me.

"Please do not say another word, Mrs. King."

Her dark eyes suddenly blazed out at me.

"You fool!" she hissed, with frantic vehemence, and turning on her heel swept back to the house.

The insult was so outrageous, so insufferable, that I could only stand staring after her in bewilderment. I was still there when my host joined me. He was his cheery, chubby self once more.

"I hope that my wife has apologized for her foolish remarks," said he.

"Oh, yes—yes, certainly!"

He put his hand through my arm and walked with me up and down the lawn.

"You must not take it seriously," said he. "It would grieve me inexpressibly if you curtailed your visit by one hour. The fact is—there is no reason why there should be any concealment between relatives—that my poor dear wife is incredibly jealous. She hates that anyone—male or female—should for an instant come between us. Her ideal is a desert island and an eternal *tête-à-tête*. That gives you the clue to her actions, which are, I confess, upon this particular point, not very far removed from mania. Tell me that you will think no more of it."

"No, no; certainly not."

"Then light this cigar and come round with me and see my little menagerie."

The whole afternoon was occupied by this inspection, which included all the birds, beasts, and even reptiles which he had imported. Some were free, some in cages, a few actually in the house. He spoke with enthusiasm of his successes and his failures, his births and his deaths, and he would cry out in his delight, like a schoolboy, when, as we walked, some gaudy bird would flutter up from the grass, or some curious beast slink into the cover. Finally he led me down a corridor which extended from one wing of the house. At the end of this there was a heavy door with a sliding shutter in it, and beside it there projected from the wall an iron handle attached to a wheel and a drum. A line of stout bars extended across the passage.

"I am about to show you the jewel of my collection," said he. "There is only one other specimen in Europe, now that the Rotterdam cub is dead. It is a Brazilian cat."

"But how does that differ from any other cat?"

"You will soon see that," said he, laughing. "Will you kindly draw that shutter and look through?"

I did so, and found that I was gazing into a large, empty room, with stone flags, and small, barred windows upon the farther wall. In the center of this room, lying in the middle of a golden patch of sunlight, there was stretched a huge creature, as large as a tiger, but as black and sleek as ebony. It was simply a very enormous and very well-kept black cat, and it cuddled up and basked in that yellow pool of light exactly as a cat would do. It was so graceful, so sinewy, and so gently and smoothly diabolical, that I could not take my eyes from the opening.

"Isn't he splendid?" said my host, enthusiastically.

"Glorious! I never saw such a noble creature."

"Some people call it a black puma, but really it is not a puma at all. That fellow is nearly eleven feet from tail to tip. Four years ago he was a little ball of black fluff, with two yellow eyes staring out of it. He was sold me as a new-born cub up in the wild country at the headwaters of the Rio Negro. They speared his mother to death after she had killed a dozen of them."

"They are ferocious, then?"

"The most absolutely treacherous and bloodthirsty creatures upon earth. You talk about a Brazilian cat to an up-country Indian, and see him get the jumps. They prefer humans to game. This fellow has never tasted living blood yet, but when he does he will be a terror. At present he won't stand anyone but me in his den. Even Baldwin, the groom, dare not go near him. As to me, I am his mother and father in one."

As he spoke he suddenly, to my astonishment, opened the door and slipped in, closing it instantly behind him. At the sound of his voice the huge, lithe creature rose, yawned and rubbed its round, black head affectionately against his side, while he patted and fondled it.

"Now, Tommy, into your cage!" said he.

The monstrous cat walked over to one side of the room and coiled itself up under a grating. Everard King came out, and taking the iron handle which I have mentioned, he began to turn it. As he did so the line of bars in the corridor began to pass through a slot in the wall and closed up the front of this grating, so as to make an effective cage. When it was in position he opened the door once more and invited me into the room, which was heavy with the pungent, musty smell peculiar to the great carnivora.

"That's how we work it," said he. "We give him the run of the room for exercise, and then at night we put him in his cage. You can let him out by turning the handle from the passage, or you can, as you have seen, coop him up in the same way. No, no, you should not do that!"

I had put my hand between the bars to pat the glossy, heaving flank. He pulled it back, with a serious face.

"I assure you that he is not safe. Don't imagine that because I can take liberties with him anyone else can. He is very exclusive with his friends—aren't you, Tommy? Ah, he hears his lunch coming to him! Don't you, boy?"

A step sounded in the stone-flagged passage, and the creature had sprung to his feet, and was pacing up and down the narrow cage, his yellow eyes gleaming, and his scarlet tongue rippling and quivering over the white line of his jagged teeth. A groom entered with a coarse joint upon a tray, and thrust it through the bars to him. He pounced lightly upon it, carried it off to the corner, and there, holding it between his paws, tore and wrenched at it, raising his bloody muzzle every now and then to look at us. It was a malignant and yet fascinating sight.

"You can't wonder that I am fond of him, can you?" said my host, as we left the room, "especially when you consider that I have had the rearing of him. It was no joke bringing him over from the center of South America; but here he is safe and sound—and, as I have said, far the most perfect specimen in Europe. The people at the Zoo are dying to have him, but I really can't part with him. Now, I think that I have inflicted my hobby upon you long enough, so we cannot do better than follow Tommy's example, and go to our lunch."

My South American relative was so engrossed by his grounds and their curious occupants, that I hardly gave him credit at first for having any interests outside them. That he had some, and pressing ones, was soon borne in upon me by the number of telegrams which he received. They arrived at all hours, and were always opened by him with the utmost eagerness and anxiety upon his face. Sometimes I imagined that it must be the Turf, and sometimes the Stock Exchange, but certainly he had some very urgent business going forward which was not transacted upon the Downs of Suffolk. During the six days of my visit he had never fewer than three or four telegrams a day, and sometimes as many as seven or eight.

I had occupied these six days so well, that by the end of them I had succeeded in getting upon the most cordial terms with my cousin. Every night we had sat up late in the billiard room, he telling me the most extraordinary stories of his adventures in America—stories so desperate and reckless, that I could hardly associate them with the brown little chubby man before me. In return, I ventured upon some of my own reminiscences of London life, which interested him so much, that he vowed he would come up to Grosvenor Mansions and stay with me. He was anxious to see the faster side of city life, and certainly, though I say it, he could not have chosen a more competent guide. It was not until the last day of my visit that I ventured to approach that which was on my mind. I told him frankly about my pecuniary difficulties and my impending ruin, and I asked his advice—though I hoped for something more solid. He listened attentively, puffing hard at his cigar.

"But surely," said he, "you are the heir of our relative, Lord Southerton?"

"I have every reason to believe so, but he would never make me any allowance."

"No, no, I have heard of his miserly ways. My poor Marshall, your position has been a very hard one. By the way, have you heard any news of Lord Southeron's health lately?"

"He has always been in a critical condition ever since my childhood."

"Exactly—a creaking hinge, if ever there was one. Your inheritance may be a long way off. Dear me, how awkwardly situated you are!"

"I had some hopes, sir, that you, knowing all the facts, might be inclined to advance . . . "

"Don't say another word, my dear boy," he cried, with the utmost cordiality; "we shall talk it over tonight, and I give you my word that whatever is in my power shall be done."

I was not sorry that my visit was drawing to a close, for it is unpleasant to feel that there is one person in the house who eagerly desires your departure. Mrs. King's sallow face and forbidding eyes had become more and more hateful to me. She was no longer actively rude—her fear of her husband prevented her—but she pushed her insane jealousy to the extent of ignoring me, never addressing me, and in every way making my stay at Greylands as uncomfortable as she could. So offensive was her manner that last day, that I should certainly have left had it not been for that interview with my host in the evening which would, I hoped, retrieve my broken fortunes.

It was very late when it occurred, for my relative, who had been receiving even more telegrams than usual during the day, went off to his study after dinner, and only emerged when the household had retired to bed. I heard him go round locking the doors, as custom was of a night, and finally he joined me in the billiard room. His stout figure was wrapped in a dressing gown, and he wore a pair of red Turkish slippers without any heels. Settling down into an armchair, he brewed himself a glass of grog, in which I could not help noticing that the whiskey considerably predominated over the water.

"My word!" said he, "what a night!"

It was, indeed. The wind was howling and screaming round the house, and the latticed windows rattled and shook as if they were coming in. The glow of the yellow lamps and the flavor of our cigars seemed the brighter and more fragrant for the contrast.

"Now, my boy," said my host, "we have the house and the night to ourselves. Let me have an idea of how your affairs stand, and I will see what can be done to set them in order. I wish to hear every detail."

Thus encouraged, I entered into a long exposition, in which all my tradesmen and creditors from my landlord to my valet, figured in turn. I had notes in my pocket book, and I marshalled my facts, and gave, I flatter myself, a very businesslike statement of my own unbusinesslike ways and lamentable position. I was depressed, however, to notice that my companion's eyes were vacant and his attention elsewhere. When he did occasionally throw out a remark it was so entirely perfunctory and pointless, that I was sure he had not in the least followed my remarks. Every now and then he roused himself and put on some show of interest, asking me to repeat or to explain more fully, but it was always to sink once more into the same brown study. At last he rose and threw the end of his cigar into the grate.

"I'll tell you what, my boy," said he. "I never had a head for figures, so you will excuse me. You must jot it all down upon paper, and let me have a note of the amount. I'll understand it when I see it in black and white."

The proposal was encouraging. I promised to do so.

"And now it's time we were in bed. By Jove, there's one o'clock striking in the hall."

The tingling of the chiming clock broke through the deep roar of the gale. The wind was sweeping past with the rush of a great river.

"I must see my cat before I go to bed," said my host. "A high wind excites him. Will you come?"

"Certainly," said I.

"Then tread softly and don't speak, for everyone is asleep."

We passed quietly down the lamp-lit Persian-rugged hall, and through the door at the farther end. All was dark in the stone corridor, but a stable lantern hung on a hook, and my host took it down and lit it. There was no grating visible in the passage, so I knew that the beast was in its cage.

"Come in!" said my relative, and opened the door.

A deep growling as we entered showed that the storm had really excited the creature. In the flickering light of the lantern, we saw it, a huge black mass coiled in the corner of its den and throwing a squat, uncouth shadow upon the whitewashed wall. Its tail switched angrily among the straw.

"Poor Tommy is not in the best of tempers," said Everard King, holding up the lantern and looking in at him. "What a black devil he looks, doesn't he? I must give him a little supper to put him in a better humor. Would you mind holding the lantern for a moment?"

I took it from his hand and he stepped to the door.

"His larder is just outside here," said he. "You will excuse me for an instant, won't you?" He passed out, and the door shut with a sharp metallic click behind him.

That hard crisp sound made my heart stand still. A sudden wave of terror passed over me. A vague perception of some monstrous treachery turned me cold. I sprang to the door, but there was no handle upon the inner side.

"Here!" I cried. "Let me out!"

"All right! Don't make a row!" said my host from the passage. "You've got the light all right."

"Yes, but I don't care about being locked in alone like this."

"Don't you?" I heard his hearty, chuckling laugh. "You won't be alone long."

"Let me out, sir!" I repeated angrily. "I tell you I don't allow practical jokes of this sort."

"Practical is the word," said he, with another hateful chuckle. And then suddenly I heard, amidst the roar of the storm, the creak and whine of the winch-handle turning and the rattle of the grating as it passed through the slot. Great God, he was letting loose the Brazilian cat!

In the light of the lantern I saw the bars sliding slowly before me. Already there was an opening a foot wide at the farther end. With a scream I seized the last bar with my hands and pulled with the strength of a madman. I *was* a madman with rage and horror. For a minute or more I held the thing motionless. I knew that he was straining with all his force upon the handle, and that the leverage was sure to overcome me. I gave inch by inch, my feet sliding along the stones, and all the time I begged and prayed this inhuman monster to save me from this horrible death. I conjured him by his kinship. I reminded him that I was his guest; I begged to know what harm I had ever done him. His only answers were the tugs and jerks upon the handle, each of which, in spite of all my struggles, pulled another bar through the opening. Clinging and clutching, I was dragged across the whole front of the cage, until at last, with aching wrists and lacerated fingers, I gave up the hopeless struggle. The grating clanged back as I released it, and an instant later I heard the shuffle of the Turkish slippers in the passage, and the slam of the distant door. Then everything was silent.

The creature had never moved during this time. He lay still in the corner, and his tail had ceased switching. This apparition of a man adhering to his bars and dragged screaming across him had apparently filled him with amazement. I saw his great eyes staring steadily at me. I had dropped the lantern when I seized the bars, but it still burned upon the floor, and I made a movement to grasp it, with some idea that its light might protect me. But the instant I moved, the beast gave a deep and menacing growl. I stopped and stood still, quivering with fear in every limb. The cat (if one may call so fearful a creature by so homely a name) was not more than ten feet from me. The eyes glimmered like two disks of phosphorus in the darkness. They appalled and yet fascinated me. I could not take my own eyes from them. Nature plays strange tricks with us at such moments of intensity, and those glimmering lights waxed and waned with a steady rise and fall. Sometimes they seemed to be tiny points of extreme brilliancy—little electric sparks in the black obscurity —then they would widen and widen until all that corner of the room was filled with their shifting and sinister light. And then suddenly they went out altogether.

The beast had closed its eyes. I do not know whether there may be any truth in the old idea of the dominance of the human gaze, or whether the huge cat was simply drowsy, but the fact remains that, far from showing any symptom of attacking me, it simply rested its sleek, black head upon its huge forepaws and seemed to sleep. I stood, fearing to move lest I should rouse it into malignant life once more. But at least I was able to think clearly now that the baleful eyes were off me. Here I was shut up for the night with the ferocious beast. My own instincts, to say nothing of the words of the plausible villain who laid this trap for me, warned me that the animal was as savage as its master. How could I stave it off until morning? The door was hopeless, and so were the narrow, barred windows. There was no shelter anywhere in the bare, stone-flagged room. To cry for assistance was absurd. I knew that this den was an outhouse, and that the corridor which connected it with the house was at least a hundred feet long. Besides, with the gale thundering outside, my cries were not likely to be heard. I had only my own courage and my own wits to trust to.

And then, with a fresh wave of horror, my eyes fell upon the lantern. The candle had burned low, and was already beginning to gutter. In ten minutes it would be out. I had only ten minutes then in which to do something, for I felt that if I were once left in the dark with that fearful beast I should be incapable of action. The very thought of it paralyzed me. I cast my despairing eyes round this chamber of death, and they rested upon one spot which seemed to promise I will not say safety, but less immediate and imminent danger than the open floor.

I have said that the cage had a top as well as a front, and this top was left standing when the front was wound through the slot in the wall. It consisted of bars at a few inches' interval, with stout wire netting between, and it rested upon a strong stanchion at each end. It stood now as a great barred canopy over the crouching figure in the corner. The space between this iron shelf and the roof may have been from two to three feet. If I could only get up there, squeezed in between bars and ceiling, I should have only one vulnerable side. I should be safe from below, from behind, and from each side. Only on the open face of it could I be attacked. There, it is true, I had no protection whatever; but, at least, I should be out of the brute's path when he began to pace about his den. He would have to come out of his way to reach me. It was now or never, for if once the light were out it would be impossible. With a gulp in my throat I sprang up, seized the iron edge of the top, and swung myself panting onto it. I writhed in face downward, and found myself looking straight into the terrible eyes and yawning jaws of the cat. Its fetid breath came up into my face like the steam from some foul pot.

It appeared, however, to be rather curious than angry. With a sleek ripple of its long, black back it rose, stretched itself, and then rearing itself on its hind legs, with one forepaw against the wall, it raised the other, and drew its claws across the wire meshes beneath me. One sharp, white hook tore through my trousers—for I may mention that I was still in evening dress—and dug a furrow in my knee. It was not meant as an attack, but rather as an experiment, for upon my giving a sharp cry of pain he dropped down again, and springing lightly into the room, he began walking swiftly round it, looking up every now and again in my direction. For my part I shuffled backwards until I lay with my back against the wall, screwing myself into the smallest space possible. The farther I got the more difficult it was for him to attack me.

He seemed more excited now that he had begun to move about, and he ran swiftly and noiselessly round and round the den, passing continually underneath the iron couch upon which I lay. It was wonderful to see so great a bulk passing like a shadow, with hardly the softest thudding of velvety pads. The candle was burning low—so low I could hardly see the creature. And then, with a last flare and splutter it went out altogether. I was alone with the cat in the dark!

It helps one to face danger when one knows that one has done all that possibly can be done. There is nothing for it then but to quietly await the result. In this case, there was no chance of safety anywhere except the precise spot where I was. I stretched myself out, therefore, and lay silently, almost breathlessly, hoping that the beast might forget my presence if I did nothing to remind him. I reckoned that it must already be two o'clock. At four it would be full dawn. I had not more than two hours to wait for daylight.

Outside, the storm was still raging, and the rain lashed continually against the little windows. Inside, the poisonous and fetid air was overpowering. I could neither hear nor see the cat. I tried to think about other things—but only one had power enough to draw my mind from my terrible position. That was the contemplation of my cousin's villainy, his unparalleled hypocrisy, his malignant hatred of me. Beneath that cheerful face there lurked the spirit of a medieval assassin. And as I thought of it I saw more clearly how cunningly the thing had been arranged. He had apparently gone to bed with the others. No doubt he had his witness to prove it. Then, unknown to them, he had slipped down, had lured me into his den and abandoned me. His story would be so simple. He had left me to finish my cigar in the billiard room. I had gone down on my own account to have a last look at the cat. I had entered the room without observing that the cage was opened, and I had been caught. How could such a crime be brought home to him? Suspicion, perhaps—but proof, never!

How slowly those dreadful two hours went by! Once I heard a low, rasping sound, which I took to be the creature licking its own fur. Several times those greenish eyes gleamed at me through the darkness, but never in a fixed stare, and my hopes grew stronger that my presence had been forgotten or ignored. At last the least faint glimmer of light came through the windows—I first dimly saw them as two gray squares upon the black wall, then gray turned to white, and I could see my terrible companion once more. And he, alas, could see me!

It was evident to me at once that he was in a much more dangerous and aggressive mood than when I had seen him last. The cold of the morning had irritated him, and he was hungry as well. With a continual growl he paced swiftly up and down the side of the room which was farthest from my refuge, his whiskers bristling angrily, and his tail switching and lashing. As he turned at the corners his savage eyes always looked upward at me with a dreadful menace. I knew then that he meant to kill me. Yet I found myself even at that moment admiring the sinuous grace of the devilish thing, its long, undulating, rippling movements, the gloss of its beautiful flanks, the vivid, palpitating scarlet of the glistening tongue which hung from the jet-black muzzle. And all the time that deep, threatening growl was rising and rising in an unbroken crescendo. I knew that the crisis was at hand.

It was a miserable hour to meet such a death—so cold, so comfortless, shivering in my light dress clothes upon this gridiron of torment upon which I was stretched. I tried to brace myself to it, to raise my soul above it, and at the same time, with the lucidity which comes to a perfectly desperate man, I cast round for some possible means of escape. One thing was clear to me. If that front of the cage was only back in its position once more, I could find a sure refuge behind it. Could I possibly pull it back? I hardly dared to move for fear of bringing the creature upon me. Slowly, very slowly, I put my hand forward until it grasped the edge of the front, the final bar which protruded through the wall. To my surprise it came quite easily to my jerk. Of course the difficulty of drawing it out arose from the fact that I was clinging to it. I pulled again, and three inches of it came through. It ran apparently on wheels. I pulled again . . . and then the cat sprang!

It was so quick, so sudden, that I never saw it happen. I simply heard the savage snarl, and in an instant afterward the blazing yellow eyes, the flattened black head with its red tongue and flashing teeth, were within reach of me. The impact of the creature shook the bars upon which I lay, until I thought (as far as I could think of anything at such a moment) that they were coming down. The cat swayed there for an instant, the head and front paws quite close to me, the hind paws clawing to find a grip upon the edge of the grating. I heard the claws rasping as they clung to the wire netting, and the breath of the beast made me sick. But its bound had been miscalculated. It could not retain its position. Slowly, grinning with rage, and scratching madly at the bars, it swung backward and dropped heavily upon the floor. With a growl it instantly faced round to me and crouched for another spring.

I knew that the next few moments would decide my fate. The creature had learned by experience. It would not miscalculate again. I must act promptly, fearlessly, if I were to have a chance for life. In an instant I had formed my plan. Pulling off my dresscoat, I threw it down over the head of the beast. At the same moment I dropped over the edge, seized the end of the front grating, and pulled it frantically out of the wall.

It came more easily than I could have expected. I rushed across the room, bearing it with me; but, as I rushed, the accident of my position put me upon the outer side. Had it been the other way, I might have come off scatheless. As it was, there was a moment's pause as I stopped it and tried to pass in through the opening which I had left. That moment was enough to give time to the creature to toss off the coat with which I had blinded him and to spring upon me. I hurled myself through the gap and pulled the rails to behind me, but he seized my leg before I could entirely withdraw it. One stroke of that huge paw tore off my calf as a shaving of wood curls off before a plane. The next moment, bleeding and fainting, I was lying among the foul straw with a line of friendly bars between me and the creature which ramped so frantically against them.

Too wounded to move, and too faint to be conscious of fear, I could only lie, more dead than alive, and watch it. It pressed its broad, black chest against the bars and angled for me with its crooked paws as I have seen a kitten do before a mousetrap. It ripped my clothes, but, stretch as it would, it could not quite reach me. I have heard of the curious numbing effect produced by wounds from the great carnivora, and now I was destined to experience it, for I had lost all sense of personality, and was as interested in the cat's failure or success as if it were some game which I was watching. And then gradually my mind drifted away into strange vague dreams, always with the black face and red tongue coming back into them, and so I lost myself in the nirvana of delirium, the blessed relief of those who are too sorely tried.

Tracing the course of events afterward, I conclude that I must have been insensible for about two hours. What roused me to consciousness once more was that sharp metallic click which had been the precursor of my terrible experience. It was the shooting back of the spring lock. Then, before my senses were clear enough to entirely apprehend what they saw, I was aware of the round, benevolent face of my cousin peering in through the open door. What he saw evidently amazed him. There was the cat crouching on the floor. I was stretched upon my back in my shirt-sleeves within the cage, my trousers torn to ribbons and a great pool of blood all round me. I can see his amazed face now, with the morning sunlight upon it. He peered at me, and peered again. Then he closed the door behind him, and advanced to the cage to see if I were really dead.

I cannot undertake to say what happened. I was not in a fit state to witness or to chronicle such events. I can only say that I was suddenly conscious that his face was away from me—that he was looking toward the animal.

"Good old Tommy!" he cried. "Good old Tommy!"

Then he came near the bars, with his back still toward me.

"Down, you stupid beast!" he roared. "Down, sir! Don't you know your master?"

Suddenly even in my bemuddled brain a remembrance came of those words of his when he had said that the taste of blood would turn the cat into a fiend. My blood had done it, but he was to pay the price.

"Get away!" he screamed. "Get away, you devil! Baldwin! Baldwin! Oh, my God!"

And then I heard him fall, and rise, and fall again, with a sound like the ripping of sacking. His screams grew fainter until they were lost in the worrying snarl. And then, after I thought that he was dead, I saw, as in a nightmare, a blinded, tattered, blood-soaked figure running wildly round the room—and that was the last glimpse which I had of him before I fainted once again.

I was many months in my recovery—in fact, I cannot say that I have ever recovered, for to the end of my days I shall carry a stick as a sign of my night with the Brazilian cat. Baldwin, the groom, and the other servants could not tell what had occurred, when, drawn by the death cries of their master, they found me behind the bars, and his remains—or what they afterward discovered to be his remains—in the clutch of the creature which he had reared. They stalled him off with hot irons, and afterward shot him through the loophole of the door before they could finally extricate me. I was carried to my bedroom, and there, under the roof of my would-be murderer, I remained between life and death for several weeks. They had sent for a surgeon from Clipton and a nurse from London, and in a month I was able to be carried to the station, and so conveyed back once more to Grosvenor Mansions.

I have one remembrance of that illness, which might have been part of the ever-changing panorama conjured up by a delirious brain were it not so definitely fixed in my memory. One night, when the nurse was absent, the door of my chamber was opened, and a tall woman in blackest mourning slipped into the room. She came across to me, and as she bent her sallow face I saw by the faint gleam of the night light that it was the Brazilian woman whom my cousin had married. She stared intently into my face, and her expression was more kindly than I had ever seen it.

"Are you conscious?" she asked.

I feebly nodded—for I was still very weak.

"Well, then, I only wished to say to you that you have yourself to blame. Did I not do all I could for you? From the beginning I tried to drive you from the house. By every means, short of betraying my husband, I tried to save you from him. I knew that he had a reason for bringing you here. I knew that he would never let you get away again. No one knew him as I knew him, who had suffered from him so often. I did not dare to tell you all this. He would have killed me. But I did my best for you. As things have turned out, you have been the best friend that I ever had. You have set me free, and I fancied that nothing but death would do that. I am sorry if you are hurt, but I cannot reproach myself. I told you that you were a fool—and a fool you have been." She crept out of the room, the bitter, singular woman, and I was never destined to see her again. With what remained from her husband's property she went back to her native land, and I have heard that she afterward took the veil at Pernambuco.

It was not until I had been back in London for some time that the doctors pronounced me to be well enough to do business. It was not a very welcome permission to me, for I feared that it would be the signal for an inrush of creditors; but it was Summers, my lawyer, who first took advantage of it.

"I am very glad to see that your lordship is so much better," said he. "I have been waiting a long time to offer my congratulations."

"What do you mean, Summers? This is no time for joking."

"I mean what I say," he answered. "You have been Lord Southerton for the last six weeks, but we feared that it would retard your recovery if you were to learn it."

Lord Southerton! One of the richest peers in England! I could not believe my ears. And then suddenly I thought of the time which had elapsed, and how it coincided with my injuries.

"Then Lord Southerton must have died about the same time that I was hurt?"

"His death occurred upon that very day." Summers looked hard at me as I spoke, and I am convinced—for he was a very shrewd fellow— that he guessed the true state of the case. He paused for a moment as if awaiting a confidence from me, but I could not see what was to be gained by exposing such a family scandal.

"Yes, a very curious coincidence," he continued, with the same knowing look. "Of course, you are aware that your cousin Everard King was the next heir to the estates. Now, if it had been you instead of him who had been torn to pieces by this tiger, or whatever it was, then of course he would have been Lord Southerton at the present moment."

"No doubt," said I.

"And he took such an interest in it," said Summers. "I happen to know that the late Lord Southerton's valet was in his pay, and that he used to have telegrams from him every few hours to tell him how he was getting on. That would be about the time when you were down there. Was it not strange that he should wish to be so well informed, since he knew that he was not the direct heir?"

"Very strange," said I. "And now, Summers, if you will bring me my bills and a new checkbook, we will begin to get things into order."

F. Marion Crawford (1854–1909)

Born in Bagni di Lucca, Italy, Francis Marion Crawford was perhaps the most cosmopolitan of all 19th century American writers. His governess taught him French as a child and he later studied Greek, German, Russian, Sanskrit, Spanish, Swedish, and Turkish in such diverse locations as Cambridge, Harvard, Heidelberg, India, and Rome.

During the years he visited India (1879–1880), he edited a paper in Allahabad, converted to Catholicism, developed an enthusiasm for the occult, and acquired the plot for what became his first novel. It was a series of events that happened to a diamond merchant of Simla who sold an unusual stone.

Two years later, at a dinner party, Crawford retold this story in such a compelling fashion that his uncle suggested novelizing it. *Mr. Issacs* (1882) was the result. It sold well and Crawford continued to write, publishing more than forty novels before his death.

As an author, he believed stories should be for entertainment only, devoid of any attempts to moralize or present a snapshot of life. A born storyteller with considerable skills at narration, dialogue, and setting, he might still be popular had he bothered to take a little more care with his works, but his extravagance and generosity required speed.

Today he is primarily remembered for short horror fiction (*Wandering Ghosts*, 1911). "For the Blood is Life," "The Upper Berth," and "The Screaming Skull," are always in print. Yet our selection, "The Dead Smile," is still relatively unknown, even though it may be his most terrifying story.

THE DEAD SMILE

I

*S*ir Hugh Ockram smiled as he sat by the open window of his study, in the late August afternoon, and just then a curiously yellow cloud obscured the low sun, and the clear summer light turned lurid, as if it had been suddenly poisoned and polluted by the foul vapors of a plague. Sir Hugh's face seemed, at best, to be made of fine parchment drawn skintight over a wooden mask, in which two eyes were sunk out of sight, and peered from far within through crevices under the slanting, wrinkled lids, alive and watchful like two toads in their holes, side by side and exactly alike. But as the light changed, then a yellow glare flashed in each. Nurse Macdonald said once that when Sir Hugh smiled he saw the faces of two women in hell—two dead women he had betrayed. (Nurse Macdonald was a hundred years old.) And the smile widened, stretching the pale lips across the discolored teeth in an expression of profound self-satisfaction, blended with the most unforgiving hatred and contempt for the human doll. The hideous disease of which he was dying had touched his brain. His son stood beside him, tall, white, and delicate as an angel in a primitive picture, and though there was deep distress in his violet eyes as he looked at his father's face, he felt the shadow of that sickening smile stealing across his own lips and parting them and drawing them against his will. And it was like a bad dream, for he tried not to smile and smiled the more. Beside him, strangely like him in her wan, angelic beauty, with the same shadowy golden hair, the same sad violet eyes, the same luminously pale face, Evelyn Warburton rested one hand upon his arm. And as she looked into her uncle's eyes, and could not turn her own away, she knew that the deathly smile was hovering on her own red lips, drawing them tightly across her little teeth, while two bright tears ran down her cheeks to her mouth, and dropped from the upper to the lower lip while she smiled—and the smile was like the shadow of death and the seal of damnation upon her pure, young face.

"Of course," said Sir Hugh very slowly, and still looking out at the trees, "if you have made up your mind to be married, I cannot hinder you, and I don't suppose you attach the smallest importance to my consent—"

"Father!" exclaimed Gabriel reproachfully.

"No, I do not deceive myself," continued the old man, smiling terribly. "You will marry when I am dead, though there is a very good reason why you had better not—why you had better not," he repeated very emphatically, and he slowly turned his toad eyes upon the lovers.

"What reason?" asked Evelyn in a frightened voice.

"Never mind the reason, my dear. You will marry just as if it did not exist." There was a long pause. "Two gone," he said, his voice lowering strangely, "and two more will be four—all together—for ever and ever, burning, burning, burning bright."

At the last words his head sank slowly back, and the little glare of the toad eyes disappeared under the swollen lids, and the lurid cloud passed from the westering sun, so that the earth was green again and the light pure. Sir Hugh had fallen asleep, as he often did in his last illness, even while speaking.

Gabriel Ockram drew Evelyn away, and from the study they went out into the dim hall, softly closing the door behind them, and each audibly drew breath, as though some sudden danger had been passed. They laid their hands each in the other's, and their strangely-alike eyes met in a long look, in which love and perfect understanding were darkened by the secret terror of an unknown thing. Their pale faces reflected each other's fear.

"It is his secret," said Evelyn at last. "He will never tell us what it is."

"If he died with it," answered Gabriel, "let it be on his own head!"

"On his head!" echoed the dim hall. It was a strange echo, and some were frightened by it, for they said that if it were a real echo it should repeat everything and not give back a phrase here and there, now speaking, now silent. But Nurse Macdonald said that the great hall would never echo a prayer when an Ockram was to die, though it would give back curses ten for one.

"On his head!" it repeated quite softly, and Evelyn started and looked round.

"It is only the echo," said Gabriel, leading her away.

They went out into the late afternoon light, and sat upon a stone seat behind the chapel, which was built across the end of the east wing. It was very still, not a breath stirred, and there was no sound near them. Only far off in the park a songbird was whistling the high prelude to the evening chorus.

"It is very lonely here," said Evelyn, taking Gabriel's hand nervously, and speaking as if she dreaded to disturb the silence. "If it were dark, I should be afraid."

"Of what? Of me?" Gabriel's sad eyes turned to her.

"Oh no! How could I be afraid of you? But of the old Ockrams—they say they are just under our feet here in the north vault outside the chapel, all in their shrouds, with no coffins, as they used to bury them."

"As they always will—as they will bury my father, and me. They say an Ockram will not lie in a coffin."

"But it cannot be true—these are fairy tales—ghost stories!" Evelyn nestled nearer to her companion, grasping his hand more tightly, and the sun began to go down.

"Of course. But there is a story of old Sir Vernon, who was beheaded for treason under James II. The family brought his body back from the scaffold in an iron coffin with heavy locks, and they put it in the north vault. But ever afterwards, whenever the vault was opened to bury another of the family, they found the coffin wide open, and the body standing upright against the wall, and the head rolled away in a corner, smiling at it."

"As Uncle Hugh smiles?" Evelyn shivered.

"Yes. I shall see him laid there too—with his secret, whatever it is." Gabriel sighed and pressed the girl's little hand.

"I do not like to think of it," she said unsteadily. "O Gabriel, what can the secret be? He said we had better not marry—not that he forbade it—but he said it so strangely, and he smiled—ugh!" Her small white teeth chattered with fear, and she looked over her shoulder while drawing still closer to Gabriel. "And, somehow, I felt it in my own face—"

"So did I," answered Gabriel in a low, nervous voice. "Nurse Macdonald—" He stopped abruptly.

"What? What did she say?"

"Oh—nothing. She has told me things—they would frighten you, dear. Come, it is growing chilly." He rose, but Evelyn held his hand in both of hers, still sitting and looking up into his face.

"But we shall be married, just the same—Gabriel! Say that we shall!"

"Of course, darling—of course. But while my father is so very ill, it is impossible—"

"O Gabriel, Gabriel dear! I wish we were married now!" cried Evelyn in sudden distress. "I know that something will prevent it and keep us apart."

"Nothing shall!"

"Nothing?"

"Nothing human," said Gabriel Ockram, as she drew him down to her.

And their faces, that were so strangely alike, met and touched— and Gabriel knew that the kiss had a marvellous savor of evil, but on Evelyn's lips it was like the cool breath of a sweet and mortal fear. And neither of them understood, for they were innocent and young. Yet she drew him to her by her lightest touch, as a sensitive plant shivers and waves its thin leaves, and bends and closes softly upon what it wants, and he let himself be drawn to her willingly, as he would if her touch had been deadly and poisonous; for she strangely loved that half voluptuous breath of fear, and he passionately desired the nameless evil something that lurked in her maiden lips.

"It is as if we loved in a strange dream," she said.

"I fear the waking," he murmured.

"We shall not wake, dear—when the dream is over it will have already turned into death, so softly that we shall not know it. But until then—"

She paused, and her eyes sought his, and their faces slowly came nearer. It was as if they had thoughts in their red lips that foresaw and foreknew the deep kiss of each other.

"Until then—" she said again, very low, and her mouth was nearer to his.

"Dream—till then," murmured his breath.

II

Nurse Macdonald was a hundred years old. She used to sleep sitting all bent together in a great old leathern armchair with wings, her feet in a bag footstool lined with sheepskin, and many warm blankets wrapped about her, even in summer. Beside her a little lamp always burned at night by an old silver cup, in which there was something to drink.

Her face was very wrinkled, but the wrinkles were so small and fine and near together that they made shadows instead of lines. Two thin locks of hair, that was turning from white to a smoky yellow again, were drawn over her temples from under her starched white cap. Every now and then she woke, and her eyelids were drawn up in tiny folds like little pink silk curtains, and her queer blue eyes looked straight before her through doors and walls and worlds to a far place beyond. Then she slept again, and her hands lay one upon the other on the edge of the blanket, the thumbs had grown longer than the fingers with age, and the joints shone in the low lamplight like polished crabapples.

It was nearly one o'clock in the night, and the summer breeze was blowing the ivy branch against the panes of the window with a hushing caress. In the small room beyond, with the door ajar, the girl-maid who took care of Nurse Macdonald was fast asleep. All was very quiet. The old woman breathed regularly, and her eyes were shut.

But outside the closed window there was a face, and violet eyes were looking steadily at the ancient sleeper, for it was like the face of Evelyn Warburton, though there were eighty feet from the sill of the window to the foot of the tower. Yet the cheeks were thinner than Evelyn's, and as white as a gleam, and her eyes stared, and the lips were not red with life, they were dead and painted with new blood.

Slowly Nurse Macdonald's wrinkled eyelids folded themselves back, and she looked straight at the face at the window while one might count ten.

"Is it time?" she asked in her little old, faraway voice.

While she looked the face at the window changed, for the eyes opened wider and wider till the white glared all round the bright violet, and the bloody lips opened over gleaming teeth, and stretched and widened and stretched again, and the shadow golden hair rose and streamed against the window in the night breeze. And in answer to Nurse Macdonald's question came the sound that freezes the living flesh.

That low moaning voice that rises suddenly, like the scream of storm, from a moan to a wail, from a wail to a howl, from a howl to the fear-shriek of the tortured dead—he who had heard knows, and he can bear witness that the cry of the banshee is an evil cry to hear alone in the deep night. When it was over and the face was gone, Nurse Macdonald shook a little in her great chair, and still she looked at the black square of the window, but there was nothing more there, nothing but the night, and the whispering ivy branch. She turned her head to the door that was ajar, and there stood the girl in her white gown, her teeth chattering with fright.

"It is time, child," said Nurse Macdonald. "I must go to him, for it is the end."

She rose slowly, leaning her withered hands upon the arms of the chair, and the girl brought her a woolen gown and a great mantle, and her crutch-stick, and made her ready. But very often the girl looked at the window and was unjointed with fear and often Nurse Macdonald shook her head and said words which the maid could not understand.

"It was like the face of Miss Evelyn," said the girl at last trembling.

But the ancient woman looked up sharply and angrily, and her queer blue eyes glared. She held herself by the arm of the great chair with her left hand, and lifted up her crutch-stick to strike the maid with all her might. But she did not.

"You are a good girl," she said, "but you are a fool. Pray for wit, child, pray for wit—or else find sevice in another house than Ockram Hall. Bring the lamp and help me under my left arm."

The crutch-stick clacked on the wooden floor, and the low heels of the woman's slippers clappered after her in slow triplets, as Nurse Macdonald got toward the door. And down the stairs each step she took was a labor in itself, and by the clacking noise the waking servants knew that she was coming, very long before they saw her.

No one was sleeping now, and there were lights and whisperings and pale faces in the corridors near Sir Hugh's bedroom, and now someone went in, and now someone came out, but everyone made way for Nurse Macdonald, who had nursed Sir Hugh's father more than eighty years ago.

The light was soft and clear in the room. There stood Gabriel Ockram by his father's bedside, and there knelt Evelyn Warburton, her hair lying like a golden shadow down her shoulders, and her hands clasped nervously together. And opposite Gabriel, a nurse was trying to make Sir Hugh drink. But he would not, and though his lips were parted, his teeth were set. He was very, very thin and yellow now, and his eyes caught the light sideways and were as yellow coals.

"Do not torment him," said Nurse Macdonald to the woman who held the cup. "Let me speak to him, for his hour is come."

"Let her speak to him," said Gabriel in a dull voice.

So the ancient woman leaned to the pillow and laid the feather-weight of her withered hand, that was like a brown moth, upon Sir Hugh's yellow fingers, and she spoke to him earnestly, while only Gabriel and Evelyn were left in the room to hear.

"Hugh Ockram," she said, "this is the end of your life; and as I saw you born, and saw your father born before you, I am come to see you die. Hugh Ockram, will you tell me the truth?"

The dying man recognized the little faraway voice he had known all his life, and he very slowly turned his yellow face to Nurse Macdonald; but he said nothing. Then she spoke again.

"Hugh Ockram, you will never see the daylight again. Will you tell the truth?"

His toadlike eyes were not dull yet. They fastened themselves on her face.

"What do you want of me?" he asked, and each word struck hollow on the last. "I have no secrets. I have lived a good life."

Nurse Macdonald laughed—a tiny, cracked laugh, that made her old head bob and tremble a little, as if her neck were on a steel spring. But Sir Hugh's eyes grew red, and his pale lips began to twist.

"Let me die in peace," he said slowly.

But Nurse Macdonald shook her head, and her brown, mothlike hand left his and fluttered to his forehead.

"By the mother that bore you and died of grief for the sins you did, tell me the truth!"

Sir Hugh's lips tightened on his discolored teeth.

"Not on earth," he answered slowly.

"By the wife who bore your son and died heartbroken, tell me the truth!"

"Neither to you in life, nor to her in eternal death."

His lips writhed, as if the words were coals between them, and a great drop of sweat rolled across the parchment of his forehead. Gabriel

Ockram bit his hand as he watched his father die. But Nurse Macdonald spoke a third time.

"By the woman whom you betrayed, and who waits for you this night, Hugh Ockram, tell me the truth!"

"It is too late. Let me die in peace."

The writhing lips began to smile across the set yellow teeth, and the toad eyes glowed like evil jewels in his head.

"There is time," said the ancient woman. "Tell me the name of Evelyn Warburton's father. Then I will let you die in peace."

Evelyn started back, kneeling as she was, and stared at Nurse Macdonald, and then at her uncle.

"The name of Evelyn's father?" he repeated slowly, while the awful smile spread upon his dying face.

The light was growing strangely dim in the great room. As Evelyn looked, Nurse Macdonald's crooked shadow on the wall grew gigantic. Sir Hugh's breath came thick, rattling in his throat, as death crept in like a snake and choked it back. Evelyn prayed aloud, high and clear.

Then something rapped at the window, and she felt her hair rise upon her head in a cool breeze, as she looked around in spite of herself. And when she saw her own white face looking in at the window, and her own eyes staring at her through the glass, wise and fearful, and her own hair streaming against the pane, and her own lips dashed with blood, she rose slowly from the floor and stood rigid for one moment, till she screamed once and fell straight back into Gabriel's arms. But the shriek that answered hers was the fear-shriek of the tormented corpse, out of which the soul cannot pass for shame of deadly sins, though the devils fight in it with corruption, each for their due share.

Sir Hugh Ockram sat upright in his deathbed, and saw and cried aloud:

"Evelyn!" His harsh voice broke and rattled in his chest as he sank down. But still Nurse Macdonald tortured him, for there was a little life left in him still.

"You have seen the mother as she waits for you, Hugh Ockram. Who was this girl Evelyn's father? What was his name?"

For the last time the dreadful smile came upon the twisted lips, very slowly, very surely now, and the toad eyes glared red, and the parchment face glowed a little in the flickering light. For the last time words came.

"They know it in hell."

Then the glowing eyes went out quickly, the yellow face turned waxen pale, and a great shiver ran through the thin body as Hugh Ockram died.

But in death he still smiled, for he knew his secret and kept it still, on the other side, and he would take it with him, to lie with him forever in the north vault of the chapel where the Ockrams lie uncoffined in their shrouds—all but one. Though he was dead, he smiled, for he had kept his treasure of evil truth to the end, and there was none left to tell the name he had spoken, but there was all the evil he had not undone left to bear fruit.

As they watched—Nurse Macdonald and Gabriel, who held Evelyn still unconscious in his arms while he looked at the father—they felt the dead smile crawling along their own lips—the ancient crone and the youth with the angel's face. Then they shivered a little, and both looked at Evelyn as she lay with her head on his shoulder, and, though she was very beautiful, the same sickening smile was twisting her young mouth too, and it was like the foreshadowing of a great evil which they could not understand.

But by and by they carried Evelyn out, and she opened her eyes and the smile was gone. From far away in the great house the sound of weeping and crooning came up the stairs and echoed along the dismal corridors, for the women had begun to mourn the dead master, after the Irish fashion, and the hall had echoes of its own all that night, like the far-off wail of the banshee among forest trees.

When the time was come they took Sir Hugh in his winding-sheet on a trestle bier, and bore him to the chapel and through the iron door and down the long descent to the north vault, with tapers, to lay him by his father. And two men went in first to prepare the place, and came back staggering like drunken men, and white, leaving their lights behind them.

But Gabriel Ockram was not afraid, for he knew. And he went in alone and saw that the body of Sir Vernon Ockram was leaning upright against the stone wall, and that his head lay on the ground near by with the face turned up, and the dried leathern lips smiled horribly at the dried-up corpse, while the iron coffin, lined with black velvet, stood open on the floor.

Then Gabriel took the thing in his hands, for it was very light, being quite dried by the air of the vault, and those who peeped in from the door saw him lay it in the coffin again, and it rustled a little, like a bundle of reeds, and sounded hollow as it touched the sides and the bottom. He also placed the head upon the shoulders and shut down the lid, which fell to with a rusty spring that snapped.

After that they laid Sir Hugh beside his father, with the trestle bier on which they had brought him, and they went back to the chapel.

But when they saw one another's faces, master and men, they were all smiling with the dead smile of the corpse they had left in the vault, so that they could not bear to look at one another until it had faded away.

III

Gabriel Ockram became Sir Gabriel, inheriting the baronetcy with the half-ruined fortune left by his father, and still Evelyn Warburton lived at Ockram Hall, in the south room that had been hers ever since she could remember anything. She could not go away, for there were no relatives to whom she could have gone, and, besides there seemed to be no reason why she should not stay. The world would never trouble itself to care what the Ockrams did on their Irish estates, and it was long since the Ockrams had asked anything of the world.

So Sir Gabriel took his father's place at the dark old table in the dining room, and Evelyn sat opposite to him, until such time as their mourning should be over, and they might be married at last. And meanwhile their lives went on as before, since Sir Hugh had been a hopeless invalid during the last year of his life, and they had seen him but once a day for the little while, spending most of their time together in a strangely perfect companionship.

But though the late summer saddened into autumn, and autumn darkened into winter, and storm followed storm, and rain poured on rain through the short days and the long nights, yet Ockram Hall seemed less gloomy since Sir Hugh had been laid in the north vault beside his father. And at Christmastide Evelyn decked the great hall with holly and green boughs, and huge fires blazed on every hearth. Then the tenants were all bidden to a New Year's dinner, and they ate and drank well, while Sir Gabriel sat at the head of the table. Evelyn came in when the port wine was brought, and the most respected of the tenants made a speech to propose her health.

It was long, he said, since there had been a Lady Ockram. Sir

Gabriel shaded his eyes with his hand and looked down at the table, but a faint color came into Evelyn's transparent cheeks. But, said the gray-haired farmer, it was longer still since there had been a Lady Ockram so fair as the next was to be, and he gave the health of Evelyn Warburton.

Then the tenants all stood up and shouted for her, and Sir Gabriel stood up likewise, beside Evelyn. And when the men gave the last and loudest cheer of all there was a voice not theirs, above them all, higher, fiercer, louder—a scream not earthly, shrieking for the bride of Ockram Hall. And the holly and the green boughs over the great chimney piece shook and slowly waved as if a cool breeze were blowing over them. But the men turned very pale, and many of them set down their glasses, but others let them fall upon the floor for fear. And looking into one another's faces, they were all smiling strangely, a dead smile, like dead Sir Hugh's. One cried out words in Irish, and the fear of death was suddenly upon them all so that they fled in panic, falling over one another like wild beasts in the burning forest, when the thick smoke runs along before the flame, and the tables were overset, and drinking glasses and bottles were broken in heaps, and the dark red wine crawled like blood upon the polished floor.

Sir Gabriel and Evelyn stood alone at the head of the table before the wreck of the feast, not daring to turn to see each other, for each knew that the other smiled. But his right arm held her and his left hand clasped her right as they stared before them, and but for the shadows of her hair one might not have told their two faces apart. They listened long, but the cry came not again, and the dead smile faded from their lips, while each remembered that Sir Hugh Ockram lay in the north vault, smiling in his winding-sheet, in the dark, because he had died with his secret.

So ended the tenants' New Year's dinner. But from that time on Sir Gabriel grew more and more silent, and his face grew even paler and thinner than before. Often without warning and without words, he would rise from his seat, as if something moved him against his will, and he would go out into the rain or the sunshine to the north side of the chapel, and sit on the stone bench, staring at the ground as if he could see through it, and through the vault below, and through the white winding-sheet in the dark, to the dead smile that would not die.

Always when he went out in that way Evelyn came out presently and sat beside him. Once, too, as in summer, their beautiful faces came suddenly near, and their lids drooped, and their red lips were almost joined together. But as their eyes met, they grew wide and wild, so that the white showed in a ring all round the deep violet, and their teeth chattered, and their hands were like hands of corpses, each in the other's for the terror of what was under their feet, and of what they knew but could not see.

Once, also, Evelyn found Sir Gabriel in the chapel alone, standing before the iron door that led down to the place of death, and in his hand there was the key to the door, but he had not put it in the lock. Evelyn drew him away, shivering, for she had also been driven in waking dreams to see that terrible thing again, and to find out whether it had changed since it had lain there.

"I'm going mad," said Sir Gabriel, covering his eyes with his hand as he went with her. "I see it in my sleep, I see it when I am awake—it draws me to it, day and night—and unless I see it I shall die!"

"I know," answered Evelyn, "I know. It is as if threads were spun from it, like a spider's, drawing us down to it." She was silent for a moment, and then she started violently and grasped his arm with a man's strength, and almost screamed the words she spoke. "But we must not go there!" she cried. "We must not go!"

Sir Gabriel's eyes were half-shut, and he was not moved by the agony of her face.

"I shall die, unless I see it again," he said, in a quiet voice not like his own. And all that day and that evening he scarcely spoke, thinking of it, always thinking, while Evelyn Warburton quivered from head to foot with a terror she had never known.

She went alone, on a gray winter's morning, to Nurse Macdonald's room in the tower, and sat down beside the great leathern easy chair, laying her thin white hand upon the withered fingers.

"Nurse," she said, "what was it that Uncle Hugh should have told you, that night before he died? It must have been an awful secret—and yet, though you asked him, I feel somehow that you know it, and that you know why he used to smile so dreadfully."

The old woman's head moved slowly from side to side.

"I only guess—I shall never know," she answered slowly in her cracked little voice.

"But what do you guess? Who am I? Why did you ask who my father was? You know I am Colonel Warburton's daughter, and my mother was Lady Ockram's sister, so that Gabriel and I are cousins. My father was killed in Afghanistan. What secret can there be?"

"I do not know. I can only guess."

"Guess what?" asked Evelyn imploringly, and pressing the soft withered hands, as she leaned forward. But Nurse Macdonald's wrinkled lids dropped suddenly over her queer blue eyes, and her lips shook a little with her breath, as if she were asleep.

Evelyn waited. By the fire the Irish maid was knitting fast, and the needles clicked like three or four clocks ticking against each other. And the real clock on the wall solemnly ticked alone, checking off the seconds of the woman who was a hundred years old, and had not many days left. Outside the ivy branch beat the window in the wintry blast, as it had beaten against the glass a hundred years ago.

Then as Evelyn sat there she felt again the waking of a horrible desire—the sickening wish to go down, down to the thing in the north vault, and to open the winding-sheet, and see whether it had changed, and she held Nurse Macdonald's hands as if to keep herself in her place and fight against the appalling attraction of the evil dead.

But the old cat that kept Nurse Macdonald's feet warm, lying always on the bag footstool, got up and stretched itself, and looked up into Evelyn's eyes, while its back arched, and its tail thickened and bristled, and its ugly pink lips drew back in a devilish grin, showing its sharp teeth. Evelyn stared at it, half-fascinated by its ugliness. Then the creature suddenly put out one paw with all its claws spread, and spat at the girl, and all at once the grinning cat was like the smiling corpses far down below, so that Evelyn shivered down to her small feet and covered her face with her free hand lest Nurse Macdonald should wake and see the dead smile there, for she could feel it.

The old woman had already opened her eyes again, and she touched her cat with the end of her crutch-stick, whereupon its back went down and its tail shrunk, and it sidled back to its place on the bag footstool. But its yellow eyes looked up sideways at Evelyn, between the slits of its lids.

"What is it that you guess, nurse?" asked the young girl again.

"A bad thing—a wicked thing. But I dare not tell you, lest it might not be true, and the very thought should blast your life. For if I guess right, he meant that you should not know, and that you two should marry, and pay for his old sin with your souls."

"He used to tell us that we ought not to marry—"

"Yes—he told you that, perhaps—but it was as if a man put poisoned meat before a starving beast, and said do not eat but never raised his hand to take the meat away. And if he told you that you should not marry, it was because he hoped you would, for of all men living or dead, Hugh Ockram was the falsest man that ever told a cowardly lie, and the cruellest that ever hurt a weak woman, and the worst that ever loved a sin.''

"But Gabriel and I love each other," said Evelyn very sadly.

Nurse Macdonald's old eyes looked far away, at sights seen long ago, and that rose in the gray winter air amid the mists of an ancient youth.

"If you love, you can die together," she said, very slowly. "Why should you live, if it is true? I am a hundred years old. What has life given me? The beginning is fire, the end is a heap of ashes, and between the end and the beginning lies all the pain in the world. Let me sleep, since I cannot die.''

Then the old woman's eyes closed again, and her head sank a little lower upon her breast.

So Evelyn went away and left her asleep, with the cat asleep on the bag footstool; and the young girl tried to forget Nurse Macdonald's words, but she could not, for she heard them over and over again in the wind, and behind her on the stairs. And as she grew sick with fear of the frightful unknown evil to which her soul was bound, she felt a bodily something pressing her, and pushing her, and forcing her on, and from the other side she felt the threads that drew her mysteriously, and when she shut her eyes, she saw in the chapel behind the altar, the low iron door through which she must pass to go to the thing.

And as she lay awake at night, she drew the sheet over her face, lest she should see shadows on the wall beckoning her and the sound of her own warm breath made whisperings in her ears, while she held the mattress with her hands, to keep from getting up and going to the chapel. It would have been easier if there had not been a way thither through the library, by a door which was never locked. It would be fearfully easy to take her candle and go softly through the sleeping house. And the key of the vault lay under the altar behind a stone that turned. She knew the little secret. She could go alone and see.

But when she thought of it, she felt her hair rise on her head, and first she shivered so that the bed shook, and then the horror went through her in a cold thrill that was agony again, like myriads of icy needles, boring into her nerves.

IV

The old clock in Nurse Macdonald's tower struck midnight. From her room she could hear the creaking chains and weights in their box in the corner of the staircase, and overhead the jarring of the rusty lever that lifted the hammer. She had heard it all her life. It struck eleven strokes clearly and then came the twelfth, with a dull half stroke, as though the hammer were too weary to go on, and had fallen asleep against the bell.

The old cat got up from the bag footstool and stretched itself, and Nurse Macdonald opened her ancient eyes and looked slowly round the room by the dim light of the night lamp. She touched the cat with her crutch-stick, and it lay down upon her feet. She drank a few drops from her cup and went to sleep again.

But downstairs Sir Gabriel sat straight up as the clock struck, for he had dreamed a fearful dream of horror, and his heart stood still, till he awoke at its stopping, and it beat again furiously with his breath, like a wild thing set free. No Ockram had ever known fear waking, but sometimes it came to Sir Gabriel in his sleep.

He pressed his hands to his temples as he sat up in bed, and his hands were icy cold, but his head was hot. The dream faded far, and in its place there came the master thought that racked his life; with the thought also came the sick twisting of his lips in the dark that would have been a smile. Far off, Evelyn Warburton dreamed that the dead smile was on her mouth, and awoke, starting with a little moan, her face in her hands shivering.

But Sir Gabriel struck a light and got up and began to walk up and down his great room. It was midnight, and he had barely slept an hour, and in the north of Ireland the winter nights are long.

"I shall go mad," he said to himself, holding his forehead. He knew that it was true. For weeks and months the possession of the thing had grown upon him like a disease, till he could think of nothing without thinking first of that. And now all at once it outgrew his strength, and he knew that he must be its instrument or lose his mind—that he must do the deed he hated and feared, if he could fear anything, or that something would snap in his brain and divide him from life while he was yet alive. He took the candlestick in his hand, the old-fashioned heavy candlestick that had always been used by the head of the house. He did not think of dressing, but went as he was, in his silk nightclothes and his slippers, and he opened the door. Everything was very still in the great old house. He shut the door behind him and walked noiselessly on the carpet through the long corridor. A cool breeze blew over his shoulder and blew the flame of his candle straight out from him. Instinctively he stopped and looked round, but all was still, and the upright flame burned steadily. He walked on, and instantly a strong draught was behind him, almost extinguishing the light. It seemed to blow him on his way, ceasing whenever he turned, coming again when he went on—invisible, icy.

Down the great staircase to the echoing hall he went, seeing nothing but the flaring flame of the candle standing away from him over the guttering wax, while the cold wind blew over his shoulder and through his hair. On he passed through the open door into the library, dark with old books and carved bookcases, on through the door in the shelves, with painted shelves on it, and the imitated backs of books, so that one needed to know where to find it—and it shut itself after him with a soft click. He entered the low-arched passage, and though the door was shut behind him and fitted tightly in its frame, still the cold breeze blew the flame forward as he walked. And he was not afraid, but his face was very pale, and his eyes were wise and bright, looking before him, seeing already in the dark air the picture of the thing beyond. But in the chapel he stood still, his hand on the little turning stone tablet in the back of the stone altar. On the tablet were engraved words, '*Clavis sepulchri Clarissimo-rum Dominorum De Ockram*'—('the key to the vault of the most illustrious lord of Ockram'). Sir Gabriel paused and listened. He fancied that he heard a sound far off in the great house where all had been so still, but it did not come again. Yet he waited at the last, and looked at the low iron door. Beyond it, down the long descent, lay his father uncoffined, six months dead, corrupt, terrible in his clinging shroud. The strangely preserving air of the vault could not yet have done its work completely. But on the thing's ghastly features, with their half-dried, open eyes, there would still be the frightful smile with which the man had died—the smile that haunted—

As the thought crossed Sir Gabriel's mind, he felt his lips writhing, and he struck his own mouth in wrath with the back of his hand so fiercely that a drop of blood ran down his chin and another, and more, falling back in the gloom upon the chapel pavement. But still his bruised lips twisted themselves. He turned the tablet by the simple secret. It needed no safer fastening, for had each Ockram been confined in pure gold, and had the door been wide, there was not a man in Tyrone brave enough to go down to the place, saving Gabriel Ockram himself, with his angel's face and his thin, white hands, and his sad unflinching eyes. He took the great gold key and set it into the lock of the iron door, and the heavy, rattling noise echoed down the descent beyond like footsteps, as if a watcher had stood behind the iron and were running away within, with heavy dead feet. And though he was standing still, the cool wind was from behind him, and blew the flame of the candle against the iron panel. He turned the key.

Sir Gabriel saw that his candle was short. There were new ones on the altar, with long candlesticks and he lit one, and left his own burning on the floor. As he set it down on the pavement his lip began to bleed again, and another drop fell upon the stones.

He drew the iron door open and pushed it back against the chapel wall, so that it should not shut of itself, while he was within, and the horrible draught of the sepulchre came up out of the depths in his face, foul and dark. He went in, but though the fetid air met him, yet the flame of the tall candle was blown straight from him against the wind while he walked down the easy incline with steady steps, his loose slippers slapping the pavement as he trod.

He shaded the candle with his hand, and his fingers seemed to be made of wax and blood as the light shone through them. And in spite of him the unearthly draught forced the flame forward, till it was blue over the black wick, and it seemed as if it must go out. But he went straight on, with shining eyes.

The downward passage was wide, and he could not always see the walls by the struggling light, but he knew when he was in the place of death by the larger, drearier echo of his steps in the greater space and by the sensation of a distant blank wall. He stood still, almost enclosing the flame of the candle in the hollow of his hand. He could see a little, for his eyes were growing used to the gloom. Shadowy forms were outlined in the dimness, where the biers of the Ockrams stood crowded together, side by side, each with its straight, shrouded corpse, strangely preserved by the dry air, like the empty shell that the locust sheds in summer. And a few steps before him he saw clearly the dark shape of headless Sir Vernon's iron coffin, and he knew that nearest to it lay the thing he sought.

He was as brave as any of those dead men had been, and they were his fathers, and he knew that sooner or later he should lie there himself, beside Sir Hugh, slowly drying to a parchment shell. But he was still alive, and he closed his eyes a moment, and three great drops stood on his forehead.

Then he looked again, and by the whiteness of the winding-sheet he knew his father's corpse, for all the others were brown with age; and, moreover, the flame of the candle was blown toward it. He made four steps till he reached it, and suddenly the light burned straight and high, shedding a dazzling yellow glare upon the fine linen that was all white, save over the face, and where the joined hands were laid on the breast. And at those places ugly stains had spread, darkened with outlines of the features and of the tight-clasped fingers. There was a frightful stench of drying death.

As Sir Gabriel looked down, something stirred behind him, softly at first, then more noisily, and something fell to the stone floor with a dull thud and rolled up to his feet; he started back, and saw a withered head lying almost face upward on the pavement, grinning at him. He felt the cold sweat standing on his face, and his heart beat painfully.

For the first time in all his life that evil thing which men call fear was getting hold of him, checking his heartstrings as a cruel driver checks a quivering horse, clawing at his backbone with icy hands, lifting his hair with freezing breath climbing up and gathering in his midriff with leaden weight.

Yet presently he bit his lip and bent down, holding the candle in one hand, to lift the shroud back from the head of the corpse with the other. Slowly he lifted it. Then it clove to the half-dried skin of the face, and his hand shook as if someone had struck him on the elbow, but half in fear and half in anger at himself, he pulled it, so that it came away with a little ripping sound. He caught his breath as he held it, not throwing it back, and not yet looking. The horror was working on him, and he felt that old Vernon Ockram was standing up in his iron coffin, headless, yet watching him with the stump of his severed neck.

While he held his breath he felt the dead smile twisting his lips. In sudden wrath at his own misery, he tossed the death-stained linen backward, and looked at last. He ground his teeth lest he should shriek aloud.

There it was, the thing that haunted him, that haunted Evelyn Warburton, that was like a blight on all that came near him.

The dead face was blotched with dark stains, and the thin, gray hair was matted about the discolored forehead. The sunken lids were half open, and the candle light gleamed on something foul where the toad eyes had lived.

But yet the dead thing smiled, as it had smiled in life; the ghastly lips were parted and drawn wide and tight upon the wolfish teeth, cursing still, and still defying hell to do its worst—defying, cursing, and always and for ever smiling alone in the dark.

Sir Gabriel opened the winding-sheet where the hands were, and the blackened, withered fingers were closed upon something stained and mottled. Shivering from head to foot, but fighting like a man in agony for his life, he tried to take the package from the dead man's hold. But as he pulled at it the clawlike fingers seemed to close more tightly, and when he pulled harder the shrunken hands and arms rose from the corpse with a horrible look of life following his motion—then as he wrenched the sealed packet loose at last, the hands fell back into their place still folded.

He set down the candle on the edge of the bier to break the seals from the stout paper. And, kneeling on one knee, to get a better light, he read what was within, written long ago in Sir Hugh's queer hand.

He was no longer afraid.

He read how Sir Hugh had written it all down that it might perchance be a witness of evil and of his hatred; how he had loved Evelyn Warburton, his wife's sister; and how his wife had died of a broken heart with his curse upon her, and how Warburton and he had fought side by side in Afghanistan, and Warburton had fallen; but Ockram had brought his comrade's wife back a full year later, and little Evelyn, her child, had been born in Ockram Hall. And next, how he had wearied of the mother, and she had died like her sister with his curse on her. And then, how Evelyn had been brought up as his niece, and how he had trusted that his son Gabriel and his daughter, innocent and unknowing, might love and marry, and the souls of the women he had betrayed might suffer another anguish before eternity was out. And, last of all, he hoped that some day, when nothing could be undone, the two might find his writing and live on, not daring to tell the truth for their children's sake and the world's word, man and wife.

This he read, kneeling beside the corpse in the north vault, by the light of the altar candle; and when he had read it all, he thanked God aloud that he had found the secret in time. but when he rose to his feet and looked down at the dead face it was changed, and the smile was gone from it forever, and the jaw had fallen a little, and the tired, dead lips were relaxed. And then there was a breath behind him and close to him, not cold like that which had blown the flame of the candle as he came, but warm and human. He turned suddenly.

There she stood, all in white, with her shadowy golden hair—for she had risen from her bed and had followed him noiselessly, and had found him reading, and had herself read over his shoulder. He started violently when he saw her, for his nerves were unstrung—and then he cried out her name in the still place of death:

"Evelyn!"

"My brother!" she answered, softly and tenderly, putting out both hands to meet his.

Robert Barr (1850–1912)

Although born in Glasgow, Scotland, Rober Barr's family immigrated to Canada when he was four. Educated in Toronto, he became the headmaster of a junior school while still in his teens.

After marrying in 1876, he moved to a job in Detroit as reporter for the *Free Press*. There he ''is said to have rifled mail bags, crossed a river on ice floes, and run a revolver gauntlet—all in pursuit of news.''

In 1881 his paper sent him to England as a correspondent. He started a British edition, made friends with Kipling and Doyle, and then in 1892 he founded (along with Jerome K. Jerome) his own magazine, *The Idler*. Though a literary and financial success, it was ended five years later by a lawsuit.

Barr remained in England, earning his living as a writer.

Today he is primarily remembered for *The Triumphs of Eugene Valmont* (1906), a volume of mystery stories about an egomaniacal French detective. However, his works are still quite readable and many can be classified as science fiction, fantasy, or horror. *From Whose Bourne* (1896) is a novel about a dead man's attempts to clear his widow of murder. *The Face in the Mask* (1895) includes what appears to be the first smog disaster story, ''The Doom of London'' as well as a humorous horror story, ''The Chemistry of Anarchy.''

For this volume, we have chosen ''A Game of Chess.'' While not well know, it features a gargantuan chessboard and a shocking climax.

A GAME OF CHESS

*H**ere follows a rough translation of the letter which Henri Dru-*
mont wrote in Boukrah, two days before his death, to his uncle, Count
Ferrand in Paris. It explains the incidents which led up to the situation
hereinafter to be described.

My Dear Uncle,

You will have gathered from former letters of mine, that, when one
gets east of Buda Pest, official corruption becomes rampant to an extent
hardly believable in the West. Goodness knows, things are bad enough in
Paris, but Paris official life is comparatively clean when brought into
contrast with Boukrah. I was well aware before I left France that much
money would have to be secretly spent if we were to secure the concession
for lighting Boukrah with electricity, but I was unprepared for the exactions that were actually levied upon me. It must be admitted that the
officials are rapacious enough, but once bought, they remain bought, or, at
least, such has been my experience of them.

There are, however, a horde of hangers-on, who seem even more
insatiable than the governing body of the town, and the worst of these is
one Schwikoff, editor of the leading paper here, the *Boukrah Gazette*,
which is merely a daily blackmailing sheet. He has every qualification
needed by an editor of a paper in Eastern Europe, which may be summed
up by saying that he is demoniacally expert with the rapier, and a dead shot
with a pistol. He has said time and again that his scurrilous paper could
wreck our scheme, and I believe there is some truth in his assertion. Be that
as it may, I have paid him at different times large sums of money, but each
payment seems but the precursor of a more outrageous demand. At last I

was compelled to refuse further contributions to his banking account, and the young man smiled, saying he hoped my decision was not final, for, if it was, I should regret it. Although Schwikoff did not know it, I had the concession signed and completed at that moment, which document I sent to you yesterday morning. I expected Schwikoff would be very angry when he learned of this, but such did not appear to be the case.

He met me last night in the smoking room of the Imperial Club, and shook hands with great apparent cordiality, laughing over his discomfiture, and assuring me that I was one of the shrewdest businessmen he had ever met. I was glad to see him take it in this way, and later in the evening when he asked me to have a game of chess with him, I accepted his invitation, thinking it better for the company that he should be a friend, if he were so disposed.

We had not progressed far with the game, when he suddenly accused me of making a move I had no right to make. I endeavored to explain, but he sprang up in an assumed rage and dashed a glass of wine in my face. The room was crowded with officers and gentlemen. I know you may think me foolish for having sent my seconds to such a man as Schwikoff, who is a well-known blackmailer, but, nevertheless, he comes of a good family, and I, who have served in the French Army, and am of your blood, could not accept tamely such an insult. If what I hear of his skill as a swordsman is true, I enter the contest well aware that I am outclassed, for I fear I have neglected the training of my right arm in my recent pursuit of scientific knowledge. Whatever may be the outcome, I have the satisfaction of knowing that the task given me has been accomplished. Our company has now the right to establish its plant and lay its wires in Boukrah, and the people here have such an eastern delight in all that is brilliant and glittering, that I feel certain our project will be a financial success.

Schwikoff and I will meet about the time you receive this letter, or, perhaps, a little earlier, for we fight at daybreak, with rapiers, in the large room of the Fencing School of Arms in this place.

Accept, my dear uncle, the assurance of my most affectionate consideration.—Your unworthy nephew,

HENRI.

The old man's hand trembled as he laid down the letter after reading it, and glanced up at the clock. It was the morning of the duel, and daylight came earlier at Boukrah than at Paris.

Count Ferrand was a member of an old French family that had been impoverished by the Revolution. Since then, the Ferrand family had lived poorly enough until the Count, as a young man, had turned his attention toward science, and now, in his old age, he was supposed to possess fabulous wealth, and was known to be the head of one of the largest electric manufacturing companies in the environs of Paris. No one at the works was aware that the young man, Henri Drumont, who was given employ in the manufactory after he had served his time in the army, was the nephew of the old Count, for the head of the company believed that the young man would come to a more accurate knowledge of the business if he had to take the rough with the smooth, and learn his trade from the bottom upwards.

The glance at the clock told the old Count that the duel, whatever its result, had taken place. So there was nothing to be done but await tidings. It was the manager of the works who brought them in.

"I am sorry to inform you, sir," he said, "that the young man, Henri Drumont, whom we sent to Boukrah, was killed this morning in a duel. His assistant telegraphs for instructions. The young man has no relatives here that I know of, so I suppose it would be as well to have him buried where he died."

The manager had no suspicion that he was telling his chief of the death of his heir.

"The body is to be brought back to France," said the Count quietly.

And it was done. Later, when the question arose of the action to be taken regarding the concession received from Boukrah, the Count astonished the directors by announcing that, as the concession was an important one, he himself would take the journey to Boukrah, and remain thee until the electric plant, already forwarded, was in position, and a suitable local manager found.

The Count took the Orient Express from Paris, and, arriving in Boukrah, applied himself with an energy hardly to be expected from one of his years, to the completion of the work which was to supply the city with electricity.

Count Ferrand refused himself to all callers until the electric plant was in operation, and the interior of the building he had bought, completed to his satisfaction. Then, practically the first man admitted to his private office was Schwikoff, editor of the *Boukrah Gazette*. He had sent in his card with a request, written in passable French, for information regarding the electrical installation, which would be of interest, he said, to the readers of the *Gazette*. Thus Schwikoff was admitted to the presence of Count Ferrand, whose nephew he had killed, but the journalist, of course, knew nothing of the relationship between the two men, and thought, perhaps, he had done the courteous old gentleman a favor, in removing from the path of his advancement the young man who had been in the position now held by this gray-haired veteran.

The ancient noble received his visitor with scrupulous courtesy, and the blackmailer, glancing at his hard, inscrutable face, lined with experience, thought that here, perhaps, he had a more difficult victim to bleed than the free-handed young fellow whom he had so deferentially removed from existence, adhering strictly to the rules of the game, himself acquitted of all guilt by the law of his country, and the custom of his city, passing unscathed into his customary walk of life, free to rapier the next man who offended him. Count Ferrand said politely that he was ready to impart all the information in his possession for the purposes of publication. The young man smiled and shrugged his shoulders slightly.

"To tell you the truth, sir, at once and bluntly, I do not come so much for the purpose of questioning you regarding your business, as with the object of making some arrangement concerning the Press, with which I have the great honor to be connected. You may be aware, sir, that much of the success of your company will depend on the attitude of the Press toward you. I thought, perhaps, you might be able to suggest some method by which all difficulties would be smoothed away; a method that would result in our mutual advantage."

"I shall not pretend to misunderstand you," replied the Count, "but I was led to believe that large sums had already been disbursed, and that the difficulties, as you term them, had already been removed."

"So far as I am concerned," returned the blackmailer, "the sums paid to me were comparatively trivial, and I was led to hope that when the company came into active operation, as, thanks to your energy, is now the case, it would deal more liberally with me."

The Count in silence glanced at some papers he took from a pigeonhole, then made a few notes on the pad before him. At last he spoke.

"Am I right in stating that an amount exceeding ten thousand francs was paid to you by my predecessor, in order that the influence of your paper might be assured?"

Schwikoff again shrugged his shoulders.

"It may have been something like that," he said carelessly. "I do not keep my account of these matters."

"It is a large sum," persisted Ferrand.

"Oh! a respectable sum; but still you must remember what you got for it. You have the right to bleed for ever all the inhabitants of Boukrah."

"And that gives you the right to bleed us?"

"Oh! if you like to put it that way, yes. We give you *quid pro quo* by standing up for you when complaints of your exactions are made."

"Precisely. But I am a businessman, and would like to see where I am going. You would oblige me, then, by stating a definite sum, which would be received by you in satisfaction of all demands."

"Well, in that case, I think twenty thousand francs would be a moderate amount."

"I cannot say that moderation is the most striking feature of your proposal," said the Count drily, "still we shall not trouble about that, if you will be reasonable in the matter of payment. I propose to pay you in installments of a thousand francs a month."

"That would take nearly two years," objected Schwikoff. "Life is uncertain. Heaven only knows where we shall be two years from now."

"Most true; or even a day hence. Still, we have spent a great deal of money on this establishment, and our income has not yet begun; therefore, on behalf of the company, I must insist on easy payments. I am willing, however, to make it two thousand francs a month, but beyond that I should not care to go without communicating with Paris."

"Oh, well," swaggered Schwikoff, with the air of a man making great concessions, "I suppose we may call that satisfactory, if you make the first payment now."

"I do not keep such a sum in my office, and besides, I wish to impose further terms. It is not my intention to make an arrangement with any but the leading paper of this place, which I understand the *Gazette* to be."

"A laudable intention. The *Gazette* is the only paper that has any influence in Boukrah."

"Very well; then I must ask you, for your own sake as for mine, to keep this matter a strict secret; even to deny that you receive a subsidy, if the question should come up."

"Oh, certainly, certainly."

"You will come for payment, which will be in gold, after office hours, on the first of each month. I shall be here alone to receive you. I should prefer that you came in by the back way, where your entrance will be unseen, and so we shall avoid comment, because, when I refuse the others, I should not care for them to know that one of their fellows has had an advantage over them. I shall take the money from the bank before it closes. What hour, therefore, after six o'clock will be most convenient to you?"

"That is immaterial—seven, eight, or nine, or even later, if you like."

"Eight o'clock will do; by that time everyone will have left the building but myself. I do not care for late hours, even if they occur but once a month. At eight o'clock precisely you will find the door at the back ajar. Come in without announcement, so that we may not be taken by surprise. The door is self-locking, and you will find me here with the money. Now, that I may be able to obtain the gold in time, I must bid you adieu."

At eight o'clock precisely Count Ferrand, standing in the passage, saw the back door shoved open and Schwikoff enter, closing it behind him.

"I hope I have not kept you waiting," said Schwikoff.

"Your promptitude is exceptional," said the other politely. "As a businessman, I must confess I like punctuality. I have left the money in the upper room. Will you have the goodness to follow me?"

They mounted four pairs of stairs, all lighted by incandescent lamps. Entering a passageway on the upper floor, the Count closed the big door behind him; then opening another door, they came to a large oblong room, occupying nearly the whole of the top story, brilliantly lighted by an electric lustre depending from the ceiling.

"This is my experimenting laboratory," said the old man as he closed the second door behind him.

It was certainly a remarkable room, entirely without windows. On the wall, at the right hand near the entrance, were numerous switches in shining brass and copper and steel.

From the door onward were perhaps ten feet of ordinary flooring, then across the whole width of the room extended a gigantic chess board, the squares yellow and gray, made alternately of copper and steel;

beyond that again was another ten feet of plain flooring, which supported a desk and some chairs. Schwikoff's eyes glittered as he saw a pile of gold on the desk. Near the desk was a huge open fireplace, constructed like no fireplace Schwikoff had ever seen before. The center, where the grate should have been, was occupied by what looked like a great earthenware bathtub, some six or seven feet long. "That," said the electrician, noticing the other's glance at it, "is an electric furnace of my own invention, probably the largest electric furnace in the world. I am convinced there is a great future before carbide of calcium, and I am carrying on some experiments drifting toward the perfection of the electric crucible."

"Carbide of calcium?" echoed Schwikoff, "I never heard of it."

"Perhaps it would not interest you, but it is curious from the fact that it is a rival of the electric light, and yet only through the aid of electricity is carbide of calcium made commercially possible."

"Electricity creates its own rival, you mean; most interesting I am sure. And is this a chessboard let into the floor?"

"Yes, another of my inventions. I am a devotee of chess."

"So am I."

"Then we shall have to have a game together. You don't object to high stakes I hope?"

"Oh, no, if I have the money."

"Ah, well, we must have a game with stakes high enough to make the contest interesting."

"Where are your chessmen? They must be huge."

"Yes, this board was arranged so that living chessmen might play on it. You see, the alternate squares are of copper, the others of steel. That black line which surrounds each square is hard rubber, which does not allow the electricity to pass from one square to another."

"You use electricity, then, in playing."

"Oh, electricity is the motive power of the game; I will explain it all to you presently; meanwhile, would you oblige me by counting the gold on the desk? I think you will find there exactly two thousand francs."

The old man led the way across the metal chessboard. He proffered a chair to Schwikoff, who sat down before the desk.

Count Ferrand took the remaining chair, carried it over the metal platform, and sat down near the switch, having thus the huge chessboard between him and his guest. He turned the lever from one polished knob to another, the transit caused a wicked, vivid flash to illuminate the room with the venomous glitter of blue lightning. Schwikoff gave a momentary start at the crackle and the blinding light. Then he continued his counting in silence. At last he looked up and said, "This amount is quite correct."

"Please do not move from your chair," commanded the Count. "I warn you that the chessboard is now a broad belt of death between you and me. On every disc the current is turned, and a man stepping anywhere on the board will receive into his body two thousand volts, killing him instantly as with a stroke of lightning, which, indeed, it is."

"Is this a practical joke?" asked Schwikoff, turning a little pale about the lips, sitting still, as he had been ordered to do.

"It is practical enough, and no joke, as you will learn when you know more about it. You see this circle of twenty-four knobs at my hand, with each knob of which, alternately, this lever communicates when I turn it."

As the Count spoke he moved the lever, which went crackling past a semi-circle of knobs, emitting savage gleams of steel-like fire as it touched each metal projection.

"From each of these knobs," explained the Count, as if he were giving a scientific lecture, "electricity is turned on to a certain combination of squares before you. When I began speaking, the whole board was electrified; now, a man might walk across that board, and his chances of reaching this side alive would be as three to one."

Schwikoff sprang suddenly to his feet, terror in his face, and seemed about to make a dash for it. The old man pushed the lever back into its former position.

"I want you to understand," said the Count suavely, "that upon any movement on your part, I shall instantly electrify the whole board. And please remember that, although I can make the chessboard as safe as the floor, a push on this lever and the metal becomes a belt of destruction. You must keep a cool head on your shoulders, Mr. Schwikoff, otherwise you have no chance for your life."

Schwikoff, standing there stealthily drew a revolver from his hip pocket. The Count continued in even tones:

"I see you are armed, and I know you are an accurate marksman. You may easily shoot me dead as I sit here. I have thought that all out in the moments I have given to the consideration of this business. On my desk downstairs is a letter to the manager, saying that I am called suddenly to Paris, and that I shall not return for a month. I ask him to go on with the work, and tell him on no account to allow anyone to enter this room. You might shout till you were hoarse, but none outside would hear you. The walls and ceiling and floor have been deadened so effectively that we are practically in a silent, closed box. There is no exit except up through the chimney, but if you look at the crucible to which I called your attention you will see that it is now white hot, so there is no escape that way. You will, therefore, be imprisoned here until you starve to death, or until despair causes you to commit suicide by stepping on the electrified floor.''

"I can shatter your switchboard from here with bullets.''

"Try it,'' said the old man calmly. "The destruction of the switchboard merely means that the electricity comes permanently on the floor. If you shatter the switchboard, it will then be out of my power to release you, even if I wished to do so, without going downstairs and turning off the electricity at the main. I assure you that all these things have had my most earnest consideration, and while it is possible that something may have been overlooked, it is hardly probable that you, in your now excited state of mind, will chance upon that omission.''

Schwikoff sank back in his chair.

"Why do you wish to murder me?'' he asked. "You may retain your money, if that is what you want, and I shall keep quiet about you in the paper.''

"Oh, I care nothing for the money nor the paper.''

"Is it because I killed your predecessor?''

"My predecessor was my nephew and my heir. Through his duel with you, I am now a childless old man, whose riches are but an incumbrance to him, and yet those riches would buy me freedom were I to assassinate you in broad daylight in the street. Are you willing now to listen to the terms I propose to you?''

"Yes.''

"Very good. Throw your pistol into the corner of the room beside me; its possession will do you no good.''

After a moment's hesitation, Schwikoff flung his pistol across the metal floor into the corner. The old man turned the lever to still another knob.

"Now,'' he said, "you have a chance of life again; thirty-two of the squares are electrified, and thirty-two are harmless. Stand, I beg of you, on the square which belongs to the Black King.''

''And meet my death.''

''Not on that square, I assure you. It is perfectly safe.''

But the young man made no movement to comply. ''I ask you to explain your intention.''

''You shall play the most sinister game of chess you have ever engaged in; Death will be your opponent. You shall have the right to the movements of the King—one square in any direction that you choose. You will never be in a position in which you have not the choice of at least two squares upon which you can step with impunity; in fact, you shall have at each move the choice of eight squares on which to set your foot, and as a general thing, four of those will mean safety, and the other four death, although sometimes the odds will be more heavily against you, and sometimes more strongly in your favor. If you reach this side unscathed, you are then at liberty to go, while if you touch one of the electric squares, your death will be instantaneous. Then I shall turn off the current again, with the result that for a few moments there will be thick, black smoke from the chimney, and a handful of white ashes in the crucible.''

''And you run no danger.''

''No more than you did when you stood up against my nephew, having previously unjustly insulted him.''

''The duel was carried out according to the laws of the code.''

''The laws of my code are more generous. You have a chance for your life. My nephew had no such favor shown to him; he was doomed from the beginning, and you knew it.''

''He had been an officer in the French Army.''

''He allowed his sword arm to get out of practice, which was wrong, of course, and he suffered for it. However, we are not discussing him; it is your fate that is in question. I give you now two minutes in which to take your stand on the King's square.''

''And if I refuse?''

''If you refuse, I turn the electricity on the whole board, and then I leave you. I will tear up the letter which is on my desk below, return here in the morning, give the alarm, say you broke in to rob me of the gold which is beside you on the desk, and give you in charge of the authorities, a disgraced man.''

"But what if I tell the truth?"

"You would not be believed, and I have pleasure in knowing that I have money enough to place you in prison for the rest of your life. The chances are, however, that, with the electricity fully turned on, this building will be burned down before morning. I fear my insulation is not perfect enough to withstand so strong a current. In fact, now that the thought has suggested itself to me, fire seems a good solution to the difficulty. I shall arrange the wires on leaving so that a conflagration will break out within an hour after my departure, and, I can assure you, you will not be rescued by the firemen when they understand their danger from live wires in a building from which, I will tell them, it is impossible to cut off the electricity. Now, sir, you have two minutes."

Schwikoff stood still while Ferrand counted the seconds left to him; finally, as the time was about to expire, he stepped on the King's square, and stood there, swaying slightly, drops of perspiration gathering on his brow.

"*Brava!*" cried the Count, "you see, as I told you, it is perfectly safe. I give you two minutes to make your next move."

Schwikoff, with white lips, stepped diagonally to the square of the Queen's Pawn, and stood there, breathing hard, but unharmed.

"Two minutes to make the next move," said the old man, in the unimpassioned tones of a judge.

"No, no!" shouted Schwikoff excitedly, "I made my last move at once; I have nearly four minutes. I am not to be hurried; I must keep my head cool. I have, as you see, superb control over myself."

His voice had now risen to a scream, and his open hand drew the perspiration down from his brow over his face, streaking it grimly.

"I am calm!" he shrieked, his knees knocking together, "but this is no game of chess; it is murder. In a game of chess I could take all the time I wanted in considering a move."

"True, true!" said the old man suavely, leaning back in his chair, although his hand never left the black handle of the lever. "You are in the right. I apologize for my infringement of the laws of chess; take all the time you wish, we have the night before us."

Schwikoff stood there long in the ominous silence, a silence interrupted now and then by a startling crackle from the direction of the glowing electric furnace. The air seemed charged with electricity and almost unbreathable. The time given him, so far from being an advantage, disintegrated his nerve, and as he looked fearfully over the metal chessboard the copper squares seemed to be glowing red hot, and the dangerous illusion that the steel squares were cool and safe became uppermost in his mind.

He curbed with difficulty his desire to plunge, and stood balancing himself on his left foot, cautiously approaching the steel square with his right toe. As the boot neared the steel square, Schwikoff felt a strange thrill pass through his body. He drew back his foot quickly with a yell of terror, and stood, his body inclining now to the right, now to the left, like a tall tree hesitating before its fall. To save himself he crouched.

"Mercy! Mercy!" he cried. "I have been punished enough. I killed the man, but his death was sudden, and not fiendish torture like this. I have been punished enough."

"Not so," said the old man. "An eye for an eye."

All self-control abandoned the victim. From his crouching position he sprang like a tiger. Almost before his out-stretched hands touched the polished metal his body straightened and stiffened with a jerk, and as he fell, with a hissing sound, dead on the chessboard, the old man turned the lever free from the fatal knob. There was no compassion in his hard face for the executed man, but instead his eyes glittered with the scientific fervor of research. He rose, turned the body over with his foot, drew off one of the boots, and tore from the inside a thin sole of cork.

"Just as I thought," he murmured. "Oh, the irony of ignorance! There existed, after all, the one condition I had not provided for. I knew he was protected the moment he stepped upon the second square, and, if his courage had not deserted him, he could have walked unharmed across the board, as the just, in medieval times, passed through the ordeal of the red-hot plowshares."